FORGED IN FIRE

A Red-Hot SEALs Novel

Montlake
Romance

Published by Montlake Romance
P.O. Box 400818
Las Vegas, NV 89140

ISBN-13: 9781612185330
ISBN-10: 1612185339

This book is dedicated to Jacqueline Marie Mousey. I was lucky to have you for the first 47 years of my life. But I still miss you every minute, of every day.

Acknowledgments

A good book is a team effort, and I had some kickass teammates in my platoon.

To Patti O'Shea, brainstorming guru: who answered all my screams of "What happens next!", who went beyond the call of CP duty by taking questions to her Northwest Airlines engineers and bringing back useable answers, who marked all those instances of repetition and slow pacing and helped keep my characters honest. Without you this book would never have taken flight.

To Roslyn Carrington: who bled red all over my pages, pinpointed my logical holes and overused adjectives/adverbs, weeded out my slow passages, and kept my characters authentic. Without you this book would never have gotten off the ground.

To Veronica Worthington (ex-police officer): who vetted all my gun stuff and action scenes and kept this book as realistic as possible while still allowing for creativity. Without your knowledge of guns and law enforcement this book would not have the ring of authenticity.

To Jolyn Palliata: who did the final read-through and precopy-edit. Without your sharp eyes noting several character discrepancies, this book would not have the depth it has now. And without your enthusiasm, unfailing support, and prelaunch promoting, half the names on my waiting list wouldn't be there.

To Cindy Oles Miller: whose comments always made me stop and think and then go back and fix. Without that early look through your eyes, this book wouldn't have had the foundation to build on.

To Matthew Pat Whalen (sixteen years of service with the navy, ten years' service with the air force—which we thank you for!): I cannot express my appreciation for your patience and unfailing kindness in answering all those e-mails I sent you. Without you this book wouldn't have the authenticity I hope it has now.

Chapter One

*L*IEUTENANT COMMANDER ZANE WINTERS SHIFTED UNEASILY against the grungy white wall across from gate C-18's ticket counter. He felt naked without his Glock. Exposed. An itchy, irritating prickle of vulnerability tightened his skin and knotted his muscles. Which was ridiculous. They were on leave, for Christ's sake, booked on a civilian flight.

Yeah, he and Cosky and Rawls had to check their weapons with their luggage, but so what? They weren't facing deployment to some godforsaken foreign jungle or burning swath of sand.

"Did they have to pick Hawaii? We have the same blue sky and warm weather in Coronado. And without the tourists."

Zane barely heard Cosky's disgusted mutter through the drone of excited voices surrounding them. With a grunt, he massaged the back of his neck and surveyed the growing crowd. More passengers were arriving by the minute. There were already too many people to keep an eye on. Too many jackets and pockets and purses. Too many places to conceal a weapon.

A stacked brunette across the gate area caught his gaze and offered a sultry smile. Zane turned away.

"Jesus." Rawls's lazy grin was a slash of white in his sun-bronzed face. "You two need to get off base more often. You're as hinky as a pair of hounds during tick season. Those are civilians y'all are glaring at, not a room full of terrorists." Bright blue eyes zeroed in on the brunette across the room. "What you need is some of *that*. Sun, sand, and sex. All the fixin's for a memorable vacation."

Cosky shot his teammate a derisive glance. "When did you become so fond of sand and sun? Sure as hell not last month, judging by your nonstop bitching."

Rawls flipped him the finger. "It's that third *s*, Cos. Makes all the difference. You should try it sometime, but without that blow-up Barbie you keep stashed beneath your bunk."

Shrill laughter erupted across the room. Zane tracked the sound, skimming an abandoned stroller and clusters of luggage. When the brunette tried to catch his eye again, he swore beneath his breath. Shifting against the wall, he gave her his back.

"See? This is why I like hanging with you, skipper," Rawls drawled. "You attract the little darlin's over, and when you turn that cold shoulder on 'em, they start buzzin' round Cosky and me."

"Leave me out of it," Cosky said. "Unlike you, I don't need to surf Zane's wake for a hookup."

"A hookup?" Rawls shook his head and smirked. "Is that any way to talk about your hand?"

Bracing his elbows against the wall behind them, he tilted his head and studied Zane's face. "Seriously, skipper, you should take her up on that offer. It's not like—" He broke off to scan Zane's face more intently. Suddenly he frowned. "You're shittin' me. That's some prime real estate over there, and you don't have any interest in her? None at all? That just ain't...natural."

Rawls was right. She *was* prime. A real looker. Long, thick mahogany hair. A tight, curvy ass. Stacked across the chest.

Enough flare through the hips to hold on to. She was the kind of woman who'd give wet dreams to any straight male between puberty and death.

Which must mean he was dead. Because he was way past puberty, yet he didn't feel even a twitch of interest. No chills. No thrills. No goose bumps.

She could be his great-grandmother, for all the attraction he felt.

Every year the numbness dug a little deeper, spread a little further. He'd been warned about this particular side effect of the family gift—or curse, depending on who was talking. But knowing about it, and living with it, were completely different animals.

"Let's hope that woman of yours shows up ASAP. Much more of this drought and you won't remember what to do with her." Rawls reached over to punch Zane's shoulder.

The moment Rawls's fist made contact, every muscle in Zane's body clenched. He froze, his breath locked in his throat. His vision blurred.

Click.

It was a subtle sound. A switch flipping inside his head. An image flashed through his mind. Quick. Brutal. Ugly.

Rawls sprawled across a bank of narrow seats. His blue T-shirt splotched with black. Blood dripping from limp fingers. A fixed stare glazing his blue eyes.

The vision vanished.

"Son of a bitch." Sheer disgust vibrated in Cosky's gritty voice. "We're on stand-down. This is a civilian flight. Regardless of that all-too-familiar look on your face, we cannot be in any goddamn danger."

Zane knew he wouldn't get anything further from Rawls, so he turned to Cosky instead and clamped a hand on his lieutenant's bicep.

This time he was expecting the vision. He tensed anyway.

Click.

He strained to capture as many details as possible as the new vision flashed through his mind.

Gray eyes locked and empty, already filming with the unmistakable haze of death. Black hair saturated with blood. Hands clenched. He was splayed across a narrow aisle, dark-blue upholstered seats rising on either side of his head.

When the image vanished, he released Cosky's arm and wrestled air back into his lungs.

"Tell me this is a joke," Cosky demanded.

Zane shook his head and gripped the back of his neck with both hands.

"What did you see?" Rawls finally asked.

Zane drew a shallow breath. "You dead. Cosky dead."

"From boredom?" Cosky asked dryly. "We *are* going to a wedding." A quick glance at Zane's face, and a glint of steel darkened his gray eyes. "Where's this going down?"

"On the bird." Zane frowned. "Couldn't tell whether she was in flight. Didn't get a good enough look."

Cosky turned to study the boisterous crowd. "When do you ever?"

Zane scrubbed his palms down his face and forced back a surge of frustration. The flashes never lasted long. No more than two or three seconds. Just enough to warn, without giving details. Just enough to raise guards, but not enough to mitigate the danger.

"Which bird? Over or back?" Cosky braced his hands on his hips and studied Zane's face. "Either fits the three-day window for those flashes of yours."

"Today." Zane nodded toward Rawls's blue-clad chest. "Same clothes."

Cosky grunted. "I don't suppose you saw who killed us?"

"When have these damn things ever been that accommodating?"

"Fuck." With a disgusted shake of his head, Cosky dropped his chin and scowled at the worn carpet. "What about the wounds?"

"Lots of blood. Could be a gun. Or a knife."

"A crash?" Rawls broke in quietly.

"Doubtful. Neither of you were burned. We're looking at some kind of weapon."

Cosky frowned. "It would be easier to smuggle a blade through security, but few people are good enough to take us on with a knife. Chances are it's a gun."

Zane pushed away from the wall. "Whatever's going to happen is bad enough to take the three of us out." The flashes never centered on him, but if Cosky and Rawls were in danger, he was as well. "We need to get hold of Mac."

As the officer in charge of SEAL Team 7, Commander Jace Mackenzie had the pull to get the plane grounded and the passengers searched.

"Question." Cosky's attention zeroed in on Zane's face. "What are we going to tell him? We don't know what's going to happen, who's behind it, or what kind of weapons will be used. If Mac gets this bird grounded only to have nothing show during the search, the backlash is gonna be a bitch."

"What are you suggesting?" Zane cocked an eyebrow. "That we skip the wedding, keep our mouths shut, and let events play out?"

"Don't be an ass. I'm *saying* it would be handy to have some solid intel to pass on for a change. Why can't you ever pick up more information if you touch us again?"

Zane shrugged. Just because he suffered through the visions didn't mean he understood their properties. "We've got some time before boarding. Maybe one of the passengers will stand out."

A wave of heat suddenly rolled through him. It started at his scalp and flowed down—a tide of molten fire that left chills in its wake. A tingling, numbing sensation followed, as though he'd been hit with an electrical shock.

"What's wrong?" Cosky's question came from a distance. Muted and warped.

Zane turned, searching for...something. The gate area spun in slow motion. That strange, electrical tingling raised the hair on his arms and down the back of his neck.

He found her in the mouth of the waiting room. She was blonde, slender. Perfect. Her cream-colored slacks and ivory blouse glowed beneath the harsh fluorescent lights, as though she stood squarely in a spotlight—lit up to catch his attention.

Her chin lifted, their eyes connected, and that strange, pulsating current shot straight to his cock. Electrified him. His libido, numb for years, reared up and howled. He took one long step toward her.

Cosky grabbed his arm and hauled him back. "Goddamn it, Zane. What's wrong?"

Zane shook his head, tried to clear the fog from his mind. The tug toward her was incredibly strong, like she was a magnet and his bones were metal. He took another step forward, his body vibrating at some strange frequency.

Cosky's hand tightened with brutal force around his forearm, piercing the primal urge to claim her.

Zane drew a shaky breath. His muscles were rigid. A vicious ache had seized his groin. His skin must have shrunk at least three sizes.

Holy shit.

It had to be her.

After all these years of waiting...this had to be her.

To go from nada to nuclear in the blink of an eye...yeah. He drew a slow, burning breath, grappling to drag his body back under control. This *had* to be her.

From listening to his brothers' stories about meeting their mates, he'd expected a strong reaction, but nothing like this whirlpool of hunger.

And he hadn't even touched her yet.

"Who is she?" Cosky demanded. "Did you see her in one of your flashes?"

The question snapped the world back into focus. The memory of those damn visions flooded his brain.

He watched, frozen, while she headed toward one of the plastic benches strewn throughout the waiting room. She was apparently booked on his flight.

His chest seized. His skin started to crawl. Christ, he couldn't breathe.

Of all the bad timing.

He'd finally found her. His soul mate. At a time when he couldn't afford the distraction. When the slightest mistake could get her killed.

Four hours earlier

Beth awoke with her mouth wide open and scream after scream piercing the dark bedroom. She jackknifed up, her heart hammering, her throat burning, horrific images of violence and death reeling through her mind.

Dark hair soaked with blood. Empty eyes staring up, a milky film clouding the emerald fire. A crimson stain mushrooming beneath a splayed, bullet-riddled body.

Oh God. Not again. This made the third time. The third time in three nights.

She ripped the comforter aside and slid from the bed, the sheets clinging to her sweaty skin. A quick glance at the alarm clock told her the dream had struck later this time. It was after three a.m. Not that the extra hour of sleep helped. A thick fog of exhaustion dulled her mind, but it would be useless to go back to bed. The dream would just start up again.

Her legs shook as she headed across the bedroom's deep pile carpet and down the short hall to the living room and kitchen. Coffee first, and then she'd jump in the shower. As she measured coffee grounds and filled the machine with water, her skin dried. Chills gave rise to goose bumps.

It was amazing that something as mundane as coffee spilled in a dream could launch a nightmare of such epic proportions. She was obviously under more stress than she'd realized. All those rush-rush-rush projects must be taking their toll. But why now? She'd been working in PacAtlantic Airlines' engineering department for seven years. Until three nights ago, she'd never had trouble leaving the job behind when she clocked out.

Maybe she just needed a change of scene, to get out of Seattle for a few days. It had been years since she'd been to the Washington coast. A trip to Long Beach would make a nice change of pace, maybe even break this stranglehold the nightmare had over her.

Once the coffee was going, she headed back to the master bath. The shower pelted her with heat and steam. Slowly, tight muscles loosened. Her thoughts drifted back to the dream, to a square face with chiseled features and grass-green eyes. He'd been just one of the passengers to die. Yet something about him resonated within her. An echo of familiarity. As though she knew him. Or should know him.

Which was ridiculous. If she'd met him, she would have remembered it. The guy was sexy as hell, not the kind of man who would slip a woman's mind. And then there was the whole hijacking. Why would her mind choose that scenario to manifest her stress?

Tilting her head back she let the water pound her scalp. Too bad it was Monday. She'd have to make it through the next five days before she could escape for some R&R. Unless...unless she put in for a couple of vacation days. God knows she was due. Maybe she could convince Ginny, Todd, and Kyle to come with her. Kyle would love the beach. They'd build sandcastles and search for seashells. As she stepped out of the shower, dried off, and donned her bathrobe, excitement stirred. A trip to the beach was exactly what she needed. Beth was smiling as she turned the corner into the kitchen and stepped into a puddle of warm water.

With a startled shriek, she jumped back and looked down. Puddles of brown liquid pooled on the kitchen's creamy tile floor. Slowly her gaze lifted and slid to the coffeemaker. She'd forgotten to put the glass carafe beneath the spout.

Just like she had in the beginning of the dream.

Her heart stuttered and then tried to climb her throat. The condo seemed to go eerily silent.

She backed up, her wet feet slipping on the tile.

It was just a coincidence. She was exhausted. Was it really so surprising she'd made such a stupid mistake? Besides, it was Monday, which pretty much explained everything.

Shaking off the unease, she went to work cleaning up the mess. She'd made an extra-large pot to ward off the exhaustion, so coffee had flowed everywhere. By the time she finished mopping up, it was time to leave for work. Racing to the bedroom, she threw open her closet and grabbed the closest ensemble of slacks and blouse. Throwing the hanger on the bed, she dropped the bathrobe, slipped into panties, pulled on socks, and grabbed the hanger, stripping off the slacks. Only then did she realize the pants were the same ones she'd worn in her dream. She glanced at the blouse. It was the same one too.

With a dry mouth, she returned to the closet and retrieved a different set of clothes.

By the time she entered the garage and climbed into her sedan, she was late.

Just like she'd been in the dream.

She pushed the thought aside and backed the car out. The voices on the radio were bright and cheerful, exactly what she needed to dispel the simmering unease. When the traffic report came on, she turned up the volume.

...southbound on Highway 509 expect delays...Southwest 116th Street from Fourth Avenue closed due to a warehouse fire, detour at Sixteenth Avenue...

Beth's fingers clenched around the steering wheel. She fought her tight chest for air.

Detour at Sixteenth Avenue.

The same detour, on the same street, for the same reason.

Her mind flashed to the nightmare. To the merciless hijackers. To the hundreds of men, women, and children who'd been slaughtered beneath a barrage of bullets.

"It's a coincidence," she said out loud, her voice so thin she didn't recognize it. But her grip didn't loosen.

Two incidents happening in exactly the same way? What were the odds of that?

She arrived at Sea-Tac Airport and PacAtlantic's employee parking at six fifteen, which meant she was officially late. After swiping her employee card, she took an empty elevator to the fifth floor and hurried to her cubicle.

Patti Oslanka, who worked in the booth to her right, swiveled in her desk chair to face her. "How was your weekend? FYI, old Ferret Face has something up his butt this morning, he's been—what's wrong?"

"I didn't sleep well last night."

"You should go back to bed. You look terrible."

Beth dropped her purse on her desk and started her computer. "Wouldn't old FF love that?"

Patti turned back to her monitor. "You need to report him. It was inappropriate to ask you out in the first place, but then to keep coming down on you because you said no? Did he bother to attend any of those sexual harassment workshops PAA keeps sending us to?"

When the login screen finally popped up, Beth typed in her user name and password, accessed PacAtlantic's database, and ran a search on flight 2077, Sea-Tac to Honolulu.

"You're not going to believe what I heard during the car pool this morning." Patti's voice droned on in the distance. "Shelby and Ryan have split!"

Beth sat frozen in front of her monitor, watching in shock as departure and arrival times scrolled down her screen. The flight existed. It actually existed and it was departing from Sea-Tac Airport, gate C-18, in just over two hours.

"Did you hear what I said?"

"What?" Beth turned her head, the world moving in slow-slow motion.

"Shelby and Ryan. They're divorcing!"

Patti's announcement didn't pierce the icy haze settling over her, even though this news too had been in her dream.

Maybe she was still dreaming.

Please, let her be dreaming.

"You've gone white as a ghost. You really should take a sick day and go home."

Beth turned back to her computer. The coffee. The detour. The fire. Shelby and Ryan. All events in her dream. Events that had come true.

What if the rest came true too?

A greasy wave of nausea climbed her throat.

Calm down, Beth, calm down. In the nightmare, you were on the plane. But you aren't flying to Hawaii. You aren't booked on that flight. You're blowing this whole thing out of proportion.

Except...she'd never blown anything out of proportion. For God's sake, her wedding had been canceled fifteen minutes before "I do" when she'd caught her groom and one of her bridesmaids necking in the coat closet. If she'd been the type to have hysterics it would have been then. Instead, she'd calmly sent the guests home and canceled the honeymoon. She simply did not have a hysterical bone in her body.

So what she needed to do now was use her brain and think.

For her own peace of mind, she had to find out whether there were guns on that plane—but quietly. If the weapons weren't there, the last thing she wanted was everyone questioning her mental health.

They'd been hidden beneath the seats. As an engineer, Todd had access to the tarmac. He could board the plane to look for them. And she wouldn't have to worry about her request becoming public knowledge, because Ginny would kill him if he breathed a word to anyone.

"Have you seen Todd?" She fought to keep her voice even.

"Not yet. Maybe he's still fighting that flu and Ginny kept him home."

"Ms. Brown," a nasal voice said from behind her. "You're late."

"I'm sick." Beth swiveled her chair to face the little weasel, otherwise known as her supervisor. "In fact, I'd like to take today as a sick day."

He scanned her face, his thin mouth puckering, and took a giant step back. "You should have stayed home. Who knows how many people you've infected."

She shut her computer down and escaped to the bathroom. Safe from prying eyes, she dug out her cell and scrolled through her contact list until she found Todd's number. The call rang and rang before going to voice mail. She left a message and tried Ginny next. That call went to voice mail too. She left another message. When she dialed their house phone, the answering machine picked up. Frustrated, Beth dropped the phone back into her purse.

According to the plane's departure schedule, it would taxi off in just over two hours. She couldn't afford to wait for Todd to get back to her. She sorted through the engineers she knew, but didn't feel comfortable approaching any of them. They'd report the incident to the boss, and lord knew what old FF would do with that kind of information.

Likely this was all a coincidence. She wasn't going to ruin her career unless she absolutely had to.

Her thoughts flashed to the green-eyed, hard-faced stranger in her nightmare. In the dream one of his friends had called him *Lieutenant*, which probably placed him in law enforcement or the armed forces. In either case, he'd have contacts, people capable of grounding the plane.

If he existed.

She could find out. As a PacAtlantic employee she could fly free. Listing herself on standby would get her inside the departure gate. She could see if he was there.

Of course, listing herself would also result in a reprimand. She swore softly and briefly shut her eyes. Employee standbys were sent to the department heads. Old FF would know she'd lied about being sick.

But the coffee had spilled.

She'd taken that damn detour to work.

The warehouse had been on fire.

Shelby and Ryan had split.

Coincidences? Maybe. But if the rest of the dream came true too, and she hadn't tried to stop it, she wouldn't be able to live with herself.

By the time she clocked out, drove the short distance to Sea-Tac's day parking, found a free computer terminal to list herself on standby, and picked up her boarding pass, she'd lost twenty minutes of her two-hour window. She lost several more minutes clearing the inbound departure gate. Her tension crested as she dodged passengers towing wheeled luggage and hurried down the tile corridor toward gate C-18.

I won't recognize anyone. This is just a huge coincidence. Ginny and I will have a good laugh about this later. Beth chanted the words to herself right up until she reached gate C-18 and got her first look at the far wall.

She stopped dead, shock searing her lungs.

Across from the ticket counter, a trio of tall, muscular men lounged against the wall. And then the dark-haired man in the middle of the knot shifted his stance against the wall, turned his head, and scanned the departure gate. His intense gaze locked onto her.

She was too far away to actually see those sharp eyes, but she knew they were green. Vibrant green. Icy chips of emerald.

Shorn hair dripping blood. Eyes locked and empty. Rough hands shoving him over, working a drenched wallet loose from the back pocket and pulling out a driver's license. "Zane Winters, just like the boss said."

Holy Mother of God...He was real.

Disbelief drowned out the low drone of voices, the shriek of jet engines climbing overhead, and the announcements over the loudspeakers.

Oh God...oh God...If they were real...what about the rest of the nightmare?

Her head went light. She staggered to the closest bench and collapsed.

"Are you okay?" a tentative male voice asked above her.

No, she was not okay. She'd gone crazy in the space of a bad night's sleep.

"There's no reason to be scared. Flying's safer than driving."

"I'm fine." She forced herself upright.

The stranger comforting her was in his mid to late thirties, tall and thin, but with a surprisingly broad span to his shoulders. Behind the wire rims of his glasses, his brown eyes were kind and bright with male appreciation.

"You don't look fine. You look like you're about to pass out." He sat down next to her and set a laptop case between his feet. "Russ Branson." He offered his hand.

She took it. "Beth Brown."

"Well, Beth Brown, what flight are you on?"

"PacAtlantic 2077, to Hawaii." Which wasn't a complete lie. She did have a boarding pass.

"Too bad." Regret darkened his brown eyes. "I'm headed to the Twin Cities myself. Minneapolis."

Across from her, an untidy pile of duffel bags spilled across the floor in front of a bench. A teenager with dirty blond hair, ripped jeans, and a hooded red sweatshirt slouched against the blue plastic.

This time the shock wasn't a hot, noisy rush—it was ice-cold and piercing.

The rat-tat-tat of machine gun fire. That dirty blond head slamming back, almost white against the dark-blue upholstery of the headrest, and then exploding in a burst of blood, brains, and bone.

He'd been in seat J32. Directly in front of Zane Winters.

"Mommy, how much longer?"

Slowly her head turned, tracking the childish voice.

A middle-aged woman shuffled past, a young child clinging to her hand. The little girl was maybe five or six with dark hair pulled into two untidy pigtails and a stuffed yellow duck clutched to the embroidered heart on her pink sweatshirt.

"Just one more flight, baby, and then we'll be home. Daddy will be waiting for us."

Mouth wide open, a young girl screamed. A duck splotched with red clamped to her rigid chest.

"Hey, maybe you better lie down. You're white as a sheet," her Good Samaritan said.

Beth barely heard him. Her gaze returned to the tallest of the trio against the wall. In the dream, Zane Winters had been intimidating enough. In real life, he was even more so. The hard planes of his face looked cast in stone. His well-washed jeans and faded blue T-shirt did little to disguise the lean, powerful frame roped with muscle. He was a warrior. She could see it in his unyielding expression, hooded eyes, and rangy physique honed to weapon-sharpness.

Hardly the kind of man to believe in ESP, or premonitions, or crazy women raving about ominous visions.

The breath she drew sounded wrenching and raw. The passengers were real. Every last one of them. Real.

The hijackers in her nightmare had been blond and jovial, only to morph into cold-blooded killers as soon as the plane lifted off.

She searched the teeming departure gate, but couldn't find them amid the clusters of chattering people. After a second sweep, she released a relieved breath. They must not have arrived yet.

"When does your flight leave?" the Good Samaritan asked.

She glanced at the clock on the wall behind the ticket counter. "An hour and a half."

Ninety minutes to convince someone to believe her and prevent a hijacking.

"You want to get something to eat?"

"I'm sorry. I'm really not up to eating."

Any other time Beth would have taken him up on the offer. He was exactly the kind of man she responded to. Gentle, a bit geeky—someone she felt comfortable around.

He reminded her of Todd. Her attention shifted to the three warriors lounging against the wall. Scratch that, two warriors. The third man, the other lean, dark, and dangerous-looking one, had disappeared. Her gaze lingered on Zane Winters's hard face. *Comfortable* was not a word she associated with him.

Her Good Samaritan followed her gaze across the room and rose to his feet.

"I see." His voice thinned, and a hint of coldness touched his eyes.

"I'm sorry."

With a shrug, he walked away.

Her attention swung back to the two men against the wall. She needed a plan. Sitting here accomplished nothing. But what exactly should she do?

She could head back to the inbound security gates, pull one of the guards aside, and explain. But explain what, exactly? That she'd had a nightmare and feared it was about to come true? They'd think she was a nut job. Besides, once they knew her name, they'd know she worked for PacAtlantic and she could kiss her job good-bye.

She could call in an anonymous bomb threat. But she'd have to do it outside of the airport and away from security cameras, with one of those disposable cell phones. Still, if she claimed a bomb was beneath the seats, someone was bound to search the plane. At least the guns would be found.

But the killers would go free.

Sure, the passengers would live. But those bastards would just do the same thing on some other flight.

Swallowing hard, Beth opened her eyes. She needed someone to believe her, or at least listen to her story with an open mind. Her attention flickered back to the two men across the room. To her surprise, Zane Winters was watching her. He snared her gaze and held it, something sensual and heated twisting between them.

She jerked her eyes away. Obviously she'd imagined *that*. She simply wasn't the kind of woman lethal men played eye-footsie with. A quick peek a few seconds later proved the assumption. He'd turned away and was leaning to the right, head cocked—listening to his blond friend.

The third man, the other dark-haired one, rejoined the two against the wall. With a subtle shift of broad shoulders and muscular bodies, the three blocked outside observation.

If she convinced him something was going to happen on the plane, maybe he could get the flight delayed, but in such a way the hijackers could be apprehended.

If he gave her the brush-off, she'd fall back on Plan B and call in the bomb threat.

Her cheeks heated as she stuffed her purse under her arm and rose to her feet. Zane Winters was going to think she was coming on to him. He was going to think she'd made this whole story up just to draw his attention. But she had to try.

She was halfway across the terminal when something icy and threatening drilled into the hollow between her shoulder blades.

The hair on the back of her neck lifted. Raw fear squeezed the breath from her lungs.

Someone was watching her. Someone ice-cold and deadly. She could feel those malevolent eyes locked on her spine.

Chapter Two

ZANE SCOWLED AT THE COUPLE SHARING THE BENCH ACROSS the room. The prick with the glasses and laptop had hit on her the moment she'd sat down. Was still hitting on her. Fuck the decision to keep her at a distance. If Loverboy moved a fraction of an inch closer, he was heading over and breaking every bone in the bastard's body.

Forcing his gaze away, he scanned the assembled passengers, studying expressions, gestures, and postures. Rawls surveyed the crowd as thoroughly from beside him. But within seconds Zane's attention migrated toward the right again. Toward that damn bench.

The pull toward her kept getting stronger. It took every ounce of restraint he possessed not to break position. He hated the loss of control.

He'd known the hunger would be strong when he found her. But he hadn't expected the sheer ferocity of the pull or the loss of his self-control. And he sure as shit hadn't expected the ugly urge to break apart any poor asshole that so much as looked at her.

But then he hadn't expected to find her in the middle of a crisis either.

What a mess.

"How you doin', skipper?" Rawls asked quietly.

"Fine," Zane snapped, ripping his attention from the bench and scanning the departure gate again. "Where's Cosky? He should be back by now."

They'd made several sweeps of the departure gate since Cosky had left to call Mac. By now they should have been able to pinpoint where the threat was coming from. If their target was an amateur, he'd be easy to spot—body posture and facial expressions would give him away. The fact that nothing struck them as odd or out of the ordinary indicated a clusterfuck of massive proportions. If the man behind the weapon was one of the laughing, chatting throng, then he was a professional and they were in deep shit.

The next time he glanced toward her, Loverboy had disappeared. Zane relaxed, at least until her gaze shifted, snaring his. A current of awareness arced between them. Son of a bitch. He *had* to get this reaction under control. But she was the one to turn away.

"She's the one, isn't she? The one you've been waiting for. Like with your dad and brothers." Disbelief rang in Rawls's voice.

"Yeah."

"And you just...know?"

"Something like that."

Although it went deeper than simply knowing. It was a tug in his bones, embedded in his cells. Hell, it spiraled right down to his DNA. It was the visceral certainty that she belonged to him.

When he caught sight of Cosky's dark head weaving through the throng of vacationers, Zane straightened.

"Mac's behind closed doors," Cosky said as soon as he joined them. "Radar wouldn't budge on disturbing him. Said to call back in thirty." He glanced at the clock on the wall behind the ticket counter. "It's tight, but workable. We've got ninety minutes before boarding." Frowning, he scanned the packed room. "Pick anything up on recon?"

Zane shook his head and scowled. "If he's here, the bastard's a pro. He isn't giving anything away."

With a twist of his shoulders, Cosky scanned the gate area. His gaze lingered on the bench in front of the main corridor and the blonde woman upon it. "What gives? You locked onto her like a guided missile the moment she entered the terminal. You can't keep your eyes off her. Yet she's sitting over there all by her lonesome."

Since there was no way he was going to admit he couldn't trust himself to remain focused if she came any closer, Zane settled for a half-truth. "We don't know what's going on. Could be someone's tracked us down and we're the targets. I don't want her anywhere near us until we've assessed the danger."

Of course it would help if he could concentrate on something besides her long enough to do his job. But his attention had splintered the moment she entered the gate room. He was acting like a goddamn adolescent with his first hard-on.

"I hate to break the bad news," Rawls said, shooting Zane a quick look. "But your little honey's on her way over."

Shit.

Zane folded his arms across his chest, set his jaw, and shifted until she faced his back. With luck she'd get the message and turn away. He couldn't afford this. Not only would her presence put her in danger, but she was enough of a distraction across the terminal. Having her up close and touchable was just asking for trouble.

"Head her off," he told Rawls and Cosky.

Heat washed over his back, flashed down to his groin.

Great. Just. Fucking. Great.

He could actually feel her behind him. Felt the tug getting stronger and stronger with each step she took.

Any other day. Any other place. But no, she had to show up today. She had to show up here. A great cosmic joke. He'd waited ten years for her, and now he couldn't even ask for her phone number.

After this was over, he'd call in some favors and get a copy of the passenger manifest. But it would take time to track her down. What if they were deployed before he found her again?

"Well, hey there, darlin'—" Rawls said.

The soft fall of footsteps ceased.

"I need to talk to you." Her voice was soft, low, thin with nerves.

Zane gritted his teeth and concentrated on his breathing.

"And I'd love to talk to you too, sweetcheeks, but we're plumb in the middle of something," Rawls told her.

"Not you. Him."

Zane tensed, focused on the crowd.

"He's married, honeycakes. Has a whole passel of brats."

"I don't care. I need to talk to him."

She didn't care?

He was losing his mind and she didn't care if he was married? He dropped his arms and turned around.

Rawls shuffled to the side, blocked her, and prowled forward, edging her back a couple of steps. "I didn't want to tell you this, considering he hasn't made it out of the closet yet. But the man's gay. No interest in women whatsoever."

Cosky, who was leaning against the wall beside Zane, choked.

Zane's gaze zeroed in on her face. It was oval, with soft cheekbones and a point to her chin. Then her eyes snared his. They were lavender. Honest-to-God lavender. The sweetest purple he'd ever seen. He was so entranced by their color it took him a second to recognize the emotion shimmering within those purple depths.

Fear.

He froze, reassessing.

"Rawls." His voice came out sharp.

Rawls shot him one quick questioning glance and stepped to the side.

She stumbled forward and reached out to touch Zane's arm. The caress of her fingertips against his bare skin set his nerves jangling. But there were no flashes, no disturbing visions. Which wasn't a surprise. Nobody in his family ever had visions that centered on themselves or their soul mates.

Heat spread out from the point of contact and shot straight to his cock. He went rock hard and aching in an instant. But not even a flicker of reaction touched her face or shimmered in her eyes.

Realization struck him dumb. She wasn't feeling the pull. His skin still sizzled from the mere brush of her fingers, but she'd had no reaction to the touch at all. No reaction to *him.*

Wasn't that just icing on the fucking cake?

"I need to warn you about...something. But they're watching."

He was so focused on her tender, trembling mouth it took a moment for her announcement to register.

She needed to warn them? Someone was watching?

"What's going on?" He tried for calm, but some of his frustration leaked into his voice and sharpened the question.

She bit her lip. "We can't talk here. They're watching. But if we flirt, they'll think that's why I came over. When we leave it won't look suspicious."

They? As in more than one threat?

"Who are they?"

"I don't know their names, just their faces. I'll tell you everything. But not here." A frown knit her forehead.

If she didn't know their names, she must not be directly involved. Maybe she'd overheard something. But that didn't explain why she'd approached him. Frowning, he searched her eyes. They were worried and wide, but held his squarely and without guilt.

Cosky shifted. "You can identify them?"

Zane shot him a quick glance. Yeah, they needed answers. Avoiding her was no longer an option. His best bet was to stick to her like a flak jacket.

She was right, though. They couldn't talk here. Too many eyes. Too many ears.

"Let's take a walk." He didn't wait for her response. Instead, he turned toward Rawls. "Stick around long enough to see if anyone follows us. Then head to the in-gate. We'll meet up by the restrooms." He glanced to the right. "Cosky? Watch our six."

He took hold of her elbow, ignoring the quiver that shook her, and swept the terminal one last time. Loverboy glared at him from across the room. Zane glared back. Time to show the little prick who had the right-of-way.

Across the terminal's main passageway and two gates down, Russ Branson watched Zane Winters—Lieutenant Commander Zane Winters, SEAL Team 7, according to the bosses' intel—escort Beth Brown down the tile corridor.

Interesting. The lady's name hadn't appeared on the passenger manifest.

While he'd been more interested in the first-class passengers and the three SEALs booked on the flight, he'd checked out the coach listings as well. He would have remembered a Beth Brown. Add in her reaction to Zane Winters and the fact the pair had hooked up immediately, and his instincts were humming.

Trouble with a capital *T* had just reared its ugly head. And unlike that fucking musical his sister Jilly insisted on playing over and over again—in this case the *T* did not rhyme with *P* and had nothing to do with pool.

It had to do with Special Operators.

He would have recognized the three even without the heads-up. He'd spent four years eating, shitting, and sleeping with such a team. He damn well recognized the vibe.

Just as he recognized a team rendezvous when he saw one—and not one of the romantic variety. Any minute the other two bastards would take off and the four of them would meet up someplace free of unwelcome eyes and ears. He could have sent someone after them, but why bother? Those SEALs were pros. They'd recognize a tail in an instant, and he'd lose the advantage of surprise.

He turned from the couple disappearing down the corridor before his interest became noticeable. One never knew who might be watching.

Sitting on a blue bench directly across from him was a child somewhere around the age of Jilly's youngest, maybe four or five. She was a cute little thing, all big brown eyes and rich mocha skin. Her frizzy hair was the color of dark chocolate. Russ winked at her, grinning as those velvety eyes widened even more.

But his smile quickly faded. The child was too frail. Pointy little elbows and knees.

His attention shifted to the fat cow in the sweat suit slumped beside the youngster. They shared the same shade of hair and eyes, but the resemblance ended there. The mother obviously consumed all the calories between the pair. Maybe if the bitch dragged her attention from the trashy magazine she was reading, she'd remember that the child needed to eat.

He turned back to the little tyke. She'd been staring at him with those huge, solemn eyes since he'd sat down. Children, in general, were amazingly perceptive, but even more so at her age. What exactly did she sense in him that brought such wariness to her eyes?

Which reminded him…

Russ dug into the pocket of his laptop case and retrieved his cell phone. As he waited for the call to ring through, he winked at the little girl again and raised his eyebrows, waggling them. The gesture had the opposite effect than he'd intended. The little one shrank back and reached for her mother's hand.

With a shrug, Russ turned his attention back to the phone.

"How are our guests?" he asked the moment his man picked up the call. "Did the packages arrive for the children? Good. Good. Are the toys keeping them occupied? Excellent."

Shifting on the bench, he glanced back down the corridor. One of the SEALs—the dark-haired one—had left his post and fallen in behind his lieutenant commander. According to intel, the black hair marked him as Marcus Simcosky. Seth Rawlings had the blond hair. He glanced toward C-18's ticket counter, but the wall opposite stood empty. Rawlings was in the wind now too.

"It's time to send a memo to our new employees. Remind them that following company policy is a requirement," Russ said into the phone. Settling back, he crossed his ankles and slouched down until he could lean his head against the bench's backrest. As casually as possible, he shot another glance down the terminal corridor. Simcosky's brisk strides were quickly carrying him from sight.

"How goes the company retreat? Are the kids getting bored? I have just the thing. The carnival's in town. At the Puyallup fairgrounds. I'm sure the kids would love a morning of fun. Three of you accompany our young guests, while the rest entertain their mothers. Make sure you take plenty of video. I want our new associates to appreciate how much effort we've put into entertaining their families during their stay with us."

He ended the call by flipping the phone shut, but he kept it in hand. He needed to update the bosses. But what exactly to tell them?

Winters, Simcosky, and Rawlings were obviously in stealth mode. The question was why.

What the hell were they picking up on?

He'd taken every precaution. He'd instructed his D–Day crew to arrive at the last possible moment. Other than his short flirtation while checking out Beth Brown, he had been sticking close to gate C-20, keeping an eye on Flight 2077's passengers from his bench next door. He knew damn well how to watch people without giving the appearance of watching. The guns were already on board. There was nothing happening in the terminal that should have tickled those bastards' finely conditioned instincts and brought down SEAL Team 7's hammer.

His gaze shifted to the front of C-18's waiting area. The bench that Beth Brown had collapsed on was already occupied. He sighed at the sight of the three children quietly coloring beside their parents, but pushed the regret aside. It was a pity there were so many kids booked on the flight, but necessity didn't care about the ages of her victims. His gaze lingered on the children's mother as she smiled and exclaimed over the picture her offspring presented to her.

Russ scowled. Somehow Beth Brown was the key. Her reaction when she'd caught sight of Winters had verged on bizarre. She'd literally stopped in her tracks. Swayed. Almost fainted. But why?

Winters's reaction to her had been almost as odd. He'd noticed her the moment she'd arrived, hadn't been able to keep his eyes off her. Yet when she'd finally approached, he'd turned his back on her. A lovers' spat? Unlikely. Special Operators didn't turn away from confrontation, even when it came to their women.

Besides, intel on Winters indicated that priests got more action. If he was hitting the mattress with some new chick, it would have been brought to their attention.

Sighing, Russ rubbed his forehead. Maybe he was reading the signs wrong.

Special Operations taught caution. The scanning and recon could be simple conditioning. If those SEALs suspected his plans for that plane, they'd have shut the flight down. But according to the reader board, the departure remained on schedule.

As for Brown, maybe she'd been struck dumb by the testosterone saturating the air. The trio had drawn a good chunk of admiring eyes—both male and female. Maybe she was looking for a vacation fling, and Winters was ready to oblige.

Except...Russ caught a flash of wheat-colored hair as Seth Rawlings trailed after his buddies. If Winters's interest in the woman was some good old-fashioned sex, he wouldn't have invited his lieutenants along for the ride. The guy was a Boy Scout, conservative to the core. He wasn't the type to appreciate a ménage.

He glanced around. The only person close enough to catch his end of the conversation was the fat cow across from him, but she was deaf, dumb, and blind to everything except the magazine she was reading.

Swearing softly, he stared down at the cell phone. After a moment, he reluctantly punched the first number in the keypad. As each successive number lit the diminutive screen, the muscles of his chest tightened until it felt like Horton the elephant was sitting on his chest.

The woman's appearance could mean nothing. But they'd gut him, cut off his testicles, and leave him to rot if things went south because he hadn't updated them on a potential problem.

A cultured voice replaced the ringing. "Our agreement was no contact until the plane was in the air."

Sweat broke out over Russ's palms. "You requested updates in the event something unexpected occurred."

A pulse of silence fell. "Continue then."

"One of our acquaintances has acquired a new girlfriend by the name of Beth Brown. She's booked on his flight."

"There is no Beth Brown on the passenger manifest," the voice coolly observed. "Which acquaintance?"

The fingers of his right hand started cramping. Russ relaxed their tense hold on the plastic casing of the phone. "LC."

A short, thoughtful pause. "Our intel suggests Lieutenant Commander Winters is unattached."

With a frown, Russ scrubbed a hand down his face. "We may need a refresher course."

A hum of agreement echoed down the line. "Do you sense a problem?"

"LC and the lady disappeared. Five minutes later, his buddies vanished as well."

"If such is the case, it's unlikely to be a lovers' rendezvous."

"Agreed."

Cold silence trickled down the line. "Had you removed this obstacle when you were advised, we would not be having this conversation."

Russ's fingers cramped again. Christ, there had been every possibility the team would deploy before the flight departed. Not to mention taking out three members of ST7 would have brought a hornet's nest down on their ass. It had made more sense to take them out on the plane. The three had no weapons. His crew was armed with submachine guns and had been given explicit instructions to target the SEALs first. Winters and his buddies wouldn't stand a chance.

"Taking action too soon would have raised...concerns."

"So you convinced us at the time." The voice chilled even further. "Considerable resources have been expended. We expect a return on our investment."

Russ chanced a quick, shallow breath. "The flight is still on schedule."

"Make certain it remains that way."

The line went dead.

Russ eased his numb fingers off the phone and dropped it into a side pocket on the laptop's case.

Ten years ago he'd taken the skills he'd honed through the military's generosity and gone into business for himself. He'd quickly discovered he had a knack for the work. Russ knew his strengths. He was good at what he did. Damn good. Maybe even the best. And that wasn't boasting. That was an honest-to-God fact. He hadn't lost an operation yet. Which was why his current employers had sought him out.

The money they'd offered had been impossible to refuse. The first half of his payment had paid off Jilly's house and her car and set up college funds for the kids. The second half would fund his retirement.

He'd handled jobs for extremists, drug cartels, and organized crime. He'd even worked with various Third World dictators a time or two. Men in power didn't scare him. There were always exit strategies. Nor had he questioned his ability to handle a troublesome employer.

Until now. Until this job.

But then he'd never taken on clients like his current masters—rich beyond imagination, political powerhouses, and batshit insane.

Their operation had taken months of planning, God only knew how much cash, and enough cogs to run a small country.

But the test flight had gone smooth as pie, bloody as a coup.

Russ didn't doubt, regardless of ST7's interference, that'd he'd get that plane down to Puerto Jardin as directed.

And once the plane landed, he'd take his fee and get the hell out of PJ. Assuming his reward for a job well done wasn't a bullet through the brain.

Beth blinked. Okay...Zane actually sounded like he believed her.

Pulling Beth closer, he slipped his arm around her waist, anchoring her to his side. Then he bent to her ear, his breath warm and moist against her neck. "Easy. We're just taking a walk, like any other couple. Put your arm around my hip."

Tingles swept down from where his breath fanned her neck and released a cloud of butterflies in her belly. Swallowing hard, she reminded herself that she'd been the one to suggest the flirting ploy. As she slipped her arm around his lean waist, she was far too fixated on his scent and how his warmth radiated up and down her side.

He didn't say another word as he guided her through the terminal, steering her around clusters of passengers and scattered luggage. To the right, a brood of shrieking children climbed a pair of benches like they were a jungle gym. She caught a glimpse of her Good Samaritan as he headed toward a bench in gate C-20. When they reached the tile corridor that ran the length of the airport, Zane turned toward the inbound security gate.

Beth frowned as she kept pace with him. "You believed me?"

"That something's about to go down? Yeah." His eyes were constantly on the move, scanning the faces they passed, inspecting the kiosks and fast-food alcoves that ran the length of the corridor.

After several seconds of walking, Beth dropped her arm and stepped to the side until a good six inches separated them.

He glanced down with a frown but let her go, his gaze lingering on her lips. "What's your name?"

Her voice caught in her throat. "Beth."

"Nobody's following," a flat voice said from behind. "You find out what the hell's going on?"

Beth started, and turned to find the other dark-haired warrior behind them. The one Zane had called Cosky. Yet she hadn't heard a sound. No footsteps. No breathing. Nothing.

"Not here." Electric-green eyes narrowed and swept the corridor, then shifted to a shallower hall that branched off the main path and dead-ended a few feet past a steel door marked *Authorized Personnel Only*. He nodded at the posted door. "There." He took Beth's elbow and steered her toward their rendezvous point. When he tried the steel doorknob, it didn't budge. "Cosky?"

Shifting up, he eased Beth in line beside him until their bodies created a barricade, blocking the main corridor's view of the door and whatever Zane's buddy was doing to it. She heard the whisper of cloth rubbing on cloth, followed by the scratch of steel on steel.

"We're in," Cosky said a second or so later.

He'd picked the lock much faster than Beth had expected. With the way her luck was running, these three probably weren't even the good guys; she'd probably accosted a trio of criminals. It suddenly occurred to her that she was about to disappear inside a room with three men she didn't even know, yet for some odd reason she felt perfectly safe.

Zane's low whistle brought Beth's attention front and center again, just in time to see his blond friend swivel in midstride and head in their direction. Zane scanned the airport corridor and waited for an Asian couple to pass. Once the coast was clear, he swung Beth around and pushed her through the open door, following her inside. Someone must have hit a switch, because bright white light exploded all around her.

They were in a supply closet. Floor-to-ceiling steel shelves stocked full of paper towels, toilet paper, and plastic soap dispensers covered three of the four walls. Against the far wall was a jumbled mess of mops, buckets, brooms, and vacuum cleaners. The interior reeked of industrial cleaner.

Although the space wasn't small, by the time Zane's two friends followed them inside and closed the door, Beth felt claustrophobic. All those huge male bodies seemed to suck the oxygen from the air.

"Boys, this is Beth," Zane said. "Beth, meet Simcosky and Rawlings." He glanced down, his hair gleaming like dark chocolate beneath the fluorescent lights. "I'm—"

It was now or never. Beth didn't hesitate. "Zane Winters," she interrupted. "Lieutenant Zane Winters. I know who you are."

Dead silence followed. All three men went still. Alert. Zane dropped her arm and stepped back.

"You know my name." Zane's tone remained controlled. "How? I'd sure as hell remember if we'd met."

"We've never met."

Simcosky and Rawlings exchanged glances.

"How do you know who I am?" Zane repeated.

Zane's green eyes shone with a different expression now. Watchfulness? Suspicion?

There was no easy way to say it, so Beth just tossed the answer out. "Because I dreamed of you. I watched the three of you die."

Chapter Three

ABSOLUTE SILENCE RAGED FOR SEVEN OR EIGHT SECONDS. To
Beth, it seemed to last forever.

"You dreamed about us." Zane's tone remained level. But his
eyes went flat and his face still, radiating skepticism.

Beth rushed the explanation out. "That's how I know your
name and rank. I heard them in the dream." She nodded toward
Rawlings. "He called you 'Lieutenant.'"

The blond man didn't look so easygoing now. With his
expressionless face and icy eyes, he looked like the warrior she'd
instinctively recognized him to be in the nightmare—the kind of
man who could kill without hesitation or regret.

For the first time a flicker of emotion crossed Zane's face. He
frowned, his forehead creasing, but his gaze remained locked on
her face. It was amazing; even the heat his big body generated felt
banked, as though his suspicions had locked him down physically
as well as emotionally.

"Tell me what you heard."

This was good, right? He was asking questions. He hadn't called
her a liar or told her to up her meds. She studied his rigid face,
the frosty gaze, the subtle distance he'd put between them. *Yeah,
right. Who was she kidding?* He didn't believe a word she'd said. She

shifted her attention to his two warrior buddies. Both regarded her with complete blankness. They didn't believe her either.

But then she'd known they'd need some major convincing.

"It was right after the three of you entered the departure gate and settled against the wall." She thought back, visualizing that moment in the dream. "Your dark-haired friend—" What had Zane called him? Simcosky. That was it. "Your buddy Simcosky said, 'He agreed to Hawaii, for God's sake. He's whipped. End of discussion.' And then your blond friend slapped you on the back and said, 'Don't know what you're complaining about anyway. At least it's not some Somalian rat hole. We're talking beaches, Lieutenant, bikinis. We've been stuck in worse places.'"

The green flecks in Zane's eyes warmed, and he shifted his attention to Rawlings. "She heard you call Cosky 'Lieutenant' and thought you were talking to me."

"You're not a lieutenant?"

"Lieutenant commander." His eyes turned distant as though he were thinking back to that moment, trying to picture her there. "I would have noticed her, if she'd been close enough to hear that," he said after a moment, the comment directed toward his two friends. More of that nonverbal communication flowed between them.

"I didn't hear that exchange in the terminal. I heard it in the dream."

"Okay. Say I buy this." Zane turned back to her, his gaze sharpening. "That still doesn't give you my name."

Beth shrugged. "Well, your friends kept calling you skipper, boss, or Zane. But I got your last name from your driver's license."

Simcosky lifted his eyebrows. "You dreamed about his driver's license?" he asked, his voice faintly mocking.

Beth stiffened and forced herself to hold his gaze. His eyes were hard, the color of concrete.

"What I dreamed," she emphasized, crossing her arms, "is that he was dead. They rolled him over and pulled out his wallet. They seemed to be confirming his identity."

Another few seconds of that intense, silent communication passed.

Zane broke the silence. "Who are *they*?"

Beth took a deep breath, but it didn't ease the tightness in her chest. She gripped her elbows harder. "*They* are the hijackers. The men who take control of the plane and kill everyone in coach."

"Hijacking?" Zane froze for a second, glanced at his dark-haired buddy, then rocked back on his heels and shook his head. "You're telling us you dreamed a hijacking? How are they going to accomplish that? Since 9/11, security at airports has quadrupled. And then there are the passengers. They aren't as complacent. They band together and act now. Box knives and bombs aren't going to control an airliner."

But there was an odd expression in his eyes. Watchful rather than disbelieving.

"They had guns, not box knives," Beth retorted, squeezing her elbows so hard she knew they'd sport bruises by evening. "And they don't try to control their passengers, they slaughter them. At least the ones in coach."

Zane ran a hand through his hair and frowned harder. Recognition kindled in his gaze. Something she'd said had struck a chord with him.

Simcosky straightened from his slouch against the metal shelving. The ice had melted from his eyes, but his face hadn't lost its impassiveness. "What you're describing requires major firepower.

We passed through security; it's state-of-the-art. Maybe a single person could slip through undetected, but multiple men, smuggling multiple weapons? No. Besides, stray bullets puncturing the hull and windows would bring the bird down."

"The guns are already on board. They're beneath the seats. All the hijackers have to do is bend down and pull them out. And bullet holes won't bring a plane down, they won't even cause decompression—which the hijackers must know." She paused, but forced herself to continue, her voice growing hoarser with each word. "Because once the plane levels out, they grab the guns and start shooting. When the gunfire stops, everyone in coach is dead."

The screams still echoed in her head. Beth scrubbed her palms down her face and pressed her fingers against her burning eyes. "I don't understand it, though." She dropped her hands. "Why kill them? It doesn't make sense. PacAtlantic would negotiate for their release."

Zane studied her face, tilted his head, and slowly shook it. "PacAtlantic wouldn't be in control. The FBI and DHS would step in." He paused a beat. "The United States government does not negotiate with terrorists. Since coach passengers were apparently no use to them, they could have been eliminating potential threats." Deep in thought, he stared at the whitewashed door. "What did they do with the first-class passengers?"

"It sounded like they were being held for ransom."

"Depending on who's flying first class, that would net some pretty hefty profits," Zane acknowledged, but the observation wasn't directed at Beth. "Where did these bastards land the plane?"

Beth thought back, trying to remember the name of the tiny country they'd diverted the airliner to. "They called it Puerto

Jardin. They blew the cockpit doors and killed the pilots. One of the hijackers took over flying."

"Puerto Jardin," Zane repeated beneath his breath. "Son of a bitch. That would explain why they targeted this flight. Seattle to Hawaii would be one of the few domestic flights that would net them wealthy passengers, expensive cargo, and enough fuel to escape to South America." He fell silent, frowning, his eyebrows a heavy black line above his hooded gaze. A moment later he glanced at Simcosky. "The MO she's describing is identical to that hijacking down in Buenos Aires last summer. They slaughtered everyone in coach but ransomed the first-class passengers. Argentina kept a lid on it."

Did this mean they were beginning to believe her?

Rawlings rubbed his palm over his flat stomach. "Zane's right—the MO's identical. The Argentinean plane was diverted to the interior of Puerto Jardin. This has to be the same crew."

"Or," Simcosky said, his voice dry. He crossed his arms over his chest and settled into a subtly challenging stance. "She could be blowing smoke up our asses. She dreamed the entire hijacking from start to finish? Including the landing? Dreams don't last that long. Nor are they so coherent. Hell, even if she did have this dream, it's more likely it was triggered by fear of flying."

"I didn't dream the whole thing at once," Beth interjected. "I had it three nights in a row, and every time I fell back asleep it would pick up where it had left off. As for fear of flying..." She held Simcosky's cold gaze. "I work for PAA—PacAtlantic," she explained when Zane frowned. "We get to fly free. I've been all over the world, so believe me, boarding a plane doesn't scare me. Besides, I wasn't planning on taking this flight."

Zane froze, every muscle in his body rigid. His head turned, and he scanned her face. "You don't have a ticket for our flight?"

"I'm on standby. Listing myself was the only way I could pick up a boarding pass."

"When did you register?" Zane asked, his voice tense, his face tight, as though he already suspected the answer and didn't like it. Not one bit.

"I don't know—maybe an hour ago." She watched his jaw clench.

"Fuck." He walked a tight circuit around the cramped room. His two friends watched in silence.

"What's wrong?" When he simply shook his head, she felt compelled to explain. "Signing up for standby was the only way I could get through the security gate and over to the departure terminal. It was the only way I could take a look at the passengers waiting to board."

"And you didn't check any baggage." Zane sounded grimmer by the moment.

Alarm skittered down Beth's spine. "Well, no. Even if a seat became available I wasn't going to take it. I was going to cancel the listing."

"Did you at least tell someone else about this dream and what you were planning to do?"

"Uh...no. The whole thing seemed so crazy...and I didn't want anyone at work to think that I was...well...crazy."

"You're buying trouble," Simcosky told him calmly. "We don't know whether weapons are stashed on that plane."

"The hell we don't." Zane squared off against his buddy, every muscle in his body radiating aggression. "You know what I—" He broke off, glanced at Beth, and shook his head. "She repeated—basically word for word—that entire exchange in the terminal. An exchange that took place an *hour* before she arrived. If she'd been listening in from somewhere, I would have known."

Simcosky focused on Beth's face. "You have these dreams often? The kind that come true?"

Beth shook her head. "Never. I'm not psychic."

"True." There was an undercurrent of dryness in Simcosky's tone. "Psychic visions aren't nearly so detailed." He paused a moment and raised his eyebrows, his gaze steady on Zane's face. "Or helpful."

Another round of silent messages shot back and forth.

Zane swung back to her. "What made you question this dream? Most people would shrug it off the next morning."

"The dream didn't start in the terminal. It started with spilled coffee and a detour to work because of a warehouse fire."

"The fire happened, so did the detour." Zane instantly picked up on what she hadn't said. "That's what sent you to the terminal to check out the passengers."

Beth nodded and coughed to clear her throat. "I started wondering about the plane. It kept niggling at me, so I took a sick day and listed myself on standby. But I never expected to recognize anyone."

With quick strides, Zane returned to her side. "We must have come as a shock."

"You have no idea."

Zane grinned, but it quickly faded. For a long moment he stared into space. "How many hijackers are we talking about?"

"There were six. Two sets of three. They were seated across the aisle from each other, in the middle of the plane."

There was a pregnant pause. Rawlings broke it. "If the guns were already on board, there has to be an inside man," he said, his face devoid of the lazy humor he'd shown in the dream.

"No shit." Zane scowled into the corner of the supply closet.

"Odds are it's someone from PacAtlantic," Rawlings said.

Zane pivoted to face Beth. "Who would have access to the plane between flights?"

"Well, of course the bag smashers have access." When Zane grinned, Beth realized what she'd said and flushed. The company didn't appreciate that particular nickname.

She held up a hand and started ticking off the possibilities as they occurred to her. "The cleaners, caterers, gate agents, mechanics, fuelers, the flight crew..." She fell silent as a final department occurred to her.

"What?" Zane asked, those green eyes locked on her face.

"The engineering department, *my* department, has access as well," she reluctantly admitted.

It felt like a betrayal to even mention it. There was no way anyone she worked with could be involved in something so horrific. But her engineers did have complete access between flights, and the ground crew wouldn't think twice about someone from engineering boarding the plane.

Although Zane didn't make a sound, the muscles across his shoulders bunched.

Simcosky watched him for a few moments before turning those steel eyes on Beth. "Tell us about this dream of yours. Start to finish. Everything."

The three men listened intently as she described her nightmare. When she mentioned the blocks of claylike substance they'd used to blow the cockpit doors, Zane hissed. "C4," he said and the other two nodded. "They're pros. Too much and they'd blow the plane. Not enough and they wouldn't breach the cockpit door." Zane's comment was followed by another round of nods. "What kind of guns?"

"I don't know." She frowned, thinking of the *Die Hard* and James Bond movies she'd been subjected to throughout the years. What was it about first dates and action movies? She eyed Zane. He probably loved those fast-paced, blow-up-everything-in-sight action flicks. "They looked like machine guns."

A slow smile spread across Zane's face, one of pure indulgence. "They couldn't have been machine guns. They're long-range weapons that require tripods."

Beth rolled her eyes. "They had lots of bullets and they killed you. What more do you need to know?"

"The make and model. That way we'll know how many bullets to dodge," the blond said, his blue eyes back to laughing.

She folded her arms across her chest and set her shoulders. They were running out of time. "Look. I don't see how the model is going to make a difference. We know they're on board. Can't you guys just make some calls and have someone check the plane?"

"The type of weapons tells us how they got them on board. You said they look like machine guns, so it's likely they're submachines. An MP5 would have to be hidden in a tote—like a toolbox. Which means the inside guy could be from maintenance." Simcosky's gaze shifted between Beth and Zane. "Or engineering," he added, his tone flat.

From Zane's tight expression, this information wasn't news to him.

She ignored the suggestion that someone from her department might be involved. They didn't know her engineers. It simply wasn't possible. "There's less than seventy minutes before the plane boards. Isn't there someone you can call to get the plane searched but without alerting the hijackers?"

The silence that fell was even deeper and more intimidating than it had been earlier when she'd blurted out his name. Beth's stomach clenched as she got a good look at the grim expression on Zane's face.

"See, we have a problem, sweetheart," he finally said, rubbing his chest. "I can make some calls. I can get that plane searched. Once you point the hijackers out, we can contain them until the white knights arrive." He fell silent, the tension solidifying the air surrounding them until it pulsed like a bass drum.

"But that's good. That's exactly what we want. I don't see any problem with that," Beth whispered, forcing the words out of her suddenly tight throat. She waited for the other shoe to drop, because something was obviously very, very wrong.

Zane sighed and shook his head, regarding her steadily. "The problem…is there's obviously an inside accomplice. Someone from PacAtlantic. Someone with access to the plane between flights. And once the FBI starts investigating, you'll rise to the top of their suspect list."

Zane watched every ounce of color leach from Beth's face.

Her eyes widened. "But I'm trying to stop it."

"I know." He shifted closer to her and ran a soothing hand up and down her spine. He could sense her fear rising. It brushed against his mind. A texture and tone that didn't originate within him.

The bond was already forming. If he could keep her close—close enough to touch—it would form faster. Physical contact accelerated the connection.

"But the agents investigating won't. One of the things they'll look at is behavior. And yours will look pretty damn suspicious."

She thought that over, the worry lines in her forehead deepening. "Why?"

"It's a combination of things. Number one, you work for PacAtlantic and in a department with access to their planes between flights. Number two, you listed yourself on standby mere hours before the flight boarded. You did this spur-of-the-moment, without telling your coworkers, and without telling anyone about your dream. Number three, this is a plane to Hawaii, but you only took one day off and brought no luggage. When they start looking into passengers, your behavior is going to stand out. It's going to look suspicious as hell."

The muscles of her throat trembled. Another surge of fear brushed against his mind. He rubbed her back again. Up and down, a slow soothing glide. What they needed was an explanation for her behavior. His hand slowed as the solution occurred to him.

He swallowed a grin. Christ, it was perfect. It would keep her tied to him as the connection grew, but it would also give the investigators a concrete reason for her behavior. They might not cross her off their suspect list, but they wouldn't look at her quite so closely.

When she pulled away Zane let her go, and that odd, whispery tickle brushing against his subconscious vanished.

"But I *don't* have access to the planes. I'm just clerical. I don't have clearance. My engineers do, although—" She shot Cosky a so-there look. "They don't use toolboxes or totes so they couldn't have smuggled the guns on board."

Zane shook his head. "If your guys have access to the plane, they could have figured out a way to get the guns on board. And you could still be involved. At the very least, they'll believe you knew about the planned hijacking but didn't come forward to report it."

"I'll explain about the dream." She lifted her chin. "If I was involved, I wouldn't be trying to stop the hijacking."

He hated the fear in her eyes, but she needed to be prepared. "They won't believe you. What they'll believe is you got cold feet and tried to back out. What they'll believe is you made up the dream to give yourself a reason for knowing something you shouldn't."

Beth gulped and bit her bottom lip, but she held his eyes. "Maybe you're right. But we still have to tell someone—even if it's going to get me into trouble. Without my dream, how will we convince someone to search the plane?"

Pride speared through Zane, followed by a healthy dose of respect. Even knowing the cost, she still insisted on intervening. She was willing to sacrifice her life for those passengers on the plane. Because at this point she had to know that if she became the major focus of such an investigation, it could well destroy her.

"We're not going to tell anyone you're the one who had the dream," Zane told her, aware that Cosky and Rawls had gone still.

They'd probably already figured out where he was going with this. From the tight expressions on their faces, they didn't like it. Which was no surprise. The real question was whether they'd go along with it.

"But we have to." Beth's voice rose with each word. "How will we get anyone to search the plane if we don't tell them about my dream?"

He smiled at her words. She'd linked them together with *we*. She didn't realize it yet, but she was already coupling them in her mind.

"You're telling Mackenzie you had the dream." Cosky's face turned stone cold.

Zane didn't deny it, just let the silence build.

Rawls was the first to break the tension. He scowled at the wall above Zane's head. "Mac's been in on enough of your"—he glanced at Beth—"hunches. He'll believe you without question."

"Yeah."

"Fuck." Cosky studied Beth's face intently before scrubbing a hand over his head. "It would get that plane searched and hijackers captured without bringing her into it."

"Who's Mackenzie?"

"Commander Jace Mackenzie. Our CO—commanding officer," Zane explained as confusion registered on her face.

Although Mac was more than their CO. He was one of Zane's best friends. Zane had served under the commander before Mac had reluctantly agreed to rank up and take a desk. Zane had even followed Mac down to Coronado and HQ1.

Son of a bitch. He didn't like lying to Mac any more than Cosky or Rawls did. It went against every instinct he had. But it was lie or serve Beth up to some glory-seeking pencil pusher out to make a name for himself. These kinds of cases drew publicity like fresh roadkill drew crows. They destroyed innocent lives.

No way was he letting Beth take the fall for this. Even if that meant lying to his superior.

If he told Mackenzie about Beth and her nightmare, the commander would make a round of calls that would result in the plane being searched. But Mac would turn her in. During the best of times, he had little use for women—apart from the obvious. When it came to national security, he wouldn't even hesitate.

Rawls cut loose with a curse sharp as a gunshot. "We better pray he never finds out about this. Otherwise we're up shit river."

Cosky stared at Beth for a long moment before turning to Zane. "I won't lie to him point-blank. If he asks me about *your dream*, I'll tell him the truth."

Zane nodded. Neither man would have agreed to this if they'd suspected Beth was involved.

"I don't know." Beth's lavender eyes were brimming with guilt and worry. "How much trouble will you get into if you get caught lying?"

Surprised, Zane turned his attention to her. He'd given her an easy out, one that would take the responsibility off her shoulders. Yet she was worried how it would affect him. Warmth spread through his chest.

"None," he assured her, which was another lie.

If Mac found out about the switch, Zane would be in a world of hurt. When Beth didn't look convinced, Zane tried again. "I'll tell Mac the same thing you told us, so the meat of what I'm telling him is true."

She apparently assumed that meant Mackenzie would understand and forgive if the lie was exposed. The worry and guilt smoothed from her face. Zane let her believe it. It was amazing how that one deception kept bleeding into others.

"So you're in the army?"

Rawls chuckled, although it sounded forced. "Bite your tongue." His gaze lingered on her mouth, and his grin eased into a more natural cast. "I'd be offended you'd confuse us with those dust-bowl wannabes if you weren't so cute."

Zane stiffened. That son of a bitch better find someplace else to stare or he wouldn't be flashing his killer grin again until the bones in his face knitted. He almost stepped forward to block Rawls's view when the absurdity stuck him. Christ, he was acting like an idiot. Rawls wouldn't poach a teammate's woman. Once she was spoken for, she was off-limits.

And Beth was his. The only one who wasn't aware of that fact was Beth.

"I'm sorry. I just assumed."

"We're with the Navy. SEAL Team 7." Zane cocked his head and waited for her reaction.

He rarely mentioned his profession to strangers, particularly women. Invariably they reacted in one of two ways. With distaste, as though the fact he was Special Operations dropped him into the same category as your average serial killer. Or they'd get this gleam in their eyes, something resembling sexual avarice, as though making it through BUD/S had endowed him with some mystical prowess.

When her expression cleared, Zane relaxed. Until it occurred to him she might not know what being a SEAL entailed.

"The SEAL program is the Navy's version of Special Forces—" he started to explain.

"I know," she broke in. "Deployed from sea, land, and air. I've read some…ah…" She coughed, her cheeks flushing pink. "… books that had SEALs in them."

TRISH McCALLAN

"No kiddin'," Rawls drawled, a mask of innocence plastered across his face. He braced his elbows on the shelving behind him and eyed her with a lazy smile. "Can I borrow them? I'm always interested in seeing how the public views our profession."

When Beth's cheeks blazed from pink to bright red, Zane's eyebrows climbed. Maybe he should borrow those books too.

"It occurs to me," she blurted out, obviously trying to side-track them from her reading habits, "even if I cancel the standby listing, it will still show up when they run the passenger manifest. I'll still be a suspect."

"Yeah, well." Zane rubbed his chin and tried not to look satisfied. "I've got a plan to make you look less suspicious."

Rawls started laughing.

Zane snapped off a glare and turned his attention back to Beth's suddenly leery expression.

"Pay attention, Cosky," Rawls drawled, managing to hold back the laughter long enough to force the words out. "We're about to witness some of the finest rationalization known to man." He started laughing again.

Zane ignored him.

Beth looked from Rawls to Zane and back to Rawls. "I'm not going to like this, am I?"

Fuck. He hadn't intended to broach the subject like this, but any good strategist knew to regroup and redeploy. "The best way to clear you of suspicion is to give you another reason to be at the airport, spur-of-the-moment, without your clothes."

Nervousness touched her face. Her eyes skittered to Rawls, who'd leaned back against one of the steel rungs of the shelving. He'd stopped laughing, but his shoulders still shook.

"I'm definitely not going to like this," she said to no one in particular.

Zane barreled ahead. "We're on our way to Hawaii for a teammate's wedding. Cosky's from Seattle. Since we're on leave, we decided to head out early, do some hiking along the trails Cosky's been bragging about, then fly out for the wedding. We've been hiking all week. We'll tell everyone that we met over the weekend and things got hot, fast. I asked you to come to Hawaii with me, but you were uncomfortable taking off with someone you'd just met. We argued. But this morning you changed your mind and decided to join me, so you listed yourself on standby."

He paused, studied her face. Was she buying his reasoning? With luck it wouldn't occur to her that they could just claim she'd come to the gate to say good-bye.

"To make this work, you'll need to call your supervisor and request the week off."

She took a deep breath and let it out; her face turned stoic. "We'll have to act like a couple."

That stoicism seriously pissed him off. Was it really that fucking hard to act like she might be interested in him? Anger prickling, he didn't try to sugarcoat his correction.

"Not a couple. Lovers. Hot and heavy lovers. The kind so hungry for each other they'd fly to Hawaii without any luggage because they'd be spending all their time in bed."

Chapter Four

COMMANDER JACE MACKENZIE DROPPED THE TELEPHONE receiver into its cradle and threw himself against the backrest of his desk chair. The metal and plastic shifted beneath his weight, squeaking like a rabid hamster on a wheel.

So, some motherfuckers thought they could grab one of America's passenger planes, did they?

He rubbed a hand over his jaw. Those fuckheads were in for a major surprise. In a contest between three of his best men and six cold-blooded killers, he'd bet every single cent he owned on his boys. Zane and company would nail those bastards to the wall and hold them there until the FBI and Homeland Security swept in for cleanup.

Slowly, the grin faded. It never paid to settle into complacency. The second you considered a situation under control it exploded in your face with the fury of an H-bomb. He'd seen it happen too many times. Some poor schmuck who'd relaxed at the worst possible moment and got his ass handed to him in the midst of a raging firestorm.

Mac wasn't afraid of death. Hell, you couldn't afford fear in his line of work. Fear paralyzed faster than a round to the spine. Besides, there were some things worth dying for. Forget that clichéd crap of love and the American Dream. Love wouldn't buy you a handful of stale peanuts. As for the American dream—that sucker had long ago withered into selfishness and a sense of entitlement. For every poor sod who appreciated the sacrifices endured in mosquito-infested swamps while your brothers-in-arms disintegrated into bloody chunks all around you, there was some other motherfucker burning the American flag.

Scowling, Mac glared at the phone.

Zane Winters was one of the calmest and most rational—yet surprisingly intuitive—men he'd served with. One of the few people, on a very short list, Mac trusted implicitly. Hell, Winters had been the one who'd talked him into stepping up and accepting this fucking desk job—which also happened to be the *only* grudge he held against the guy. As for those freaky visions of his... well, fuck. They'd saved their asses more than once.

So if Zane said something was going to happen on that plane, then something was going to happen. He'd been on the receiving end of Winters's intuitive flashes enough to trust his LC's judgment. Yeah, this might be the first time his buddy had actually dreamed an event, and hell yeah, that might make it even freakier than normal, but if Winters said there were guns on that bird, and six men intending to grab it and divert to Puerto Jardin, then Mac would get the FBI and DHS out there pronto.

Because Zane Winters didn't lie.

Which made it a fucking bitter pill to swallow knowing his best friend had just spent the better part of the past five minutes lying to him.

Oh, he didn't doubt for an instant that there were guns stashed beneath those seats and six bastards intending to escort the passengers into the afterlife. No, he didn't doubt the bulk of what his

LC had told him, but something about that conversation didn't ring true.

Winters wasn't the only one with kickass intuition. And Mac's bullshit meter, which had been fine-tuned through the years, had warped into the red zone. Although what, exactly, he was picking up on, he didn't have a clue.

Staring down, Mac picked up a pen and glared at his stained, battered, and scuffed steel desk. His one and only contact in the FBI had retired the previous year, which meant he had absolutely nobody to call from the Rolodex in his mind. However, he had HQ1's secret weapon a push button away.

He reached out to punch the intercom button as the conversation with Zane played through his head. Something niggled at him, but he couldn't put his damn finger on it, and considering the plane was due to lift off in an hour, he didn't have time to pin it down.

"Get hold of someone from the FBI," he said the moment he heard the door open, "and not some fucking junior agent. I need someone with clout, someone who can get things done."

The measured footsteps across the room paused, as though he'd managed to startle the old goat for a change. Mac glanced up, hoping to see surprise on that weathered face, but not a chance. His assistant, Radar, had his intractable image to preserve.

"What division?" Radar asked. With his ears sticking out the way they did, and his triangular face and thickened, earth-toned skin, he looked like a bat that had been staked out to dry in the sun.

Mac tapped the pen against the top of his desk. "Counterterrorism. Out of the Seattle Field Office. I need someone on that line ASAP."

"Perhaps you should contact Captain Gillomay first?" Radar offered bluntly.

Yeah, no doubt he should—the proper channels and all that shit—but then he would have to explain. While Gillomay had heard of Zane's neat little trick, he hadn't been on the receiving end of the visions, which meant there would be some convincing to do, which meant there'd be a hell of a lot of arguing. The plane would be in the air before the spineless ass took action. Rear Admiral McKay, on the other hand, had firsthand experience with Zane's flashes. He'd back Mac's play.

"There isn't time. I'll inform McKay after the FBI's rolling."

Radar's thin lips pursed, but he merely nodded, pivoted with military precision, and retreated into the quarterdeck with his customary economical stride.

Mac watched him go. He'd inherited the old goat from his predecessor. While he wasn't completely certain how Radar had earned his nickname, he suspected it had something to do with the old *M*A*S*H* sitcom. Like his namesake of the television show, his assistant had an uncanny ability to read his mind and know exactly what Mac was going to need and when he was going to need it. If anyone could get hold of a top-ranking FBI official, it would be Richard Anderson, a.k.a. Radar, HQ1's secret weapon.

As he waited, Mac continued glaring down at his desk. From what Zane had described of the hijacking, it sounded like the same crew who'd grabbed that plane down in South America. Too bad the details had been so sketchy. No description of the men in question, since they'd butchered all the first-class passengers once the ransom had been paid.

The intercom buzzed and Radar's raspy voice came through the machine. "John Chastain, Senior Agent in Charge of Seattle Field Office's Counterterrorism Division, is holding on line one."

Mac glanced at the clock above the door. It had taken Radar less than a minute to get someone on the phone. That had to be some kind of record. He snatched the receiver up and punched the button.

"Agent Chastain? This is Commander Jace Mackenzie, HQ1 out of Coronado. We've got a big problem in Seattle. Sea-Tac airport to be specific—Flight 2077, Seattle to Hawaii. We've just received intel indicating this flight is about to be hijacked."

Dead silence greeted this declaration.

Mac hardened his tone. "I'm not fucking with you. This is good intel. Fresh as a fucking daisy. This bird is about to be jacked, the guns are already on board, and we're running out of time. Liftoff's in seventy minutes. Boarding starts in forty. You need to get on the wire, get this flight delayed, and get someone out there to search that plane."

He paused, listened for a few seconds, his pen tapping against the desk with increasing frequency. "I'm fully aware of how difficult it is to smuggle guns on board an airliner. I'm also aware that no matter how difficult, it can be done. Those guns *are* on board. They're about to be used on a plane full of American citizens. Somebody needs to get their asses out—"

Breaking off, he tossed his pen onto the desk and threw himself back in his chair. It squawked violently beneath him. "That long ago, huh? You including 9/11 in those statistics? Yeah? Well, maybe you better check with your buddies in DHS before making stupid-ass assumptions."

He scowled at the rising voice on the other end of the line and broke in. "A flight out of Argentina was hijacked last year. Our intel indicates it's the same crew. You drop the ball on this, you go down for it."

After listening for a moment, he said. "Glad to see you're finally showing some fucking sense." He laughed. "You go right ahead. Oh, and Chastain? As coincidence would have it, three of my best men are booked on that flight. If anything happens to them, and I do mean *anything*, I'm going to rip your lungs out through your ass. You'll be using them as a fucking umbrella."

He listened a second, shook his head, and massaged the tight skin across his forehead. Dealing with arrogance and stupidity left him with a headache.

"No, we weren't conducting ops on mainland soil. They're on their way to a wedding. However, they've been apprised of the situation. They'll be monitoring the passengers until you get your team into place. Fine. I'll be flying up myself. Yeah, sure, you do that. It's spelled M-a-c-k-e-n-z-i-e—make sure you get the spelling right." Without saying good-bye, he slammed the phone down.

Chastain had to be fucking kidding. Could the prick really be so stupid he'd blow off fresh intel from a black op? Christ Almighty, he'd run into arrogance and territorialism before, but this guy took the prize, and considering the jackass headed up Seattle's counterterrorism unit, they were in a shit-can of trouble.

The door to the office opened as he pushed his chair back and stood up. "Get me Admiral McKay."

"Of course, Commander. I've taken the liberty of booking you on the first flight out. It leaves in two hours."

Of course he had. No doubt he'd known a trip to Seattle was in Mac's future before Mac had. He didn't bother to tell the man to cancel his appointments and reschedule. Knowing Radar, he'd already done so.

As he waited for the call to ring through, his thoughts returned to Zane. What the hell had Winters gotten himself into? He might not know what his LC had lied about, but he knew the lie was there. There was something else he was certain of. Somehow, in some way, this lie involved a woman. When it came to by-the-book operators like Zane Winters, only a woman could trip them up and send them reeling into the gray zone where lying became an option.

When you added in Zane's family history and all that crap about soul mates—well hell, the man had a weak spot a mile long.

Beth had described her dream several more times before Zane was satisfied. At which point he'd kicked her and his two friends out of the storage closet. She suspected the bid for privacy was meant to protect his friends from *the lie*, as she was beginning to think of it.

The deceit still bothered her. If they'd had more time, she would never have allowed him to take that step, but their window of opportunity was shrinking. Besides, his story would be believed more quickly than hers, which was essential with only an hour left until boarding.

"Why don't you tell us about your coworkers?" Cosky's flat tone turned the question into an order. He braced his shoulder against the wall beside the closet door and turned so he could keep an eye on the airport's main corridor.

"You mean do I work with anyone capable of cold-bloodedly murdering hundreds of people?" Beth asked drily, knowing where this line of questioning was headed. "Why are you jumping to the conclusion that their inside guy is in engineering? It makes more sense to recruit one of the bag smashers or techs."

"Do you know the baggage handlers or techs?" Cosky asked, studying her face.

"Well, no." Like any big corporation, PAA's departments were pretty insular. She knew everyone who worked on her floor, and a few people who worked on the floors above and below, but nobody who worked out in the hangars.

"But you do know your engineers, so we'll start with them. Is there anyone who comes to mind as being capable of this?"

Sure, there were people she didn't care for. Every job had them. Her coworker from hell, the tech writer in the cubicle beside her, sprang to mind. He talked incessantly, took overly long lunches and breaks, and told the same stupid joke over and over again. But his transgressions were a far cry from something this inhumane.

For the most part, the engineers in her department were complete geeks walking around in a daze. She tried to imagine Todd hiding the guns and bit back a laugh. Knowing Todd, he'd get distracted by some equation in his head and sit down to work it out. The guns would still be there, beside him, in plain view, when the flight crew arrived.

"Nobody I work with could possibly be in on this," Beth said. "It's not like any of them live on the fringe. We're a department of boring nine-to-fivers, with families and mortgages and car payments."

"You're making assumptions." His gaze met hers before shifting back out to the corridor where an elderly couple had appeared.

The fact that he studied the couple as they slowly walked past, arm-in-arm, told Beth how serious he was. The pair had to be in their seventies.

"The hijackers are male, mid to late thirties," she reminded him.

Cosky turned his head and stared at her, his gray eyes hooded. "Those people are on our flight. They were waiting at the departure gate, yet they've left...why?" He turned his attention back to the corridor. "It's a mistake to assume innocence based on gender or age."

Ouch. As if that jab hadn't been directed at her, which didn't surprise her. Of the three men, Simcosky was the coldest. The hardest. The most intimidating. Zane radiated calm, Rawlings good-natured charm, but this one exuded ice.

When it came to the two men, she much preferred Zane's calm over Simcosky's chill. Spending too much time with Zane's friend was likely to give her a bad case of frostbite.

"You were telling us about your coworkers," Cosky prompted.

She hadn't been, but she could take a hint. "Trust me. You're barking up the wrong tree. The accomplice can't be in my department. The only people with access to the tarmac or the planes are the engineers, and the planes are their babies. They take it personally anytime anything happens to one of them. There is no way one of my guys would be involved in something that could damage or destroy one of their precious planes."

The closet door opened on the last sentence.

Zane stopped in the middle of the doorjamb. His eyes were dark as a pine bough. Flat. "You're wearing blinders and making assumptions. You can't afford either," he said. "They leave you vulnerable."

Beth caught the quick glance that passed between his two friends. So did Zane.

"You two have a problem?" he asked, his voice as inflexible as his face. His expressionless gaze shifted between the two men across from him.

They simply stared back, their faces unapologetic, and somehow Beth knew this silent standoff was all about her.

"What did your boss say?" Beth asked, breaking into the macho posturing since neither of his friends seemed willing to interrupt the silence.

"His boss is the navy," Rawlings said.

Beth rolled her eyes. "*Excuse me*, your superior officer."

"Mac's contacting the FBI. There should be movement on that plane within fifteen minutes. We need to head back to the departure gate. Make sure your hijackers don't decide to abandon ship."

She was too relieved to protest the *your hijackers* comment. "So he believed you?"

"Yeah." A shadow slipped through his eyes.

It was the lying, Beth realized. He hated the lying. He'd done it, because he had this odd need to protect her, but he'd hated having to lie. Which she could appreciate. A woman would always know where she stood with such a man. She might not always like what he had to say, but she could trust it was the truth.

"When we get back to the terminal, you'll have to point these assholes out. There will be plenty of men who fit your descriptions." Zane stepped up and wrapped his arm around her shoulder. "From here on out, we're going to be lovers."

Beth frowned. His eyes had lightened and started to glitter, and somehow she knew the phrasing had been deliberate. Not we're going to *pretend* to be lovers, but we are going to *be* lovers. A declaration of intent. He was obviously looking for a fling.

A frisson of electricity slid down her spine. She wasn't sure whether it was because of his touch or his words. "We're going to *pretend* to be lovers."

From the gleam shimmering in those emerald eyes, he'd understood her gauntlet as easily as she had understood his.

Rawlings started whistling and tilted his head back to stare at the ceiling, his posture screaming *I am so not getting into this.*

Beth flushed, abruptly realizing where they were having this contest of wills. "So how am I supposed to point the hijackers out without them noticing?"

"Stop walking, turn your back to them, and tug my head down like you're going to kiss me. But at the last moment turn your head slightly, brush your cheek against mine, and whisper where they are in my ear. If they're watching, they won't be able to see exactly what you're doing or saying."

She nodded her understanding, but Zane's eyes darkened again, something edgy and raw drifting across the hard planes of his face.

"I don't like this," he told her, "but there's no other choice. You're the only one who can point them out. Besides, you need to be waiting at the departure gate with us. It's the only way the feds will buy this story we've concocted."

He was worried about her, Beth realized, warmth spreading through her chest.

"Which reminds me." His arm tightened around her shoulders as they started walking toward the main corridor. "You need to call your supervisor and ask for the week off."

She sighed; there went the last of her vacation days. They returned to the departure gate in silence, flanked by Zane's equally silent friends.

Beth spent the time trying to ignore the tingles that swept through her every time their hips or legs brushed. Lord, her hands were actually perspiring, and she was pretty certain *that* had nothing to do with terrorists or hijackings.

Zane stopped walking in front of gate C-18. "You up for this?" he asked, cupping her cheek, the strength of his hand belied by his gentle grasp.

She took what was supposed to be a deep, calming breath, which turned out to be a big mistake because she inhaled the erotic combination of scents she associated with Zane—clean, fresh soap and smoky male musk. The double whammy had the same effect on her heart as his touch.

"I'm fine." Which might have sounded convincing if it hadn't come out so breathless.

From the satisfaction on his face, he knew exactly what he was doing to her. He bent his head to nuzzle the side of her neck, and the pulse of his breath against her ear sent a shower of sparks down her spine. Her nipples tightened.

"When you see them, squeeze my hand," he breathed against her skin before straightening.

The brush of his lips only lasted a second or three, but it was enough to steal every milliliter of air from her lungs and zap all her erogenous zones to life. Holy Mother of God, there were places suddenly tingling she hadn't known existed.

Remnants of that heat persisted as Zane escorted her into Gate C-18's waiting area and the teeming, chattering hordes of people. The laughter and drone of voices verged on deafening.

Slowly, worry pushed aside the hunger.

What if she was wrong? What if there were no guns?

She tensed as she scanned the terminal for the hijackers. Panic flared. Even if they existed, how in the world was she going to locate the killers in this swarm of humanity? Seconds later the question became moot as a cluster of college-aged men headed for the left wall and a gap opened in the crowded terminal. Her gaze shot through and fell on the three men standing in the far corner. She recognized them instantly.

Before she could squeeze Zane's hand, the tallest of the three—the one with the cell phone plugged to his right ear—turned his head and stared straight at her. Even across the room she could see the viciousness in his intense gaze. The furious knowledge on his lean, aristocratic face.

He knew. Somehow he knew that they knew.

How was that possible?

Panic crested, a white-hot pulse through her chest. Her muscles locked and trembled.

She forced her gaze away and squeezed Zane's hand—hard. Maybe she'd imagined the exchange.

"Son of a fucking bitch." Zane's growl was so low Beth barely heard it.

Clearly she hadn't imagined that vicious glance. Zane had caught it too.

"We've been made," he continued, a note of urgency beneath the calm. "Move. They're about to break."

"Where are the other three?" Rawls asked. He turned to Beth, his face tense, blue eyes burning with intensity. "Do you see the rest of their crew?"

Beth cast a frantic look around the terminal, but there were so many people. Clusters of people. "I don't see them. But they could be sitting down, hidden from view."

"They're splitting up," Cosky said, his voice flat. "I'm going left." With that he disappeared into the crowd.

Beth shot a glance toward the corner, but the three men from her dream had vanished.

"Rawls? Go right," Zane snapped. "Beth? Don't move an inch. Do you hear me? Not an inch. Scream bloody murder if anyone so much as talks to you." Without glancing in her direction he slipped through the crowd.

She watched him go, mesmerized by his fluid, lethal grace.

"Due to a mechanical issue, Flight 2077, Seattle to Honolulu, has been delayed."

The announcement came over the loudspeaker as a hand clamped over Beth's shoulder.

Chapter Five

B Y THE TIME ZANE WINTERS AND HIS ENTOURAGE RETURNED, Russ's crew had arrived. He'd considered instructing his men to avoid C-18 until the plane started boarding but decided against it. He needed to know whether the operation had been compromised. So he'd split his team—sending three to the gate and telling them to hang back, out of sight. The other three he'd ordered to wait at surrounding areas.

If the flight boarded without a hitch, his remaining crew was close enough to arrive at the ticket counter in time for boarding. However, if something had triggered Winters's suspicion and this operation *was* compromised, he had backup reserves in place.

The passengers, along with the scientific data they carried, needed to be acquired one way or another. Anything less would bring consequences that Russ had no intention of facing.

With his laptop open on his knees, Russ angled his body on the bench so he had a good view of the airport corridor and the gate next door.

Zane Winters had his arm around Beth Brown's shoulders, his body language both protective and territorial. They were playing the lovers card to the hilt.

Or at least *he* was.

But how much of the behavior was for show? The guy's stance screamed *mine, back off.* Maybe he really had latched onto her.

The woman, though…Russ shifted on his bench, punched a few random numbers into his laptop's keypad, and studied her stiff body…She was throwing off more conflicted signals. Not such a good actress, that one. Or perhaps she was uncomfortable with public displays of sexuality.

Aware that eyes were on him, Russ glanced up. His young friend on the bench across from him met his smile with solemnity. Which was a crime. A child so young should be full of giggles and laughter. His gaze shifted to her uninterested mother. Someone needed to put a bullet through that lazy cow's brain. They'd be doing the kid a favor, freeing her from such a joyless childhood. If not for the timing, he'd take on the task himself. Pro bono. Unfortunately, he couldn't afford the distraction.

With a sigh, he turned back to his targets. Simcosky and Rawlings had joined Winters. All three men and the woman were slowly winding their way through Gate C-18, their heads swinging from side to side, eyes scanning.

Obviously looking for someone.

Russ frowned, pinching his chin. If they were looking for someone, then they hadn't tapped his operation. His crew remained unidentified. Nobody had survived the test flight, so nobody knew what they looked like.

Whatever Winters and his crew were up to, it was unlikely that it had anything to do with his plans for that plane.

His tense muscles loosened. Russ relaxed against the back of his bench, stretched his legs out, and crossed his ankles. When his cell phone started vibrating against the leather of his laptop case, he fished it out and glanced down. Tension pinched again when he recognized the number flashing across the screen.

Swearing beneath his breath, he let the phone numb his hand for a few moments before flipping it open.

No news, in this case, was good news. This contact had strict instructions to call once the plane was in the air and negotiations were underway. The only reason he'd be calling early was if something had gone wrong.

He hit the green call button and pressed the cell to his ear. "What?"

With absolute stillness he listened to his FBI contact's tale of HQ1 interference and Commander Jace Mackenzie's demands to shut down the flight and search the plane.

Just like that, his operation tanked.

Without missing a beat, Russ switched to Plan B. "You'll be receiving a list. Make sure the passengers are available."

He hit the disconnect button and punched in another phone number. His crew chief picked up on the first ring.

"Our party's been crashed. Pass the word. We'll be moving to our second venue." He didn't wait for acknowledgement, simply disconnected the call.

How the fuck had those bastards stumbled onto his operation?

The woman had to be the key. Nothing else made sense. The four had disappeared, and minutes later the commander of SEAL Team 7—who just happened to be Winters's CO—had called the FBI, insisting fresh intel indicated that the flight was about to be hijacked?

Beth Brown must have passed the information on to Zane Winters, who'd passed it on to Mackenzie.

But how the fuck had she found out?

Maybe his PacAtlantic conduit had squealed. It was always a risk working with amateurs. The man was of no use to them anyway at this point, a thread that needed snipping. But before he took the bastard out, they'd have a little chat about the benefits of confidentiality. As for Beth Brown...His gaze lingered on the woman's profile. Suddenly she stopped dead. Winters dropped his arm from her shoulder and turned in the direction she stared. Russ turned in that direction as well, and swore softly as he caught a glimpse of his crew chief before a swarm of passengers swallowed him again.

Quick as a muzzle flash, the three SEALs melted into the crowd, in obvious and hot pursuit.

Russ turned to stare at the abandoned feminine figure.

How in the fuck? How in the goddamn fuck had she managed to identify his crew?

There were no pictures. No descriptions. Not one fucking person alive from the Argentina flight who could have identified them.

Damn it, he'd ordered the death of all those poor kids just so this wouldn't happen—so there would be no possibility of his crew being identified.

He forced himself to breathe again, wrenched his gaze away, and punched another number into his cell. With the SEALs in pursuit, she was alone. Vulnerable.

"Did you get a look at our associate's girlfriend?" he asked without preamble. "Good. He appears quite fond of her. It would benefit us to make her acquaintance. Yes. Now."

He needed answers and he needed them fast. How deep did this fucking leak go? The bosses were going to demand answers, and if he didn't have them he could forget about taking an early

71

retirement. Unless it was into a shallow grave to swap stories with the worms.

Beth Brown had the answers. She'd been the one to identify his crew. As a side benefit, she'd make excellent leverage. If Winters wanted to spend any time between those long legs, he'd do exactly as he was told.

───────────

"I'm with airport security. You need to come with me," a man said from behind Beth, his voice brusque, scratchy, and faintly familiar.

Beth's heart—which had started hammering the moment she caught the lead hijacker's eyes across the crowded terminal—suddenly froze in midbeat. She glanced back, recognizing the man immediately. He wasn't particularly tall—no taller than her—but twice her width, with the muscled chest and bulging biceps of a wrestler. She flashed back to the dream and his gloating smile as he'd plowed bullet after bullet into Zane.

"You're not with airport security," she said, Zane's order running through her mind. "And if you don't let go of my arm, I'm going to scream."

A scowl twisted his flattened face. He yanked on her shoulder and dipped his head. His breath, ripe with the smell of onions and greasy hamburger, blasted her in the face.

"You're gonna come with me now, or I'm gonna take this gun out of my pocket and blow your fucking head off. Got it?" He kept his voice low, but the words and the threat came hard and fast. Perfectly clear.

There was no way she could overpower him *and* hold him until the FBI arrived, but there were plenty of men in the crowd who could. Passengers react to a perceived threat nowadays. If she could incite the same reaction...

She threw back her head and screamed. She screamed as loud and as hard as she could, until her throat burned and her voice seized and her ears were ringing. The shrillness of her shriek pierced the chattering, laughing crowd, and instant silence fell.

Hundreds of startled, curious faces swung in her direction. The man beside her cursed.

She screamed again—just as loud, just as hard. When she finally fell silent, a confused hush consumed the departure gate.

The hand grinding the bones of her elbow dropped. The guy was about to bolt; she could sense it.

Oh no, he wasn't. Beth stepped into him, tangling her feet in his.

"He's got a gun!" she shouted. "Somebody stop him. He's got a gun!"

An uneasy buzz swept through the crowd. Eyes sharpened and swung toward the man she'd accused, but nobody stepped forward to restrain him. In fact, the fool might have escaped if his survival instincts hadn't kicked in. Rather than playing the amused or surprised or irritated bystander, he gave Beth's shoulder a hard shove and leapt back.

His instinctive reaction looked guilty as hell. Several men stepped forward, their focus locked on the clearly rattled would-be hijacker. In a move that looked almost choreographed, the approaching men fell into a loose pack formation, moving forward and splitting to the sides as though they intended to circle him— cutting off any avenue of escape.

"You okay, miss?" one of the men asked.

Before she had a chance to respond, her attacker made another snap decision. Rather than making a run for it, he leapt forward and grabbed Beth by her hair. Yanking her head back, he wrapped his arm around her throat and squeezed—hard.

She gagged, clawed at his arm, and tried to turn her head to bite him, but she couldn't angle her head enough to reach his flesh. She kicked back with her heels, but there wasn't enough leverage to inflict any damage, and while her elbows connected with a bit more force, it wasn't enough to gain her freedom. Instead, he cursed and squeezed even harder.

This time the black dots dancing across her vision had nothing to do with shock and everything to do with lack of blood and breath.

"Everyone stay back!" he snarled as her vision started to gray. "Stay back or I'll break her fucking neck."

Russ swore as Beth Brown screamed. The surrounding gates went still as death, every eye swinging in her direction. Which by default included Dietrich. The attention brought him into focus like a blinding white spotlight.

That alone was reason enough to kill the stupid bastard.

She was a smart cookie. No way in hell was Dietrich dragging her out now. Not with the entire fucking airport watching.

It shouldn't have been that difficult to get the woman to leave willingly. All Dietrich had to do was present himself as an authority figure. Demand that she accompany him. If one presented themselves as someone in authority, people tended to follow along like pathetic little lambs—at least in the beginning. By the time she'd realized her mistake, it would be too late. Without her SEAL contingent protecting her, the woman had been vulnerable. Easy pickings.

Swearing beneath his breath, Russ turned from the drama taking place like a runaway train across the corridor. He typed a command into the keyboard of his laptop that would wipe the computer clean, leaving it a useless lump of plastic and metal. Although nothing was ever truly wiped clean. If the FBI or DHS techs got their hands on it, everything that had just vanished could be resurrected, but it wouldn't matter—there was nothing on the computer that would lead them to Russ's doorstep anyway.

Of course if he intervened, his laptop wasn't the only thing he could kiss good-bye. He'd lose any possibility of escape as well. Since he wasn't booked on Flight 2077, it was doubtful he'd have been hauled in for questioning.

While they'd separate and hold the passengers of the compromised flight for interrogation—hell, he was counting on it—there would be no reason for the FBI to quarantine the surrounding gates. He would have been free to catch his plane to the Twin Cities.

Except he needed that fucking woman.

Since Dietrich had lost his opportunity, that left Russ to step up and take charge. Of course, by taking action he'd bring himself to the feds' attention, but they wouldn't discover anything detrimental. His military record had been erased years ago. Even if they did fingerprint him, his prints were on file under the Russ Branson persona, thanks to a carefully crafted arrest report charging the man with a DUI.

He should update the bosses. Explain why the operation was moving to door number two. A pulse of pure tension shot through him. He took a deep, calming breath. He'd take care of that unpleasant task as soon as he corrected the situation across the corridor.

Moving without haste, he zipped the laptop into its case and rose to his feet. He stretched, worked the kinks out of his shoulders, and smoothed the wrinkles from his slacks. A quick tuck-in of his shirt and he was ready for battle. Breathing easily, calmly, he picked up the laptop case and tucked his cell into the pocket of his slacks.

Russ scanned the gate area as he started across the corridor, but Beth's screams had drawn a crowd, and dozens of frozen passengers obstructed his view. Too bad. He'd bet Jilly's entire Broadway sound track collection that those screams had set off some interesting physical reactions in Zane Winters's physiology.

When he finally got a good look at the pair occupying everyone's attention, he stopped and stared. What a fucking idiot. All Dietrich had to do was laugh her off as an unstable, hysterical girlfriend. All he had to do was walk away. Instead, he'd grabbed her by the neck, proving to the watching passengers that he was dangerous. No doubt everyone was wondering if he did have a gun beneath his shirt.

Un-fucking-believable.

Once this job was over, he'd hunt down the bastard who'd vouched for the fool and stuff that glowing recommendation down the asshole's slit throat.

Half a dozen men had formed a loose circle around the pair. Russ picked up his pace. Adrenaline crested, along with the razor-sharp awareness he remembered from those long-ago Special Ops days. His senses sharpened. His vision brightened. His hearing crystallized until he could hear the hard thump of his heart.

It felt good to be so alive. Back in the action.

He'd been stuck in the prep and flow of strategy for so long he'd forgotten how much he loved these heightened moments just before the kill.

———————————

Zane locked his gaze on the target and slipped between the laughing, chattering, milling clusters of people. The ages of the passengers ran the gamut from frail seniors leaning on canes to a jostling crowd of college-aged males who'd staked out a section next to the wall and were tossing a football back and forth. A knot of Koreans in three-piece business suits to the right were yammering away. To the left, another group of passengers with fair hair and light skin were decked out in colorful sweaters and denim jeans.

In some eerie way, deploying through the crowd felt like deploying through the ocean—but rather than the buoyancy of the waves, you were carried along by the rise and fall of voices.

Zane lost the tango when the blond hijacker faded into the crowd. He parked it and waited for the asshole to move. From his position he'd know the moment the guy went right or left.

Within minutes his target lost patience and moved. He was easy to track. His head jutted a good six inches above most of the passengers and his white-gold hair shone like a beacon.

Zane had the advantage in this skirmish. For one thing, the target had been waiting at the back of the departure gate, with no exit behind him. To escape into the airport, and from there out to the street, he'd have to come forward—directly toward Zane. It was a serious tactical error. In tight quarters, the smart man buddied up to an exit.

The target slipped between the college kids and a cluster of Middle Eastern businessmen, and then turned toward the mouth of the terminal. Zane shifted over to block him.

No escape here, asshole.

The hijacker must have realized that himself. He abruptly pivoted and eased in behind the kids, who'd clumped together and were busy shoving each other amid boisterous slurs regarding sexual performances.

There was a ribbon of space between the boys and the wall. If Zane dodged left, the target would go right, skirt the kids, and break for the mouth of the terminal. If Zane went right, the guy would dodge left—with the same effect. From his smug expression the idiot apparently thought he'd acquired the upper hand.

Amateur.

There wouldn't be much risk if Zane used the students to fence the tango in. The asshole was unarmed, and these boys looked to be in good shape.

"Guys," he said loud enough to pierce the terminal's din and with enough authority to bring instinctive compliance. A dozen pairs of eyes swung in his direction. "I need you to split this group down the middle. Step to the right and left. Use your bodies as a barrier. Do not let that asshole behind you get past." When they stared at him with startled confusion, he injected steel into his voice. "Move. Now."

They reacted instantly to the authority in his voice. The group split down the middle.

The hijacker settled back on his heels and crossed his arms over his sweatshirt-clad chest. With just the right amount of bewilderment, he watched Zane advance.

"Is there a problem?" the guy asked, confusion in his voice, but his eyes gave him away. They were too sharp, too focused. He knew exactly what was going down.

"I need a couple of you boys to strip off your shoelaces. The longer the better," Zane said, without taking his eyes off the tango's face.

"Who the hell are you to give us orders?" one of the college students asked, bravado quivering in his voice.

"Yes," the hijacker agreed, his gaze assessing. "I'm rather curious of that myself."

A whisper of unease prickled and Zane frowned. Some deep, raw instinct insisted he check on Beth. He blocked the urge. He couldn't afford to lose focus. The moment his attention wavered, the situation could explode.

The simplest method to capture this asshole was to use these kids to contain him while Zane moved in for the takedown. But they needed to know exactly what they were up against.

"I'm Lieutenant Commander Zane Winters with the United States Navy. And the asshole behind you is a terrorist. Intel suggests he and his team intended to hijack this flight."

There was a hiss of breaths and a stammering of questions. Zane kept his attention locked on his target. The hijacker's eyes had narrowed as Zane spoke. Now they filled with frustrated fury.

"I haven't done a damn thing. You can't hold me," he said, his voice perfectly clear despite the noise surrounding them.

Zane smiled. There was the scuffle of more feet against carpet. Through his peripheral vision he caught the flash of movement as several students backed up.

"Then I'm sure you won't mind sticking around to answer some questions," he countered in an agreeable voice, even as an odd, urgent tension swelled inside him.

He fought the urge to check on Beth. She was fine. She'd scream if she were in trouble. Forcing himself to concentrate, Zane shook the foreboding aside.

"But I do mind," the target said, and while his tone might have been conversational, his hazel eyes were hot and mean. "It's against my constitutional rights."

Wasn't that just sweet. Another jackass hiding behind the Constitution.

"Uh-huh. What about the constitutional rights of the passengers you intended to use those MP5s on?"

From the flash in the tango's eyes, it was obvious MP5s were stashed on board. Good to know. Even better to know that Beth's dream had been right on target; when the plane was searched those guns would be found. He'd already accepted the possibility of reprimand if the weapons weren't located. Acting on her information had been a calculated risk, but it had been the only option he could live with.

After that telling instant of shock, the target's face tightened. A scowl furrowed his forehead and pinched his eyebrows together. "You have no right to hold me. I can walk out of here right now, and you can't do a fucking thing to stop me."

Another surge of foreboding rolled through him. Sharper this time. Stronger. Christ, he needed to end this and find Beth.

He dropped his smile and matched the hijacker stare for stare. "I can break both your legs. Consider it a citizen's arrest."

"Hey, man," a nervous voice said to Zane's left, "here's those shoelaces you asked for."

Before Zane had a chance to reach for the bindings, the tango's nostrils flared and his eyelids flickered. The guy was about to make a break for it. Zane loosened his muscles, shifted his weight over the balls of his feet, and eased down slightly...waiting.

Just as the hijacker's thighs bunched—a dead giveaway that action would follow —a wave of fear ripped through Zane. The hair along the back of his neck lifted. His heart gave one frantic thump and stopped cold. There was no doubt who that fear belonged to and it wasn't him.

He'd already experienced the bond acting as a conductor when he'd been touching her. And his dad had told him that once the link was fully formed, couples could transmit images—even words. But he hadn't expected to experience the connection so soon. Christ, Beth was clear across the room. He shouldn't be able to sense her so distinctly. Still, every instinct he possessed insisted that he abandon this asshole and head to the rescue.

Only, the target attacked.

Launched by pure adrenaline and the need to end this skirmish ASAP, Zane dropped to the ground, bracing his palm on the floor so his weight was balanced on his right shoulder and arm. The hijacker hadn't expected the movement and led with a punch that sailed harmlessly above Zane's head. Zane waited for the guy's forward momentum to carry him closer and kicked out—hard. The heel of his boot connected with the bastard's knee, but at a slight angle. There was a sickening crunch, followed by series of pops, and the hijacker's right leg folded.

Without hesitation Zane struck again, taking out the left knee. He needed to make sure this bastard was incapable of movement.

Another sickening crunch and the target dropped, screaming in agony.

Zane swarmed him. Forced him onto his belly. Dragged his arms behind his back.

"Laces," he snapped, holding up his hand.

A scream pierced the terminal.

Feminine. Familiar. *Beth.*

His chest burning, his breath locked in his throat, Zane cinched the guy's wrists in record time. He didn't bother with the ankles. The guy wouldn't be walking anytime soon. Fear a black mist choking his brain, he rocketed to his feet and spun around just as some motherfucker leapt forward and wrapped his arm around Beth's neck.

Time screeched to a stop. He could see her clearly from his vantage point across the gate room. Her face was turning gray.

Fear shot directly into terror. Was it his or hers?

He'd faced countless situations where death hovered an instant away. He'd faced those moments with absolute calm and no discernible acceleration to his heart rate. Until today, when he couldn't seem to catch his breath or get his fucking body to *move*.

The hijacker across the departure gate started backing away, dragging her limp body with him.

Suddenly Beth's admirer from earlier stepped into view. His thin face tense, his glasses sliding down his narrow nose, he slowly raised a laptop case above his head. He moved with painstaking stealth, although he needn't have bothered; Beth's attacker was so fixated on the men crowding him in front that he wasn't paying the least attention to his back.

He watched his rival raise the laptop case even higher and then tilt it at an angle, so the sharp edge pointed down. Relief mixed with disgust. Hell, the asshole was actually going to rescue her, and Zane was too far away to help.

Her rescuer brought his makeshift weapon down with stunning force. Even across the shocked silence of the terminal Zane could hear the muffled thud as the case connected with bone. The arm fell from Beth's throat and her attacker dropped like a brick.

Beth would have dropped too, if Loverboy hadn't let go of his weapon and caught her around the waist. Zane's heart stuttered back to life as her arms and legs started to move. Her head rolled against his shoulder, the ash-blonde tangle of hair looking tousled and blonder than ever against the dark blue of Loverboy's cotton golf shirt.

The relief that she was alive and unharmed barely had a chance to settle before the sight of her in another man's arms started needling him. He growled low in his throat, a surge of heat blasting the ice from his veins. His gaze locked on those masculine arms cradling *his* woman and he stomped on the urge to kill.

"Relax," Cosky said dryly, appearing beside him. "He's not one of our targets." He paused. "Besides, looks to me like he saved her."

Yeah. Like *that* was helping.

A scowl built as he glared across the terminal. Beth was upright. Standing on her own two feet, but that bastard still hadn't dropped his arms. If he wanted to keep them, he'd better rectify that mistake pronto.

"She looks unsteady," Cosky said. "I'm sure that's why he's still hugging her."

"You might think about shutting the fuck up." A swarm of blue-suited security guards came trotting down the airport corridor. About fucking time. "Where the hell's Rawls?"

"Right here, skipper," Rawls drawled from behind him. "Target acquired, contained, and awaiting transport. I heard the scream. Came to see if I could—" He broke off and released a strangled cough. "Well, would ya look at that? Loverboy's back and he's gettin' downright *friendly.*"

Zane's gaze didn't budge from the pair as he stalked forward. *Jesus Christ! Was that son of a bitch actually rubbing her back?*

"Is he rubbin'...?" Rawls wheezed alongside him, easily keeping pace.

Considering that Rawlings worked out a gazillion hours a day and was in better shape than all of ST7 put together, Zane knew damn well all that gasping had everything to do with holding back his amusement and nothing to do with exhaustion.

"Why don't you two head back and keep an eye on our tangos," Zane said, his tone more of a demand than a request as he tried to mask the aggression in his voice.

"No offense, skipper." Rawls picked up his pace. "But my guy's down. He ain't goin' nowhere and no way am I missing this."

Suddenly his rival raised his head and stared straight at him. No question he picked up on Zane's territorial urge to maim because his chin reared back and his shoulders tightened. But he didn't let go of Beth. Instead, his gaze narrowed and he glared back. Then deliberately cradled her closer.

No. Way. In. Fucking. Hell.

"Jesus." Rawls's tone had distilled to complete and utter ice. "That fucker's challenging you."

"Obviously the guy's got a death wish." Cosky's voice was just as cold.

Some of the tension seething through Zane eased. That was team life for you. Your crew always had your back, no matter the war.

The security force swept in, several converging on Beth and Loverboy.

One chubby guard bent and put two fingers against the neck of Beth's attacker. The coarse cloth of his blue uniform strained across his distended belly, he glanced up at his partner and shook his head. The news that Beth's attacker was dead didn't surprise him. From the angle of the head and his complete stillness, it was obvious the hijacker wouldn't be getting back up.

By now Zane was bearing down on the couple.

"I've got her," he told Beth's rescuer in a brusque voice, reaching out to wrap his fingers around Beth's upper arm.

But the asshole just stared at him, challenge in the brown gaze behind the glasses. "And you are?"

"Her fiancé," Zane snapped, crowding in.

He gentled both his grip and voice when he noticed the minute spasms raking her slender frame.

"You can let go." When it didn't look like the jackass was going to take the hint, his voice hardened. "Now."

For a moment it looked like the little prick was going to ignore the demand. Some latent instinct stirred as Zane held the challenging gaze. There was more to this guy than met the eye. Very few men could stare him down, but this one was giving it his damnedest.

Beth stirred. "Zane?"

She pulled away from Loverboy's hold and tried to turn. Slowly, with obvious reluctance, those grasping hands released their grip and his arms fell away.

"I'm here." Zane carefully folded her into his embrace. "Let me check you out."

"I'm okay. My neck hurts. And my shoulder and my arm and my elbow really hurt." Her voice gained strength.

She let Zane tilt her head back and winced at the hiss that shot out his mouth. "It probably looks worse than it is," she said stoutly.

Considering the entire length of her neck was livid red, it looked pretty bad.

"Rawls?" Zane eased Beth to the side so Rawlings could get a look at her. "Rawls is ST7's corpsman." He paused at Beth's blank look. "Our medic. He's as good as a doc, has four years of medical school behind him," he told her, forcing gentleness into his voice.

"Any trouble breathing?" Rawls asked, probing along the length of her neck.

"No." She flinched, visibly relaxing as Rawls's hands dropped.

"Soft tissue damage. It's gonna swell and look mighty colorful, but won't leave any permanent damage," Rawls reported. "How 'bout I take a look at your elbow?"

"It's fine." She caught Zane's lifted eyebrow and frowned. "He twisted my arm, so the elbow's sore, but it's not broken. I can move it—see?" She brought her arm up, albeit gingerly, and straightened it out.

"Good. That's good. Why don't ya let me take a look at it now?" Rawls asked, reaching for her extended arm.

She snorted her opinion of that request and shifted out of reach. "Because you'll just poke and prod, making it hurt even worse and then tell me it's *just* soft tissue damage."

Zane grinned in relief at the asperity in her voice. She was getting stubborn, which had to be a good sign.

"Who's going to tell me what happened here?" The security guard who asked the question was on the far side of middle-aged, with the competent air of someone used to giving orders and having them obeyed without question.

Just how much had this guy been told? Zane went with the assumption he didn't know enough.

"I'm Lieutenant Commander Zane Winters, United States Navy." He nodded toward Rawls and Cosky. "Lieutenants Seth Rawlings and Marcus Simcosky. We've been advised through Central Command that Flight 2077 has been compromised. When the suspects attempted to flee the terminal, we detained them."

The security chief's graying eyebrows lifted. "They still alive?"

"Alive, but in need of medical attention," Zane responded blandly. "This gate needs to be sealed. Nobody in. Nobody out."

With a slight nod, the security chief motioned several of his guards over and issued quick, flat orders. Instantly his men spun and jogged to the mouth of the terminal, setting up sentry duty. Zane watched with approval. The guy ran a tight ship, which would make containment easier.

"And him? I take it he was one of your suspects too?" The security chief glanced at the motionless figure at their feet.

"Was?" Beth jolted in Zane's arms and tried to look down. "He's dead?"

Zane frowned. The injury shouldn't have killed. A blow to the top of the head rarely proved fatal, particularly when the object used was a laptop case. He glanced down, studying the discarded computer. Of course Beth's rescuer had twisted the case so the corner had been the impact point, but even so...

"Yeah," Zane slowly said. "He tried to grab Beth."

"You killed him?" the security guy asked, not sounding like he cared. More like he wanted to get his facts straight.

"No." Damn it. "I didn't arrive in time."

The security chief rocked back on his heels and planted his fists on his hips. "Then who—"

"I didn't mean to kill him," Loverboy stammered. "He had the woman by the throat. I just wanted to stun him, so he'd let her go."

Zane frowned again, his instincts buzzing. The guy had challenged him. He wouldn't get all stammery over some run-of-the-mill questioning. Besides, he'd twisted that case for maximum damage—something most civilians wouldn't think to do.

"You'll need to come with us." The security officer motioned a couple of his guards forward.

"Of course." With a final glance at Beth, Loverboy followed the two security escorts down the corridor.

Still frowning, Zane watched them go.

"I didn't get a chance to thank him." Beth shifted in Zane's arms and turned to face their questioner. "I hope he won't get into trouble. He saved my life." She touched her throat and flinched. "I couldn't breathe."

The security guy shrugged. "That's for the feds to decide. But I doubt he'll be charged with anything." He shifted his attention to Zane. "How about you show me where the rest of these suspects are?"

Zane indicated Rawls with a jerk of his head. "Lieutenant Rawlings will take you to them," he said absently, his gaze tracking Loverboy's thin frame as it ambled down the hall. He nodded at the admonishment to stick around for debriefing, but his gaze never left his rival.

Cosky waited until the guards had wandered off before easing closer. "What's up?" he asked quietly, following Zane's gaze to Loverboy's disappearing figure.

"There's something off there," Zane said just as softly.

Cosky glanced at Beth. "Was he in your dream?"

With a lift of her head, she frowned. "You mean Russ? No. Why?"

"Russ?" Zane's eyebrows snapped together. He ignored the dry glance Cosky shot him.

"Russ Branson, that's his name."

"And what else did Russ Branson tell you?" Try as he might, he couldn't smooth the sharp edge from his voice.

Beth drew back at his tone. "Well, he's not one of the hijackers, if that's what you're implying." Her voice sharpened. "He wasn't in the dream. In fact, he's on his way to Minnesota."

"How the hell would you know that?" *Jesus Christ!* What was wrong with him? Zane tried to back off, but she'd been entirely too comfortable in that bastard's arms.

"Because he told me. Earlier. When I first got to the gate room." Beth glowered back.

"He could be lying."

"Why would he lie? This was before I even talked to you. And in case you've forgotten," her voice rose with each word, "he saved my life."

Yeah, like he was ever going to forget that.

"Let's recap," Cosky broke in placidly. "He wasn't in her dream. He approached her before she approached us. He's booked on a different flight. And it's likely he saved her life." He paused, shook his head, something close to sympathy gleaming in his dark eyes. "Sorry, boss, looks like your instincts are off on this one."

Zane swore and raked a hand through his hair. Maybe Cosky was right. Maybe that instinctive buzz was caused by something more primal—the reaction of a male sensing a rival for his mate.

Because when it came right down to it, knowing Beth was his soul mate didn't mean shit.

A life with her wasn't something he could count on. The visions never flashed to warn of a soul mate's danger, as proved by the fact he'd almost lost her already. Nor was there any guarantee that the woman you bonded with would want you back.

Or, Christ, even if she did, that she'd live long enough for something to develop.

Webb's tight, raw face flashed through his mind. His empty eyes and silence since he'd lost Marie. Zane had thought he'd understood his brother's pain.

But he hadn't understood shit. Not until now. Until Beth.

Chapter Six

*O*KAY, SO CHALLENGING THE BIG BASTARD HADN'T BEEN THE smartest choice he'd ever made.

Russ matched his stride to his security detail's, aware that Zane Winters's eyes still drilled into his spine. He could feel the suspicion in that sharp gaze, the realization there was more to Russ Branson than appeared on the surface.

He'd spent his career avoiding such suspicion. Inviting closer observation led to unmasking, which led to...well, nothing pleasant, that was for sure.

He knew better, damn it.

He should have played it cooler. Handed the woman over quicker.

The reason behind the challenge had been solid. He'd needed to find out whether the woman actually meant something to Winters. Whether it would benefit him to keep her alive after they'd extracted the information they needed. It would be a shame to kill her if she could provide leverage over HQ1.

He bit back a laugh.

Yeah, that question had been answered. Winters was completely and utterly attached. And jealous as all fuck. There had been murder in those eyes when they'd locked on Beth Brown and found her in the arms of another man.

Absolute murder.

His reaction had been immediate. Instinctive. Something that couldn't be faked. Not at such a visceral level.

And now, thanks to those few seconds of stupidity, Lieutenant Commander Zane Winters was suspicious of him. Which translated to—Naval Spec War being suspicious of him.

Luckily, the airport security guards didn't share Winters's razor-sharp instincts. Russ idly considered taking the men out. There were only two of them. Police academy washouts. If he jumped them, he'd be out of the airport before anyone knew he'd escaped.

Of course such action would alert everyone to his involvement in the attempted hijacking. Even with his FBI and DHS contacts, someone he didn't control might get curious and uncover things best left buried, which would interfere with his acquisition of the required passengers.

So best to go with the flow. Keep an eye on Plan B from the airport. Besides, Chastain might find it difficult to acquire Beth Brown on his own. Winters wasn't going to let her out of his sight. It might prove useful to have two people working in tandem to grab the woman.

His blue-suited escorts had shown him through a door marked *Airport Personnel Only* when his cell vibrated against his thigh. He fished it out and checked the window display.

The bosses.

Fuck.

If he didn't pick up, they'd wonder why. The original plan hadn't involved any direct action on his part, which had left him available for spur-of-the-moment updates. He couldn't afford to have them start questioning his capabilities. He needed to touch base long enough to downplay the change of venues and assure them everything was still on track.

Russ glanced at the guards. They wouldn't be able to hear the bosses' side of the conversation, and he could couch his replies carefully enough to ensure these two clowns wouldn't pick up on what was actually being said. But if he waited much longer, he might find himself trapped in a room monitored by some kind of electronic listening device.

The guards glanced at him as he lifted the cell phone to his ear, but didn't try to stop him.

"Hey," he said, "I was just about to call and warn you. It looks like I'll be arriving later than expected."

Cold silence throbbed down the line. "We are told the plane's been grounded."

So they had their own contacts within PacAtlantic, or perhaps the FBI.

"Yeah, it was the damnedest thing. There was some kind of altercation at the gate across from mine. A woman was attacked. Airport security poured in and started detaining people."

The silence chilled to ice. "You're in custody?"

Best to own the information and play it how he wanted. "I tried to help the woman." He forced a rueful laugh. "Got detained for my efforts. I'm sure it's just a formality, but I suspect I'll be taking a later flight than expected. It shouldn't affect our plans. I'll still arrive in time for the convention."

"You've switched to the alternative?" A different voice broke in. Flat rather than cold.

"Yes. I'll give you a call as soon as I know more."

"You do that," the flat voice said. "In the meantime, you should call your sister and let her know your flight's been delayed."

Russ's stride faltered. He almost stopped dead in the hall before he caught himself. "My sister?"

"Jillian Michaels. You've got quite the collection of nieces and nephews too, don't you?" The voice paused, and Russ's stomach twisted. "We've found in the past that it's in our best interests to know the people we do business with."

The line went dead.

Very slowly, Russ closed the cell and shoved it into his pocket. His sudden tension, he was relieved to see, hadn't registered with the guards. Unlike cops, security details weren't trained to look for signs of stress—like the sudden dampness gluing his shirt to his spine or the tightness of his fingers.

He'd taken supreme effort to make sure his true identity never surfaced. He'd masked his fingerprints. Altered his appearance. Changed his name. Paid to have his true identity erased from every data bank in existence. The price to delete himself had been exorbitant but well worth the cost. Because he had a huge weakness that could be used against him.

A sister.

A twin.

How in the hell those bastards had tracked down his true identity didn't matter.

They had. End of story.

And if he didn't deliver exactly what he'd promised, he might not be the only one suffering the punishment of failure.

Jilly and the kids could end up suffering alongside him.

Beth was handling the whole someone-just-tried-to-kill-her-thing fine, until she glanced down to find her attacker glaring up at her. Her dead attacker. His muddy brown eyes were starting to glaze, but remained fixed on her face with uncanny focus.

A chill started at the crown of her head and slowly, steadily drained down, crystallizing every cell in its wake, immersing her from ears to toes in glacier water. She broke off in midargument with Zane and started to shake. She shook so hard she thought her bones were going to shatter, so hard her muscles ached.

"Hey." Zane's scowl vanished. Concern darkened his eyes. He drew her into his arms, running his palms up and down her rigid, trembling back.

"I'm fine."

Which was a stupid thing to say, considering her body had frozen into a giant block of ice. Desperate to soak in his warmth, Beth pressed closer, but this time his heat didn't penetrate the permafrost enveloping her.

"Shock," Rawls murmured, and she felt a pair of hands that weren't Zane's touch her face and reach for her wrist.

"Her pulse is fast, a little thready. She should be sitting down."

Rawlings's voice came from a distance. Somehow it seemed important that he'd lost his southern twang, and she realized that she was using his accent as a barometer—he seemed to lose it when things got tense.

"I'll find a blanket. Get her down on the floor."

Suddenly she was moving, but without her legs doing any of the work. And then they were back against the wall, sitting on the floor, with her cradled like an infant in Zane's lap.

She burrowed closer to his hot body, pressing her face against his chest, the cotton of his T-shirt soft and warm against her cheek, and she concentrated on the steady, strong thump of his heart.

How embarrassing.

She hadn't expected to fall apart like this. She had always been the go-to person in emergencies. The person everyone relied on. Of course, surviving a murder attempt was a lot different than dealing with a broken window or leaking washing machine. She didn't have any practical experience when it came to life-and-death situations.

Unlike the man cradling her in his lap.

His heart rate remained slow and steady. His breathing even. His skin warm and dry. There was no sign of adrenaline. No sign of fear. No sign of shock.

But then he was a SEAL, and if she could believe the romances she'd read, the men who graduated onto the teams were a breed apart. His training would have heightened his natural predisposition toward calm action in emergencies. Still, she would have expected some sign of adrenaline.

The fact it was completely absent illustrated what polar opposites they were. While the situation had thrown her into a full-blown panic attack, his pulse hadn't even accelerated. What in the world would a man like that want with a woman whose life was so dull that fixing a leaky water pipe constituted an emergency?

But then it didn't really matter, did it? Her body might be in an epic battle with her brain, it might crave everything he was offering, but her brain knew better. Sizzling heat burned out as quickly as it flared, leaving nothing but ashes and regrets in its wake. She wasn't cut out for a fleeting, albeit raging, affair. She wanted the slow, steady, lifelong burn. The kind that started as friendship, morphed into love, and lasted forever. A true partnership. Like what Todd and Ginny shared.

"Here, tuck this around her," Rawls said from somewhere above her head.

A lightweight, crinkly space blanket was draped over her shoulders. Zane anchored it in place by clamping the edges beneath his armpits.

"I'm fine, really," she said, relieved the words were coherent.

His arms tightened, locking her in place. "Relax. You're white as snow and still shaking. This material will reflect our body heat. It's the quickest way to warm you up."

She was already warming up, almost toasty, as a matter of fact.

"I'm sorry about wigging out on you," she told his chest, the ice giving way to lethargy.

He ran a hand down her spine. "Someone tried to kill you. You're entitled."

"You didn't freak out."

"No one tried to strangle me." His hand continued that slow, comforting glide. Up. Down. Up. Down. She focused on his hand, the gentle strength of his fingers. Russ had rubbed her back too, but his caress had felt alien. Foreign. Zane's touch felt...perfect.

She pushed the comparison aside and scrunched her nose in disgust. He wouldn't have freaked out even if all three terrorists had tried to kill him—at the same time. He would have dispatched them with his habitual calm and coolly cleaned up the mess.

He must have read her mind because he gave a ghost of a laugh and a quick hug. "There's a big difference, sweetheart—I'm trained for combat. You're not. Trust me, you're handling yourself just fine."

She sighed and snuggled closer. "I'm surprised nobody's questioned us."

"They're waiting for the feds." Zane shifted her weight, easing her away from the ridge of hard flesh pushing against her bottom.

Good Lord, the man had an erection.

To her surprise, an answering rush of heat softened the flesh between her legs and her nipples started to tighten. Apparently now that her muscles were warming up, her libido was too.

Lovely.

"Where do you think they'll take us?" Not that she cared, but they needed something to distract them.

"It will depend if they have a large enough area here to hold everyone and enough rooms to separate people during interviews. They may end up shuffling everyone to a different location."

He cocked his head slightly and studied her face, then stroked her cheek with his knuckles. Whatever he saw must have satisfied him, because he visibly relaxed.

"Your skin's picking up color."

"I told you, I'm fine."

She should be moving, but it felt so good to be held like this. Too good, actually. Her reluctance to distance herself was a clear sign she needed to.

Straightening, Beth forced herself to back out of his lap. His arms tightened, but just for a moment, then released her. She shook off the weird sense of loss and scrambled to her feet.

"We should be looking for the other hijackers," she said, concentrating on folding the silver blanket.

"We won't find them. They've been warned off." He rose to his feet with economical ease.

Beth's hands stilled; slowly she raised her head and searched his face. "Warned off? By who?"

"By whoever warned our three. They were in full flight by the time we got back to the terminal."

"They knew their operation was compromised," Cosky agreed, his voice grim. The gaze he turned on Zane was flat. "We've got a leak."

"Not us. Mac didn't go through channels. He called the FBI directly. The leak didn't come from HQ1. It had to be the feds."

"Wait a minute," Beth protested. "That seems too convenient. I mean, how likely is it that your superior would go directly to the people working with the hijackers? Even if the hijackers did have someone on their payroll, the chances they are the same agents your boss talked to is...well...astronomical."

"Think about it." Zane turned his head toward Beth. He was in full warrior mode again. Expressionless. Cool. Competent. "Hijacking's considered an act of terrorism. It wouldn't take much to find out which agency would be assigned to the investigation. If you control the people assigned to the case, you'd control the investigation and ransom negotiations."

Cosky surveyed the crowd of curious passengers—dozens of eyes were locked on their small group by the wall—and lifted a dark eyebrow. "Who did Mac talk to? That will give us a place to start looking."

"I don't know, but you can bet your ass he'll be asking his contact some hard questions."

Rawlings cleared his throat. With a lazy nod, he drew everyone's attention to the main corridor.

Beth's gaze deviated to the left. She breathed a sigh of relief on finding a silver hump where she'd been attacked. Somebody had covered the hijacker's body with a blanket identical to the one Zane's friend had brought her.

"They found the guns." Cosky watched impassively as an army of blue suits and plainclothes approached.

Beth turned to stare at the cluster of men. "How can you tell?"

"There's too damn many of them for anything else."

"Surprised?" Beth asked, a sense of vindication stirring. She got the distinct impression that Simcosky still didn't believe her.

He turned his head toward her, those black eyebrows climbing. That small telltale gesture seemed to be the only expression he allowed himself. He was taking the whole Spock thing to extremes.

"I attacked a complete stranger. Knocked him out. Trussed him up like a Thanksgiving turkey. If I hadn't believed you, he'd still be on his feet."

Okay, then…Beth didn't have a clue what to say. *Thank you* didn't quite fit under the circumstances. Luckily Cosky didn't seem to expect a response.

"Game's on." Zane stepped up and wrapped his arm around her shoulder. "You remember how we met?"

Obviously he wasn't talking about their *real* meeting. "Over the weekend, while hiking." She frowned; they needed more of a story than that. "What trail? What time? What was I wearing? How did we actually meet? What did we have for dinner? Breakfast the next morning? What time did we leave on Sunday??"

"Toleak Point, Olympic National Park. We met Saturday morning, at a stream, filling up water bottles. We hit it off, hiked the trail together, camped together. Dinner was beef stew and chili. Breakfast was bacon and eggs. We left at noon. You were wearing jeans and a T-shirt. Pick a T-shirt."

She cast her mind over her wardrobe. "I've got a Pink Panther T-shirt." That would be easy enough to remember.

"Pink Panther. Got it." He bent to nuzzle the side of her neck, and chills feathered across her skin.

They'd expect her to know more personal information about him too, wouldn't they? Even if they'd just met, an exchange about family would have taken place at some point. She tried to convince herself the sudden rise of curiosity was because of what the agents might ask. "Have you been married? Any kids? Do you have brothers? Sisters? Where did you grow up? Are your parents still alive?"

He straightened and cast a quick glance across the gate room. "No. No. Four brothers—Chance, Webb, Gray, and Dane—no sisters. I was a navy brat, so I base-hopped. Both parents alive." Interest sharpened his gaze. "You?"

"Never married, but engaged once." She felt him tense. Frowning, she waited, but when he didn't comment she continued. "No children, raised here, in Burien. No siblings, and I lost my mom years ago."

For a moment it looked like he was going to say something. His hand rose toward her face, but before it made contact he shifted and shot another glance toward the corridor. When he turned back, his face had gone flat. Professional.

His arm tightened around shoulders. "Relax. You'll be fine."

Beth wasn't so certain; their story seemed awfully sketchy. What if someone asked her a question that wasn't on their list? Plus, she'd spent the weekend at home. Granted she'd been alone, inside the condo, and her car had been parked in the garage. Still, one of her neighbors could have seen her. What if the authorities actually checked into their story and someone contradicted their account? A dozen terrifying possibilities loomed in her mind.

"We should just tell the truth." She dropped her voice and leaned toward Zane. "Eventually someone's going to expose us, and we'll both be in trouble."

Zane shook his head and smiled reassuringly. "It's too late. Changing the story affects more than us. Mac told the FBI the info was picked up through border-op intel."

Well, crap, he was right. Plus, they'd identified and subdued the hijackers on the basis of her dream—which meant they had no pictures, no descriptions, no actual proof that the three men Zane and his buddies had incapacitated were a danger to anyone. If she confessed, they'd let the hijackers go. At least this way the terrorists would remain in custody until they found enough proof to nail them.

His attention drifted down to her mottled neck and his eyes darkened. "How are you feeling?"

Beth reached up to brush her throat, wondering how bad the bruises looked. Pretty ugly, she suspected.

"I'm fine. Really." Which was surprisingly true. The shaking had vanished and while her neck felt a little swollen and achy, it was easy enough to ignore.

"What do you think's going to happen next?" She turned to stare across the terminal. An army of blue-suited police officers was gathering in the mouth of the gate room.

"They'll start moving everyone. Separating people. Conducting interviews."

He glanced toward the front of the terminal. The cops were mingling with the security guards and heads were turning in their direction.

After a few minutes of discussion, two overweight men in dark slacks and ill-fitting jackets broke away from the cluster of law enforcement and approached them.

"Lieutenant Commander Winters?" the taller of the two said. "I'm Detective Sheridan. If you and your group would follow me."

They were escorted through a series of corridors and hallways until they were deep within the bowels of the airport. Minutes later they arrived at a conference room. A pair of uniformed officers flanked the double doors. Their detective escorts ushered them inside, only to disappear back down the hall.

The room was moderate in size with a long, rectangular table and plastic orange chairs. Rather than taking a seat, the three men stood with their backs against the spackled wall. Did they have some weird distaste for sitting? With a disgusted shake of her head, Beth marched over to the table, pulled out a chair, and plopped down. After a pregnant pause, Zane joined her.

Maybe a quarter of an hour crawled by before the conference room doors finally opened and two hard-faced, middle-aged men strode in.

"Feds," Cosky said, without lowering his voice.

Beth wondered how he could tell. Other than the fit of their clothing, they looked like the detectives who'd escorted them through the terminal. Sharp, assessing eyes surveyed the group before zeroing in on Zane.

"Lieutenant Commander Winters?" the agent to the left asked as he headed in their direction. His voice remained cool yet respectful. "I'm Senior Agent Aaron Haskell with the FBI's Counterterrorism Division."

Zane nodded and introduced his men. When he came to Beth, he presented her as his fiancée. She suppressed a jolt. She vaguely remembered him claiming her as his fiancée earlier—to Russ—but why? It would be easier to pull off a spontaneous hookup than an engagement.

"We need to ask you some questions. If you'll follow us?" Haskell turned and indicated the door with an abbreviated gesture. "Your fiancée can wait here with Lieutenants Simcosky and Rawlings. Another agent will take their statements."

With one last sweep of the conference room, Zane started to nod, his arm loosening around Beth's shoulders. Suddenly he froze. "Beth comes with me," he said, his voice uncompromising.

The agent frowned. "Miss Brown will be interviewed separately. At the moment we're more interested in the men your commander claims were attempting to hijack the plane—"

"She comes with me."

Beth stared at him, puzzled. He'd warned her they'd be separated during the interviews, so why this sudden intractability? Didn't he trust that she'd stick to their script? But then he'd broken their script already, hadn't he, with this bogus engagement? Maybe that's what had him worried, that their engagement accounts wouldn't match. Except he wasn't looking at her.

Curious, she followed his gaze and realized his attention wasn't focused on the FBI agents either, but farther back toward the door. She shifted to the right until she could see around the agent in front of her and discovered that Russ Branson had entered the room.

Russ broke into a relieved smile as he caught sight of her and started forward.

"Son of a bitch," Zane snapped.

The agents looked at each other and turned in unison.

Agent Haskell's eyebrows shot up. "Considering Mr. Branson saved Miss Brown's life, I'm sure you'll agree he's no threat to her."

Zane shifted his glare to Haskell, who took a half step back. "There are still two hijackers unaccounted for. She's obviously a target. She stays with me."

A pulse of silence fell. The two agents frowned, glanced at each other. Apparently, by osmosis, they came to some sort of agreement because Haskell turned back to Zane.

"Fine." He gestured toward the door again.

They'd barely started walking before Russ intercepted them. The FBI agents halted and glanced between Russ and Zane with quizzical eyes.

Russ frowned, ran a hand down his face, and pinched his chin. His gaze lingered on her throat. "I just wanted to make sure you were okay."

"I'm fin—"

"She's just hunky-dory," Rawls drawled. "Her *fiancé* is taking real good care of her."

Haskell's lips twitched, and he exchanged amused glances with his partner. Beth wished the floor would open up and swallow her. Did Zane *have* to play the jealous lover? This confrontation was beyond embarrassing.

Pasting a bright smile on her face, she turned to Russ. "I wanted to thank you for what you did. I hate to think of what might have happened if..."

Russ shot a quick look at Zane before refocusing on Beth. "It's lucky I got there when I did. A second later and it would have been too late."

Zane's shoulders stiffened. "We're on our way out," he told Russ brusquely.

Haskell coughed and brought a hand up to cover his mouth.

TRISH MCCALLAN

Beth turned her too-bright smile on Zane's glowering face and fought back a glare. "I'm thanking—"

"You can thank him later," Zane snapped, his lips tight. He glanced up and suddenly froze, his face smoothing into an expressionless shell.

"What?" Startled by the change, she followed his gaze but wasn't tall enough to see over the FBI agents.

"Commander," Zane said, the rank a greeting.

"Radar must have got you on the first plane up." Rawls stepped forward.

"He had them hold the plane for me," a rumbling voice full of grit and gravel responded. "Commander Jace Mackenzie," the raspy voice continued, by way of introduction.

Tensing, Beth withdrew into the security of Zane's loose embrace, listening as the FBI agents introduced themselves. The last thing she needed was the owner of that harsh voice focusing on her.

"Where is she?" Mac demanded.

Beth's breath stuttered. Zane's arm tightened around her shoulder. Rawls and Cosky silently stepped to the side, opening a path, and she tried to reassure herself that they hadn't just thrown her to the big bad wolf. She caught a glimpse of Russ's sharp face as he turned toward the new arrival, and then she got her first look at the owner of that grating voice.

Eyes so dark they looked black locked on her face and shot from there to the arm Zane had wrapped around her shoulders. An almost murderous expression flashed across his lean, chiseled face. It was gone so quickly she tried to convince herself she'd imagined it.

Mackenzie's skin was deeply tanned, the hard planes of his cheekbones and jaw lending an almost brutal cast to his features.

106

Mac waited until the doors closed behind them, stuck his hand in his jacket pocket to thumb on the voice scrambler, and rounded on Zane. "Imagine my surprise to find you engaged, particularly when I spoke with you mere hours ago and you failed to mention the good news."

He tried for a silky tone, but it sounded more like someone had pushed the words through a cheese grater. The rasp came courtesy of a damaged larynx, which he'd picked up thanks to a garrote wielded by a Taliban rebel back in Afghanistan. He'd been lucky; as a freshly finned minnow straight from SQT it could have been his first and last op.

"I was going to tell you once things settled," Zane told him flatly.

"Why is it I've never heard of Miss Brown before?"

Zane held his gaze. "We met over the weekend. I asked her to marry me this morning."

Mac tried not to grind his teeth. There had been no hesitation in the statement. No wavering in Zane's gaze. Yet he was absolutely certain the bastard was lying to him. Again.

"Did you now? After three days?" He let the disbelief echo in his voice.

With a lift of his eyebrows, Zane stared back. "You've met my dad? My brothers?"

The dry reminder pulled Mac up short, but just for a moment. Talking to his LC would get him nowhere. His men were conditioned to withstand hardcore interrogation techniques. If he wanted to find out what the hell this bitch had dragged his team into, he needed to talk to the woman.

"I'll speak with your fiancée now." When Zane's face tightened, Mac hardened his voice. "Alone."

A muscle twitched in Zane's cheek. "We're on our way to a debriefing."

"You take the interview. I'll take her."

The muscle twitched again. Stronger. "She doesn't leave my side."

"Commander," Rawls broke in, his voice tight, his blue eyes watchful. "She's had a tough time. Take a look at her neck. Zane's just feeling a mite protective."

Mac hauled in a deep, calming breath. He held it for five seconds and released it slowly. The pressure didn't ease. "I've got eyes, Lieutenant. I can see her neck."

Not to mention that he'd heard the story from three separate people. How the hell an attempt on her life fit into this mess, he wasn't sure. But if the hijackers wanted her dead, there had to be a reason.

Such as: she'd double-crossed them.

"This isn't a request. I will talk to her. Alone. Now."

Zane's face went hard as stone. It was an expression Mac remembered from their black-op days but he'd never seen it turned on him before.

What the fuck had the bitch done to him?

"Mac—" Cosky started to say.

"Not one more word, from either of you." Mac issued the warning through his teeth. He didn't take his gaze off Zane's face. "Do I need to make this an order, Lieutenant Commander Winters?"

"We're on leave."

"I'm still your fucking commanding officer."

Zane opened his mouth, and Mac knew with gut-wrenching certainty that his best friend was about to throw himself in front of a fucking Zodiac and all because of a goddamn woman.

Except that the woman in question slammed her elbow into Zane's chest hard enough to shut the bastard's mouth. As Zane shifted his glare to her, she turned toward Mac and pinned him with disgusted eyes.

"If you two Neanderthals are finished with this useless display of testosterone, I'd like to remind you that the only person who has any say over what I do and who I do it with—is me." She turned her glare back on Zane. "If I want to speak with Commander Mackenzie, I'll speak with him."

Sheer frustration flashed across Zane's face. "Goddamn it, Beth."

Her mouth dropped open, outrage flashing in her eyes. "Did you just swear at me?"

Zane took a deep breath. Held it. Considering the combination of frustration and fury flashing across his normally calm countenance, the technique didn't work any better for him than it had for Mac.

The woman turned her back on her fiancé and yanked herself out of his arms. The glare she turned on Mac didn't look any friendlier—which didn't fit with how she should have been acting, according to his profile.

Surprisingly off balance, he watched her approach.

"Commander Mackenzie," she said, a militant look on her face, "of course I'll speak with you."

"Beth—"

She shot his LC a sharp glance. "But Zane remains with us."

Mac scowled and stepped forward threateningly. "Alone."

Crossing her arms, she rocked back on her heels and lifted an eyebrow. "You do realize that I am *not* under your command. You *cannot* order me around. If I talk with you, it's because I choose to, which will only happen if Zane remains."

Reassessing his approach, Mac studied her face, measuring the depth of her determination. She looked pretty damn determined. And since he didn't have any jurisdiction here, he couldn't force her compliance.

"Fine," he growled.

She nodded, abruptly regal. "We'll be right with you, after we speak with these FBI *gentlemen*."

Her emphasis on the last word was a blatant dig at his less-than-gentlemanly behavior. Mac rubbed his lips to hide their sudden twitch. Christ, she was a snippy little thing.

"Cosky and Rawls will be happy to take this turn with the feds," Mac said as the door to the conference room opened. Apparently their five minutes were up. "You may not be under my command"—a fucking pity—"but they are, and they'll be happy to take this turn with the feds. Won't you, boys?"

"Yes, suh." Rawls's drawl was more pronounced than ever.

"I'm certain the FBI would like some say in who *they* interview."

The woman obviously liked getting her way. Too bad. He always got his.

"Absolutely," Mac mimicked her pronunciation and watched her eyes fill with frustrated temper.

He turned to the approaching agents. "I need to speak to Lieutenant Commander Winters. Lieutenants Simcosky and Rawlings will accompany you for the debriefing. I'll send Zane once I'm done with him."

Mac waited until the agents escorted Simcosky and Rawlings out of the room. As soon as the double doors closed, he took the scrambler out of his pocket and showed it to them before shoving the cylinder back in his pocket.

"It's a scrambler," Zane explained to the woman in a low voice. "It scrambles any electrical signals. Bugs. Microphones. Cell phones. Cameras."

"Which means we can talk freely, so why don't you explain to me what the fuck's going on?"

Zane watched him with absolute stillness. "You know what's going on. They found the guns."

"I'm not talking about the guns. Or the hijacking. I want to know what the fuck you've got yourself involved in, what you're lying about."

Something flickered across Zane's face. Although it was gone instantly, Mac knew with raw certainty that his best friend was about to lie to him...again...because of a fucking woman.

"Don't you *dare* lie to me. I know you better than that." He wondered if it sounded like a plea. It sure as hell felt like one.

For one long moment Zane stared back. Mac could read the regret on his face, in his eyes. Yeah. He was going to lie, and nothing would be the same between them.

"Tell him the truth." Beth broke the tension-filled silence.

Slowly Mac turned his head in her direction.

Zane's breath hissed between his teeth. He raised his hands and scrubbed them down his face. "Beth...just stay out of this."

She put a hand on his forearm. "I told you this was a mistake. If you'd told him the truth in the beginning, we could have avoided all this." She waved her hand back and forth.

"What's going on?" Mac asked again, only this time he directed the question to the woman. "The guns were exactly where he said they would be. That plane was about to be hijacked. I'm confident when the targets they apprehended are identified, they'll prove to have been responsible for taking down the Argentina plane. So what the fuck is he lying about?"

She breathed a ghost of a laugh and held his stare without flinching. "You see, that's the lie."

"Beth, for Christ's sake. You don't need to do this."

Mac frowned in confusion. "What's the lie?"

"That the guns were where he said they'd be. That he was the one who identified the hijackers."

Mac put two and two together instantly. "You were the one who knew."

The news didn't surprise him. He'd suspected as much. The big surprise was that she'd admit it.

"You were the one who knew this flight was going to be taken, who knew where the guns were, who knew what the hijackers looked like. You passed this information on to Zane."

She squared her shoulders and nodded.

Zane cursed softly, staring at Mac with grim frustration.

"So Zane didn't dream any of this. The dream was the lie."

She shook her head. Shot a fleeting glance toward his lieutenant commander. "No. The dream was the truth. The lie was who had it. Zane isn't the one who dreamed about the hijacking. I was."

————————————

With a muttered curse, Zane watched Mac's spine turn to stone.

What a disaster.

"You dreamed the hijacking," Mac repeated with a total lack of expression. His dark head tilted back until he was staring at

Beth down the barrel of his nose. "You're serious? You're going with that psychic bullshit?"

From Beth's resigned expression, the question didn't surprise her. It didn't surprise Zane either. Mac's very DNA was wired with suspicion. As a kid he'd probably done perimeter searches before letting anyone out on the playground, checked beneath swings and slides and merry-go-rounds before climbing up to play. His Special Operations training had taken that inherent caution and ratcheted it up several degrees, turning him into a razor-sharp, deadly operator. There were few people Zane would rather have at his back.

But when you needed him to suspend that suspicion, it was like trying to convince a hungry lion not to take down an injured gazelle—completely against his nature.

"You have these psychic episodes often?" Mac asked dryly.

Beth snorted and blew a wisp of hair off her forehead. "Didn't we just do this?"

"What?" Mac's chin came down a notch.

"The explanations. Suspicions. Doubts. Accusations. No, I am not psychic. This was the first—and hopefully the last—time I've ever dreamed something that came true."

"So you just happened to dream about this flight. Wait. Let me guess. You dreamed it because Zane was on board, your soul mate."

With an audible slap, Beth's palms came down on her hips. "Considering I didn't know Zane existed until this morning, I'm guessing your theory sucks saltwater."

Zane groaned and waited for the shit to hit the fan.

"You need to keep track of your lies, sweetheart. You met him over the weekend—"

"I'd know when I met him better than you, and it was—" She consulted her watch. "Just over three hours ago."

Mac paused, his eyebrows bunching as he worked the pieces into place. "You're not engaged."

"Give the man a cookie." She frowned. "We were going to play the couple so the hijackers wouldn't question why we were leaving the departure gate." Her frown deepened. "Beats me how that escalated into an engagement."

Mac shot Zane a grim look. "Why'd you approach Zane in the first place?"

"I heard Rawls call him 'Lieutenant' in the dream. I hoped that meant he had contacts. Someone who could get the plane grounded and searched." She held Mac's gaze. "Like you."

"Jesus Christ." The muscles in Mac's forearms bunched as he rounded on Zane. "How the *hell* could you fall for this?"

"I knew something was wrong an hour before she arrived." Zane tensed, fighting to keep his tone calm.

"That's not the point, which you fucking know. I don't doubt those flashes of yours were at work. But she has to be involved in this."

"She's not."

"You don't know that." Mac's voice sharpened. "You're compromised. You've convinced yourself she's the one. It's your blind spot."

Whoa. This conversation needed to switch focus fast. He wasn't explaining his family's quirks to her in the middle of an argument.

"You're not seeing her clearly," Mac snapped.

"I'm not the one wearing blinders." Zane folded his arms across his chest. "She's not your mother. Or your ex. Or Jenn."

"What the *fuck* do they have to do with this?" Mac's voice deepened and rose, until it rumbled through the room like a Blackhawk on liftoff.

"You know damn well what I'm talking about." He watched Mac's eyebrows slam down over the bridge of his nose. "You don't know her, yet you're already lumping her into the same category as all the other women in your life. You're already assuming she's up to no good."

"That's the *goddamn point*. I don't know her. Neither do you. You met her three hours ago, and you're already claiming an engagement. You don't think that's cause for concern?" He stalked forward, fury vibrating off him in waves. Lifting his index finger, he pointed it like a gun. "You roped me, Cosky, and Rawls into this lie, and all to protect some broad who has to be involved."

"Well, you know the truth now," Beth pointed out tartly. "You can tell everyone how you found out about the guns and your conscience will be clear."

Zane could just imagine the feds' reaction to that bit of news. He reached out to take her hand, craving the feeling of her skin against his. Her fingers entwined with his.

Christ, he'd just found her. No way in hell was he losing her.

"Yeah? How's that going to work?" Mac swung toward Beth with a snarl. "The feds think the info came through fresh intel. If I reveal the *fresh intel* was your dream, how long do you think those assholes my boys nabbed are going to stay in custody? Not to mention Zane will spend a good share of his life rotting in the stockade, and ST7 will become the butt of every stand-up routine for the next year."

"How this works," Zane interrupted flatly, "is you trust me to know she isn't playing us. You trust me to know the difference."

"Trust you?" Mac's voice swelled. "When you're basing every decision on the fact she's your predestined mate, the woman you've been waiting ten fucking years for?"

For a second sheer silence reigned. Zane had one raw, wrenching moment of hope—maybe she hadn't been paying attention.

And then her mouth dropped open.

"*What?*" Her voice climbed shrilly.

Son of a bitch.

"Didn't he tell you? See, Zane's the psychic. Hell, his whole family is. And the men in his bloodline have this handy-dandy little trick—they can sense the woman destined to be their wife, their soul mate, the mother of their children."

Beth's eyes rounded with each word. She jerked her hand from his and stepped back. Zane's chest clenched. It was too soon. She wasn't ready to hear this. He needed more time, the chance to prove to her how good they could be together.

Goddamn it. With a deep breath, he refocused.

He could hardly call the happy tidings back, so he'd have to play the hand Mac had dealt. Besides, the sparks were still there, the heat between them as fiery as ever. He could use that.

Mac's furious gaze settled on her dismayed face and he suddenly frowned, looking uneasy.

Before Zane had a chance to move in with some major damage control, the door flew open. The feds had been remarkably accommodating, even respectful. Something of a surprise, considering the amount of posturing that normally accompanied cross-departmental interaction. For them to barge in without warning meant that something had changed.

Had the jammer been compromised? Someone was constantly coming up with new ways to circumvent stealth equipment. Had the feds been listening in?

The man who filled the doorway scanned the room with sunken brown eyes; his gaze lingered on Mac for a second before shifting to Zane.

Deep grooves scored his face. His hair was mahogany, graying in streaks, but the quality of the suit marked him as someone high on the food chain.

"Miss Brown." His gaze fell on Beth.

Zane tensed as the new arrival raked Beth from head to toe. There was more than interest in those eyes. There was suspicion as well.

Silently Zane crossed to her side and slid an arm around her waist. He half expected her to pull away, but she must have sensed the danger because she didn't flinch as he drew her against him. Heat flared where their bodies touched. Christ, it felt good to hold her again.

"I'm John Chastain, Special Agent in Charge of Seattle's Counterterrorism Division. You need to come with me."

"Chastain." Mac stepped forward and held out his hand. "Commander Jace Mackenzie. We spoke on the phone."

Zane caught a faint trace of contempt in Mac's voice. The fed acknowledged the introduction with a nod and an abbreviated handshake, but his attention didn't budge from Beth's face, which told Zane everything he needed to know.

Beth had moved onto their suspect list.

Zane was psychic?

Mac's voice echoed in Beth's mind. She'd wondered why Zane and his teammates had believed her so quickly. Apparently Cosky and Rawls had bought her story because of Zane, because he was psychic. But if this were true, wouldn't he have known something was going to happen on the plane?

Her memory flitted back to the closet, to when she'd first told them about the dream, to all those quick glances and intense silences. Something had passed between them. She'd even sensed it at the time.

Maybe he had known. Maybe all three of them had known. And then she'd come along with her hijacking dream...Rawls and Cosky must have believed her because of Zane. Because he was convinced she was his predestined mate. His soul mate.

Predestined mate.

Soul mate.

The words rolled round and round Beth's mind, a pair of pinballs that knocked every other consideration out of her head. They were all she could think about, which was aggravating considering she needed to focus on the FBI agents across the table.

The room to which this newest pair of federal agents had escorted them was a lunch room. A large round table swallowed the middle of the room. There was a refrigerator in the back corner. A microwave on a cart next to it. A stained but clean Formica counter ran the length of the back wall. Cupboards climbed the wall above and below the counter.

It was similar to engineering's lunchroom. Except this one felt like an interrogation room.

The fact they'd allowed Zane to accompany her was a surprise. Was he under suspicion now too?

She suspected the agents were trying to throw her off balance with their silence, hoping to unnerve her. Hoping her fear would escalate until it weakened her resolve and she blurted out confessions just to fill the void.

Any other day the tactic might have worked. Today it barely registered. All she could think about was that she was the supposed soul mate of a gorgeous, sexy stranger. A man she'd only known for three hours, a man with whom she had absolutely nothing in common.

The very fact he believed in such fairy tales was a clear indication of how unsuited they were. Soul mates were nothing more than pre-pubescent fantasies. Real relationships flourished by getting to know each other, by learning when and how to compromise, by learning your partner's quirks and habits, by accepting their tastes and brushing off the idiosyncrasies people accumulated through the years.

Real relationships took work.

They didn't depend on some lazy, mythical connection to hold a couple together. Putting faith in the soul mate theory was the surest path to divorce court, the surest path to raising a family on your own.

She couldn't believe—could *not* believe—that Zane put stock in such complete and utter nonsense. Soul mates? He was a SEAL, for God's sake. To survive such life-and-death missions he had to have a core of common sense.

Where was that common sense now?

She took a deep, calming breath, vaguely aware the new agent—Chastain—was watching her with puzzlement. Perhaps he'd expected a confession by now, but then he wasn't aware of the four-ton white elephant Zane had dropped on her head. Although, to be fair, Zane wasn't the one who'd pitched the bomb.

His butthead boss had. So maybe it wasn't even true. Maybe Mackenzie had been spewing a boatload of crap.

She breathed easier. Okay, yeah, that made sense. Zane was too sharp to believe something so foolish.

"Miss Brown," Chastain said, apparently tired of waiting for the silence to jolt a confession from her. "It's come to our attention that you work for PacAtlantic."

With a slight nod, Beth settled back in her chair. "That's right, going on seven years now."

Her relaxed reply earned a narrow-eyed look from the agents across from her. Apparently suspects were not supposed to chill out once the interrogation started.

"In the engineering department." He opened a manila folder and consulted a paper inside.

"Yes," she agreed.

Chastain frowned and rubbed his chin. The poor man looked awful. Huge circles shadowed the skin below his eyes. Grooves were carved into his forehead and alongside his mouth. His skin almost looked gray. From the way his suit hung off his shoulders, it was obvious the man had lost weight. Maybe he was ill.

"You listed yourself on standby for Flight 2077 an hour before the plane was due to board, but there's no record you checked any baggage or asked for time off work," he said abruptly, his tone an accusation.

So Zane had been right. Her behavior had been flagged as suspicious.

"I didn't intend to take the flight. I only listed myself on standby so I could get into the departure gate and see Zane off."

Before she could continue with the rest of their story, the agent nodded. Obviously the explanation made perfect sense to him. Why hadn't they gone with that excuse in the first place?

Chastain leaned back in his chair, absently reaching into his pocket. His brow suddenly furrowed and he pulled his fingers out again. With casual interest he unfolded a slip of paper and glanced down, only to freeze—the muscles of his chest, shoulders, and arms visibly contracting. His lips tightened until a white line ringed his mouth. For what seemed like an eternity he sat there, rigid, eyes locked on that slip of paper.

"John?" The other agent, a slender, almost effeminate man with slicked-back red hair and a fastidiously trimmed goatee, leaned to the left with a frown and glanced at the note.

The movement snapped Chastain out of his trance. He crumpled the paper and shoved it back into his pocket.

"Sorry. Shopping list," he said in a voice that lacked breath.

As Chastain turned back to her, she caught something raw and haunted in those sunken eyes. Something hurting.

"You work in the engineering department?" he asked again, jotting something down inside the file.

From the confused frown his partner sent him, Beth wasn't the only one wondering why he'd asked that question a second time.

"Yes." She left it at that.

His fingers tightened around the pen. "Are you familiar with a Todd Clancy?"

She stiffened. Why were they asking about Todd? Something told her this sudden interest in her coworker had serious ramifications.

"Why?"

He regarded her with complete flatness. "Are you friendly with Todd Clancy?"

"Yes. It's through him I got my job," she whispered through suddenly dry lips.

Zane's hand tensed within her grip, his fingers clamping around hers. "Ginny—Todd's wife—and I have been friends since kindergarten. I'm godmother to their son, Kyle."

Zane's fingers relaxed.

"You've been to their house?" Chastain bent over the folder, scanned a page, and flipped it over. Beth craned her neck, trying to get a look, but he closed the folder over the piece of paper.

"Of course. What's this about?" she asked, tired of their games, of the posturing, of the lack of answers. "If you think that Todd had anything to do with this—" She waved her arm around the room. "You couldn't be more wrong."

"Why do you assume we think he's involved?"

She snorted. "Because you're asking about him."

His forehead crinkled and he jotted something down on the inside flap of the folder. What had he written? That she was uncooperative? Defensive?

"You guys are completely off track. Todd is the kindest, gentlest person you'll ever meet. There is no way, *absolutely no way*, he'd stash those guns and make it possible for the hijackers to take that plane."

Dead silence fell. Chastain stared down at his folder and for a moment his shoulders seemed to hunch. "The east gate login shows Todd Clancy accessed the tarmac at approximately four thirty a.m. His shift didn't start until six a.m."

Beth relaxed, expelling a puff of relief. "The engineers come in early quite often. If they need to check something on a plane they have to do so preflight or between flights. I'm sure he has a perfectly good explanation."

Chastain cocked his head and watched her intently. "We have a witness, Miss Brown. A witness who can place Mr. Clancy outside Flight 2077 with a parts crate. Can you think of a reason why Todd Clancy would show up at the plane with a parts crate?"

Beth swallowed, retreating into her seat. An engineer hauling around a parts crate was much harder to dismiss. Engineers didn't touch the actual mechanics of the plane. It was forbidden. Only the maintenance department was allowed to work on PAA planes, and even they kept detailed records, per FAA regulations. Of course, it was probably a case of mistaken identity. Thousands of people worked for PacAtlantic. In all likelihood, their witness had mixed Todd up with someone else.

She leaned forward again and met Chastain's grim gaze. "Then your witness is wrong."

"Our witness is a camera. The camera focused on gate C-18 specifically. It clearly shows Mr. Clancy boarding that plane—with a crate."

Her chest tightened and her hands started to sweat. He wouldn't need a parts crate for any legitimate work he had on that plane.

This couldn't be true. It couldn't be. Her gaze flipped back and forth between the two men before her. "I don't believe it. I know Todd. He wouldn't do this."

The agent withdrew a photo from the folder, set it faceup on the table, and slid it across to her. The sibilant hiss of plastic against wood echoed in her ears.

"Is this Todd Clancy, Miss Brown?"

She didn't want to look. Oh God, not Todd. He couldn't be involved in this. Vaguely she felt Zane's hand tighten around her own, but the sensation was distant, out of focus.

Swallowing hard, she glanced down, instantly recognizing that sandy sprout of hair.

Oh, Jesus.

"Is the man in this picture Todd Clancy, Miss Brown?" Agent Chastain's flat tone made it clear he already knew the answer to that question.

Beth didn't answer. Instead, she ran a gentle finger down the face in the photo, grief and shock rolling through her like a tidal wave. Her heart hurt. So did her head. This didn't make sense, none of this made sense. Todd would cut off his arms and legs rather than hurt anyone—especially Ginny and Kyle—and this— this was going to kill them.

"Miss Brown, is this Todd Clancy?"

Beth's finger trembled as she stroked that glossy face again. "You know it is."

He didn't deny it, just leaned back in his chair and studied her face.

Zane scooted his chair closer to hers, the plastic feet screech- ing against the floor, and wrapped an arm around her waist, giving her a one-armed hug. Without saying a word, he leaned in to kiss the side of her temple, his lips gentle against her skin. Beth closed her eyes and breathed in his musky male scent, tried to push aside the whirlwind of disbelief and confusion.

"How well do you know the Clancys?" the agent to the left asked, his pale blue eyes assessing her, and Beth knew he was wondering if the friendship she shared with Todd and Ginny had extended into a business arrangement.

"I told you. I've known Ginny forever. We grew up together. They're my best friends," she said, stunned disbelief solidifying inside her. "Why would Todd do something like this? It doesn't make sense."

The agent with the well-groomed goatee answered. "Money? It's a prime motivator." But he didn't sound like he believed it himself.

Beth shook her head. "They don't need money. Todd's an avid fly fisherman. A couple of years back he invented a lightweight collapsible reel for hikers. Some company paid a fortune for the design. Since then, he's invented a couple of other things and sold those as well. They've got more money than they know what to do with. The only reason he works is because he loves planes." She paused, stared down at the picture, and shook her head again. "If he did this, there's a reason behind it. A good reason."

Chastain glanced down as he slowly closed the folder. "Do you have any idea where he might have gone?"

With a deep breath, Beth tried to focus. This development meant they'd be looking at her more closely. She tried to stir up some worry over the possibility, but all she could think about was how this was going to shatter Ginny and Kyle.

"Have you tried his house? Ginny will know where he is." *Oh God, Ginny.* Tears stung as she imagined the horror and disbelief Ginny must be feeling. This nightmare was about to swallow her whole family.

"You can't find the wife and kid?" Zane asked.

She was so caught up in her own thoughts it took a moment for Zane's question to register. She must have missed something.

"He took the family and disappeared?" Zane dropped his arm from her waist and shifted until he was facing the federal agents again.

The silence in the wake of that question sent chills crawling up Beth's spine. Neither agent was agreeing with Zane's assessment. When she caught the brief, haunted skim of emotions across Chastain's lined face, she suddenly knew why.

Oh God. God, no.

Horror compressed the air from her lungs and crawled up her throat until she felt like she was suffocating. She flashed back to the last time she'd seen them. To Ginny's laughing blue eyes. To Kyle's shy grin and chubby little body.

Nonononono.

"*Oh, God.*" With a jerky motion she reached into her purse and pulled out her cell phone. She expected the feds to prevent her from making the call, but they just sat there and watched. She tried Todd first. It rang a couple of times and went to voice mail. Ginny next. Same thing. Just like the calls that morning.

A cold, heavy sludge settled in her chest.

"What's happened to them?"

"We don't know that anything has. We're trying to determine the situation," Chastain said.

But Beth didn't believe him. Not with that raw, sickened expression in his eyes.

"When's the last time you saw Virginia or Kyle Clancy?" Chastain's voice was very quiet in the icy room.

Beth tried to think back, but terror squeezed the memory from her mind. "I don't...I don't know. A week ago? We were supposed to have dinner at their place this past Friday, but Todd canceled. He said Kyle had some kind of..." Her voice trailed off, suddenly remembering how odd the call had been.

Todd never remembered such things, and Ginny had learned early in their relationship to pass the information along herself or to check in later and make sure Todd had made contact. More often than not, he hadn't. So she'd expected Ginny to call later in the day, to make sure Todd had delivered the message.

When she didn't, Beth had assumed she'd been busy taking care of Kyle.

"What about Todd? Have you noticed any changes in his behavior, his appearance, or his habits during the past few weeks?"

Todd's face came into focus. Hollow cheeks. Red-rimmed eyes. Getting thinner and thinner every day.

"He said he picked up Kyle's flu." Her voice dropped to a whisper. "He wasn't sick, was he? I should have known something was wrong."

"Hey." Zane cupped her chin and waited until her gaze shifted to his. "This isn't your fault. There is no way you could have known."

"*You* would have known," she said.

Zane would have sensed that something was wrong immediately. Tracked down the problem and taken steps to rectify it.

She took a deep, shuddering breath and pulled her chin free. Bracing herself, she turned back to Agent Chastain. "The hijackers have them. That's why Todd put the guns on board."

"We don't know that. All we know for sure is no one's at home. According to Kyle's elementary school, his father called earlier in the week and told them Kyle was going on a trip with his mother. No time frame was given."

"Is it possible Mrs. Clancy took their son and left? Was the marriage in trouble?" Chastain's partner asked.

He was speaking in the past tense. Her breathing hiccupped.

"No. They have a strong marriage."

A true partnership. They'd been together since high school and knew each other inside and out. Their relationship was the kind Beth hoped for. The kind based on respect, understanding, and an endless depth of love. The kind of marriage in which to raise children.

Chastain rubbed his palms down his face. "We need you to walk through the Clancys' residence. Since you're familiar with their home, you may notice if anything is missing."

Although Beth nodded her agreement, she was already certain they'd been taken and used to force Todd to smuggle the guns on board. It was the only thing that made sense. There was no way Todd would have planted the weapons unless he'd been trying to protect his family.

What would happen to them now? With the hijacking plot exposed and the guns discovered, would Ginny and Kyle become excess baggage to dispose of as soon as possible?

Were they already dead?

A rush of nausea climbed her throat and her scalp started to tingle.

What if, by stopping the kidnappers and exposing the guns, she'd caused the death of her best friend?

And Kyle. *Oh, God.*

Kyle could be lying dead somewhere. Those shy blue eyes empty of life. That chubby little body still.

A hot, heavy pressure settled in her chest.

Because of that damn dream, a plane full of strangers was safe, but her best friends and her godchild were, in all likelihood, dead.

Because of that damn dream.

Chapter Eight

B Y THE TIME COSKY AND RAWLS RETURNED FROM THEIR debriefing, Mac had fielded multiple questions from a variety of agencies. Agent Britta of Homeland Security was the most insistent, demanding to know the circumstances under which the intel had been acquired and how they'd identified the hijackers. Since no passengers had survived the Argentinean incident, there was no record of what the terrorists looked like.

Christ, the clusterfuck swirling around them threatened to swallow the whole team. He could hardly admit the information had come from a fucking dream.

As soon as Cosky and Rawls stepped inside the room, he activated the jammer and got down to business. "Report?"

Cosky shrugged and leaned a shoulder against the wall. "Lots of questions we couldn't answer. We cited classified and held fast."

Mac grunted, watching as Rawls perched on the edge of the lunch table. "They're pushing for the source. It won't be long before they hit up Command Central."

"What did you tell Gillomay?" Cosky regarded him with a level stare.

"I told *McKay* that *Zane* had a dream." Mac stomped on another surge of betrayal.

Captain Gillomay wouldn't have accepted Mac's interference and confrontation with the FBI without busting him back a rank, which was exactly why Mac had gone to McKay. The admiral had personal experience with Zane's visions. Or at least his grandson did, since one of Zane's flashes had saved the kid's life during his first deployment. McKay had called Gillomay and smoothed the waters.

Of course Admiral McKay had been going on the same false assumption as Mac. Namely that Zane hadn't lost his fucking mind and been lying through his teeth.

Cosky cocked his head and watched Mac in silence. "So he knows our information didn't come from a source we can hand over?"

Mac wouldn't go that far. He had every intention of handing over the fucking *source*, but after he'd cleared his team from potential fallout. He practiced some deep breathing to counter his spiking blood pressure.

Cosky and Mac stared at each other for one throbbing moment.

"How the *hell* could you let him do this to us?" Mac finally asked through gritted teeth.

Cosky didn't flinch. "It was the only viable option."

"Bullshit." Mac unclenched his teeth long enough to force the words out. "He should have told the truth. You know damn well I would have moved on the plane."

"And her."

The two words hung there, an accusation in the charged air.

A blast of shock sucked the air from his lungs. Frustrated rage filled them back up again. He stalked to the corner of the room and back. "Don't fucking tell me you believe her?"

"Yeah, I do," Cosky said in that same level tone as he watched Mac pace. Mac stopped in front of Rawlings and scanned his face. "You too?" He didn't wait for Rawls's silent nod. Grinding his teeth, he took another trip to the far corner. "What the fuck did that bitch do to you three?"

"Beth." Cosky's voice chilled. "Her name's Beth."

Mac spun around. "And you don't find *Beth's* sudden appearance a little too convenient?"

"Because of her, we're not lying in a pool of blood twenty thousand feet up. Because of her, we have three targets in custody."

"I'm aware of that—" Mac broke off, took a deep, calming breath, and regrouped. "She's lying. She has to be involved."

"You weren't there, Mac," Rawls said, his gaze watchful. "She was scared. Confused."

Mac snorted. "Which makes her a damn fine actress."

Cosky tilted his head and studied Mac's face. "Why are you having such trouble with this? You accept that Zane knows things he shouldn't. You trust those visions of his. What's the difference?"

"Fuck no. You're *comparing* the two? I know Zane." He squared off against his lieutenant, feeling like he was bracing for a nuclear sub charge. "I've experienced his flashes. We don't know a goddamn thing about this woman."

With a lift of his eyebrows, Cosky shook his head dismissively. "You barely knew Zane the first time you trusted one of his visions. It was your first op together. Trusting him saved your ass. Why not give her the same benefit of the doubt?"

If that didn't beat the bull—the jackass was lecturing him. Had his whole team gone crazy?

He ground his teeth and tried to shout some sense into them. "We don't know this—" Christ, he sounded like a broken record.

"Zane knows her," Cosky cut in. "If we're gonna trust his flashes to keep us alive, then we trust this too."

"Big difference, buddy. Zane's hung up on her. He's compromised."

Cosky straightened against the wall and pinned him with a sharp look. "I'm not. Neither is Rawls. Back off. *She's not involved.*"

Mac bared his teeth. "You don't see what she's up to? She's convinced him to lie to his commanding officer. Next, she'll separate him from the teams. A year from now, she'll convince him to retire and play nursemaid to some fucking security firm."

Whoa. He broke off. *Where the hell had that come from?*

With a snort, Cosky stepped away from the wall. "The lie's on Zane's head. She's been against it from the beginning. As for separating him from the team—" he paused, regarded Mac steadily. "She's not the one pushing him out. You are." When Mac stiffened, Cosky's gaze hardened to slate. "He's been waiting ten fucking years for her. You think he's going to give her up? Even for the teams? You need to stand down. She's one of ours now."

Clearly a warning. *Son of a bitch.* Mac scrubbed his hands down his face. "She isn't one of ours yet. He's still got time to grab hold of his senses."

"Ain't gonna happen," Rawls drawled, sliding off the table. He stood, lifted his right arm above his head, and worked his left shoulder. "Better him than me, though."

"No shit." Cosky's lips twisted.

Mac took another turn around the room. Obviously the woman had cast some kind of spell over Cosky and Rawls too. More accusations would just drive a wedge between them. Best to back off and wait. Eventually she'd show her true colors, and they'd see the little bitch for what she was. He relaxed as a plan took shape. He'd feed her some rope and watch her dangle from it.

"So what's the word?" Rawls asked.

"We're free to go, but we've been asked to remain available tomorrow morning—for questioning." Mac shrugged. "We're hands-off. Keep your eyes open, though. Something hinky's going on."

"Who leaked?"

"Figured you'd pick that up." Mac tossed Cosky a predatory grin. "First thought was Chastain. The bastard's reaction to the initial call didn't fit." He delivered a concise replay of their conversation over the phone.

"What kind of asshole blows off fresh intel?" Rawls asked.

Very slowly Cosky shook his head, his gaze dark and distant. "Doesn't track. Anyone with an ounce of sense would realize such a reaction would raise flags."

"You'd think." Mac eyed his lieutenants with satisfaction. Zane, Cosky, and Rawls were as sharp as they came. "I pulled his file. The SOB's a fucking Boy Scout. Twenty years on the job. Commendations up the ass. He's taken hardware twice. And get this—before he went federal, he spent time on the teams."

With each word, Cosky's brows lowered further, until they looked like a bushy black V, perched above the bridge of his nose. "Who'd he serve with?"

"Semper Fi."

"No shit?" After a moment Cosky shrugged. "Even Marines go south."

"This guy doesn't read like that. Reads stand-up. Lost his family to a drunk driver back in the eighties. Pulled into a gas station, filled up the tank, went inside to pay. While he's waiting in line some asshole skids into the family wagon and pins it against the pumps. Whole thing bursts into flames. One minute he's got a wife and three kids. The next, his family's gone."

"Jesus," Rawls said.

All three men fell silent.

After a moment Mac continued. "Poor bastard lived the job after that. Handled some ugly cases. Routed the Mafia out of the San Francisco garbage union. Took one of those bullets there. After 9/11, he transferred to Counterterrorism. Three years ago they appointed him special agent in charge of the West Coast Unit."

"A guy like that…" Cosky shook his head and cursed softly. "Doesn't have much to lose. Maybe that's how they turned him."

Mac frowned. "That's the thing. He remarried, started a new family—in his forties no less. He's got two kids now. Boys. Can't see him risking his second family by getting in bed with these motherfuckers."

Even as the words hit the air, Mac froze.

He flashed back to his first sight of Chastain. The deep lines bracketing his mouth. The loose hang of his clothes. And then there was how accommodating the man had been. For Christ's sake, he'd allowed him to talk to his men before the feds had even interviewed them. From his escort's stunned reaction, that alone had to be unusual.

"Jesus," he breathed, watching the same realization creep across Cosky's and Rawls's faces.

How hard would it be to compromise a man who'd lost his first family, lost his first run at happiness? How hard would it be to use his second family, his second chance, against him? Suddenly that strange reaction to Mac's phone call made an ominous sort of sense. It had been a deliberate flag, a signal.

"Son of a bitch," he said quietly. "The bastard was trying to warn us."

———————————

The Clancys' home was an expensive tri-level in a gated community fifteen minutes north of the airport. Any other day the place probably looked impressive with its rolling lawn, clipped hedges, stained-glass entrance, and towering brick walls. Today, however, the legion of FBI agents emptying closets, upending drawers, and searching every square inch muted the mansion's majestic appeal.

It was obvious Beth knew her way around the house. Within minutes of passing through the front entrance she'd found Ginny Clancy's purse, which was stuffed in a cupboard in the laundry room.

"There's no way Ginny would have left the house without this," she told Chastain as he reached for it with hands gloved in latex. "It has everything she'd need. Her cell phone. Her debit card, her credit card, her checkbook."

Chastain withdrew the items she mentioned and lined them up on the laundry room counter above the dirty-clothes bins. When he withdrew a plastic, L-shaped object and set it on the counter, Beth's voice caught.

"Kyle's inhaler." Her voice dropped to a whisper. "She wouldn't have left voluntarily without Kyle's inhaler."

Chastain picked up the cell phone and pressed the power button. Nothing happened. "The battery's dead."

He put it back down and transferred everything from the counter back into the purse, then handed off the bag to one of the techs.

They toured the second floor, which consisted of the kitchen, dining room, and living room, next. Beth didn't see anything that looked out of place so they continued on to the next level. With each step up, her shoulders pulled forward until she was practically vibrating with tension. Zane itched to pull her close and comfort her. But it was pretty damn obvious she'd withdrawn from him.

He'd noticed it during the trip over. They'd been sitting side by side, yet an emotional vacuum separated them. She'd avoided contact, shifting her thigh away if it brushed his, leaning against the passenger door with her arms tucked tight against her sides. Her eyes were guarded when they touched his. Her voice polite but cool. All signs she'd distanced herself.

Nor could he feel her emotion anymore. He could see her grief, but he couldn't feel it. She'd shut herself down so tight she'd blocked the link. He could pinpoint the moment she'd withdrawn. After Mac had dropped the soul mate grenade.

He needed someplace private to work on damage control, to prove how good things could be. Unfortunately, there wasn't much chance of that, not at the moment, not with an FBI escort and a crowded house.

In the master closet she pointed to a set of luggage.

"Those are Ginny's suitcases." She pushed aside several hangers and waved at the clothes quivering on the rods. "And these are some of her favorite clothes. She would have taken at least some of these with her…given the chance."

Chastain nodded, pulled a pen and notebook from his breast pocket, and jotted something down. The next room was a guest bedroom, which Beth barely glanced over. But when they stepped through the door at the end of the hall, she stopped dead—her body going rigid. Her breath escaped her in a soft huff and her shoulders curled in, as though absorbing a blow.

Zane followed her gaze to a twin bed, covered in a comforter shaped like a rocket. A threadbare, stuffed fluff of gold sat against the pillows. It took him a moment to identify the shape. The fluff of fabric and yarn resembled a dog.

Beth moved forward, her shoulders still hunched and her breathing erratic. She sank down on the mattress, reaching for the stuffed toy. "He left Buddy. He would never have left Buddy."

"Who?" Chastain asked from the doorway.

"Kyle." Beth's voice was thin. She pulled the ragged animal closer and cradled it against her chest. "Kyle took Buddy everywhere. Everywhere. He would never have left him behind."

She looked so lost sitting there. So fragile. The walls surrounding her, with their vibrant painted images of planets, stars, and spaceships, seemed to dwarf her.

Zane turned to Chastain. "Give us a minute."

Chastain glanced toward the bed, nodded, and waved two agents who were poking through a white bookcase out of the room. Zane closed the door behind them and headed for the bed. Beth had drawn her knees up to her chest and wrapped her arms around her thighs. She was silently rocking.

Zane crossed to the bed and picked her up then sat down, cradling her on his lap. She didn't fight him, just melted into his embrace. Twisting in his arms, she pressed her face into the hollow at the base of his throat, her arms going around his waist.

With wordless murmurs of comfort Zane stroked her hair and rocked her. He could feel the grief pouring out of her. A heavy black pressure pushing against his mind and heart.

"I gave him Buddy," she mumbled against his chest, her voice raw and broken. That heavy black pressure worked its way into his mind until the pain was his too. "He wanted a dog for his birthday. But Ginny said no, that he was too young. So I gave him Buddy and told him Buddy would keep him company until I could get him a real dog."

Zane glanced at one of the framed photos sitting on the table beside the bed. Beth was sitting on the grass, a fragile red-haired child cradled in her lap.

"He's barely six. Just a baby," she said, her voice thick.

Tears dampened the skin of his throat. He wished he could assure her that her friends were fine. That goodness would prevail and innocence would win in the end. But he'd seen far too many good people murdered. So he tightened his arms instead and tried to absorb her grief.

The kiss started off as comforting. Or at least it was meant to.

He lifted her chin and dropped a gentle kiss against her wet eyes, then pressed his lips, still damp from her tears, against her trembling mouth. That's all he intended. One kiss. Comfort rather than craving.

Except she was so soft and warm and perfect in his arms— she fit so perfectly against his body. And Christ, she smelled like strawberry shortcake.

Even so, he would have tightened his leash and kept it comforting, kept it gentle, kept his hunger out of it, if her lips hadn't moved beneath his. If they hadn't blossomed and then parted. If her breath hadn't filled his mouth and her scent his head.

If he hadn't felt her hunger stir and then rear up, sparking his.

Her arms tightened around his waist, and her tongue brushed his. And then she rubbed herself against his chest. That's all it took.

One touch of her tongue and one sensual shimmy, one brush of her thoughts to find the hunger had turned ravenous, and comfort was the last thing on his mind.

With a muffled groan, his mouth hardened, opened over hers, forcing her lips apart even farther. Their tongues tangled, rubbed—past teasing, past patience—straight into urgency. His embrace tightened, crushed her against him, reveling in the way she responded, the way her arms clamped around his waist until they burned like fire.

He was about to take her down to the mattress when the door to the bedroom opened. Someone coughed.

Son of a bitch.

His muscles howled in protest, but he eased back from her mouth. Her eyes opened. They were dazed, heavy with sensual heat.

The cough sounded again. Louder.

Yeah. Yeah.

Zane sucked in a strangled breath—and got a lungful of strawberry. And damn if his dick didn't sit up and beg. Regulating his breathing, he rested his forehead against hers for a moment and then drew back.

"You okay?" he asked, watching with regret as her eyes cleared and pink touched her cheeks.

"Fi—" Her voice came out strangled. She coughed. "Fine." She pushed against his chest and scrambled out of his lap, rocketing to her feet. Avoiding Chastain's gaze she tucked her blouse into her slacks and gestured toward the bed and the abandoned stuffed animal. "Kyle wouldn't have left Buddy behind."

His arms felt empty without her cradled against him. With a soft curse, Zane rose to his feet too. He would have reached for her, except she shied away, her expression shuttered, her arms tight across her chest.

"We're done here," Chastain said. "I'll take you back to the airport."

They retraced their steps through the house and out to the feds' company-issue Cutlass in silence. Beth climbed into the back seat beside him, but distance stretched between them again. A chasm even wider and deeper than before. The kiss had seriously set him back. Still, he didn't regret it. Not one heated moment of it. Considering how often he'd had her in his arms today, it was a miracle he'd held off kissing her as long as he had.

All bets were off now.

He'd had his first taste of her and he wanted more. A lot more. He wanted all of her.

"We appreciate your cooperation, Miss Brown, Lieutenant Commander Winters." Chastain twisted in the front passenger seat and held Zane's gaze. "Your teammates have been released; they're waiting for you at the airport."

Zane stared back. "The bureau's finished with us?"

"For today. We'll need to go over your statements tomorrow. Your CO's already promised the three of you will present yourselves at the Seattle Field Office tomorrow morning." The agent's attention shifted to Beth. "We'd appreciate your presence as well, Miss Brown." He faced front again at Beth's silent nod.

"What about our luggage?" Zane asked. No doubt Mac had already arranged for transportation and lodging. But it would be nice to have a change of clothes. Even nicer to have his Glock.

"Luggage hasn't been released. We're still going through bags," the red-haired, cool-eyed agent driving the sedan informed him.

Damn. Zane settled back with a frown. He could manage without the change of clothes. However, the lack of a weapon was a constant, uneasy itch.

Mac, Rawls, and Cosky were waiting for him in the parking garage. Zane and Beth climbed out of the fedmobile. He studied Mac's face. No doubt some major discussions had taken place concerning that damn lie. But at least Mac had chilled some. He no longer resonated with the intensity of a bomb about to detonate. In fact, he didn't even glance in Beth's direction, just fixed those fierce black eyes on Chastain.

"After tomorrow morning, how much longer are you jackasses planning on keeping my boys?" Mac demanded, his voice echoing within the concrete dome of the parking garage. He braced his hands on his hips. "They've got a damn wedding to attend."

Zane's lips twitched. The disgust in his commander's voice as he said "wedding" mirrored the tone he'd used when discussing the hijackers, but then Mac viewed the female half of the population—at least from puberty on—as an army of domestic terrorists.

Chastain shrugged. "Depends on what they have to say."

Translation: *Depends on whether they stick to the same story.*

Mac scowled, his gaze sharp and knowing. "You've already heard what they have to say."

"I want to hear it again," Chastain retorted, but his tone held patience rather than confrontation. "Nine a.m. At the Seattle Field Office. Do you need directions?"

Cosky shook his head. "We're good."

"What about a ride?"

"We've got one coming," Cosky said blandly.

"Fine. I'll see you tomorrow." Dismissing them, Chastain headed toward the airport entrance, his auburn-haired partner trailing a step or two behind.

As soon as the feds were out of range, Mac turned to Zane. "We've rented a vehicle. It's parked above. Cosky's mother's gonna put us up for the night." He cocked his head and glanced toward Beth then lifted an eyebrow.

"She's coming with us." Beth stirred and opened her mouth, protest plain on her face. Zane frowned. "There are still two hijackers loose. It's a safe bet they know who you are. You aren't safe on your own."

That stopped her, but just for a moment. "Then you can drop me off at a hotel. I'll pay cash so they can't trace me."

"You're safer with us," Zane said flatly. "They're professionals. Odds are they'll find you."

"I'm not going to force myself on some poor woman I've never even met. That's rude."

"Mom knows you're coming. She's expecting you." Cosky cast a long glance around the garage and headed for the elevator to the right of them. "We need to get moving."

"What about your friends?" Rawls fell into step beside Beth.

When her jaw trembled, Zane reached out, entwining their fingers. He was surprised when she didn't pull away. "It looks like they were taken," Zane said. "She found Ginny Clancy's purse in the laundry room and a stuffed toy the boy wouldn't have left behind."

"They may not have been the only ones." Mac's voice was grim and low. He ignored the elevator in favor of the concrete staircase and took the flight leading up at a fast clip.

"Who?" Zane asked, his concentration split between Mac's voice and the feel of Beth's fingers clasping his as she climbed the stairs beside him.

"Our leak. Chastain."

That caught Zane's attention. "They grabbed his family? Forced his compliance?"

"It's a good guess. He's the perfect target. You control him, you control the investigation."

"Have you looked at him?" Beth suddenly asked. "He's lost weight. You can tell from the fit of his clothes. And he looks exhausted, like he hasn't slept in ages." She glanced at Zane, darkness in her eyes. "He reminds me of Todd."

Mac stopped at the next level to prop open the steel door with his hip. The look he shot Beth held a mixture of suspicion and surprise. "She's right. He looks like hell."

Zane thought that over as he escorted Beth through the door. Jesus, the ramifications were endless. If they could get to Chastain…"Where's this leave us?"

"In the shitcan." Mac let the door fall shut behind Rawls. "If they can get to him, they can get to anyone."

"Christ." Zane swiped a hand down his face. This damn thing kept getting uglier and uglier. "He must think his team's compromised."

Mac's jaw tightened. He dug into his pocket and pulled out a key ring, which he tossed to Cosky. "You're driving." He turned back to Zane. "Not just his team—the FBI itself. Otherwise he would have taken it up the ladder."

Beth's eyebrows knit. "Maybe they threatened to kill his family if he told anybody."

"His chances of getting them back alive are stronger with the full resources of the FBI behind him," Cosky said as he punched the red button on the key chain and headed toward the Ford Expedition that beeped and flashed its taillights. "The fact he's made no effort to utilize those resources means he thinks the agency's compromised."

"We're talking about hundreds of lives." Beth looked unconvinced. "Would he really put his family's welfare above all those passengers? Why wouldn't he go to Homeland Security?"

Zane opened the back door of the SUV and put his hand on the small of her back to guide her in. Then slid in beside her. "If they can infiltrate the FBI, they can infiltrate DHS."

Cosky smoothly took over. "In an ideal world, he'd report what happened, but this is a guy who already lost one family..."

"The poor bastard's hands are tied." Rawls slid in next to Beth on the opposite side of the SUV and grabbed his seat belt. "He doesn't know who's safe to approach. The wrong choice and his family's dead."

"He has to know the kind of bastards he's dealing with." Mac slammed the front passenger door and clicked his seat belt into place. "They showed no mercy in Argentina. Killed everyone. Including the kids. With the hijacking aborted and the kidnappers scrambling, he's got to be wondering what this means for his family."

Beth flinched, her face haunted, and Zane knew she was wondering the same thing about her friends.

———————————

Russ shifted in his plastic chair, watching what remained of the restless, milling passengers of Flight 2077.

If he hadn't been detained and questioned, he wouldn't have had the opportunity to get up close and personal with his FBI moles. Agents, thus far, he'd only had contact with on the phone.

Well, admittedly, just one of the agents, since Chastain hadn't bothered to show up yet.

Russ smiled toward the senior agent with the FBI's Counterterrorism Unit who'd interviewed him earlier. Perfectly styled russet hair gleamed beneath the harsh fluorescent lights. Looking at the spit-polished, tailored, and oh-so-polite senior agent, you'd have no clue how riddled with rot the man was.

Of all the buttons Russ had available for pushing, this particular FBI agent was by far his most volatile—and invaluable. They wouldn't have gotten to Chastain without him, wouldn't have been able to control Chastain once they'd grabbed his family, wouldn't have had eyes and ears on the inside monitoring the situation.

It was too bad the guy was so fucking unstable. Never a healthy trait in someone you needed to rely on.

However, obsessive characteristics had one saving grace: if you played to that obsession, you controlled their actions. In this case, the obsession centered exclusively on Chastain. Their mole hated Special Agent in Charge John Chastain—detested him with vitriolic intensity. Indeed, he'd undertaken his end of this operation solely to destroy his superior—destroy his reputation, his career, his family, even take his life.

Russ didn't know what Chastain had done, or what the SOB *perceived* Chastain had done. The bosses hadn't bothered to share with him that information. And nothing—absolutely nothing— had turned up during the research he'd done on the pair. In fact, on paper, the two men appeared to be good friends. He'd been best man at Chastain's first and second marriages. He was godfather to one of Chastain's sons.

Their mole only had three conditions for setting Chastain up. He insisted on being the one to take Chastain out once they were done with him and that Chastain's sons' bodies be delivered to their father before his death. But the third demand had raised the most eyebrows—Amy Chastain was to be released alive at the end of the operation.

One would think his concern for Chastain's wife indicated a depth of feeling for her. But one would be mistaken. Whatever the guy felt for Amy Chastain, it had nothing to do with love. Revenge, perhaps.

He would have felt sorry for the woman except she wouldn't be alive long enough to suffer whatever the obsessed bastard had planned.

Amy Chastain had to die once the operation was concluded. It was a pity, but it couldn't be helped. Like any good strategist, Russ had done extensive research on his targets. It had turned up a couple of pesky problems. She'd been FBI prior to her marriage. And a good agent at that. An intractable one. She was smart, loyal, and stubborn. She'd latch onto the investigation like a bulldog. She wouldn't rest until she dug up why her family had been targeted and who was responsible for taking them from her.

Without her, eventually, after a massive internal investigation into the aborted hijacking and the events surrounding it, the FBI would shelve the case pending new evidence. They'd sweep it under the departmental rug and try to pretend that one of their own hadn't been integral in such a colossal fuckup.

But if Amy Chastain was around to stir things up…If the woman lived, she'd never let the investigation be swept aside or let her dead husband be used as a scapegoat. She wouldn't stop digging and badgering until she'd uncovered the truth and exposed everything.

Chapter Nine

THEY STOPPED OFF AT A SMALL MARKET WHERE THE MEN FILLED up a metal cart with a case of Coors Original and six huge steaks. Beth insisted on adding a large bag of salad greens, some potatoes, a bottle of dressing, and a loaf of bread to the basket.

"Believe me," she said in response to the dry glance Cosky sent Zane. "Your mother will appreciate something besides beer and steak for dinner."

Cosky nodded toward the salad in a bag. "She's got a fridge full of that crap. Believe me, she doesn't need any more."

Beth ignored him. It still bothered her to be foisted off on the poor woman. But Zane was right. She was safer with them, at least until the hijackers were behind bars. Besides, the thought of being left alone, in silence, with no distractions and all the time in the world to think...yeah...no. She'd be a basket case by morning.

Of course the arrangement meant she'd be spending a lot more time in Zane's company...Her thoughts skittered to his CO's taunt about psychics and soul mates, followed by that hot-as-Hades kiss. Her muscles softened and warmed even as her mind shied away from the memories. She obviously needed to have a bracing talk with the man—set him straight on a few points—but that didn't have to happen now. While it was undoubtedly pure selfishness on her part, she couldn't stand the thought of spending the night alone, obsessing over what might be happening to Ginny, Kyle, and Todd. In any other circumstances, she'd have headed over to see Ginny, but…

Beth cut that thought off, concentrating instead on her soon-to-be hostess. She could at least offer the woman a small token of appreciation and apology.

"Does your mom like flowers?" They'd passed by some nice bouquets toward the front of the store.

"She's got a whole yard full with flowers." His tone made it clear she didn't need any more.

"She likes wine," Zane said. "Merlot." The smile he sent her held understanding.

That was good enough for Beth. With Zane beside her, she detoured to the wine section and picked out her favorite label. By the time they arrived at the front of the store, Zane's teammates had already checked out and were waiting in the car. Zane paid for the wine while Beth was still pulling her wallet from her purse, and they headed out to the parking lot. Mac twisted in the passenger seat and pinned her with an impatient stare as she slipped into the SUV. Jeez, you'd think she'd kept him waiting all day.

"At least we can arm up at the house," Cosky said as he pulled out of the parking lot. "Dad collected guns, so we've got some nice pieces to choose from."

Cosky's mother lived in a subdivision in Federal Way. Her home was an older ranch style that looked recently painted—a rich blue-gray with charcoal trim. The front yard was small, more flower beds than lawn, and studded with ceramic birdbaths and colorful birdhouses.

As everyone piled out of the Expedition, the entry door swung open. The woman who stepped onto the raised landing sported a cloud of silver hair and a sweat suit of peach.

Beth liked her on sight, which was somewhat of a surprise considering she was Mr. Chilly's mother, but Mrs. Simcosky radiated warmth.

"Mom." Cosky set the case of Coors down and bent to kiss her cheek. His accompanying hug lifted her off the porch.

The move was so natural Beth didn't doubt it was habit, which forced a reassessment of Zane's buddy. Any man who loved his mother enough to show his affection couldn't be as unemotional as he wanted the world to believe.

Cosky set his mother back on her feet and nodded toward the men behind him. "You remember Zane? Rawls?"

"Of course, dear." She swatted his arm. "I haven't gone senile yet." She headed for Rawls.

Beth choked on a giggle as Rawls shot a panicked glance in Cosky's direction, dropped his bag of groceries, and froze, submitting to the hug with a deer-in-the-headlights glaze to his blue eyes.

"I just pulled some brownies out of the oven," Mrs. Simcosky said as she released him. "You go right in and help yourself." She moved on to Zane.

Her curiosity rising, Beth watched the exchange. Zane not only accepted the affection, he returned it with another hug that cleared Mrs. Simcosky's feet from the porch. Zane, apparently, was a man used to female attention. Was his ease with women due to motherly affection or a girlfriend in every port?

SEALs, she suspected, visited *a lot* of ports.

A sharp spurt of irritation jabbed her, which brought a jolt of surprise. Good Lord, she was jealous. She was actually jealous over a man she hadn't even known a full day.

"This is Mac, Mom. Commander Jace Mackenzie." Cosky watched with a gleam in his eyes as his mother headed across the porch.

Mac's eyebrows slashed into a scowl and a furious glare lit his dark eyes.

With determined cheerfulness she reached up and grabbed hold of his shoulders, tugging him down. After one long moment of pulling back, Mac conceded—grudgingly. Arms stiff at his sides, he bent at the waist and submitted to her hug. From the contorted expression on his face, you'd think the effort was killing him.

Cosky's hard lips quirked.

"This is Beth Brown, Zane's fiancée," Cosky introduced smoothly as his mother turned in Beth's direction.

"You're engaged? Congratulations! You couldn't ask for a better man—except for my Marcus, of course."

She wrapped Beth, wine and all, in a surprisingly hard hug before Beth could contradict the whole engaged thing. Why in the *world* did everyone keep claiming this bogus engagement? She obviously needed to have a talk with more than just Zane. But now was hardly the time, so she let the introduction stand.

They followed Mrs. Simcosky into the house and down a bright hall lined with family photos—where Cosky aged from infant to adult.

The kitchen was huge and old-fashioned, with worn oak cupboards and scuffed tile on the floor. But the shimmering stainless-steel appliances looked brand-new. An oak table was positioned in an alcove beneath a huge window dripping with sunlight.

Directly in the middle of the table was a platter stacked high with brownies.

"We need to borrow some of Dad's guns," Cosky told his mother as he crossed to the table and snatched up a brownie.

"It's your collection now, dear." A shadow slipped through his mother's eyes. "Why do you need guns? Does it have anything to do with why your flight was held over?"

Cosky made a beeline toward a narrow door at the back of the kitchen, with Rawls, Zane, and Mac hard on his heels. "We have a situation," he said over his shoulder. "I'll explain in a minute."

Mrs. Simcosky watched the men disappear through the door and shook her head. "Boys and their toys. They never really grow up." She turned to Beth with a warm smile. "Let me show you to your room, dear."

"I'm sorry for the imposition, Mrs. Simcosky." Beth offered the bottle of wine.

"Don't be silly. Zane's practically family, which makes you family too." She took the wine, set the bottle on the counter, and caught Beth's hands, squeezing them once and releasing them. "Please, call me Marion. Marcus is determined not to give me a daughter-in-law, so believe me, I'm *thrilled* for some female companionship."

She linked her arm through Beth's, patted her hand, and drew her out of the kitchen, through a well-lived-in family/dining room, and down a long hall at the back of the house. The last door on the right was already open. Marion dropped Beth's arm and bustled over to the huge bed, straightening the quilt and plumping pillows.

"Here you go, dear. And just so you know, I'm not one to make judgments. Zane's welcome to the room as well." She shot Beth a wicked grin, and Beth felt her face heat.

Lord, she hadn't even thought about sleeping arrangements. But of course Marion would expect them to share a bed. She thought they were engaged, for God's sake.

Marion showed her the attached bathroom and how to work the tricky hot and cold faucets. By the time they returned to the kitchen the men had taken over the table and were discussing the merits of one gun over another. An arsenal lay strewn across the table, and all four men were sprawled out in oak chairs, dismantling or assembling the various weapons.

The brownie platter had been pushed to the back, where it sat empty and forgotten.

Zane shifted in his chair and scanned her face as she crossed the kitchen toward their hostess, and she gave him a quick smile.

"I saved you a brownie, dear." Mrs. Simcosky gestured toward the counter, where a huge brownie swallowed a saucer.

The rich, fudgy scent drew Beth like a hummingbird to nectar. It wasn't until Cosky's mother picked up a saucer and moved toward the sink that Beth noticed the book lying open—facedown—on the tile counter. She recognized the green and gold cover immediately. Both author and title were among her favorites.

"Do you read?" Mrs. Simcosky asked, catching Beth's glance toward the novel.

"My favorite pastime." Beth nodded toward the book. "It's one of her best."

"I'm rather partial to her first." She sent Beth a wicked smile. "That Alex, he curled my toes. Such a shame he didn't get his own book."

Beth laughed, marveling at how easy it was to fall into book discussions with complete strangers when both parties shared a love of romances. "Have you tried—"

She broke off as Rawls approached and set the empty platter on the counter beside the book.

"Could you hand that over, sweetie?" Mrs. Simcosky said. "I'll put it in the sink."

As Rawls picked the platter up again, the edge caught the corner of the book and flipped it off the counter.

With a murmured apology, Rawls handed the platter off and bent, picking the book up. As he straightened, he absently scanned the text. His movements slowed. His head bent. Slowly his ears turned pink. A hint of red frosted his cheekbones.

Beth glanced toward Cosky's mother, who winked.

"Love scene," she mouthed.

Oh. Ohhhhhhhhhh. Beth grinned. If memory served, that particular book had been smoking hot.

"Rawls," Cosky's dry voice broke over the silent corner. "If you're done checking out my mom's porn, maybe you'd like to help me get the barbeque started?"

Rawls dropped the book as if he'd been caught digging through a bag of crack.

"You can take it with you," Mrs. Simcosky offered.

"That's okay." Rawls sidled toward the table, his ears getting pinker by the moment.

"Are you certain? Because—"

"He's sure." Cosky nailed his buddy with a derisive look that clearly warned if he responded with anything but no, he'd never hear the end of it.

The wicked smile on Mrs. Simcosky's face collapsed into a frown. She crossed her arms and glared at her unrepentant son.

"Believe me, the four of you would benefit from reading some of my romance novels. They'd give you a better idea of what women are looking for in a relationship."

Cosky snorted, reassembling a big black gun with quick, sure movements. "We're doing just fine on our own."

"Then why don't I have grandchildren?"

Cosky won the argument by ignoring the question and stepping out the kitchen's sliding door to the brick patio beyond. It took Cosky, Rawls, and Zane to haul the mammoth barbeque from the side of the house out onto the patio, while Mac stood around offering advice.

"You should drag that thing to the dump, while you're at it," Mac said and tipped his head back to take a long pull on his bottle of Coors. "You'd be doing your mother a favor."

"He's right," Marion conceded in a low voice to Beth. "That damn thing's older than Cosky is. And I can't do a thing with it myself."

Beth glanced at the monstrosity in question. "Why don't you get rid of it? They make small, easy-to-use ones now."

Marion shook her head, her eyes softening as they rested on her son. "Cosky's father made it. And my son...well, he's... attached to it."

Attached or not, it took fifteen minutes of swearing before the propane started flowing. Beth helped her hostess toss the salad and set the table, and by the time the grilling was done, the bread was warm and they were ready to eat.

The men devoured the meal like they hadn't eaten all day. Which Beth suddenly realized was probably true. She hadn't eaten all day either and discovered she was surprisingly hungry.

They took turns filling in Marion on the day's events. When Zane reached Todd's role in the aborted hijacking and the sudden disappearance of Ginny and Kyle, Marion gasped and reached across the table to grasp Beth's hand.

"How awful." She squeezed Beth's fingers hard before letting go. "Thank God Zane was there for you. I can't imagine going through something so terrible on your own."

Beth's gaze fell on Zane's hands as he worked his knife and fork. They were huge compared to hers, with long fingers and bluntly shaped nails. Capable hands, just like the rest of him. She quivered at the memory of their clasp as he cradled her cheeks. They'd been so warm against her skin, slightly abrasive, but incredibly gentle.

Marion was right. He had been there for her. He'd been there for her every minute of this horrible day.

Even those heated, hungry moments in Kyle's bedroom had been about her, at least in the beginning. His embrace had been comforting, not sexual. He'd kept his attraction in check. His arms and kiss had been soothing.

She'd been the one to change the parameters. She'd been the one to open her mouth and use her tongue and turn the embrace into something sexual.

Oh, he wanted her. She didn't doubt that for a moment. She'd sensed it well before those moments on Kyle's bed. His hunger showed in the glitter that struck his eyes when he looked at her, in the way he'd glued himself to her side, how often he touched her, as though he craved the feel of her skin.

She'd have to be an idiot not to pick up on all the subtle and not so subtle clues he broadcasted. Zane didn't keep his need hidden. At least not when it came to her.

But he hadn't acted on that need. Not once.

Maybe he was just looking for a vacation fling. A couple of drive-by trysts to scratch a persistent but temporary itch. But some deep instinct told her that wasn't the case. And then there was this whole soul mate nonsense, not to mention their completely unnecessary and bogus engagement. Zane seemed honestly invested in her, seriously invested, for such a short space of time. He'd lied to the FBI, to the DHS, to his commanding officer to protect her.

These weren't the actions of a man with a temporary relationship in mind.

They needed to have a discussion about more than the night's sleeping arrangements.

He had to realize a relationship wasn't possible. She had a great job, a condo she loved, good friends, a godchild she wanted to watch grow up—all in Seattle. She pushed aside the onslaught of fear at the thought of Ginny and Kyle.

The point was, she had a life in Seattle and he had one in Coronado. When he was even in Coronado, when he wasn't stuck in some turbulent country doing God knew what, for God knew how long.

So where would that leave them? Weekend lovers—if he happened to be in the States for the weekend? Best case they'd be looking at an on again, off again, long-distance relationship, which was bound to fail. It was difficult enough keeping a relationship alive when both parties were living together. They wouldn't stand a chance when hundreds of miles separated them.

To make the relationship work, one of them would have to give up their life. It was that simple and that destructive.

What would happen when the chemistry faded? When they realized there was no foundation beneath the sparks, that they had nothing in common, that their values, ideals, even their vision of the future were poles apart.

Because fireworks didn't last forever. They blazed across the night in one intense burst after another, but they eventually vanished. And when they did, they left regrets and resentment in their wake. Like the ugly split between her mother and father. Like what had happened between her and Brad.

Her mother had found herself abandoned and alone, with sole responsibility for an infant. Beth had been luckier. Her first brush with sexual attraction had left her humiliated and broke, but her life hadn't irrevocably changed.

Not the way it would have if she'd given up a great job and moved down to San Diego.

"Hey," Zane said in a low voice. He set down his fork and squeezed her thigh. "You're miles away. You okay?"

His hand burned through her linen slacks and illustrated the core realization she'd come to. There was more going on between them than simple attraction, at least on his end. A hand on the thigh was an intimate gesture. One a man gave a lover, not one you'd give a woman you'd known less than a day.

They definitely needed to talk.

Marion glanced between Beth and Zane, warm understanding in her eyes. "Beth, why don't you show Zane where you'll be sleeping."

Dead silence hit the table.

Her cheeks hot, Beth forced herself to hold her hostess's gaze. "I'll help you clean the kitchen."

As they worked side by side in the kitchen rinsing the plates the men brought them and sticking them in the dishwasher, Marion dropped her voice. "I didn't mean to embarrass you, dear. With everything going on, I just thought you and Zane could use some alone time."

Beth murmured a vague reply. Cosky's mother was right about that, but not for the reason she assumed.

Once the table was cleared, the food put away, and the dishes stowed, Beth had no excuse other than procrastination to avoid Zane. So when he headed out to the garage with an armful of empty beer bottles, Beth followed him.

She caught up with him next to a silver Lexus as he dropped the Coors bottles into a recycle bin against the wall. He straightened and turned to her, his gaze guarded.

"We need to talk." She worked at keeping her voice steady, nonconfrontational.

He didn't move, just watched her with absolute stillness. "I'll be bunking with Mac and Rawls."

That stopped her, but just for a moment. She hadn't expected anything less. Zane wasn't the kind of man to sneak his way into her bed. "This isn't about the sleeping arrangements."

Something flickered in his eyes.

"What did Mac mean about that soul mate thing?"

Zane's face went blank. "You don't need to worry about that."

"I think I do." Beth chose her words with care. "I think you have unrealistic expectations. I think you're building a relationship in your mind that doesn't exist in reality."

"Nothing's going to happen that you don't want to happen."

She didn't doubt that, actually. But that was the whole problem with sexual heat. You wanted it while the flames were churning. It was afterwards, when the flames gutted, that the regrets set in.

"Just so we're clear. I have a job I love. A home I love. Local friends I love. I'm not looking for a long-distance relationship."

Frustration slipped through his eyes. "You're getting ahead of yourself. I'm not asking you to make choices."

Not yet, maybe. "So you're just looking for a vacation fling, a roll in the sack, and then we'll go our merry ways?"

His eyebrows snapped together. "Hell, no."

"Then you aren't looking for any relationship at all?" She asked point-blank.

This time the frustration touched both his face and eyes. He swore beneath his breath. "You know better than that."

Yes, she did, which was the whole purpose of this conversation.

"Look," he said, raking a hand through his hair. "Let's take this one step at a time. We'll worry about the hows when we get to that point."

When they got to what point? After they were emotionally invested? When a split would cause untold pain? The thought of never seeing him again already brought a twinge and she'd only known him a matter of hours. How much more would it hurt to lose him after a couple of days? Weeks? Months?

She needed to nip his expectations in the bud. Quickly and cleanly. "Look, I'm already involved with someone, okay? Seriously involved. I'm not interested in a relationship with you."

A thundercloud rolled into his eyes. "Bullshit," he bit out. "You wouldn't have used your tongue on me like that if you were seeing someone else."

Beth's eyes widened and then narrowed. How incredibly crass. "I was imagining I was with him," she snapped.

"Really?" A muscle in Zane's cheek twitched. He took a step toward her, the movement blatantly threatening. "Are you thinking about him now?"

Okaaaay, claiming a prior relationship was obviously the wrong tact. She watched in alarm as an expression of pure possessiveness slipped over his face.

"Noooo." She took a cautious step back.

"Good."

He moved so fast she didn't have time to react. One moment he was facing her, the next she was locked in his arms—crushed against him. His rock-hard chest burning through her clothes.

He took her mouth like a marauder. His lips hard. Insistent. His mouth opened over hers. The tip of his tongue probing the seam of her lips—a silent demand that she let him in.

And she wanted to. Oh Lord, did she ever want to. She wanted to taste him, drown in the rich headiness of him, wallow in that sexy male musk his skin emitted. Her muscles were already softening, her breasts swelling, her nipples pebbling. Tingles and chills swept her spine. But the very strength of her hunger brought a spurt of unease.

This was exactly the kind of reaction—the kind of chemistry—that got a person in trouble.

So she braced herself and clamped her lips together, a silent denial.

A low growl rumbled up his throat and throbbed against her lips like a threat, but he broke contact and eased back.

Beth relaxed. Clearly he'd gotten the message. Except he leaned down and nipped her bottom lip. Not enough to sting, just enough to send a message—along with a rush of blood to her head—just enough to let her know that…yeah…he had no intention of playing by her rules. She tried to pull back, but he lifted her and turned, pinning her against the SUV, the thick column of his arousal pressing hard against her belly…which…really…she should *not* have found so sexy.

This time the growl that broke from him held a predatory rasp. He nipped her bottom lip again, then caught the sensitive flesh in his teeth and tugged. A hot rush flooded her veins.

He nipped again. Harder. A sensual sting that shot straight to her throbbing nipples and liquefied the moist heat between her legs.

Dear Lord.

She sucked in a shocked, aroused breath. His tongue surged in before she could rectify the mistake. And good God, he used his tongue with the same finesse as he'd used his lips. Stroking, rubbing, and prodding until her blood whipped through her veins in a frenzy. She lost track of where they were, what she'd been trying to accomplish, and what loomed ahead.

The fireworks of before were nothing compared to the sensual storm he dragged her into this time. In seconds he had her weak, clinging, the heat boiling through her as though someone had dialed her internal thermostat to scorching.

She swallowed a whimper as he pulled back.

He caught her chin in an iron grip and forced her eyes to meet his. The gaze staring back was hard, determined. Lethal. "You can fight what's between us all you want. It won't change a thing. You're mine. And sweetheart, you don't want to bring another guy into this, not unless you want to watch him bleed."

"*Excuse me?*" The chills and tingles vanished as though she'd been dowsed in ice water. Beth's jaw would have dropped if he hadn't had hold of her chin.

A wave of intense disorientation swept over her. For a moment she was convinced she was dreaming. That she'd fallen asleep while reading one of JR Ward's *Black Dagger Brotherhood* paranormal romances and had inserted herself into a dream based on the book. Any moment now he was going to start growling *Mine Mine Mine* and let loose with some spicy bonding scent. Or flash a massive set of fangs.

Except...if she was dreaming, wouldn't he be a jacked-up, massively muscled vampire warrior rather than the testosterone-laden, far-too-alpha—but human—pain in the derriere?

She concentrated on the hard fingers under her chin, and the sense of disorientation dissipated. Oh no, this was real. And it just went to show that literary escapism did not translate well into reality. The last thing she needed, or wanted, in real life was a bonded alpha male. Romantic fiction aside, they were serious jackass material.

"You're mine," he said again, his voice flat, yet in that you-just-need-to-be-reasonable-about-this tone that men had been driving women crazy with throughout history.

She told herself she shouldn't even respond to that insane claim, but the words just burst out. "I am not yours. You don't even *know* me."

He gave her a hard, confident smile. "I know you weren't thinking about anyone else while your tongue was wrapped around mine."

She choked. Okay, this was getting them nowhere. She pushed hard against his chest, relieved when he loosened his arms and stepped back. God only knew what might have happened if he'd decided to push the matter—she had no self-control when it came to the man.

As she straightened her clothes and willed her overheated body to chill out, she avoided his satisfied expression and tried to convince herself that she hadn't just lost about a million miles in ground.

———————————

Early the next morning, after Marion Simcosky kicked them out of the kitchen so she could cook breakfast in peace, the discussion turned to Chastain and the FBI's leak. Zane watched Mac pace back and forth in front of the pool table, his footsteps heavy on the basement's concrete floor. He understood his commander's frustration. They could hardly accuse a highly decorated FBI veteran of leaking classified intel. Not without hardcore proof.

Yet they couldn't let the situation stand either.

Regardless of the circumstances, if Chastain was feeding information to the assholes who'd intended to hijack Flight 2077, then his pipeline needed to be blocked.

But therein lay the crux of the problem—if.

They knew the leak was there, but they couldn't be sure it was coming from Chastain. Yeah, the pieces fit and it made an ugly sort of sense, but they had no proof.

They were debating what to do when footsteps sounded on the wood stairs leading down to the basement. The door opened and Beth stepped inside, followed by the very agent under discussion. Without making a sound, he turned and closed the door behind him. Then he just stood there, his hand resting on the knob, his head bent—frozen in place as though he'd forgotten where he was or why he'd arrived.

Zane exchanged a grim glance with Cosky as complete silence fell over the room.

Christ, the guy looked like hell, like somebody had pounded the living shit out of him—but without leaving bruises. When he finally stepped back, he did so slowly, carefully, as if every bone in his body ached and every muscle burned.

New lines carved the face he turned toward them, some cutting so deep they looked anchored to the bone. Sunken brown eyes were rimmed with red. Vacant. Broken.

A soft curse echoed in the room. It could have come from any of them.

Chastain's head turned toward Mac. "I need your help."

Mac raised his eyebrows, his eyes watchful. "How did you find us?"

"I guessed. Lieutenant Simcosky is the only one with family in the area. I tried Miss Brown's place first, but no one was home." Chastain sounded exhausted.

Mac's attention didn't budge from that wrecked face. "If you're looking for our source, you're SOL. HQ1 doesn't share sensitive information with other agencies, particularly when those agencies are compromised." He paused, his gaze sharp. "Or at least some of their agents are."

Chastain held the black burn of Mac's stare. "I'm sure you're aware you have one of those agents in front of you now."

Surprised silence filtered through the room.

Zane glanced at Beth. She was watching Chastain, sympathy in the soft lines of her face.

"How'd they turn you?" Mac's expression remained blank.

"You must have figured that out for yourself." A hint of hardness tightened Chastain's voice. "How 'bout we get down to business?"

So he wasn't going to make excuses. No apologies either. Zane wasn't sure whether to applaud the man or deck him.

Chastain shoved trembling fingers through his hair. "I don't know how deep they've infiltrated the agency, but they've got their claws into someone else on my team. No," he added as Mac opened his mouth. "I don't know who or how many. All I know for sure is that they turned at least one other member of my team. Someone dropped a note in my jacket pocket. They did this while I was wearing it. While we were at the airport. The only people with that kind of access are members of my team."

A sharp silence fell.

"What did they want?" Mac finally asked.

"They wanted me to make sure the plane was given safe passage through US airspace. I was to negotiate with the airline, government, and families. To convince the president that the hijackers were not a threat to national security and there was still a chance of getting the passengers back alive."

Zane frowned. Since 9/11, if a flight seized by terrorists couldn't be forced to the ground, it was subject to termination. To get the plane down to Puerta Jardin, it would have been crucial to have someone negotiating safe passage.

Chastain paused, shook his head. "However, their demands have changed since the flight's been grounded."

Mac rocked back on his heels, his eyes narrowing. "The plane's grounded. Their crew's in custody. An investigation's underway. They're missing a couple of propellers if they think they can grab that flight now."

"They're not after the flight." He paused, scrubbed shaking hands down his face, and took a deep breath. He seemed to force himself to continue. "The note contained the URL to a video. Of my family. Plus a list of names. Seven people—all from first class. I'm to make them available if I want to see my family again."

Silence fell.

"You're telling us this was never about the plane? It was about the passengers?" Zane finally asked, raking a hand through his hair.

Cosky frowned. "We can't be sure of that. Could be they're after ransom."

Chastain shook his head. "The passengers they're demanding aren't among the wealthiest in first class. They aren't even close."

"So why them?" Zane cocked his head and studied the fed's face. It made no sense. Why hijack a plane just to grab seven people? There were easier ways to kidnapping someone. "What do those seven names have in common?"

"I don't know, at least not yet."

"When did they grab your family?" Cosky's eyes flashed silver.

Chastain's shoulders lifted beneath a tight breath. "Six days ago."

Mac tilted his head. "Who'd you report it to?"

"I didn't." When Mac simply lifted an eyebrow and stared, Chastain bared his teeth. "I tried. Went to my director. He was un-fucking-available. Within minutes someone sends a picture of my son to my phone. My youngest. He's zipped up in a body bag. Just his face showing—only he's laughing, like it's a game. The caption says, 'Next time he won't be laughing.'"

Grim glances circled the room.

"You try DHS?" Zane asked. He tried to imagine what he'd do if their positions were reversed, if it had been Beth taken... Beth's life at stake.

The agent's head swung in his direction, his red-rimmed eyes exhausted. "No, I didn't go to DHS. What if they're compromised too? That asshole wasn't joking. The wrong word to the wrong person..." He broke off, took a deep breath and held it, then exhaled in a soft hiss. "You four I can be certain haven't been tapped. You're of no use to them. You can't even operate on US soil." He turned back to Mac. "When you called, warning me the plane was about to be taken, I knew you had to be clear."

"What about the three we took down?" Zane asked. "Did you get anything from them?"

"Denials and counteraccusations against you three."

"What of Clancy?" Mac shot an undecipherable glance in Beth's direction.

With a tight shoulder roll, Chastain shook his head.

Ah, hell.

Zane turned, but from the lack of shocked grief on Beth's face, it was clear she hadn't grasped what Chastain's gesture indicated. He took hold of her hand. Her fingers tensed in his, and she started to pull away.

He tightened his grip. "How did he die?"

Beth's hand froze, her sharp inhalation piercing the room.

"Gunshot to the back of the head. He was discovered last night. In the parking lot. In his van. I'm sorry, Miss Brown. I know he was a friend of yours."

When she flinched, Zane let go of her hand and wrapped her in his arms. She came docilely, underscoring the depth of her shock and pain.

Zane sighed. "They're cleaning house."

A tremor shook the slender frame cradled against him and he knew Beth was wondering where that left Ginny and Kyle. No doubt Chastain was wondering the same thing about his family, which explained his visit, along with the full reveal.

"You have any idea who's pulling the strings?" Zane asked, burrowing his fingers into the hair at the back of Beth's head and massaging her scalp. She leaned into his hand and slowly the tremors ceased.

"No clue. He's smart. Communicates through prepaid cells and e-mail."

"We'll assume you traced the e-mail account," Mac said, then watched without expression as Chastain's lips tightened. "What about the phone?"

"Nothing."

Nobody in the room looked surprised.

"I told you. The bastard's sharp."

Beth stirred and shifted to stare at the fed. "He can't be that smart. He picked an engineer to hide his guns rather than someone from maintenance. He was lucky Todd managed to find a parts crate."

Chastain hesitated and gave a what-the-hell shrug. "Your friend did double duty. They picked him because of his net worth. All those inventions paid off. He's been liquefying assets for the last four days. This morning he transferred five million into a holding account."

"Ransom," Zane murmured.

When Beth stepped back, he forced himself to relax his hands and let her go, trying to ignore the feeling that she was slipping away from him as easily as those cool strands of hair were slipping through his fingers.

"What do you need from us?" Mac asked.

Chastain closed his eyes. When he opened them again they were hard with determination. "I need you to run down a clue."

"We don't have the authority to act within a law enforcement capacity," Mac reminded him quietly.

"Are you saying no?"

"That's not what he's saying." Cosky didn't glance at Mac for confirmation. "We don't have legal standing. If anything comes from this clue, you chance a good lawyer shredding the prosecution's case."

With a silent snarl, Chastain turned on Cosky. "I don't give a fuck about the *prosecution*. Those bastards weren't wearing masks. Got it? They angled the lens so I couldn't see their faces. But Amy and the boys could. They aren't worried about identification, which means they don't plan on leaving anyone alive to identify them. You're the best shot I have of getting my wife and kids back alive. My son sent me a clue, but I can't track it down myself. They're watching me." He paused, took a deep, gulping breath. "You'll be acting beneath my authority."

Zane shot a quick glance at Mac and received an abbreviated nod. "What's this clue?"

Chastain's muscles loosened. "Yesterday afternoon those assholes took my boys to the carnival. I checked; since it's spring break, the carnival's in town through this weekend. It's at the Puyallup Fairgrounds. Those bastards took video, and Brendan, my eldest, tried his luck at the shooting booth. The vendor might remember him." Desperation and hope warred in his eyes. "Brendan's a sharp kid. He'll have left a message. A clue. Something."

Zane glanced at Cosky, saw the same doubt in his eyes. "How old's your boy?"

"Ten." Chastain's mouth tightened at the glances traveling the room. His voice rose. "It's the best fucking chance I've got."

"The odds this vendor will remember your son are astronomical." Zane kept his voice calm, reasonable, even as raw emotion flooded the haggard face across from him. "They must get hundreds of kids a day."

"Brendan insisted they take footage of this booth. He'd have made sure the vendor remembered him. He'll have left a clue behind to follow."

Zane doubted it. Even the smartest of kids would find it difficult to leave a message with a watchdog on his tail. Nor would the kidnappers have sent the footage if there'd been a chance of it exposing them.

Mac glanced at the floor and shook his head slightly. When he looked back up his eyes were grim but steady. "We need to see the film."

Chastain twitched, his teeth clenching so hard they caught his bottom lip and drew blood. "I'll give you a description of the vendor."

Sourness crawled through Zane's belly. It didn't take a rocket scientist to figure out why Chastain didn't want them to view the video footage. The kidnappers must have shot video of the wife too, only it sure as hell hadn't been at the carnival. To alternate the assault on the wife with the carnival footage took a seriously twisted mind.

"John," Mac said, and with the transfer to first names, a corner was turned. "We need to see that tape. You're too close to this. You'll miss things. Details that might help find them."

Chastain's face twisted. For a moment only ragged breathing filled the room. After one last hard breath, he scrubbed his palms down his face and rocked back on his heels. "Fine." He held Mac's gaze without flinching. "But just you. We'll need to access it from my laptop, which is in my car."

"Was Kyle on the video? Ginny?" Beth asked hoarsely. From her ashen face and the horror swimming in her eyes, she'd figured out what was on that tape too and was wondering whether her friend had suffered the same fate.

"No." Chastain's voice smoothed as he pulled a shroud of composure into place.

"You said the footage was taken yesterday?" Zane glanced at Cosky. From the grimness in his teammate's eyes, they'd arrived at the same conclusion.

Chastain nodded. "Midafternoon from the time stamp."

Which meant it had been taken after the hijacking had been aborted. The timing made sense. The terrorists had wanted to deliver a reminder of what was at stake. But that didn't mean the hostages were still alive.

"Show me the video," Mac said.

Without saying a word, Chastain headed for the basement door with Mac on his heels. Though nothing was said, everyone knew what they'd be watching. The knowledge permeated the room like a thick, ugly haze.

Thirty minutes later Mac returned, face rigid and skin pale. His hands clenched into fists. Fury and livid disgust burning in his eyes.

Chastain didn't return with him.

"McKay's given the green light," Mac said. "Chastain gave me photos of his kids. We'll roll as soon as we've eaten. The timing should be perfect. Chastain says it's a forty-five-minute drive. We'll arrive just as the gate opens."

Zane frowned and glanced toward Beth. He wasn't leaving her behind. There were two hijackers unaccounted for; if Chastain had found them, the second mole could as well. She'd be safer with them at the carnival.

Mac followed Zane's gaze. "She waits here."

No way in hell. "She comes with us."

Mac's jaw set. "She's a civilian. She waits here."

In any other circumstances, he would have agreed. You didn't bring civilians on missions. Period. But this was more recon than a penetration, with no real danger attached. The kidnappers would be long gone by the time the team arrived at the fairgrounds.

"She's not safe here," Zane said flatly.

Beth stirred. "I can speak for myself and I'm going. I've got pictures of Kyle and Ginny in my wallet. I can show the pictures around, ask if anyone's seen them, while you guys question the booth attendant."

Mac ignored her. "Marion can keep an eye on her."

"Mom's coming too. If Chastain tracked us down, chances are anyone in the bureau can. I'm not leaving her unprotected."

"Fine. Stay home and babysit," Mac snapped. "This isn't open for discussion."

Beth raised her voice. "You're right, this isn't open for discussion. I'm going," she said, finality ringing in her voice. "If I have to, I'll call a cab as soon as you leave and head over on my own."

"Jesus Christ." Mac's face twisted into a snarl. He tried to intimidate her with a glare. When that didn't work, he swung to Zane. "Keep her out of the fucking way."

Turning on his heel, he stalked toward the stairway. The door opened as his hand touched the knob and Chastain's haggard form filled the doorway.

"If you find anything," he told them, "run it down. Don't call in. Just follow it."

"And if we get a location?" Mac asked, his face still.

"Move on it." Chastain didn't hesitate. "I'll take full responsibility. Just nail those bastards."

Mac nodded his understanding and waited for the fed to move out of the way. Zane rested his hand on the small of Beth's back, the tightness in his chest easing as the warmth of her skin heated his hand.

Chastain's promise to cover them amounted to a whole lot of hot air.

Once this mess hit the public's eye, Chastain wouldn't be able to protect himself—let alone ST7. The poor bastard would be well and truly fried. Regardless of the circumstances, he'd cooperated with terrorists. He'd be lucky to avoid time in the pen.

At this point, they could only hope that when Chastain took the hit and fell, he didn't drag them down with him.

Chapter Ten

*T*ODD WAS DEAD.

The words rolled through Beth's mind, an endless litany. She felt trapped in a nightmare, one that grew more hazy and terrifying by the hour. First the damn dream, then Todd's involvement, then Ginny and Kyle's kidnapping, followed by Todd's death and what had likely been done to John Chastain's poor wife.

Please...please...please...don't let that have been done to Ginny.

Staring out the window of the Expedition the men had leased, Beth watched the streets of Burien streak past as they followed Marion to the friend she'd decided to visit rather than accompany the men to the carnival. The blurred houses, cars, and people deepened the sense of dreaming, the rift from reality, the feeling of being trapped in a bad case of déjà vu.

This can't be happening. Please don't let this be happening.

Zane shifted beside her, his jeans squeaking against the leather upholstery, his heat simmering along her left side from shoulder to thigh, his scent a smoky musk in air saturated with new-car smell.

His warmth grounded her, anchored her—prevented her from splintering into a billion pieces. She turned her head, latched onto his presence with something akin to desperation, and tried to concentrate on the voices rising and falling in the cramped interior.

"If anything comes from this," Cosky said as he slid back into the driver's seat after seeing his mother inside her friend's house, "we'll need to arm up. You've seen my dad's collection. We've got a small arsenal on hand if needed." He executed a neat U-turn and headed back the way they'd come.

Mackenzie snorted. "The odds are better we'll catch the Tooth Fairy than uncover a clue to find them."

Rawls, who was sitting to Zane's left, glanced over to Beth and then Zane. "How 'bout you, skipper? You picking anything up?"

He meant psychically. Beth half twisted to look at Zane's face. She still wasn't ready to touch that soul mate nonsense, but the ESP bit..."Is it true? Are you psychic?"

Dead silence blanketed the car. Someone cleared his throat.

"Sometimes," Zane said calmly, green eyes steady on her face. "I get flashes of things to come. They're quick. Never last longer than a few seconds."

Beth digested that in silence. She thought back to her full reveal in the closet back at the airport and the glances flying back and forth between the three men. "You knew. You already knew something was going to happen on that plane. That's why you believed me so quickly."

"I got a flash just before you arrived at the gate—saw Cos and Rawls dead." His intense gaze held hers like a magnet. "But I didn't see who did it or what caused it."

Suddenly she wanted to laugh. She choked the amusement back, suspecting it would have a hysterical edge, but she couldn't stop the small snort that escaped. "I don't believe this. Here I had the stupid dream, but *you're* the psychic. So how often do you get these..." What had he called them? "...flashes?"

Something about that question brought back the sense of déjà vu. It took her a second to pin the reason down. She'd been asked almost the exact same question, in the exact same tone, at least twice in the past twenty-four hours. Once by Cosky. Once by Mac.

This time she couldn't hold the laughter back, and yep—there was definitely a hysterical edge to it, judging by the concerned expression on Zane's face. She let him cuddle her closer and relaxed as he stroked her hair. The laughter sputtered and died.

With each caress of his hand, the dream haze faded. By the time they arrived at the Puyallup fairgrounds, Beth had herself under control.

They parked toward the front of the parking lot and everyone piled out.

"Show these around." Mac handed Zane and Cosky a couple of wallet-sized photos of two dark-haired boys. "Cosky and Rawls will start at the back of the grounds. You two start at the front. I'll find the shooting booth."

Beth dug into her purse and dragged out her wallet. "Everyone take a picture of Kyle and Ginny too." She quickly sorted through the plastic sheaths of photos.

"She's beautiful," Rawls said, his gaze lingering on the photo Beth handed him.

Yes, she was. Ginny was one of the most beautiful women Beth knew—inside and out. As she stared at the photo in Rawls's hand, her throat tightened and tears blurred the radiant image. With a deep breath, she forced the grief aside and concentrated on what needed to be done.

Pictures in hand, everyone headed for the front gate, but the men's longer legs quickly outpaced Beth. Zane held back, matching his stride to hers.

"They're more than friends, aren't they?" Zane asked as they walked. "The only pictures you have in your wallet are of Ginny, Kyle, and Todd."

That wasn't true. She did have pictures of her mother, just not that many of them. And even fewer of them together.

"They're my family," Beth admitted. "My dad left when I was a baby. Mom took extra shifts or second jobs to support us. She was rarely home, and when she was, she was so tired…Ginny and her family lived next door. Her mom used to babysit me. They sort of unofficially adopted me. I spent far more time with them than I did with my own mother while growing up. And then Mom died when I was fifteen." She shook her head slightly, shying away from the ugly memories. "Ginny's family took me in."

Zane digested that in silence. "She's more of a sister."

Ginny *was* her sister, in every sense that mattered. Just as Kyle was her nephew. Beth tightened her grip on her purse strap and stared at the entrance to the fairgrounds. The last time she'd been here had been with Ginny and Kyle. Todd had skipped out on them in favor of some new project in his garage.

A fresh burst of grief lit her chest.

How was Ginny going to handle Todd's death? He'd been her best friend. Her partner. They'd had the perfect marriage. Exactly the kind Beth wanted, where difficult decisions were made together and resources were pooled.

From here on out, Ginny would be a single mother. Nor would she have the cushion of savings and investments since Todd had depleted their financial resources in the hopes of getting the two of them back.

God, it was so unfair. Ginny deserved better.

Zane slowed even further. "You want to talk about it?"

About what? The bomb the dream had dropped on her? The bomb the FBI had dropped on her? The bomb his commander had dropped on her? The way her world had been turned upside down and shaken—until the very foundations of her life felt warped and unstable?

No. No. And no.

"We should hurry," she said instead, lengthening her stride. "Your friends are leaving us behind."

"Beth." Raw frustration throbbed in his exhaled curse. He caught her elbow and swung her around. "Look..." His voice trailed off as his attention fixed on her lips.

Oh, boy. She recognized the gleam flickering to life, sparking those green eyes until they glowed. This was not good. Not good at all. She tugged at her hand, but he just dragged her closer. The two hands he used to cradle her face were surprisingly tender.

Warmth flared in her cheeks where his rough palms held her. Her blood heated and thickened, sweeping downward in a lazy wave, from cheeks to toes, warming everything in its path. Her legs lost strength as he bent his head.

His lips were gentle, stroking carefully against hers as though she were delicate china capable of shattering at the slightest pressure.

Except...she didn't want gentleness. She didn't want careful. She wanted intensity. A bonfire. Sparks so strong they'd gut the grief and this creeping sense of being lost in the fog.

Going up on her toes, she wrapped her arms around the strong column of his neck and rubbed her breasts against his chest.

Her nipples tightened. Her breasts ached. Her thighs quivered. Tingles coursed up and down her spine. It felt so good she did it again. With her second rub, fire coiled, flickered through her, whip-sharp and intense.

He groaned as she opened her mouth to the taste of him. The heady dark chocolate of him. His smoky musk swirling around her, through her, the effect intensifying as his skin heated.

His mouth hardened and his tongue surged forward, stroking, thrusting, rubbing—fanning the sparks. He groaned again, the sound filling her mouth, and her legs went rubbery. Her breath caught as he broke from her lips and nuzzled a path to the tender patch of skin below her ear, where he stopped to suckle and then nip before soothing the sting with butterfly kisses.

With each press of his lips or nibble of his teeth or stroke of his tongue, the ache coiled tighter. The bonfire leapt higher.

A whimper caught in her throat.

"Christ, you feel so good. Taste so good." He groaned against her neck, his breath a hot, erotic blast against her ear.

"Get a room," a young male voice jeered. A cacophony of laughter followed.

Beth was vaguely aware of bodies sweeping past them, the sound of more laughter, of shoes crunching on gravel. She lowered her heels back to the ground and loosened the tight clasp of her arms.

Zane took a deep breath and lifted his head but kept his arms around her. A good thing, considering how shaky her legs were. She wasn't sure they were capable of holding her up on her own.

As the haze of desire dissipated, she got a good look at his face, and a chill of unease pushed the last of the hunger aside.

He looked far too satisfied for a man whose erection still throbbed against her stomach, far too complacent for a man whose body had to be aching to the point of pain.

Far too possessive for a man who hadn't actually claimed her.

Beth wrenched herself out of his arms. "Let's go, we need to start showing the pictures around."

———————————

If not for the circumstances, it would have been a perfect day.

The sky shone brilliant and blue overhead. A gentle breeze teased Beth's hair and swept the heat from the fairgrounds before the temperature climbed past warm. The scent of caramel candy, corn dogs, and funnel cakes hung thick and heavy in the air. In the distance, muted screams broke out as rides took to the skies. Clusters of children raced from booth to booth, thrusting wadded-up bills or pockets full of change at the bored attendants.

With Zane beside her, Beth got in line behind a young family of three at a food booth.

"My brothers and I used to race each other like that," Zane murmured, watching as a pack of young boys sprinted down the grass corridor between the carnival stands. "Had more fun racing around than the games themselves, I think. There's nothing like a fair to wear a youngster out."

Beth followed his gaze, watching as the kids disappeared between two booths. What had he been like as a child? "You said you were raised on navy bases. Your parents were in the service?"

"My dad was. We spent time at Coronado, Virginia Beach, even Hawaii for a stint. But no matter where we landed, Mom always found a fair or carnival. We'd go at least a couple of times every year."

She digested that, absently watching as the man in front of them hoisted a young boy onto his shoulders. Father and son, she deduced from the wiry brown hair sprouting from both their heads.

"Your father was a SEAL?" She wasn't surprised by his nod. "Did your brothers follow him into the service as well?"

"Yeah, Dad's retired now—they're living down in San Diego—but we all took the trident." Zane half turned and scanned the grounds before turning back to her. "Chance and Dane are stationed at Little Creek. Webb's at Dam Neck—" He chuckled as she raised her eyebrows. "That's the base, Dam Neck, Virginia. Gray's down in Coronado with me."

A family of SEALs.

That had to be an anomaly—all five sons? The SEAL teams were said to comprise the strongest, most lethal candidates. What were the odds all five brothers would have made it through training? Zane obviously came from an extraordinary family.

And then there was the psychic ability Mac had spoken of, the one that supposedly ran through their bloodline. Knowing where the danger was coming from had to be handy when you were headed into battle.

Which reminded her of what else they supposedly knew...

She shied away from that thought.

Zane squeezed her hand. "You okay? You looked freaked all of a sudden."

Beth glanced down at the strong, tanned hand holding her own. He hadn't let go of her since *the kiss*. It felt good to hold hands like this. Right. As though they'd been walking hand in hand since the beginning of time, even though she'd only known him a day.

The couple in front shuffled forward several paces, their young son's voice rising excitedly above them. As the woman turned to smile at the child, Beth caught a glimpse of a tautly rounded belly.

"When's your baby due?" she asked.

The woman shifted toward Beth. "Eight weeks. We wanted to give Jackie a special day before his sister arrives." She smiled, serenity shining in her dark eyes. "While I'm still able to walk."

Beth smiled back, listening as the youngster chattered nonstop from atop his father's shoulders. "Sounds like you've accomplished that."

"I hope so." The woman looked up at her son, and the corners of her eyes crinkled. "It's one of my favorite memories, going to the fair with my parents and sister. I hope he remembers his time with us as fondly."

A swelling pressure, one of regret, tightened Beth's throat.

Of all the things she'd missed out on during her childhood, this one brought the most sorrow: the memories. She didn't have any memories of time spent with her mother. Not just to the fair, but holidays, vacations, the movies, walks in the park. Her mother had been so busy surviving she hadn't had time to live.

That wasn't to say she hadn't gone to the movies or been taken to the fair. She just hadn't gone with her mother. So while she had memories of racing beside Ginny from booth to booth, they were tainted with the knowledge she'd been a fourth wheel, taken through kindness and charity. She hadn't actually belonged.

They weren't her real family.

For a while Beth had thought she'd found her family with Brad. A partner. Someone to raise children with. To create new, happy memories in young minds.

Instead, she'd discovered what her mother had learned before her, that passion was the great deceiver. The ultimate betrayer. Pure animal attraction, along with its accompanying tingles, butterflies, and chills, masked people's character. It tricked you into believing you saw something that wasn't really there. Convinced you there was a foundation beneath the sparks.

That there was love.

"You okay?" Zane asked as the small family in front of them stepped up to the counter. "You look sad."

"I'm fine." She tugged her hand loose in the pretense of brushing a strand of hair from her eyes.

Beth shook the memories aside and glanced down at the pictures she held. Kyle. Ginny. Chastain's family. The reasons they were here.

She needed to remember that.

When the family in front took their corn dogs and Cokes and wandered off, Zane and Beth stepped up to the window. Beth spread the pictures across the Formica counter. "Have you seen these children?"

The girl gave the snapshots a cursory glance and shook her wildly teased mane of bleached hair. "What did they do?"

Zane pushed the pictures closer. "Take another look. Do you recognize any of them? It's important."

This time the teenager bent her head and took a good look. Finally she popped her gum, straightened, and pushed the pictures back. "Sorry."

As Beth scooped the pictures up, Zane slung an arm around her shoulders and gave her a squeeze. "We've still got plenty of booths to check."

But booth after booth brought the same answer. Nobody recognized the photos.

They caught glimpses of Cosky and Rawls as they threaded their way through the crowd. From the frustration stamped across their faces, they weren't having any better luck.

"We're headed to the shooting gallery," Cosky said when they met up in the middle of the fairgrounds. "You two want to hit the rides?"

Canvassing the rides took next to no time. Still, when they arrived at the shooting gallery, a crowd had gathered.

"Man, he hasn't missed once," a weedy teenager said.

"Neither did the other one," someone to the teenager's right responded.

They slipped between a balding man who reeked of cheap cologne and a brassy-haired woman who reeked of cigarettes. Beth gagged and held her breath.

"You wanna bet they're cops?"

"I doubt it, dear. Those muscles didn't come from donuts."

They weaved their way through a flock of teenage girls wearing shorts that skirted the edge of decency and discovered that the front of the crowd consisted of children.

They broke into the open as Rawls leaned down and handed a plastic doll to a tiny Asian child in a frilly sundress.

"Here ya go, darlin'," he said, his blond head gleaming like platinum in the sunlight. "I'd have got pink to match that purty dress—but pink's Cosky's favorite color."

"I'm not the one asking for dolls," Cosky said with a pointed glance at the half dozen Barbie knockoffs clutched in tiny hands.

Beth glanced over the front row of children; they all held an array of cheap toys. Her gaze lingered on a little red-headed boy and the purple dinosaur he cradled to his fragile chest. Her heart started aching. Something about him reminded her of Kyle. Maybe it was the shyness in the dip of his chin or the way he avoided everyone's eyes or that bright red hair.

"What?" Zane's gaze was locked on Rawls's grinning face. "You decide to break the vendor by winning all his toys?"

Rawls looked up and shrugged. "The guy we came for isn't here yet. Since he's not answering his phone, we figured we'd try our luck while we waited. Might as well give the rug rats some mementoes."

"We'd have upgraded these cheesy toys by now if Rawls would spend more time shooting and less flirting with the ladies." Cosky winked at the cluster of grade-schoolers.

"Cosky's just jealous." Rawls shot his buddy a smirk. "Poor bastard couldn't hit the hull of a sub from the dock."

"Pay attention, pretty boy"—Cosky slapped a five-dollar bill down on the waist-high counter and waited for the scowling attendant to scoop it up and move out of the way—"while I show you what real shooting looks like."

He raised the BB gun to his shoulder. A steady *phuffitt, phuffitt, ping, ping* filled the air, and the metal ducks toppled over in a massacre of sunny yellow.

Beth stared at the rifle. According to Chastain, his son had used one of those guns. Touched one of those guns...

She'd read various books through the years that had featured psychic heroes or heroines, and then there were all the television shows. In the movies and books, just touching an object could spark a vision. It was hard to believe she was actually considering the idea—Lord knows she'd never put much stock in psychic phenomena. But it was a little hard to dismiss the possibility, considering everything that had happened since that damn dream.

She turned to Zane and lowered her voice. "Can you pick something up off the rifle? Agent Chastain's son must have touched one of them."

He glanced at her, surprise flaring in his eyes. "It doesn't work like that, at least not for me. I've never gotten anything from an object."

"Oh," Beth murmured, surprised by the quick rise of disappointment.

Zane studied her face for a moment and then turned back to the counter.

It wasn't until the last target fell and the puffing, pinging sounds dissipated that Beth heard the excited whispers rising from behind. She turned to find half a dozen teenage girls admiring Cosky, Rawls, and Zane's long, lean frames. Several of the girls adjusted their blouses to display maximum cleavage.

"Hell," Mac said from the sidelines where he stood with his arms crossed and his feet spread. "You call that shooting? Took fifteen seconds to take them down. If they'd been snipers we'd be dead by now."

Snipers?

Beth stared at the smiling yellow ducks and swallowed a snort.

Dropping his arms, Mac stepped forward and snatched the BB gun from Cosky's shoulder. This time Beth couldn't hold back the snort. Good Lord, they'd regressed to kindergarten. Her gaze shifted to Zane. Well, at least three of the four had. Zane appeared to be the only one—

She dumped that comparison when Zane stepped forward and made a grab for Rawls's gun. As Mac started shooting, and that oddly rhythmic *phuffitt* of escaping air and *ping, ping* of metal hitting metal once again filled the booth, Zane dug into his pocket and pulled out a money clip.

Beth glanced at the prices affixed to the post in the middle of the booth and did some quick mental gymnastics. A snicker escaped. If her calculations were correct, it cost two bucks to win a prize that cost about fifty cents at the dollar store.

"If you want to impress Beth with some fancy shooting," Rawls drawled, "you better let me keep the gun."

"Not another one!" The waif-thin teenager manning the booth groaned as Zane dropped a wad of bills on the counter. The attendant walked over to the rope that stretched the length of the booth and plucked down the peach-colored pony Mac pointed to. He fired the stuffed animal to the commander and threw up his hands. "Why don't you just give me your wallets and I'll hand over the prizes. It'll save time."

Mac caught the pony and handed it off to a dark-haired sprite in a yellow dress. "We want to upgrade these shitty toys."

As Zane brought the BB gun up to his shoulder, another man pushed his way through the crowd.

"What the fuck?" Freckled, skeletal hands plunked down on bony hips. He glared at the multitude of toys in the first row and then transferred his ire to the booth attendant. "You giving them away?"

Mac glanced over and froze, then lowered his BB gun to the counter. Beth turned toward the new arrival. From the commander's reaction, he had to be the man they'd come to see. Zane set his gun down as well, and just like that all four men morphed from competitive schoolboys to steely-eyed men on a mission.

"A word." Ignoring the disappointed groans sweeping the bystanders, Mac reached into his pocket, pulled out a photograph of Brendan Chastain, and held it in front of the vendor's face. "This kid was here sometime yesterday afternoon. Recognize him?"

He shook the photo slightly, as though the movement might jog the vendor's memory.

The booth attendant barely glanced at the picture before he swore again. "Let me guess. You're related to the little bastard. He was almost as obnoxious as you."

Surprise froze Mac in place. "You remember him?"

"Sure. He didn't miss." With a swipe of his hand the vendor pushed the picture aside. "What the hell's this about?"

"How many people were with him?" Zane took a step forward.

For a moment it looked like the booth attendant was going to refuse to answer. Beth watched the four SEALs tense in coiled threat.

The vendor must have sensed the danger as well. He shrugged and took a careful step back. "There was another kid with him."

"Which child?" Beth showed him colored photos of all three kidnapped kids. Her heart sank when he silently pointed to Chastain's younger son.

"How many adults?" The question shot from Mac with the ferocity of a bullet. Their witness's eyes widened. "Three adult men. Why?"

"We need to locate this boy. Anything you can tell us would be helpful." Cosky's voice was hard, commanding rather than requesting.

The vendor's forehead furrowed. "They weren't bodyguards?"

Zane leaned forward slightly, his eyes narrowing. "Why would you assume that?"

"Because they hovered. Wouldn't let anyone near either kid. Wouldn't let the kids talk to anyone. The only reason the oldest was allowed to shoot was because he raised such a stink about it. I figured they were a pair of Richie Riches. But man, that kid could shoot. Said his dad taught him." He studied Mac's face. "You the dad?"

Mac shook his head. "Did he say anything else?"

"Didn't get a chance. Every time he opened his mouth one of those guards stepped in. Figured the parents had told them to keep their spoiled little brats away from everyone. You know"—His voice dropped to a sneer—"so's our trailer trash stink didn't rub off."

Cosky swore. So did Zane. "He didn't say anything?"

The vendor shook his head. "Not that I recall."

This time Mac was the one to swear. "What about the younger one?"

"Nah, that little bugger didn't say a word. Just squealed every time the older one hit something." The vendor scowled. "Which was too fucking often."

Although their controlled faces didn't reflect any emotion, Beth had spent enough time around the four men to pick up their frustration. It seethed in the air surrounding them. The same disappointment clotted in her chest, tightening her throat. So close, they were so close, only to walk away with nothing.

Scowling, Mac glared at the endless march of yellow ducks. Suddenly he frowned, cocked his head to the side.

"What?" Zane asked quietly.

Mac continued staring at the ducks. "You have to hit ten targets to claim the prize."

Zane glanced at the metal targets. "Yeah?"

With a shake of his head, Mac frowned. "On the video, he said I got all eight of them. Emphasis on the word *eight*."

Falling silent, Zane thought about that, only to shake his head. "He's a kid. Could have miscounted."

Mac nodded slowly, but he didn't look convinced. "We know there were three men shadowing the boys here at the fair." Grimness flickered over his face and his jaw clenched. "Three more on the video with the wife. That makes six. There could have been two more with Clancy's family."

Cosky frowned, tilted his head to the side. "You think he was giving his dad a head count? Hell, could mean nothing."

"Maybe." Mac suddenly swung around and stared at the BB guns resting on the counter. "The kid held the gun up and said he wanted one just like it for Christmas, but Chastain said he has a pellet gun."

"A pellet gun's superior to a BB gun," Zane said thoughtfully.

In unison, all four men swung around and headed for the counter and the BB guns they'd discarded.

"Which gun did he use?" Zane asked.

The vendor followed them to the counter. "First time he used the one on the right. Second time he used the one in the middle."

"Has anyone used the gun in the middle?" Zane asked his men.

"No." Cosky shifted closer to the counter. "We've been shooting from the ends."

Zane picked up the BB gun under discussion and studied it. "Did he have trouble making the target with the first gun?"

"Hell no. Little bastard made contact every time."

"So he wanted that one." Cosky nodded at the gun in Zane's hand. "Question is why? They're identical."

An arrested expression settled over Zane's face. "Not quite." He turned the gun upside down, exposing a thick crack running the length of the plastic stock. "You wouldn't see the defect from above."

Everyone watched as Zane opened the barrel, shook out the extra BBs, and tilted the gun toward the sky, until a shaft of sunlight pierced the crack in the plastic. His hissed exhale filled the sudden silence.

"What is it?" Beth asked, stepping closer, trying to peer into the crack herself.

"Some kind of paper. It's wedged in tight. We need something to dig it out."

With shaking hands, Beth unzipped her purse and dug around for her travel-size first-aid kit. Once she found it, she popped the lid and rummaged through Band-Aids, Neosporin, and baby wipes until she found a pair of tweezers. Silently she handed them to Zane.

"Give him room," Mac snapped when everyone pressed closer.

It took Zane a few seconds of wiggling the tweezers back and forth before he worked the ragged slip of paper free. He handed the tweezers back to Beth and carefully unfolded his prize.

For one long moment he just stared at it. "Son of a bitch," he finally said, pure disbelief in his voice. "The kid left us an address."

Chapter Eleven

ASSUMING THE KID WAS PASSING ALONG A BODY COUNT, WE'RE outmanned two to one." Cosky flipped on his blinker and took the Federal Way exit. "Plus, while there's some damn fine weapons in my dad's collection, those assholes stashed MP5s on that plane."

"If they've got MP5s, we're outgunned no matter what your dad collected. We need a distraction," Zane said in a matter-of-fact voice. "Bottle bombs come to mind."

"Bottle bombs?" Beth felt a sinking sensation in her chest. Anything with the word *bomb* attached to its name sounded like something to be avoided.

"Molotov cocktails. Beer bottles, tampons, and gasoline, and you're set. It wouldn't take long to whip up a six-pack."

He had to be kidding! She caught the round of nods traveling through the car. *Or not.* "What about Kyle and Ginny and Chastain's family? They could get caught in the blaze or pass out from smoke inhalation."

"Depending on furnishings, flooring, and interior composition, we've got four to seven minutes before spread and smoke become a problem." Zane shot her a reassuring glance. "Plenty of time to get in, get them, and get back out again."

Four to seven minutes? Plenty of time? Good God.

"I've got a better idea." She sat up straighter. "Why don't we call the police?"

What made perfect sense to her, apparently, made no sense to her fellow passengers, because they shook their heads in unison.

"It could tip off the kidnappers," Zane told her quietly.

Oh, come on. The hijackers couldn't have their hooks into everyone. Chances were the police hadn't been compromised. And the more people who swarmed the house, the safer everyone would be.

Beth tried again. "It's unlikely that anyone in the police department is corrupt. It makes sense that they'd go after Agent Chastain or Todd since both men served a purpose, but the cops wouldn't be able to help them take that plane."

Zane glanced at her. "A corrupt cop would be a gold mine. They could direct patrols away from the neighborhood where the hostages are stashed, bury reports if something leaked. And the more cops you add to the mix, the more likely something will go wrong. There's a reason we work in smaller teams."

"Besides," Cosky glanced in the rearview mirror, "the police aren't going to take our word on this. They'd contact the FBI. Any hostages would be killed within minutes."

"If your friends are alive, we're the best shot they have," Zane told her. "We're trained for extractions. We'll get in and get them out."

But at what cost? If Brendan Chastain's cryptic comment had been a head count, they were going up against eight kidnappers. Eight ruthless, heavily armed kidnappers.

Ginny's face flashed through her mind, followed by Kyle's. God, she wanted them safe. She wanted them free from this nightmare, but not at the expense of Zane's life or the lives of the other three men in the car.

"We'll need to stop and grab supplies," Mac said.

They were going to do this with or without her help.

Beth took a deep breath and let it out slowly. "I've got tampons in my purse."

Cosky sent her an approving look via the rearview mirror. "We've got the empty beer bottles from last night, and mom has a gallon of gas in the garage. We'll need to strip the rest of the weapons. They haven't been touched since Dad died."

Marion hadn't returned from the visit with her friend, but Cosky had a key to the house.

"Zane, you know where the garage is—how 'bout you start on the bottles. There's some paint thinner on the counter from when we painted the house last fall. The rest of us will sort through the weapons." Cosky made a beeline toward a narrow door at the back of the kitchen, Rawls and Mac hard on his heels.

Putting together the Molotov cocktails sounded fairly easy from Zane's description, something she could handle while the men concentrated on the weapons.

"If you'll show me how to do the first bottle, I'll do the rest," she told Zane. "It would give you guys another pair of hands sorting through the guns."

Zane's eyes softened. "Good plan."

He led her out of the kitchen and into the attached two-car garage. The space was empty since Marion hadn't returned yet. But the interior was spotless. Tools neatly fixed to white pegboard, garden and yard tools hanging from the walls. A waist-high counter ran the length of the back and left walls.

"You'll need wire and wire clippers," Zane said as he headed toward the recycle bin. "There's a coffee can and paint thinner on the counter. Dump the paint thinner into the coffee can. Drop the tampons inside. I'll find four beer bottles."

Beth found both the can and paint thinner. The turpentine filled the coffee tin a third of the way up. She quickly rummaged through her purse, removed the tampons, and dropped them inside the can.

"You painted this house?" She spotted the wire and wire clippers hanging from the pegboard and reached up to release them.

"Rawls and I gave Cosky a hand."

Painting a house was tremendous work. He must have given up an entire leave to help Cosky out. The realization warmed her. He was a good friend. A good man.

A red plastic gas can sat in the far corner. She lugged it over to the counter, arriving as Zane lined up the beer bottles in a neat row on the cement.

"Fill them with gasoline. I'll start sealing them with duct tape."

While Beth filled the bottles with fuel, Zane rummaged through the drawers running the length of the counter. He hit pay dirt on his second try and returned with a roll of duct tape. Ripping a chunk off, he slapped it over the mouth of the bottle and pressed it tight, smoothing the edges down the neck. Once the liquid was sealed inside, he set the bottle on the counter and went to work on the second cocktail.

"I thought the tampons were taking the place of rags," Beth said as she filled the last bottle. Setting the gas can down, she confiscated the tape from him and went to work sealing the last two.

"The paint thinner and cotton will act as a wick. The minute the glass breaks, the burning tampon will detonate the gasoline. The tape prevents fumes, spillage, and premature detonation."

He picked up the wire cutters, clipped off six inches of wire, plucked a drenched tampon out of the coffee can, and attached it to the neck of the bottle by winding the wire repeatedly around the two. When he was done, the wire strapped the tampon to the neck of the bottle.

Simple enough.

When Zane stepped away from the counter, Beth slid over to take his place. But instead of heading back to the kitchen, he moved in behind her, wrapped his arms around her waist, and nuzzled the hollow between her neck and collarbone.

"How are you holding up?" He dropped a whisper-soft kiss on the side of her neck.

A shiver skated through her as his cheek rasped against her neck, his day-old bristles scratchy yet strangely erotic.

"I'm okay." The shiver turned to a quiver as he pressed another light kiss to the sensitive skin.

"We'll find your friends." His arms tightened around her waist, his breath a sensual tickle against her heating skin. "We'll bring them back to you."

He wasn't promising they'd be alive, but then how could he promise something like that? Something he had no control over?

He must have sensed the tension that suddenly gripped her, because his arms tightened even more. "Beth—"

"I can finish the rest of the bottles. You should go help your friends," she broke in.

With a sigh, his arms loosened and he stepped back. "I'll be in the kitchen."

She listened to his footsteps cross the garage, the opening and closing of the door, and found herself surrounded by silence. She was used to being alone, but somehow the emptiness surrounding her felt more intense without Zane's larger-than-life presence beside her. Warning bells rang. If her life already felt emptier without him beside her, and she'd only known him a day, how much worse would the loneliness be after days, weeks, even months?

The garage door rolled up as she finished the last Molotov cocktail.

Marion parked her Lexus as the door to the kitchen opened and Zane appeared. Beth waved him away and waited for her hostess to join her.

"Oh, dear," Marion said in a faint voice as she caught sight of the gasoline-filled bottles. Her face lost its healthy glow. "This can't be good."

But she helped Beth hunt down a plastic bucket. They packed the bottles in tight, using wadded-up newspaper to brace the glass.

Back in the kitchen, she listened to the rise and fall of calm voices discussing insertion points, fallback positions, and other tactical strategies she didn't understand. An arsenal lay strewn across the table. Rifles and shotguns to the right and left, and an assortment of handguns in the middle. The four men ringed the table, dismantling or assembling the weapons.

Zane shifted in his chair and scanned Beth's face as she followed her hostess across the kitchen.

"Mom." Cosky glanced up. "You and Beth need to hang out at your friend's place. The one you're watering the plants for. It should be safe. There's nothing to connect you to that address."

He didn't wait for her reaction, just turned back to the table. Before long, they were loading the guns with various rounds of ammunition and distributing the weapons among themselves; all four men took a shotgun or rifle, as well as a pair of handguns.

The sheer volume of weapons they were stuffing beneath waistbands or belts set Beth's stomach churning. They were preparing for war.

"We need two cars," Mac said as Cosky spread a map across the table. "There isn't enough room in the rental for the four of us, two women, and three kids—assuming they're there."

"Mom—"

"Of course, dear. Although you'll have to drive us to Vivian's."

"I can drive one of the cars," Beth said, taking a step toward the table.

"Cosky can drive one. Mac the other." Zane didn't look up.

Beth took another step forward. "They're my friends. They might need me. Besides, if the women have been...abused... they'll need another woman on scene. Not a bunch of strange men."

Zane straightened from the table, regarding her with an implacable expression. "We're trained for this. You're not. You'd be a liability."

"I'm not stupid," Beth snapped. "I'm not saying I want to go in with you. I'll wait in the car, a couple of blocks away. You can call me once it's safe."

Zane shook his head, his implacable expression unbudging. "At best, you'd be a distraction. At worst, someone could grab you and use you against us. You don't know who might see you."

"Then I'll wait in a place full of people. A store or something."

"We'd have to wait for your arrival before we could leave. Your *friends* might not have those minutes to spare. *We* might not have those minutes."

"We're wasting time." Mac shot Beth a glance full of disgust. "Lock her in the fucking closet if you have to. Let's move."

He was right. She was being selfish and foolish and risking everyone's lives, and for what? Because she wanted to do something?

Sometimes the best way to help was by doing nothing at all.

"Beth." Zane headed toward her, his face tight. "You can't—"

"I know." She released a long sigh. "I'm sorry. I'm being foolish. Where will you take them?"

"To the closest ER. They'll need to be checked out." His gaze dark, he searched her face.

With a reassuring smile, she reached up to stroke his cheek. It was warm and bristly beneath her fingertips.

"You don't need to lock me in the closet. I promise I'm not going to turn stupid. I won't go anywhere." She ignored Mac's disbelieving snort. "Just promise you'll call as soon as you have them."

He gave a slow nod and reached up to take her hand, holding it against his face in an iron grip.

After a moment he glanced over at Mrs. Simcosky. "Your friend won't mind if you and Beth hang out at her place?"

Cosky's mom patted his arm and smiled at Beth. "Of course not. She's in Australia visiting her daughter. We'll be perfectly safe there while you boys are working."

Working. Quite the euphemism.

Zane snatched a pen off the counter, tore off the bottom of a grocery list, and jotted something down. He handed the slip of paper to her.

"My cell."

After Beth stuffed the scrap of paper into the pocket of her slacks, he took her hand again.

By the time they reached the porch, Cosky had the garage door open and was backing his mom's Lexus out. He tooted the horn impatiently.

"Don't forget the bottles. I put them next to the garage door," Beth said.

She followed Zane to the car Cosky was driving and climbed in the backseat, sliding over so Cosky's mother could sit beside her. Marion gave her son directions to her friend's house and they were off.

The SUV Mac had leased dropped back until it disappeared from view and followed them via directions issued through Zane's cell phone. When they reached their safe house, Mac showed back up again. He pulled up next to where Cosky had parked along the side of the road.

Rawls rolled down the passenger window. "We're good. Nobody followed."

Cosky and Zane insisted on checking the house before leaving, so the four of them headed toward the back entrance and the key Marion said was hidden beneath the rock ledge. Once the house had been given the SEAL of approval, they gathered in the front entrance. Cosky gave his mother another hug, kissed her cheek, and loped down the brick walkway toward the street.

"You'll be safe here. I need to know you're safe." Zane turned toward Beth and hauled her into his arms. With a soft sound, he took her mouth in an urgent kiss.

A kiss full of promise.

The promise that he'd be back. That there would be more kisses. More time.

And then he was gone.

With her fingers pressed against her lips, Beth watched him climb into the Lexus's passenger seat. The Ford Expedition took off and Cosky fell in behind it. Beth stood there watching the car's taillights bleed into a single crimson eye.

Her lips still throbbed. Ached for his touch.

Her mind flashed to the dream—to his body crumpling beneath a hammering spray of bullets. To the thick, red spread of blood and the milky sheen of death filming those gleaming emerald eyes. In the nightmare, he'd died in the air.

In reality, it could take place in some crappy little house across town.

Panic rose, clogging her chest and paralyzing her. She couldn't breathe.

Mrs. Simcosky, her eyes a rich, turbulent gray, reached out to grab Beth's hand. She gave it a hard squeeze. "Try not to worry, dear." She cast one last look down the empty street and turned toward the open door behind them. "Why don't we see what Vivian has in her cupboards? The boys will be hungry when they return."

Chapter Twelve

S ON OF A BITCH," ZANE SAID BENEATH HIS BREATH AS HE lowered the binoculars they'd liberated from the gun safe.

Taking care not to disturb the drooping boughs, he sank to his knees. The cushion of pine needles matting the ground gave beneath his weight, releasing an alpine-scented perfume of such strength it smelled like someone had spritzed the place with air freshener. He aimed the binoculars through a break in the dense foliage and studied the football-field expanse of lawn stretching from the edge of the forest to the concrete path leading up to the front of the house.

The situation didn't look any better on the second scan.

With a frustrated grunt, he passed the binoculars to Cosky, who crouched beside him.

"We're good and fucked." Zane kept his voice low, barely above a whisper. Sound traveled, even within the confines of heavy vegetation.

The two pairs of military-grade binoculars they'd found amid the guns had been the last piece of good fortune they'd been blessed with before things had taken a detour into fucked up.

Apparently the good citizens of Enumclaw didn't believe in numbering their mailboxes, driveways, or even their goddamn houses. Nor had the worthless piece of shit the rental agency called a GPS system been able to direct them to the address on that slip of paper. The system had guided them toward a driveway that didn't exist. They'd wasted twenty minutes looking for a mailbox with a street number and then counted their way up from there.

"This has to be the place." Cosky aimed the binoculars toward the left edge of the house and the two cameras mounted to the trim just below the gutters.

"No shit."

The cameras and windows were a dead giveaway. Zane took the binoculars back and peered at the sheets of plywood stretched across the glass. No way in hell were they gaining access through there. Not without a crowbar and some serious muscle. He turned the binoculars toward the upper-left quadrant of the house. One of the cameras was aimed out, surveying the endless stretch of emerald lawn, while the other was angled in, toward the windows, front door, and two-car garage.

He scanned the yard again. At least two acres of flat lawn. No trees. No shrubs. No rock. No dips or swells. Which equaled no cover. Yeah, they were well and truly screwed.

Out of the blue, Zane found himself wondering where Beth lived. Did she live in a rural setting or the heart—

Christ, he needed to get his mind back on the mission. Scanning the entryway again, he forced Beth out of his mind.

No steps. No shrubs. No decorative trees.

Son of a bitch.

"At least we don't have to worry about neighbors. The last thing we need is some poor bastard out mowing his lawn taking a stray slug." Cosky didn't lift his gaze from their target.

"Or calling the police." Zane lowered the binoculars, foreboding prickling.

The house was a good three-quarters of a mile from the main road and surrounded by a thick stand of maple, pine, and fir. They couldn't ask for better cover, at least back here, but once they left the shield of the trees, they'd be completely vulnerable. The residence's position gave a tactical advantage to its inhabitants. With those cameras on the roofline and the lack of cover, the kidnappers would know the second someone launched an attack.

No doubt the house's defendable position was one of the reasons this place had been chosen. But he could think of another reason.

Nobody would hear any screaming.

His phone started vibrating against his thigh. He fished it out of his pocket and pressed it against his ear, sealing it tight, so no sound escaped.

"Yeah." The word was more breath than sound.

"We got eyes all the way around. No cover," Mac said, his voice hushed.

Zane wasn't surprised. "Copy." He snapped the cell phone closed by making a fist, shoved it in his pocket, and turned to Cosky. "Cameras ring the place and cover's no better out back."

Cosky swore beneath his breath and plucked the binoculars from Zane's lax hand. He trained the lens on the front door. "Reinforced steel."

Zane scowled at the front entrance. The door was hardly a surprise. Boarding up the windows had been a clever tactic. They'd limited access to the interior of the house. They'd hardly blow that advantage by using wood doors—three good blasts from a shotgun and you'd have a manhole. Those same blasts against reinforced steel just left a couple of impressive dents.

"We'll have to take out the frame," Zane said, his voice grimmer by the second.

Even reinforced steel had its weakness; the doors were hinged to a wood frame. The frame could be chipped away. Once the wood was destroyed, access was assured.

But it would take time, and a hell of a lot of bullets.

Zane shook his head in disgust. They could scratch any possibility of a blitz attack. With cameras recording every move they made, the kidnappers would be waiting for them long before the door fell in. Rocking back on his heels, he scrubbed both hands down his face, then got his toes beneath him and slowly rose to his feet.

"This has to be the right place," he said, the lack of numbers still bothering him.

"Probably," Cosky agreed, and then his voice turned dry. "Or whoever's inside could be batshit crazy and cooking meth in the garage."

"Hell." But Cosky was right. He could think of a dozen illegal activities requiring these kinds of security measures.

"We're fucked," Mac said tightly as he fell in behind them.

"That's the consensus," Zane agreed, his voice just as tense.

"We might as well just walk up to the door and knock." Mac raised the second pair of binoculars and scanned the area in front, then shook his head. "Same distance front or back. Rawls and I will take the back. You two take the front."

"We'll have to shoot out the frames. Kick the doors in," Zane said.

Mac swore beneath his breath and glared across the lawn. "We could blast our way through the garage door."

Zane and Cosky shook their heads in unison. "If they've stashed the hostages in there, we'll end up killing the people we came to release. Besides, we can't be certain this is the right place."

All four men turned to glare across the grass.

"Is it too fucking much to ask that people number their damn mailboxes?" Mac braced his fists on his hips. "How in the hell did the kid get the address, anyway?"

Zane had been wondering the same thing. "We need to get them to open the door," he said after a moment of silence. "Lure them out."

With a disgusted snort, Mac dropped his hands. "Yeah? How the hell we gonna do that? Tell them we're selling Girl Scout cookies?"

"Everyone shut the fuck up," Cosky suddenly snapped.

Zane turned to find him standing with his head cocked, listening. A moment later the rest of them heard it. The low, prowling growl of an engine. The crackle of tires rolling over gravel, the ping of rocks chipping away at an undercarriage.

A car was headed up the driveway.

Zane shot a quick glance at the house. If they were actually parking their vehicles inside the garage, that car could be their only chance of accessing the target without fatalities. In unison, they turned and sprinted deeper into the woods, rifles thumping against shoulders, moving as silently as possible while maintaining speed. The driveway cut through the forest in a lazy arch. There were two bends—the first less than a klick from the main road, the second just before the narrow lane broke into the open and cut a swath through the lawn.

They didn't have a shot in hell of reaching that car before the first bend, so they had to intercept it before the second one.

This time Mother Nature and the property owner's stinginess smiled on them. The driveway was a rutted, washed-out mess, impossible to navigate with any kind of speed.

They reached the straight section between bends before the vehicle finished navigating the first turn. Cosky and Rawls darted across the rutted strip of gravel and melted into a pocket of shrubs. Zane and Mac took cover in the dense underbrush opposite, shed their rifles, and crouched.

If their luck held, the car doors would be unlocked. They could hardly shoot out the tires; the report would alert everyone within a five-klick radius. Nor could they afford to render the car unusable. Stepping in front would just invite a hit and run. Their best bet was to yank open those doors and jerk the bastards out.

As the car turned the first bend, the odds shifted in their favor. Peering through a slit in the surrounding vegetation, Zane got a good look at the approaching vehicle. It was white, an older model Chrysler sedan, and the driver's window was down. A muscled forearm rested on top of the door. They could yank the asshole out the window if need be.

There were two people in the vehicle. The passenger was smaller, slighter, with dirty-blond hair. The driver was a big bastard—heavy through the shoulders, his dark hair spiky and short. A ripple of movement caught Zane's attention as the car passed beneath a break in the canopy, and a beam of light shimmered across the exposed bicep. Crimson and black ink undulated beneath the sun's rays. Some kind of tattoo.

A low, menacing growl rose from his right. From Mac.

Zane froze, his heart slamming into triple digits. It was a sound unlike anything he'd heard before. Menacing. Inhuman.

Like a rabid bear or a Rottweiler on steroids. The hair lifted along Zane's forearms and down the back of his neck.

The car rolled closer, bumping across the ruts, and the ink flashed again.

That low, guttural growl broke the stillness once more.

Jesus Christ!

What the *hell* had gotten into Mac? But he couldn't afford to check and see. The vehicle was so close; the shiver of branches on a windless day could give them away. Hell, that fucking growling could give them away. If the bastard hit the accelerator, they'd never get him out of the car.

The Chrysler rolled closer.

Ten feet.

Five feet.

Three.

Zane gathered himself, every muscle tensing, but before he took that first step, Mac leapt forward, flying through the thicket like a cannonball.

His attack was brutal and eerily silent.

———————

As the Chrysler bumped its way down that narrow, pitted lane, an image exploded in Mac's mind. A slender, pale neck. Feminine. The muscles bulging as she fought to lock the screams inside. Finger-shaped bruises mottled the white skin like some obscene choke chain.

He tried to shake the vision aside, to focus on the job, but with every flash of that fucking tattoo, the image bloomed in his mind. And it was flashing a lot as the car hit patch after patch of sun. Just as it had flashed in that video Chastain had shown him.

Violence wasn't new to him. Brutality and black ops shared the same leech-infested swamps and burning stretches of sand, but there was something about the viciousness that had taken place in that bedroom…something about her white neck and furious courage, her stubborn refusal to give them the satisfaction of her screams.

The car rolled closer, the tattoo shimmered and—

Flash.

"Scream, bitch. Scream. Tell me how much you like it and maybe I'll let those two brats live after we're through with you."

Mac shook the memory aside. Burying it within his subconscious where it coiled, waiting to strike—an oily, black serpent belching rage and repugnance.

He could sense Zane tensing beside him as the car rolled closer, but at the three-foot marker, Mac's muscles took on a life of their own and he found himself flying through the air without the memory of taking the first step. He hit the driver's door like a rocket, yanked it open, grabbed the driver by the back of the head, and slammed him face-first into the dashboard to the right of the steering wheel.

The car slowed and rolled to a stop.

"You hit that car horn and we're fucked," Zane said from behind him. "Drag him out."

Hell. He hadn't even thought about the horn. It was a miracle the driver hadn't hit it when he'd connected with the dashboard. He needed to get his head back in the game.

Grabbing a handful of muscle shirt, Mac yanked the bastard out of the car. Zane leaned in to shove the gear into park and set the emergency brake. Cosky, he saw with a quick glance across the seats, had already dragged the passenger clear.

As the driver's shoulders hit the gravel, he shook off the dashboard-induced lethargy and lunged for the .357 SIG tucked into the waistband of Mac's jeans. With furious satisfaction, Mac slammed his fist into the asshole's face.

"Scream, you bitch. Tell me how much you like it and maybe I'll let those two brats live after we're through with you." He waited long enough for recognition to stir in the bronze eyes below before lifting his arm again.

Zane caught his cocked fist in an iron grip. "Jesus, Mac. What the fuck? Stand down. We need him functional."

For one long moment Mac strained against Zane's grip, the serpent coiled inside him vibrating with the need to strike. This bastard had savored the agony he'd inflicted.

"He was on the video," Mac said. "With Chastain's wife."

When Zane let go, he eased back on his knees and yanked the SIG loose from his waistband, aiming it at the driver's head.

Zane stared down at their captive. "You said his back was to the camera. How can you tell?"

"The tat." Mac forced calmness into his voice.

Cosky crouched, taking a closer look at the tattoo. Mac didn't bother checking it out. He already knew what he'd find—a harvest moon pierced by a dagger, tears of blood dripping from where the knife ripped into the moon's flesh.

Swearing, Cosky rose to his feet. "There's letters inside the tears. It's some kind of fucking trophy."

Did the harvest moon symbolize women? Each tear representing a rape? Chastain's wife's name was Amy. Was the bastard planning on adding an *A* to his trail of tears? A *G* for Beth's friend Ginny? Mac's finger tightened on the SIG's trigger. He forced it to relax. Out of the corner of his eye he saw Zane head to the open driver's door.

"At least we know we're at the right place." Zane braced a palm against the hood and leaned inside. "There's a garage door opener clipped to the visor. We can use it to gain entry."

The driver stared hard at the unwavering hold Mac had on the weapon, then rolled onto his left shoulder and spit out a loogie thick with blood.

"You've got the wrong guy." He turned his head and shot off another wad of bloody spittle.

"That's not what your tat says," Mac growled. "Or what the DNA will say."

"We can get into the garage with this." Zane jerked his chin at Mac's captive. "Tattoo here can drive. Rawls, you're the same size and coloring as your new friend." He nodded toward the kidnapper Rawls held at gunpoint. "You should be able to pass as him long enough to get us inside the garage." He leaned into the car and popped the trunk. Gravel crunched underfoot as he walked to the rear of the car. "There's enough room back here for me and Cosky. Mac can stretch out across the backseat."

"Works for me." Mac gestured at the driver with the gun. "Get up. You've been drafted."

Tattoo studied Mac's face, and his swollen lips twisted. "I don't see any warrants."

Mac shot him a nasty grin. "Sue me."

"We should assume they have protocols in place." Cosky's icy gaze locked on Tattoo's face. "Some kind of code to alert their crew to trouble."

"No doubt." Mac thumbed off the SIG's safety, his smile showing plenty of teeth. "But our new friend's going to provide every code necessary to get us into that garage. Aren't you, motherfucker?"

The kidnapper offered another smirk. "You bet. What are friends for?"

"You think I'm blowing smoke up your ass?" Lunging forward, Mac jammed the .357 against Tattoo's left knee. "Maybe you need some convincing."

The driver's smirk shifted to a sneer. He glanced down at the gun pressed against his leg and rolled his eyes. "You think I'm a fucking idiot? The FBI's nothing more than glorified Boy Scouts. Get serious. What the fuck are you going to do if I say no? Kill me? I don't think so."

As Mac stared at the asshole across from him, he knew with absolute certainty that they couldn't trust the bastard. First chance he got, the motherfucker would bungle the code and lead them into an ambush.

They needed a different driver.

Rawls's captive had a different temperament. Controllable. Rather than superiority, there was wariness in his watery blue eyes. He'd make an excellent chauffeur. After some conditioning.

As the driver shifted his weight from one shoulder to the other, his tattoo flickered. Mac's gaze darted toward it, then back to his captive's swollen but smug face.

"You keep looking at the tat. You like? I bet you got off on that video, didn't you. I bet you liked what we did to that bitch. How we made her scream."

That damn image mushroomed in Mac's mind. A slender, arched neck. The muscles corded. Eyes locked on the ceiling. Endurance and courage.

"But she never screamed, did she? Not once," Mac said, the darkness inside him stirring again. "You couldn't take that from her."

Tattoo's bronze gaze went flat. Utterly cold. "She would have. By the time I was finished with her she'd have screamed herself hoarse."

The bastard had been on his way back for another round. The serpent coiled tighter and tighter around Mac's chest, squeezing the breath from him. Without conscious thought, the SIG migrated north.

"Give it up," Tattoo sneered, glancing down as the gun moved. "You can't do a fucking thing. You sure as hell aren't gonna kill me."

Flash.

The driving punishment of male hips hammering between spread thighs. Bloody tears dripping down a harvest moon.

All those tears. Over a dozen of them. Each tear an initial. A name.

"You're right," Mac agreed with eerie calm. "I'm not going to kill you."

He smiled and watched sudden wariness flare in the eyes across from him.

In a smooth, unhesitating move, he jammed the .357 against the driver's crotch. As panic flooded the guy's face and the tattooed arm lunged forward, making a sudden grab for the gun, Mac plunged forward, slapping his palm over the guy's mouth. The force of his grip slammed the driver's head down to the gravel.

The guy's legs scissored. Both hands clamped onto the gun in a desperate attempt to force it away. Mac climbed onto the bastard's knees, pinning him to the ground.

As he settled onto the kidnapper's legs, the tattoo bulged along with the guy's bicep, and with each flash of ink, the rage burned hotter, darker.

"I'm not FBI. Nor was I a Boy Scout." He angled the SIG's barrel for maximum damage and held it in place by sheer force of will as straining, panicked hands tried to force the weapon aside. "And no, I'm not going to kill you. I want you to remember this every fucking minute you have left."

He pulled the trigger.

The gunshot was muffled by the flesh beneath, but still loud enough to echo amid the trees.

The two hands clamped around the SIG went lax. The body beneath him convulsed and screams pounded against his palm.

A throbbing silence fell as the report faded.

"Jesus fucking Christ!" Cosky's harsh voice splintered the silence. "You want to go Lorena Bobbitt on him, use your goddamn knife. At least you wouldn't give our position away."

Mac leaned into his palm, forcing the screams back down the bastard's throat. "Who's screaming now, you motherfucker? Although we can't call you that anymore, can we?"

"The report was muted," Zane said, his voice as calm as ever. "It's over a klick to the house, through the trees. The windows are boarded. It's unlikely they heard anything."

"We can't be sure of that," Cosky snarled.

"No. But it's done. We'll deal." Gravel crunched as Zane stepped closer, and Mac could feel him staring down. "He won't be adding any more tears to that tat." There was satisfaction in the even tone.

Mac shook his head, a sudden wave of dizziness rolling over him. The condensation from the driver's breath was slicking his skin, breaking the seal between flesh, and some of the screams were leaking out, although they were too weak to carry much range. He adjusted his grip and the guttural cries dried up.

Shifting his weight, he glanced up. Their second captive was trying to drag Rawls across the hood of the car. Although Rawls had the passenger's arm in an iron grip, he wasn't paying attention to the kidnapper's frantic bid to escape. Those sunny blue eyes were darker than Mac had ever seen and locked in disbelief on Tattoo's bloody crotch.

"Rawls, bring your guy over," Mac said.

Their second captive let out a low, plaintive moan. But Rawls didn't budge, nor did his gaze lift from the blood spreading across Tattoo's hips and down his thighs.

"Rawls," Mac tried again, but it was Cosky who stepped over and grabbed the passenger by his elbow, dragging him forward. As their captive's plaintive moans grew more urgent, Mac's patience snapped. "Shut the fuck up, or you'll be joining your buddy in eunuch land."

The moans snapped off in midwail.

"You're taking the driver's seat." Mac stared directly into their captive's horrified eyes. "You're going to get us into that house. So let's try this again. Are there any protocols in place?"

The passenger nodded. "We call. Just before we get to the house, we're supposed to call. They open the garage door for us."

Gravel crunched as Zane walked back to the open car door and leaned in to flip down the visor. "You don't use the opener?"

Their captive's gaze flitted to the gun Mac still held against Tattoo's mangled crotch. "No, they open the doors from inside."

"What would happen if someone used it?" Cosky asked.

The passenger's eyes flickered toward Cosky only to compulsively shift back to the .357 SIG. "They'd know something was wrong. They'd split into two groups. One would kill the hostages. The second would set up in the garage, waiting for us."

So they'd arrive to a massacre. "It's a damn good thing you're not going to touch that opener," Mac said. "How many are waiting in the house?"

"Six."

"So you two would have made eight," Zane said with a quick shake of his head. "I'll be damned, that kid *was* giving us a head count." He turned his attention back to their new driver. "Have you called in yet?"

Their captive shook his head. "We were just about to, but—" He broke off and glanced at his buddy on the ground.

"Get him into the driver's seat," Mac ordered, and for the first time took a good hard look at the bloody mess below him.

Another wave of dizziness swept over him. He shook it off. "I need something to stuff in this bastard's mouth. And the duct tape. Somebody find our bucket."

They'd left the bottle bombs at the edge of the forest before they'd embarked on their wild flight toward the car. While Zane tore a swatch of cloth from the bottom of his shirt and Rawls guarded their new driver, Cosky melted back into the forest in search of their Molotov cocktails. By the time Cosky returned, Tattoo had stopped struggling.

Cosky handed the tape to Zane and stowed the bucket in the backseat. Mac stuffed the SIG back in his waistband and accepted the hunk of cloth his lieutenant commander passed to him. It took seconds to gag and bind this captive. The tattoo, smeared by blood and dirt, didn't flash once.

"Let's get him into the bushes," Zane said.

For the first time since that car had started bouncing toward them, Mac turned to meet his best friend's gaze. He wasn't sure what he'd expected to find in Zane's eyes—maybe concern that his OIC had turned into a fucking schizoid.

Instead, Zane watched him with calm understanding.

Oddly relieved, Mac lifted Tattoo onto his shoulders and carried him into the forest, dumping him behind a thick tangle of bushes. The limp body didn't stir as it hit the ground.

By the time he pushed through the shrubs and emerged back onto the driveway, someone had kicked a mountain of dirt over the pool of blood.

"Zane, take the passenger seat." Mac joined his team beside the open driver's door. "You've got the same length and color of hair—at least you will, after you've messed it up some. With the driver blocking the camera you should be able to fool them into thinking you're Tattoo long enough to get inside."

Cosky turned to Zane and his face went tight. A pulse of silence fell. "Fuck, get it over with. Might as well test those fucking visions of yours now. There may not be another chance."

Zane, green eyes splinter-sharp, reached for Rawls's arm. Nothing touched the calm stillness of his face, so he must not have been hit by one of those freaky visions. He let go, turned toward Mac, and lifted a dark eyebrow. After a grudging hesitation, Mac stepped forward, bracing for his buddy's touch. Hell, all these years later, and he still couldn't get used to this damn ritual. Knowing your own death, even if it could be averted, just felt… wrong.

But apparently his death wasn't on the roster today. Zane moved on to Cosky.

This time when his hand landed, every muscle in his body convulsed. He froze. His face rigid, eyes blank.

"Son of a bitch." Cosky raised disgusted eyes to the bright blue sky and jerked his arm free. "This day just keeps fucking with me."

Mac waited until awareness flooded the green eyes across from him. "What did you see?"

With an abbreviated nod toward Cosky, Zane dragged in a raw breath. "Blood, lots of it. Orange shag carpet."

"Damn it." If he benched Cosky, it put everyone at risk. They were already outmanned and outgunned. They couldn't afford to lose another operator. He turned his attention to his disgusted lieutenant, "You're on our six. For Christ's sake, look sharp."

Cosky snorted his opinion of that order.

Zane held the gun on their captive while Mac and Cosky levered themselves up and climbed inside the trunk. It was a tight fit, but Rawls managed to close the lid.

"Showtime," Mac said as darkness descended.

Chapter Thirteen

W HAT'S YOUR NAME?" ZANE EASED THE GLOCK BACK A FRACTION. He shot a quick glance over his shoulder. Rawls lay flush with the floor mats, hidden from view. So far, so good.

"Little Mike." Their captive simply sat there, face ashen, hands tight around the steering wheel. "Chino's cell's in the cup holder." With a nervous tic of his eyelid, he slid a wary glance toward the passenger seat.

Zane checked the console between the bucket seats. Sure enough, a flip phone was tucked inside the plastic cup holder.

"Pick it up. Who's Chino?"

Their captive loosened one rigid hand from the steering wheel and reached for the cell. "Chino's the guy your buddy...ah—" His breath turned choppy and whistled through the gap between his front teeth. "Tattoo."

Yeah, no need to go there. Judging by the trembling fingers and tight face, their new pal was teetering on the brink of a melt-down. It wouldn't hurt to do some soothing.

"You do what you're told, you've got nothing to worry about. Make the call."

"They won't be expecting me to call. Chino does the driving and talking."

This kind of info was exactly why this guy had been the right choice. Sure as hell Chino wouldn't have volunteered that little secret.

"Is Chino a drinker?" Little Mike's nod didn't surprise him. Tattoo had the look of a man who spent a good chunk of his life in the neighborhood bars, with periodic trips home to beat the shit out of the wife and kids. "If your buddies ask"—and they probably would—"tell them Chino knocked too many back at the bar and he's passed out beside you. Sell it. Because I guarantee you won't like the results if you don't."

Their hostage nodded and swallowed so hard his Adam's apple bobbed, but his hand was steady as he highlighted a phone number and punched the call button.

"Hey," he said into the phone, his voice strained but level. "You want to let us in?" He tilted his head and listened, his sandy brows knitting. "Yeah. That's not gonna happen. Chino went on a bender. I tried to stop him…but, well…you know Chino." He paused, shook his head. "Nah, he passed out before anything slipped. The bartender helped drag him to the car." His voice rose a pitch. "Hey, when you report this, make sure the boss knows this wasn't on me—okay? Thanks, man." His tone leveled out again. "We'll be there in a minute." He snapped the cell closed.

"Hand it over." Zane took the phone and tossed it into the backseat. "Now drive."

With a quick twist of the key, the Chrysler's engine roared to life.

"There must be a door from the garage into the house?" Zane raised his voice to compete with the sedan's rumbling engine. "Where's it lead?"

"Into the laundry room. From there into the kitchen." The car started to roll down the rutted lane.

Shit. Most laundry rooms were small and narrow, full of bulky machines and lots of cupboards, which left little space for cover. Maybe they could access the house through one of the exterior doors. "You got guards on all the doors?"

Their captive nodded.

Son of a bitch. "Who watches the camera feeds?"

"Each camera feeds into a separate laptop and is monitored by the guard assigned to that door."

So they'd be spotted the moment they approached, which meant the front and back entrances were still out. "Give me a layout of the place. Where are the rooms in relationship to each other? How many guards on each door?"

The hostage slowed for a huge, deep rut running the width of the gravel drive. The sedan rattled over a dozen smaller furrows before hitting the big one, and Zane gritted his teeth as the Chrysler rocked violently. No wonder the car had been going so slow. The piece of shit had no shocks, which meant each roll of its worn tires was an exercise in isometrics.

"Living room and bedrooms to the left. Kitchen and dining room to the right. A hallway separates the two sections. The front access through the living room, back through the dining room. One man per entrance."

"You got someone on the garage?"

"Yeah, Joey." The car picked up speed as it came out of the grand canyon of ruts.

So they'd have eyes and ears the moment they hit the garage.

"You're going to get Joey over to the car." Zane shoved the SIG hard enough against Little Mike's side to leave a circular imprint on the guy's kidney. "Tell him you need help getting Chino into the house." He pitched his voice louder. "Rawls, I'll have to curl into the passenger door. Tattoo and I are close enough in size and coloring to fool them from the back. But if they get a look at my face—we're fucked. You'll need to cover our new friend."

"Copy." Rawls's cool voice floated up behind them.

Zane turned his attention to their chauffeur's tense face. "My boy back there has a Smith and Wesson .500. You ever looked down the barrel of one of those babies? It's like staring into a cannon. Leaves a crater the size of a pizza box. He's got that sucker pressed against the back of your seat, and while traveling through all that foam and fabric might slow it down some, that bullet's still gonna disintegrate a good chunk of your spine and turn your guts into soup." He twisted the gun against Little Mike's ribs. "You copy me?"

Their captive gave a jerky nod.

Turning to the passenger window, Zane rolled it down and angled the side mirror until he had a lock on the driver's face. Then he hunkered down, curling his shoulders toward the door, but elevating his chin so he could keep an eye on the mirror.

The sedan turned the corner and broke into the open. Sunlight splintered the lacy shadows of the canopy overhead.

Christ, he hated going in blind. If their captive decided to grow a set of balls, he'd do so now, while Zane's back was turned. But the cameras needed to record what their chauffeur had described.

"You said there were eight of you." Seven now with Chino out of the picture. "Three guarding the doors. Where are the other men stationed?" Out of the corner of his eye, he caught flashes of movement as the forest spiraled past in an endless ribbon of green.

"We rotate, six on, two off. Me and Chino were headed back to cover our shift."

Zane clenched his teeth against the urge to turn and make sure a firing squad hadn't lined up to serenade their arrival.

"There's a guard on each family. Sixth man's a floater." The car sped up as the ruts smoothed out.

Standing orders were likely to kill the families the minute trouble reared. They'd be hard-pressed to reach the civilians before their guards started firing. "Where are the families?"

"They keep to the bedrooms."

He swallowed a groan. The civilians were on the opposite end of the house, with an army of armed guards between them and the insertion point. Great.

The driver suddenly slowed and honked.

Zane went rigid. "What the fuck was *that?*"

"We always honk." Little Mike's voice climbed. "To let them know we're here."

"Which you didn't mention," Zane snapped. "Which is the kind of thing that gets a man killed."

"I forgot!" His tone skated the edge of the ozone layer, high and thin.

Zane regulated his breathing and forced himself to relax. A grating rumble sounded as the garage door rolled up. When the sound ceased, the car eased forward again.

"Hey, Joey," their driver called as the car rolled to a stop. "You wanna help me get Chino into the house?"

"We should just leave…" The rumbling of the garage door as it came down drowned out the voice.

Their chauffeur waited until the door touched down. Dusk descended as the last patch of sunlight fractured and dissipated.

"Yeah, well. You want to be the one to explain to him why we made him sleep it off in the car?"

"Serves him right," a clipped voice said, each word gaining strength and clarity as the target neared the car. "Drinking on a job? What was he thinking? He'll be lucky to have his balls when the boss hears about this."

Little Mike made a choking sound. Zane tightened his grip on the Glock.

Footsteps rounded the hood of the car.

"Hey, what the—" The exclamation came directly above the passenger door. Zane shot his arm through the open window, grabbed the target by his scruffy T-shirt, and jerked him forward, slamming him face-first into the doorframe. An ugly crack sounded. Blood spritzed the air. And then Zane was out of the sedan, weapon pressed to the bastard's throat.

"Not one word," Zane whispered as he scanned the interior of the garage. No cameras. He shot a quick glance toward the laundry room door.

Closed.

Their newest draftee must have shut it behind him. How considerate of him.

Rawls had the driver out and down on the floor. Zane grabbed the duct tape as Mac and Cosky joined him. It took seconds to bind ankles, wrists, and mouths. After collecting a 9mm off their second captive, they dragged the pair behind an upright freezer.

Three down, five to go.

After a few moments of whispered strategy, they were ready to deploy. As they passed the sedan, they each grabbed a bottle rocket, stuck it beneath their armpit, and positioned themselves on either side of the entrance leading into the house.

Mac, his shoulders flush with the wall, turned the knob. A sliver of space opened between door and frame. Mac stretched forward, took a look, then pulled back and swung the door toward Rawls, who caught it and eased it back against the Sheetrock paneling.

The next time Mac leaned forward, he kept going. Hunched over, his weapon extended, he disappeared into the laundry room. Zane swung in behind him. The space was narrow: a washer and dryer to the left, a wall to the right. Floor-to-ceiling cupboards sandwiching the machines. No door ahead. Just an open, airy archway.

No cover anywhere.

They glided up the hall, feet silent on yellowing linoleum. Directly across from them sat a horseshoe-shaped kitchen. A sink, stove, and refrigerator were positioned against the back, with counters curving to the right and left.

"Start dinner," a harsh male voice said from somewhere to the right. "You've been screwing around long enough."

Mac and Zane froze.

"What would you like?" a voice asked. Female. Calm. Controlled.

"Something high in energy. You girls are going to be busy tonight, wouldn't want you to fall asleep on us." His tone shifted from taunting to loud and irritated. "Hey, Joey. What the fuck's keeping you?"

"You want me to go look?" a gravelly voice asked from the left of the door.

"Yeah. Go."

Shit.

Spinning around, Mac hard on his heels, Zane warped back down the hall. Cosky and Rawls had already disappeared into the garage. Zane and Mac followed suit, taking position to the left of the door.

Heavy footsteps drew closer. Cosky passed his Molotov cocktail to Rawls, who knelt and set it against the wall. As Cosky tensed, Mac shifted into position opposite him.

"Joey?" A bulky shadow filled the doorframe. Light spilled down from a bare bulb, flickering off wheat-blond hair.

Suddenly the guy's head swung in Mac's direction. Cosky sprang. Before the target had a chance to shout a warning, an arm coiled around his bullish neck, crushing the carotid artery. Cosky clamped his left hand over the bastard's mouth and dragged the struggling target into the garage.

Muffled shouts were crushed beneath Simcosky's punishing grip. The tango twisted, his boots scraping concrete. Mac slid over to the open door and took a quick look only to freeze for a split second before jerking out of sight.

Son of a bitch. Someone must be in the laundry room.

Zane waited for the alarm to sound. Instead, there was a metallic pop, and light footsteps padded away. A flapping sound echoed down the hall.

What the hell?

The kidnapper's struggles weakened.

Zane caught Mac's gaze, jerked his chin toward the open door, and arched his eyebrows. Mac signed the letters for *FBI* and *wife*. Amy Chastain then. So she knew they were in the house. As ex-FBI, she'd be invaluable on the inside.

The target slumped, his body limp. Cosky continued the compression hold until the barrel chest stuttered and stilled, then dragged him behind the freezer, dumping him against the wall.

They didn't bother binding or gagging this one; he wouldn't be getting back up.

Zane rubbed his tight chest and forced himself to take a couple of deep breaths. Tension flickered through his bloodstream, lit a bonfire in his gut.

They'd neutralized four. The odds had shifted in their favor, but the memory of Cosky's dead face kept flashing through his mind.

At least the chairs in the interview room at Seattle's Field Office were more comfortable than the chairs at the airport. Russ settled into the roomy, well-upholstered rolling chair and studied the drawn face opposite.

John Chastain.

His ace in the hole. Even if the bastard hadn't returned one of Russ's phone calls this morning.

He looked like hell. Deep grooves sectioned his face, his auburn hair hung limp, and thick wrist bones punched up against his sallow skin. He looked like a skeleton in an expensive suit.

No doubt the video had etched some of those furrows in the man's face. Had he figured out yet he wouldn't be getting his family back? At least not alive? Had that knowledge carved the rest of those deep, raw trenches?

It was too bad about the boys. He hated killing kids, but they could identify his men. He couldn't afford to lose his crew this early in the game, which meant none of the hostages could survive. Including the kids.

He'd do them quick, though. Take care of it personally. Make sure they didn't feel a thing. Hell, he'd even take them someplace special beforehand—maybe to Chuck E. Cheese's. Jilly's kids loved that damn place.

"Did Miss Brown's attacker say anything before you hit him?" Chastain glanced up from the file folder and studied Russ's face. "Give any indication why he attacked her?"

Russ shook his head. Since the situation called for concern, he allowed a frown to form. "He was going to break her neck. Hey, I'm not in any trouble, am I? Do I need a lawyer or something?"

Chastain cocked his head and stared back. "Why would you need a lawyer?"

"Well, I did kill someone. I didn't mean to, but I did."

"We're still assessing the situation. However, eyewitness accounts support your statement. It's doubtful charges will be filed."

"Good. That's good." Russ gusted out a relieved breath, even though the response was nothing less than he'd expected. "Hey, when do I get my laptop back?"

"We'll need to hold onto it. As evidence. I'm sure you understand."

Russ didn't give a rat's ass what happened to the laptop. He'd wiped the hard drive. He'd be long gone before they managed to salvage anything.

However, an insurance adjustor whose entire professional life was in that hard drive would have a different reaction. "I don't think *you* understand!" Russ raised his voice. "I need that laptop. It has all my client files. All of my pending cases. My schedule for the conference."

A frown pulled at Chastain's eyebrows. "You don't have your files backed up?"

Russ threw up his hands. "Well, sure, but not on me!"

"You need these files for your conference?" After a quick glance at his wristwatch, Chastain ran a tense hand over his limp hair.

"Not the files, but the conference schedule."

"You can pick up another schedule on-site." Chastain dropped his head to scan the neatly printed notes. "You're headed to Minneapolis, is that correct?"

"Yes. To the National Insurance Adjustors convention."

"What hotel are you booked at?"

Russ thought the question was filler until Chastain looked up. Beneath bloodshot lids, his brown eyes were sharp and searching.

"At the Marriott. It's the host hotel." He held that demanding gaze, surprised to find his agent in charge hadn't checked out of the game after all. "I'm reserved through Sunday."

If Chastain bothered to look, he'd find a Russ Branson registered at the conference and reserved at the Marriott. If he opted to dig deeper, he'd find a handful of credit cards, a valid Social Security card, and a driver's license that expired on his next birthday—which was coming up fast.

Or at least the real Russ Branson was about to hit the big four-zero. Not that he'd be doing much celebrating, being dead and all.

"You met Beth Brown earlier yesterday morning, before the incident, is that correct?" Chastain suddenly asked.

Russ eyed him curiously. Where was he going with this line of questioning? No sense in lying about it. The lady herself would have told them he'd approached her earlier. "Yes, at the gate area."

"What brought her to your attention?"

TRISH McCALLAN

With a shrug, Russ stroked his chin. "I felt sorry for her, I suppose. She looked scared. Shaken. She's an attractive woman." He offered an embarrassed, can't-really-blame-me-for-trying grin.

His gaze sharpened as Chastain's attention drifted back to his wrist. This made the second time he'd checked his watch since he'd sat down at the table. "How is she?"

The real question was where the hell was she? Beth Brown, along with her SEAL contingent, had inconveniently vanished. Although he could guess where she was, along with the rest of those bastards. They'd been held over for questioning and only one of the three SEALs had family in the area. No doubt they were camped out there. In familiar territory. On high alert.

He had no intention of tipping his hand by sending a man to keep an eye on them. They'd spot a shadow. Besides, eventually they would have to show up at the Seattle Field Office. At some point she'd be separated from her escort. He'd make sure of it.

Chastain picked the folder up, tapped the corner against the surface of the desk, and pushed back his chair. "She's fine," he said once he gained his feet.

Russ forced a smile. "Glad to hear it."

"If you think of anything else, please give me a call." Chastain reached into his jacket pocket, pulled out a business card, and dropped it on the table.

"Sure. Anything to help."

Chastain offered another of those bland, annoying smiles. "We appreciate your cooperation, but you're free to leave. Pac-Atlantic will arrange a seat for you on the next flight to the Twin Cities. If further questions arise, we'll contact you."

And just like that the bastard ripped away Russ's excuse for sticking around.

Russ's cell phone started vibrating as he walked across the FBI's parking lot to his rental car. *Unknown caller* flashed across the screen. One of his crew. He summoned a casual expression and kept walking. "Hey. What's up?"

Tyler Carey, one of the men assigned to guard duty, cut loose with an urgent stream of updates. Russ's hand tightened so violently around the phone, his fingers cramped. *Goddamn it.* He knew where those fucking SEALs were now. They were trying to free his hostages. But how the fuck—*how the goddamn fuck*—had they found them?

He flashed back to Chastain. To those quick glances at his watch.

The fucking asshole. He was behind this. He must have provided the location.

But how—

Russ froze for a moment and then forced himself to keep moving. The video. There must have been something on the video, something Chino had missed. A clue. One leading to the location of the safe house.

Tyler's voice rose as he described finding Chino bound, gagged, and covered in blood. Russ allowed himself one moment of vicious satisfaction. If Chino had been standing in front of him, he'd have castrated the fuckup himself.

With a tight breath, he shoved the rage back. Forced himself to think. To do what he did best. Evaluate. React. Strategize. He couldn't afford to lose Chastain's family. If he lost the hostages, he lost his leverage over the FBI. If he lost control of the FBI, he lost access to those first-class passengers. If he lost those passengers, he lost his life. Jilly and the kids could very well lose theirs too.

As Tyler stuttered out urgent questions about doctors and hospitals and Chino, Russ ran prognosis simulations. One thing became urgently clear.

He could not lose those hostages.

The men funding this operation did not accept excuses...or failure.

"No." He forced calm into his voice. "Head over to the house and help with the remodeling. It's essential that we retain as much of the furnishings as possible. Remind our work crew of that."

Russ ended the call on another round of questions concerning Chino. The fuckup's dick could rot for all he cared. It served the bastard right.

He dialed Jilly's home number as he reached his rental car. There was a stash of cash in the safe at his apartment. His sister knew the combination. It would give her and the kids the means to vanish. At least until this damn thing was over and they weren't caught in the crosshairs of this fucking disaster.

Her voice mail picked up.

Swearing, he punched in a second number and started talking the moment the call was picked up. "You still have a line on the woman? What house? Are you sure she's in there? Fine, check it out. If she's there grab her. Meet me at M67 when you're done."

He hung up without waiting for a response. If those bastards defeated his crew and released his hostages, he had one last shot of getting them back before he lost control of the FBI.

It paid to know your enemies. It had been simple enough to get a line on Marion Simcosky. His man had tailed her until an opportunity presented itself, then knocked her purse to the ground and dropped the tracker in while helping the woman pick up the contents. It was one of the oldest tricks in the world— because it worked.

As long as she had her purse, they knew where she was, and they could grab her. If Simcosky wanted to see his dear old mom again, he'd betray his teammates and turn over Chastain's family. By the time the bastard realized his mother had already paid the price for SEAL interference, it would be too late. The hostages would be back under his thumb. And Marion Simcosky would be dead.

The snap of wet fabric echoed down the laundry room.

Mac peered around the edge of the doorjamb. Amy Chastain had planted herself just past the open archway, in the middle of the hallway between the laundry room and the kitchen. She shook a child-sized T-shirt, and another damp snap sounded.

The living room with its guards would be down the hall to her left. The dining room, with its guard, to her right.

There were no cupboards above the east kitchen counter, which allowed whoever was cooking to interact with guests in the dining room. An open floor plan, which meant the kitchen would be visible from the dining room.

Mac swore beneath his breath. The laundry room walls would provide some cover, but that open archway limited their options. Only one man could take position at a time. The entryway was too narrow and visible to support a second man.

A second female joined Chastain's wife in the hall. Both were redheads, but the shade and cut varied. Amy Chastain was shorter in height, with hair more strawberry than auburn and cut no-nonsense short. Ginny Clancy—who towered above her siege-mate—was willow thin, with long auburn hair.

Great. As of now, the success of this operation revolved around two traumatized women keeping their mouths shut.

"Joey? What the hell you doing back there, boy?" a voice said from somewhere to the right.

"He can't hear you." Amy glanced in the direction of the voice. "Neither of them can. They're in the garage with your buddy. It looks like they could use your help."

Surprised, Mac scrubbed a hand down his face. Her response had been damn close to clever. If the asshole took her advice and headed back, it would give them a chance to grab him. If he remained at his post, he'd likely relax. She had, after all, just encouraged him to check out the garage. Nor was she attempting to escape.

"You'd like that, wouldn't you?" the guard asked, and sure enough the tension had drained from his voice. "Bet you're hoping you can get this door open and escape the party we have planned for you tonight." His voice hardened, sharpened to a jeer. "Start dinner. We want your brats in bed early."

Mac stiffened, waiting for the feminine meltdown. The tall, slender female flinched, which sparked an ugly laugh from the guard. Mac's fingers tightened around his weapon. Christ, he'd love to plug that bastard's mouth.

To his surprise, other than the flinch, the women ignored the taunt. Which would have been admirable—if they'd fucking move. They stood directly in the line of fire.

"If you want to start dinner, I'll finish the laundry," Amy told Ginny.

Unfuckingbelievable. They were turning all domestic.

"What should I make?" Ginny asked with a tremor in her voice.

"Something with lots of protein," the target in the dining room drawled. "For stamina."

Amy Chastain turned to the taller woman and squeezed her arm, then stretched up on her toes to whisper in her ear. Ginny's eyes widened. She turned her head, glancing toward the laundry room, eyes widening even farther as she caught sight of Mac. When Amy's hand clamped down hard on her arm, the woman wrenched her gaze away.

"What the fuck are you two whispering about?" the guard snapped.

Amy glanced toward the dining room. "Just girl talk."

She turned back to Ginny. "Why don't you check the fridge, see what we have. I'll help as soon as I've finished folding the boys' clothes."

With that, she headed for the laundry room. Mac stepped out from behind the doorjamb to meet her.

Once she was hidden from view, her pace picked up. She dumped the T-shirt on top of the dryer and punched the button to start the machine. The rhythmic rumble of tumbling clothes filled the air. The sound would mask any talking, and the excuse of folding laundry had bought her some time.

Maybe not such a nitwit after all.

He crossed his arms, rocked back on his heels, and watched her approach, his gaze lingering on the bruise shadowing one cheekbone and her raw, swollen lips. Something tightened inside him. Shook with rage. He battened it down.

She halted maybe a foot from him, pointed at the gun in his hand, and wiggled her fingers.

"Where are the kids?" He kept his voice low, ignoring her silent demand.

"Locked in the bedroom." Her gaze didn't budge from his .357 SIG. "I need a gun."

"What kind of weapons are the guards carrying?" Little Mike had told them the guards were all equipped with submachine guns. Joey, unfortunately, had been carrying a 9mm. They sure could have used one of those MP5s.

"Submachines," she said in a flat voice. "Now give me the damn gun."

"Oh, for Christ's sake. Give it to her," Cosky whispered from behind.

That bright head of hers snapped up. Mac wasn't sure what he'd find in her eyes. Maybe shame. She had to know they'd found her through the video. Maybe rage; a burning need for revenge. And while she had every right to blow that motherfucker straight to hell, if he handed the gun over and she used it on the target in the dining room, they'd lose any chance they had of getting those kids out alive.

But when her hazel eyes locked on his, he found calmness. Resolve. Cool intelligence.

She stepped closer, so close her body heat registered against the bare skin of his arms. The hair at the back of his neck lifted. His scalp tingled. Something stirred inside him. A loosening. A thick, raw prickle.

Shaken, Mac jerked back and stomped on Cosky's foot.

A curse echoed behind him.

"The boys aren't allowed out of the bedrooms, which are on the opposite end of the house," she told them in a low voice. "There's a hall between us and them. Guards at the end of the hall. Guards on the bedrooms. The moment you move, they'll kill the kids. You won't have time to stop them, but I can get into that bedroom. With the gun, I can protect them. It's the only shot we have of getting them out alive."

Mac scowled down at his weapon.

"You give me a gun and three minutes and I'll get the kids into a defendable position. You did bring a backup weapon?" she asked dryly, one ember-red eyebrow arching.

He searched her eyes. Calm focus filled her gaze. Intelligence.

She was right. The best shot they had of getting everyone out alive was by planting someone in the bedroom to protect those kids. She'd been FBI before her marriage. She knew how to handle a weapon, knew when to turn off emotion and focus on the situation. She'd also be able to enter the room, no questions asked.

With a quick motion, he thumbed on the safety, reversed the gun, and handed it to her butt first.

She accepted the SIG without a word, lifted the hem of her navy-blue turtleneck, and shoved the weapon into the waistband of her jeans. He caught a glimpse of luminescent skin marred by ugly bruises.

That goddamn video flashed through his mind, her eyes locked on the white ceiling. The fixed set to her face.

"You've got a guard to your right, in the dining room," she whispered, adjusting her shirt until the soft fall of cotton hid the slight bulge against her waist.

The neck of her turtleneck dipped and a row of dark smudges caught Mac's eye. Fingerprints. A fucking choke chain of finger-prints. Fury ignited in his gut, rolled out in waves. He'd see every last one of them dead.

She caught and held his gaze. "You've got one guy in the wind, though. He left an hour ago to hit the store. Should be back any minute."

The news cleared Mac's mind like a splash of cold water. "How will he access the house?"

"He'll call Joey."

Mac swore silently. Joey wouldn't be answering.

"Give me three minutes to get the kids covered." Beneath the whisper, her voice remained cool. Collected.

Admiration tugged. He scrubbed a hand down his face and watched her pivot. She headed back down the laundry room with a no-nonsense stride.

"You might want to arm yourself and move into position," Cosky hissed behind him. "Or better yet, trade places with me."

Fuck. He yanked his backup piece out of his waistband, clicked off the safety, and moved up, taking position next to the entrance to the hallway.

Amy joined Ginny in front of the sink. He waited for the women to offer some excuse that would get them out of the kitchen and into the boys' bedroom. Instead, Amy glanced at the food sitting on the kitchen counter and turned toward the refrigerator. "You forgot the ketchup. Brendan won't eat anything unless it's drenched in ketchup."

"Maybe if you stopped spoiling the little brat, he'd eat what he was told," their guard said, the edge back in his voice.

Mac frowned as she opened the refrigerator. What the hell was the woman up to?

Once the door blocked the guard's view, she lifted her shirt and yanked out the SIG.

Ah, hell. Fuck no.

"Hey," she said to Ginny. "Can you come grab this for me?"

Ginny hesitated and then stepped forward, joining her house-mate behind the cover of the refrigerator's door. Chastain's wife yanked up the woman's sweater and shoved the gun into the waistband of her slacks.

"Son of a bitch," Cosky whispered. The words sounded like they'd been forced through his teeth. "What the *fuck* does she think she's doing?"

Mac shook his head. *What* she was doing was pretty obvious. *Why* was the question.

You didn't arm civilians and send them into battle. He'd passed the gun to Chastain's wife because she had the training and expertise.

Of course, he'd based that decision on the assumption that she wasn't batshit crazy. Ginny slowly bent and listened as Amy whispered in her ear. The two straightened. In unison, they backed out of the refrigerator.

"Why don't you get the boys ready for dinner? I'll finish up here," Amy said, her voice the epitome of casual.

"Sure." Ginny placed the ketchup on the counter and smoothed a strand of sleek red hair behind her ear. Mac watched those slender fingers quake, and shook his head in disgust.

"Make sure Brendan washes his hands." Amy closed the fridge door and slid over to the sink.

"You better not make grilled cheese again," the voice in the dining room said. "I don't give a shit if it is the only thing those spoiled brats of yours will eat. Make some adult food for a change."

Clancy's wife passed so close on her way down the hall, Mac could have snagged her elbow and dragged her to safety. At least they'd have one of the damn fools safe. But they'd lose the kids.

She hurried past, glancing at him out of the corner of her eye. A minute ticked by. Amy fussed with various jars. Unscrewed lids. Picked up a butter knife. Another minute ticked by.

"Where the fuck's Joey? And Gustav?" The guard suddenly snapped, tension sharpening his voice. "It shouldn't take this long to get Chino out of the car."

Amy put down the knife and turned. "I can check if you want."

"You stay put."

Shrugging, she bent and pulled open the bottom cupboard.

"What the fuck are you doing?" the guy snapped.

When she straightened, her right hand grasped a cast-iron skillet. She arched a slender eyebrow.

"Cooking dinner," she said in a nonconfrontational tone, "like you told me to."

"Go back to the bedroom. You can finish dinner after I've checked the garage."

A hiss of static echoed down the hall and then the guard was speaking again, his voice flat. Professional. "I'm sending the second bitch back. I need to check the garage. Gustav and Joey have been gone too long. Copy?"

Another burst of static, followed by a distant, metallic voice. "Copy."

They were officially out of time. If they launched an attack, they'd face immediate fatalities. The target was suspicious, his eyes likely fixed on the laundry room. To line up a shot, they'd have to expose themselves long enough to sight on the target. An MP5 held dozens of rounds. They'd be riddled with bullets in seconds.

There wasn't room for Cosky to slide up beside him and provide cover. Amy Chastain no longer had a gun. They could toss one to her, but the bastard would see it. Nor would she be able to get her head above the counter to line up a shot.

Fuck. If they moved now, they'd be dead the moment they left the protection of the laundry room wall. They needed a distraction. He looked down at the bottle tucked beneath his armpit. Throwing the Molotov cocktail would prove useless since he couldn't sight on the target.

He glanced at Chastain's wife, waiting for her to follow the guard's order and split for the bedroom. This time he'd snag her as she passed.

Instead of leaving, she grabbed hold of the skillet with her left hand, wrapping her fingers around the handle just above the grip her right hand held. Instantly Mac knew what she had in mind. He flowed in sync with her movements, so even as she rocked back and then forward and sailed that skillet across the room like a fucking Frisbee, he rolled up, exposing just enough of his face to line up his shot.

"What the—" The guard's attention was completely focused on the skillet. He jumped to the side, just before the cast-iron pan slammed into the wall inches from his face.

"You fucking—"

Mac locked onto the target's sternum and squeezed off two quick shots.

At the last possible millisecond, the guard spun and dropped to one knee. The rounds plunged into the wall above his head with a hollow *thwack-thwack*.

Son of a fucking bitch.

Amy Chastain shot him one disgusted, disbelieving look and dropped to the ground.

Before he could line up a second shot, the bastard sprayed the surrounding area—from the kitchen to the laundry room—with a burst of submachine fire. Mac ducked out of sight.

"Jesus Christ," Cosky roared from behind him. "You fucking missed?"

Mac glanced to the left, in the general direction of the living room. There went their stealthy infiltration. Those bastards guarding the kids would be on the move now.

He hoped to God that Amy knew what she'd been doing when she'd passed the SIG off. Because, sure as hell, Ginny was going to need it.

Chapter Fourteen

YOU'RE GOING TO LOVE THIS," MRS. SIMCOSKY SAID, LEADING Beth into a generous room ringed with bookcases. "Vivian's library is almost as well stocked as mine. Which isn't a surprise, I suppose, since we've been in the same book club for almost twenty years." She paused and smiled. "When we get back home, I'll show you my library—or, as Mason liked to call it, my love den." She drifted to one of the floor-to-ceiling bookshelves and trailed her fingers down a bevy of colorful spines. "He used to call my books 'the other men.'"

When she turned to Beth, there was a mixture of bittersweet amusement and loss on her face. Beth gave her hand a comforting squeeze before stepping farther into the room. The cherry finish of the bookcases glowed beneath the lamplight.

Although her condo served her needs for the moment, eventually she'd intended to buy a bigger place. A home with some character and a lot more space. She'd planned to convert one of the rooms into a sanctuary, where she could sink into an overstuffed couch and read those cold, rainy days away.

Her dream library had looked much like this, with the same big-screen television stashed in the corner and well-worn furniture just waiting to welcome someone into their comfortable depths. Not to mention the bookcases, with row upon row of colorful spines.

Drawn to the overflowing shelves, Beth stared at the rainbow assortment of books. She recognized many of the titles, even more of the authors. It felt like arriving at a new acquaintance's party and discovering a dozen good friends. Except...the familiar titles and authors didn't offer the same appeal as they had in the past.

Somehow, immersing herself in a fantasy didn't hold the same allure. Maybe because she'd tasted the real thing. Felt the press of Zane's hard body against hers. Breathed in his smoky, musky scent. Listened to his deep, calm voice.

She swayed as the realization hit. She missed him.

Missed his heated presence beside her, warming her from the inside out. Missed that steady, confident tone. The tingles his touch set off. The fire in those molten kisses.

How was that possible? How she could miss a man she'd only known a day? A man she had nothing in common with? A man she had no real relationship with?

Even more insidious was the worry for him. Fear of what he might be facing, what *they* might be facing. She tried to shake it aside. If anyone could take care of himself, it was Zane. He and his buddies were trained for hostage situations. They'd faced combat and emerged unscathed. Look how easily they'd taken down the hijackers at the airport.

Except—a sneaky voice whispered—the hijackers at the airport had been unarmed. God only knew what kind of weapons they were facing at the moment.

Beth turned back to the bookshelves in the hope of distracting herself. It wasn't fair to let her fear infect Marion. Zane wasn't the only one risking his life out there. Three other men were right there beside him, and one of them was this woman's son.

"Try not to worry," Marion said, her gray eyes as dark and turbulent as storm clouds just before the thunder rolled. "If you give in to it—the fear—it will chew you up inside."

So much for her determination not to worry the woman. Beth stared at the rows of colorful titles occupying the shelves. At least half of the books were romantic suspense. Love and danger, they went hand in hand in such books. But in real life, the mix wasn't nearly as satisfying.

"Does it get any easier? Watching that door close behind them?"

A pulse of silence fell.

"No," Marion finally said. "If anything it gets worse, as you start calculating the odds. The smart woman learns how to deal with it."

Beth stared at the hundreds of books lining the walls. Hundreds of covers full of happily-ever-afters. Was this how Marion had coped? By sinking into imaginary worlds every time her husband walked out the door? Every time her son walked out it now? Had she buried herself in a mirror reality in the hope of escaping the ugly one surrounding her? Buried herself in imaginary worlds where she could count on the bad guys being defeated and the good girls getting their man and everyone living happily ever after?

Where she could count on the literary hero walking through the door at the end of the book, even if she couldn't count on her own hero doing so at the end of his shift?

A familiar cover caught her attention. Beth gently wiggled the book free. *Mackenzie's Mountain*, one of her favorite books. A comfort read. One she'd read so many times her copy was tattered and torn. Yet it offered no comfort now. She put the book back.

"Was he a SEAL, like Cosky? Your husband, I mean?"

"No," Mrs. Simcosky said, her voice thick with grief. "He was a cop when I met him. A detective when he died."

"How did he die?"

The laugh that echoed through the room was raw with irony. "Not in the line of duty, if that's what you're wondering. Cancer took him. Lung cancer. Even though he'd quit smoking years earlier, long before I met him." She walked over to Beth and stared at the dusted and polished shelves. "All those years of worrying," she murmured, "of terrifying myself every time a knock sounded on the door. Only to lose him in a hospital. In a bed."

The echo of past fears seemed to swell in the room, the pulse of fresh grief.

Suddenly all those colorful spines seemed to suck the oxygen from the air. She was suffocating. Suffocating beneath the knowledge that somewhere across town four good men were most likely under fire. Possibly injured, or even dying.

Because in real life, people died who didn't deserve it. Women were raped. Sons lost their fathers, and wives their husbands. In the real world, life wasn't fair and you couldn't count on a happy ending. Good men died. Families were fractured. Whether because of cancer or a bullet in the family van or submachine fire in some crappy little tract house across town, they died.

As though she understood Beth's sudden panic, Marion Simcosky linked their arms and drew her into the warm kitchen, fragrant with the aroma of baking brownies.

"I do wish Vivian had had the double fudge mix," Marion confided, dropping Beth's arm and picking up a pot holder.

"They're Marcus's favorites. No matter, the timing should be perfect. They'll have cooled enough to take back home by the time the boys return. No doubt they'll have worked up an appetite."

A bubble of hysteria formed in Beth's throat. *Worked up an appetite?* As though they'd participated in some kind of extreme sports competition?

As Marion focused on the brownies, Beth turned to the sink. Her eyes were drawn to the window looking out over the backyard. On the other side of the glass, above a round table carved from some kind of reddish wood, hung a spiral set of metal wind chimes. They spun in the light breeze, rotating in and out, and an airy melody drifted through the kitchen window.

Beth breathed in the light, harmonic sound. Her tight muscles slowly loosened. How soothing. Her condo had an outside porch. She could pick up a patio set and hang some wind chimes. Why wait? There was no reason—

A blur of movement to her left caught her attention and she turned her head, expecting to see a bird flitting through Vivian's backyard. Or maybe a cat stalking the bird or perhaps a dog chasing the cat. Which reminded her of that old nursery rhyme—*there was an old lady who swallowed a fly.*

She was still smiling when the blur of movement took shape. It stepped out of a swath of bushes to the left. She swayed, dropped her hands to the sink to steady herself. Stared so hard her eyes burned. It was an animal, all right. Of the most lethal variety. A two-legged monster. In muscled arms, he cradled an MP5.

Beth dug her fingers into the metal sink, the stainless steel cold and damp against her fingertips. The bubble of hysteria took shape again, climbed her throat.

She must be dreaming. Dreaming while awake now.

His face was flat. A thin, jagged scar curving along his hairline. Hair cut short and stubby, in some kind of military cut. She recognized the face, the muddy sheen to his eyes, even the weapon he carried. She recognized them all. From the nightmare.

"Mrs. Simcosky?" Her voice emerged eerily calm.

But then this couldn't be happening. They weren't at the airport. They weren't even at Cosky's mother's home. This was a private residence. How would the hijackers know where to find her?

"Please, call me Marion." The oven door creaked and a rush of heat baked Beth's backside.

"Marion? Would you come here?"

The brutal face turned in her direction. Flat, dead eyes locked on her face.

"In a moment, dear." The metal baking rack rattled. "As soon as I turn off the oven and get these—"

"Now." Beth's voice rose as the man in the window lifted his arm and spoke into a device strapped to his wrist. "I need you to come here *now*."

Marion must have dropped the brownie pan, because there was a metallic bang behind her. The oven door slammed shut and the billowing heat evaporated.

"Do you see him?" she asked the moment Marion joined her at the sink.

"You mean the man with the Uzi?" Marion's voice was so matter-of-fact, it reinforced Beth's disbelief.

"It's not an Uzi. It's an MP5," Beth corrected, and that bubble of hysteria almost escaped in a giggle.

"Well, don't just stand there." Exasperation edged Mrs. Simcosky's tone. "Let's skedaddle."

To the left, toward the front entrance, came a crash. The tinkle of shattering glass. The screech of splintering wood.

The devil in the window raised his gun.

Mac scuttled back, the urgent *rat-tat-tat* of the MP5 echoing in his ears. The doorjamb detonated into mangled chunks of wood and lethally sharpened slivers. Amy scrambled on her hands and knees toward the refrigerator as the cupboards and counters to her right erupted into wood pulp.

"Me and Cos are headed out front," Zane said from behind him. "We'll take down the front door."

Mac grunted in acknowledgement. With luck, Zane's attack would keep the guard in the living room so busy he wouldn't get a chance to take out the kids.

"Give me your backup." Mac stuck his hand back.

He grabbed the weapon Zane pressed in his palm, crouched, and slid it to Amy, who'd yanked open the refrigerator and was huddled behind the door. As the gun slid across the linoleum, he stuck his Glock around the mangled doorframe and fired. The bastard in the dining room jammed down the trigger of his MP5 and rattled out another dozen rounds.

Amy snatched up the gun, gave it a quick once-over, and clicked off the safety. She listened, head cocked, and at a lull in the gunfire scooted to the edge of the fridge door, stuck her arm out, and fired.

A cacophony of bullets struck the cupboards and counters in front of her. Dust, wood pulp, and tatters of linoleum misted the air.

Mac frowned. MP5 rounds could penetrate wood. Their position remained secure since the laundry room shared a wall with the garage rather than the dining room. The fridge provided Amy a measure of safety. But some of those rounds could have penetrated the west wall and riddled the room beyond. If that room happened to be where these bastards had stashed the kids, they could be looking at fatalities.

At a break in the submachine fire, he thrust his arm out and snapped off a round. Another prolonged bombardment hammered the laundry room's arch. The doorjamb shrunk by a couple more inches. Swearing, he glanced at Amy. Neither of them could expose their heads long enough to line up a shot.

They needed a distraction.

He set his gun on the floor and grabbed the Molotov cocktail. It was far from an ideal choice. Once the weapon detonated, they'd have five minutes—give or take—before flames and smoke took their toll. The linoleum would slow the blaze and the bedrooms were on the opposite end of the house. Still, he hated like hell using fire with kids in the house. But he didn't have much choice. They had to break this stalemate. He couldn't count on Zane and Cos busting down the front door in time to turn the tide. Without some kind of movement, the kids wouldn't be the only casualties.

Bottle bombs had one huge advantage. On impact, the gasoline sprayed outward. If the target was within a four-foot radius, he'd go up in flames.

Down the hall, on the opposite end of the house, a steady barrage of gunfire broke out. Zane and Cosky were chipping away at the front entrance. Amy Chastain flinched at the sound. Her head jerked toward the front room. She started to rise.

"My men," Mac shouted at her. "They're taking down the front door."

She glanced toward the laundry room, her eyes skimming past Mac, and visibly relaxed.

He skidded the Molotov cocktail across the floor toward her. She was closer to their tango, with a direct shot into the dining room from across the kitchen counter.

Hope flared in her eyes. She stretched her fingers toward the rolling bottle.

Mac dug into his pocket, tossed a Bic lighter at her, then snatched his weapon back up and glanced over, checking on his female partner—Christ, who would have thought it?

She crouched there. Frozen. Bic in one hand, Molotov cocktail in the other. Slowly her head turned toward the kitchen wall, and Mac knew she was thinking about her kids. When her head swiveled back, he caught the determination in her eyes.

Her hands were steady as she sparked the lighter and set the tampon ablaze.

He'd wasted six rounds so far, which left four in the magazine. And he didn't have a backup piece. The rest of his shots had to count.

Another quick glance at Amy. Those calm hazel eyes were locked on his face, waiting. He nodded, rolled toward the doorjamb, thrust the Glock out, and started firing.

The MP5 coughed to life with that fucking *rat-tat-tat* and the doorframe shuddered. Out of the corner of his eye, he saw her take a quick peek above the counter and lob the bottle.

A muffled pop sounded as something punched through his palm. His gun went spinning, clattered across the floor. Numbness swallowed his hand, crept up his forearm. Swearing, he jerked back, fell on his ass, and discovered a wood sliver the size of a steak knife pierced his palm from front to back.

In the dining room, glass shattered. There was a whoosh and the acidic stink of igniting gasoline. The submachine fire went wild. Chunks of Sheetrock and insulation rained down.

And then a male voice started screaming.

"My turn." Rawls grabbed him by the collar and dragged him back, then stepped over him to take point.

Bracing his wrists against the doorjamb, Rawls snapped off a couple of shots.

Amy Chastain popped up as well and fired from behind the counter. The screaming fractured in midshriek.

Swearing, Mac glared down at his hand. Numbness extended from his palm into his fingers and up his wrist. His tingling fingers dripped crimson.

Gingerly he rolled onto his knees, careful not to jar the injured appendage.

Rawls shifted positions and glanced down the hall toward the living room. He gestured at Amy. She nodded and turned, firing down the hall.

"We can't assume that bastard's dead." Mac forced himself to his feet. The movement set the wound off, and the Novocain sensation dissolved until his entire hand throbbed like a mother-fucker.

"He's up in flames, Commander."

Rawls's backup weapon was plugged into his waistband and bulging against the white cotton of his T-shirt. Mac yanked the material up and liberated the piece.

"You're right-handed." Rawls's hooded gaze dropped to Mac's bloody hand.

"Ambidextrous." Mac thumbed off the safety.

Amy fired down the hall and Rawls darted across the narrow space between the laundry room and kitchen.

Mac checked out the dining room. A bonfire leapt from a charred, motionless bundle. The flames escalated from a hiss to a roar and the ceiling caught fire. In seconds, the blaze resembled a hellish mushroom. Clouds of smoke spiraled toward the hall.

His eyes started to burn. They needed to get moving.

Gunfire still pounded the living room. God only knew which side was taking the brunt of that heat. Time to get their asses down that hall. He shifted into a half crouch.

"Cover me," Amy shouted, then stepped around Rawls.

Like fucking hell. Mac sent Rawls an urgent *grab her* gesture and relaxed as his lieutenant latched onto her arm, hauling her back.

"Rawls," he said, his eyes tearing.

"Got your back." The words were coughed more than spoke.

Mac's lungs began to burn. They needed to get the fuck out of this smoke. He glanced back at the dining room. The ceiling blazed. Flames licked toward the kitchen. Christ, that sucker was escalating faster than it should have.

Crouching, his weapon extended, Mac headed down the hall.

The first wave of unease hit Zane as he ducked beneath the garage door while it was rolling up. His heart stuttered, then warped into overdrive. Cosky's dead face flashed through his mind. Whatever was going to happen would happen soon. His stride faltered.

Cosky slowed beside him and shot him a quick, hard look. Zane picked up speed again.

Out of the blue, an urgent impulse to call Beth slammed through him. He locked the compulsion down.

They shot out the cameras as they raced along the outside wall. No need to hide their presence, but submachine rounds penetrated wood as easily as flesh, and the cameras would give their location for cluster shooting.

They took up position on either side of the door. Cosky reached out and tried the knob. It didn't budge. Big fucking surprise.

Together, they aimed their weapons at the sweet spot on the doorframe that housed the door's bolting mechanism. The wood disintegrated beneath the barrage of bullets. It took a full clip each to chip the bolt free. They paused to reload.

There had been no return fire, but without the cameras, the kidnappers wouldn't know where to concentrate their shots. They could be conserving ammunition.

Cosky glanced at him and moved into position in front of the door. Zane flanked him, weapon ready. One hard kick of Cosky's booted heel broke the door loose. Zane fired the moment it started moving. Cosky joined in. The door flew forward, crashed into the wall behind, and bounced back.

Still no return fire. *What the fuck?* Maybe the living room guard had joined the fray in the kitchen. Or maybe he'd headed for the kids. Too many fucking maybes.

Cosky stepped to the right. Zane moved to the left, until they straddled the entrance. They crouched low, leaned back slightly, weapons extended. With the toe of his boot, Zane nudged the door open. This time a burst of gunfire greeted him. He ducked back.

Toward the back of the house, amid the rattle of MP5 fire, someone started screaming.

Cosky stuck his weapon through the opening between the door and frame and fired off a couple of rounds. Return fire thunked against the doorjamb. Cosky snatched his arm out as the edge of the door splintered.

Son of a bitch. They were getting nowhere.

The distinct scent of gasoline, smoke, and charred flesh wafted out to him. Mac must have used his Molotov cocktail. Zane discarded the possibility of doing the same. Unlike the dining room, the living room was carpeted, which decreased their window by several minutes. It was also right next to the bedrooms. They'd be blocking the kids' only avenue of escape.

He'd have to go in fast and low. Drop the target with his first shot.

Zane lowered himself into position.

A whistle snapped his head up. Cosky made a fist. Thumped his chest.

The memory of blood flashed through Zane's mind, shag carpet. He shook his head. Cosky swore, thumped his chest again, his eyes blazing.

Glaring back, Zane pointed at the door and held up five fingers. At the five-second mark, Cosky's boot hit the door and he thrust his weapon around the doorjamb, holding it high. Submachine fire battered the jamb next to Cosky's arm. A muffled *thunk*. A hiss from Cosky. Simultaneously Zane launched himself through the door. He came in hard and low. Sighted on the bald, burly tango in the corner. Fired. Twice. Heard the twin wet *thwacks* of his rounds striking home and the *pluck pluck pluck* of MP5 rounds plowing into the wall behind his head. He hit the carpet—fucking orange shag—and rolled, came up shooting, reassured by the sound of Cosky's Smith & Wesson as it coughed out bullet after bullet to his left.

The figure in the corner grunted, wheezed out a death rattle, and slowly pitched forward.

Zane scanned the living room. "Clear."

Cosky swung through the door in a half crouch, gun extended, a streak of blood bright against his forearm. "Are you fucking crazy? You forget you have someone to live for now?"

Yeah. Like he was going to let Cosky or anyone on his team take all the dangerous ops from now on.

"You're hit," he said. But one quick glance assured him the wound wasn't serious. He started for the motionless, splayed body in the corner. They could use that MP5.

Sudden movement across the room sent them diving for cover behind a couch.

"Don't shoot. Don't shoot!" Ginny Clancy shouted. "I've got the kids. Don't shoot."

Zane swore, his heart slamming against his chest. He eased his finger off the trigger. Jesus, he'd been a twitch away from coming up shooting.

"Christ," Cosky said from behind him, his voice just as shaken.

"Don't shoot. We're coming out," the woman yelled again.

Zane started to rise, but a wave of foreboding slammed through him. He froze. It was unlike anything he'd felt before. It rolled through him with the force of a tsunami, sucking the breath from his lungs and the strength from his limbs. Burying him beneath a tidal wave of fear.

Intense, soul-sucking terror. Beth's terror.

He felt the bright, white heat of Beth's presence in his mind. Images started flashing. *Vivian's kitchen. A window. A hard-faced man with cold eyes. Thick arms cradling an MP5. Marion's fragile back as she fled down a hall.*

Frozen, sweat breaking out across his back, Zane rode the flashes out. *Jesus. Jesus. Jesus.* Panic screamed through him, zapping every nerve alight. Something was wrong…Something was terribly wrong and he wasn't there to protect her.

"What's—" Cosky started to ask.

"Look out! Behind you!" Ginny screamed as two shots rang out behind them, from the direction of the open front door.

The unmistakable wet *thwack thwack* sounded of bullets plowing into flesh. Cosky grunted and pitched forward, his body a huge, smothering weight collapsing on top of Zane. The gun coughed again. A third round shook Cosky's body. He coughed out a thick groan.

Jesus. Jesus. Cosky hit. Cosky down.

Even as he shifted—those fucking images still reeling through his mind like a silent movie—the gun coughed again. Cosky's body twitched, but without a sound.

Jesus. Jesus. Jesus. How bad? How bad?

His vision finally clearing and Beth's presence receding from his mind, Zane felt the warm, wet spread of blood soaking into his shirt. His jeans.

Cosky's blood.

Smelled the metallic, sweet scent of looming death.

Zane focused. Tightened his blood-slick fingers on the Glock and shoved Cosky's dead weight aside. But even as he twisted to face the threat, he knew he wouldn't get his shot lined up before that fucking gun went off again.

For a moment Zane's image was so clear in Beth's mind he could have been standing beside her. She felt his warmth. Sensed his cool, calm focus. And then she blinked and his face fractured, disappearing.

The hijacker raised his arms and the black barrel of the MP5 swung in her direction.

"This way." Marion grabbed her hand and tugged her into flight.

Heavy footsteps pounded across the living room, from the entryway.

A surge of adrenaline flooded her. Panic crested, then suddenly vanished, as though a door had been thrown, trapping the fear beneath. Her mind cleared. There had been two hijackers missing at the airport. The guy in the backyard was one of them. It seemed reasonable that the guy pounding down the hall was the other.

But there could be other men waiting outside.

"Marion." She matched her stride to her hostess's shorter legs. "Where are we going?"

A crash echoed behind them. The tinkle of glass hitting tile. Beth's heart climbed her throat. The guy in the backyard must have broken through the sliding glass door in the kitchen.

"To the garage." Marion's voice was surprisingly strong and calm. "There's a door there."

"Someone could be waiting in front of the garage," Beth said, surprised to hear her voice emerge as cool and rational as Cosky's mother's. "We need a window. One that's close to shrubs so we can hide. Like the arborvitaes at your house."

"They're junipers, dear." But Marion abruptly changed direction and led Beth down the same hall they'd taken earlier to see her friend's library.

Marion slowed as they neared the end of the hallway and ducked into the last room on the left. Beth closed the door behind them. While her hostess ran to the huge window next to the bed and dragged the drapes out of the way, Beth glanced around for a phone. She could dial 911 and leave the receiver off the hook. It would bring the cops.

Except there was no phone.

Footsteps started down the corridor.

They were slower, cautious. A door opened, a long pause. The door closed again.

She looked for something to brace against the entrance, but the only thing heavy enough to act as a barricade was a thick dresser next to the door, and by the time she shoved it into place, their attackers would be inside the room.

Best to just get out of the house.

She turned toward the window, which Marion was struggling to open. Beth leapt forward, adding her strength. It gave with a loud groan and squealed as they wrenched it up.

The footsteps in the hall paused and then pounded closer.

Beth bent, grabbed Marion's ankles, and boosted her up, throwing her out the window. As the door creaked behind her, she braced her hands on the window ledge, jumped up, and shimmied through the open square. The bedroom door slammed open, banging against the wall.

She tucked her shoulders and rolled, the yard spinning wildly around her, and then bounced up. She stopped long enough to yank Marion to her feet. Together they dived into the hedge dividing the properties. From behind came the unmistakable clattering of gunfire from her nightmare, and the vegetation surrounding them exploded into bright green confetti.

———————————

As Zane twisted, trying to line up a bead on the shooter behind him, a torrent of gunfire erupted from the hallway leading into the kitchen. Multiple strikes sounded. A grunt followed and a heavy thud hit the carpet behind him.

Zane spun on his knees, but their shooter was already down. From the blood and brains decorating the wall, the bastard wouldn't be getting up again. He spun back toward the direction the gunfire had sounded and found Mac, gun still extended.

Cosky.

He turned back to his teammate, his heart slamming in his throat. Blood stained Cosky's blue T-shirt. Tie-dyed it a strangely harmonic pattern of crimson on blue. He rolled the limp, heavy weight over. Worked the soaked cloth over the still head.

Jesus. Ah, Jesus. There was blood everywhere.

He pressed shaky fingers against Cosky's neck. Found a thready pulse.

"Rawls!" he bellowed as he stripped off his shirt, wadded it up, and pressed it against the worst of the wounds—a gaping hole to the left of the sternum, bubbling froth and blood. He leaned down hard in an effort to slow the bleeding. "Man down."

Rawls dropped to his knees, brushed Zane's hands aside, and lifted the edge of the makeshift pad. Instantly he slapped it down again. Zane went back to leaning. Without saying a word, Rawls stripped his shirt over his head and unbuckled his belt, ripping it loose from the loops.

"How bad?" Mac asked, looming overhead.

"Bad," Zane managed around the concrete block in his throat. Christ, he'd known this was coming. He should have stopped it.

"We'll have to risk moving him. This place is about to go up." Grimness shadowed Mac's face. He turned toward the cluster of women and children hovering a few feet away. "Everyone clear out."

Zane rose to a crouch, wrapped Cosky's limp arm around his shoulder, and lifted him into a fireman's hold.

"What about the guards on the kids?" Rawls kept pace with Zane as they headed for the front door.

"Chastain's son took them out." Disbelief echoed in Mac's voice. "Amy Chastain sent the gun to the boy."

The sunshine burned so bright it watered Zane's eyes. He carried Cosky's limp body fifty feet from the house and eased it down on the lush grass. Squatting, he held his breath as he checked for a pulse.

"He still with us?" Rawls pressed Zane's bloody shirt back over the chest wound, adding his own to the compression pad.

Zane found a pulse. *Weak...so fucking weak.* "Yeah."

For the moment.

He pushed Rawls's hands aside. "He took a couple of rounds to the leg."

Rawls grunted. As Zane went back to leaning on the chest pads, he moved down to Cosky's blood-soaked thigh.

Mac stuck his weapon into his waistband, fished his cell out of his jean pocket, and hit 911.

Zane watched as Rawls slipped the belt beneath Cosky's thigh and cinched it tight.

A redheaded child crept closer, stared at the blood welling between Zane's fingers. "Is he going to die?"

Yeah, he almost certainly would. Zane swallowed and forced the knowledge aside. He recognized the kid from the pictures—Kyle Clancy. At least Beth wouldn't be losing any more people she loved.

"Of course not, sweetheart, he's going to be just fine." But the gravity in Amy's eyes undermined the reassurance.

His throat so tight he couldn't swallow, Zane leaned down harder, his fingers squishing into the blood-soaked shirts, and reached out with his mind, trying to reestablish that fleeting connection with Beth.

Nothing but emptiness greeted him. Her warm, bright presence was gone.

But he'd know if she was hurt, wouldn't he? Wouldn't he?

With a snarl, Mac snapped his phone shut. "The birds are all taken. They're sending an ambulance."

Zane shook his head, numbness creeping over him, watching his best friend's life ooze out between his fingers. Cosky would bleed out before the ambulance arrived.

His fault. He'd known, damn it. He should have stopped it.

Mac spun, sprinting for the garage. He was going for the sedan, Zane realized. The Chrysler was their only shot at getting Cosky to the ambulance in time. Marion's SUV and Chastain's company car were a good five minutes out. Cos didn't have five minutes.

"Ginny and I can apply pressure," Amy Chastain said as she dropped to her knees beside him. "Your buddy's going to need help in the garage."

As her hands replaced his, Zane pushed up and raced after Mac. Although no flames flickered in the interior of the garage, the air shimmered like hot pavement on a scorching day.

He shoved Mac away from the sedan's open door and dove inside. The Chrysler roared to life with the first twist of the key. *Thank Christ.* Slamming the gear into reverse, he punched the accelerator and backed onto the lawn.

As he parked the Chrysler next to Cosky's limp body, Zane knew he'd have to drive. Mac couldn't take the wheel, not with that fucking spike sticking out of his hand. They needed Rawls in back, keeping Cos alive.

He cursed beneath his breath. His heart a cold weight in his chest. Beth was out there somewhere. In trouble. And he was as useless to her as he was to Cos, who lay dying at his feet.

Chapter Fifteen

MAC WATCHED THE SEDAN FLY DOWN THE DRIVEWAY.
The tourniquet had slowed the bleeding from Cosky's leg, but the double tap to the chest...Christ, so much blood. Too bad they hadn't been able to tourniquet that son of a bitch.

He rubbed his abdomen, trying to ignore the raw burn, but his gut knotted with the knowledge he was about to lose a good friend.

"I'm sorry about your teammate." Amy Chastain's tone was thick with sympathy, as though Cos was already gone and they were just waiting on a casket draped in Uncle Sam to make it official.

Which wasn't far from the truth, considering the amount of blood he'd lost...was still losing. *Ah, Christ. Not Cosky.*

With a shake of his head, Mac turned away, concentrating on the two bound and gagged kidnappers they'd dragged from the garage. What the hell was he supposed to do with those motherfuckers? He needed to get to the hospital, not play babysitter to the FBI's fuckup.

After a moment's consideration, he headed for the woods and the two cars they'd stashed off the main drag. Their hostages weren't going anywhere. Let Chastain deal with them.

Amy fell into step beside him. "Maybe we should have waited for the ambulance."

Mac shot her an irritated glance. Weren't women supposed to be the intuitive sex? Why the fuck couldn't she *intuit* that he didn't want to talk?

"He'd be dead before they arrived." He locked an upsurge of grief behind a kick of temper. Pointedly he turned his back on her and picked up his pace.

In all likelihood Cosky would bleed out before they got him to the ambulance, but at least he had a chance. Zane would drive like a maniac. Rawls would work every trick in his not inconsiderable medical arsenal—hell, even Ginny would be contributing with those compression pads. He, on the other hand, was of absolutely no use to them. Not with this fucking spike sticking out of his hand.

He concentrated on the screaming burn radiating from his palm down into his fingers. At least the physical pain pushed aside the numbing sense of loss and that familiar storm of frustration. Once again he was stuck on the outside: watching, arranging, ordering. Sending good men off to die while he watched from afar.

"You think that sliver's going to jump out of your hand if you glare hard enough?"

Mac turned his scowl on her. "Maybe you should call your *husband*. I don't know—tell him you and your boys are *alive*."

"Why didn't I think of that? Now if only…" She turned in a slow circle staring at the trees and shrubs surrounding them. "There was a phone…"

Mac dug into the pocket of his jeans, clamped onto his cell phone, yanked it out, and tossed it to her. "You couldn't just fucking ask?"

She snatched the phone midair. "You scared me, with all that scowling."

Smartass. He suspected nothing scared the damn woman. Mac tried to ignore the easy way she fell into step beside him as they started walking again. Her tight, compact body moved smoothly, not with grace, but with power. With fluid control. With supreme confidence.

He snapped that line of thought off, thankful that as soon as they reached the hospital they'd go their separate ways. It couldn't happen soon enough for his peace of mind.

He deliberately eavesdropped when Chastain picked up the call.

"We're out," she said, her voice brisk—all business. "I'm fine. The boys are fine." Her voice suddenly softened, quavered. "We're all going to be fine."

Something in his chest clenched, throbbed in time to his heart.

She tipped her head away from him. Beneath a bright swath of red hair, slender fingers trembled.

"I know. I know you did, but we'll get through this." Her voice thickened. "The boys are on their way to the hospital with Ginny and Kyle. No. They're not hurt. We wanted to get them somewhere safe, away from the house. There wasn't enough room in the car for all of us." She caught up with Mac and shot him a sympathetic glance. "One of the men you sent took several direct hits. They're meeting the ambulance."

Mac's jaw tightened. He increased his stride.

She matched it easily.

"I'm with Commander Mackenzie. We're on our way to the car." She stopped to listen. "I know. I know, John. Ssshhhhhhh. I know."

There was such gentleness in her voice. Such love.

Mac's fingers twitched. So did his heart. Because of his wound, he assured himself. His hand throbbed like a motherfucker.

"We're headed to Sacred Hearts in Enumclaw. I'll see you there?" She released a long, slow breath. "I love you too. Oh, and John?" Her tone turned professional. "We left two of those bastards bound and gagged outside on the ground." She gave him the address. "And the house is on fire." With a last good-bye, she snapped the phone closed.

As Mac reached out to take it, a gunshot cracked. Something plowed into his left shoulder, spinning him around, sending him crashing—shoulder first—to the forest floor. His shoulder popped and searing agony engulfed him.

He spit out a mouth full of grit and forced his body to move. His left shoulder screamed in protest. Pine needles crunched beneath him as he flopped onto his back. Jesus, his entire left side was on fire.

"Step away from him, you fucking bitch," a raw, breathless voice said from above Mac's prone form.

His eyes wouldn't focus. Mac blinked and tried to move his arm. Pain exploded, sucking him into a vortex of blackness and screeching agony.

"You move one fucking inch and I won't bother going for your crotch. I'll go for your head."

Ah, hell. Mac blinked again and an image took shape.

A wavering figure towered over him. Mac's gaze skimmed up black combat boots, knees caked with mud, blood-soaked thighs—and an even more blood-soaked crotch.

"Hey, Tattoo." He tried for a snarky smile. "You find your dick anywhere in that mess?"

With a hidden grimace, he ran a quick assessment. The Glock was still beneath his belt, to the left of his zipper. He tried to reach for it and agony engulfed him. Christ, his left arm wouldn't budge. And the wooden sliver through his palm made it impossible to grasp anything with his right hand.

This time, when the pain receded and his vision cleared, Mac raised his gaze to Tattoo's eyes. They were wide and bright, insane with rage and pain.

Tattoo wavered, but the compact weapon he'd aimed at Mac's chest remained steady. As the bastard's hand tightened around the grip of the gun, Mac knew he'd run out of time, but damned if he was meeting his maker without at least trying to save his ass.

Sliver be damned.

The first shot rang out before his right hand cleared the forest floor.

"This way," Marion hissed.

Her pulse thundering in her ears, Beth tunneled through the thick vegetation toward her hostess's voice.

The whine of the bullets as they peppered the hedge, shredding the branches, sent her adrenaline skyrocketing. For the love of God, they were shooting the hell out of the shrubs, in broad daylight, in the middle of a residential neighborhood. What were they thinking?

Cold terror coalesced in her belly. If any of the neighbors came to investigate, they'd end up dead. Heading toward the nearest house for help was out.

Marion apparently realized this as well. Instead of running for the house next door, she darted across the yard. Beth followed and they plunged into another thicket of shrubs, adding another layer of bloody scratches to their arms.

Behind them, something heavy crashed through the hedge. They flew across the next yard at a dead run.

This new property was ringed by lilac bushes. Marion took the yard at an angle, racing toward the back of the property. They pushed through the bushes at the very back of the property, darted across a narrow alley, and plunged into another yard. Somewhere to the left, a dog started barking. A deep, full-throated baying. Another dog took up the alarm. Then a third. They crossed several more yards and darted across a narrow residential street before they slowed down.

"I think we've lost them," Beth whispered as they stopped within the concealing branches of a weeping cherry in someone's backyard and tried to catch their breath. "We need to find a phone."

"Mrs. Micelles lives a few doors down. If we stick to backyards, we should be safe enough, don't you think?" Marion braced her palms against her knees and puffed the words toward the ground.

Beth didn't see how they had a choice. They needed to find a phone.

They reached the Micelles house with no sign of their pursuers.

Marion led Beth through the overgrown backyard and they banged on the back door until a tiny, wrinkled woman pulled the drapes aside to peer out the window. The drapes fell back into place, but it seemed like forever before the door croaked open.

"Marion Simcosky, as I live and breathe," a quavering voice said. "What a nice surprise."

The woman had to be at least a hundred years old and, from the way she hung on to her walker, mobile only because of modern technology.

"I'm so sorry to barge in on you like this, Jane. But we have a situation and need to use your phone."

"Of course, of course. Come in." It seemed to take the woman a century to edge her walker out of the way.

Beth followed Marion inside the house, closing and locking the door behind her.

"Let me put a nice pot on," Jane said, inching her way across the kitchen toward the stove.

"That's really not necessary. As soon as we've called the police, we'll be out of your hair."

"Not the police," Beth said. "Those men could be monitoring the emergency dispatch frequencies."

"Well, we need to call someone," Marion said. "I left Vivian's stove on."

Not to mention the splintered front and back doors. Zane's face rose in Beth's mind.

"I'll call Zane," Beth said, heading for the old-fashioned wall phone. "He can call the police."

She dug in her pocket and pulled out the slip of paper with Zane's cell phone number. According to the clock on the stove, it was after four p.m. The men had been gone for hours. Surely they'd rescued the hostages by now? But what if they hadn't? What if the ringing phone gave them away and got someone killed?

Or…what if he didn't answer at all?

He could be lying dead somewhere. All four of them. Dead.

A cold, heavy weight numbed her chest.

She shook it off. Took a deep breath, uncurled her fingers, and started dialing. He was a SEAL for God's sake. He wouldn't be stupid enough to leave his cell phone on in the middle of battle.

He picked up on the first ring. "Beth?"

Her name was an urgent roar blasting down the line. The sound so welcome, she went limp and closed her eyes.

"Yes," she managed around the lump in her throat.

"Where are you?" Rather than easing, his tone climbed. He must have tried Vivian's phone number.

"We're at a friend of Marion's—" she started to explain, but something about his ragged breathing gave her pause. Her senses sharpened.

"You're okay?" His voice leveled out. "I thought…"

"I'm fine," she said slowly, her hand tightening around the receiver. There was more than worry in his tone. There was something rough and hurting as well. "Is it over?"

A long, raw silence crawled over the line. Ice prickled her spine.

"Yeah." He sounded exhausted. Tense. Not the slightest bit relieved.

The chill spread from her spine across her chest and filled her heart with its cold, hard weight. "Ginny? Kyle? Chastain's—"

"They're fine."

From the tightness to the words, *someone* wasn't fine. She glanced up, caught Marion's worried gaze. "Where are you?"

"The emergency room. At Sacred Hearts." Another long, raw silence seethed down the line.

"Zane." She dropped her voice and turned her back to the fear flooding Marion's face. "Are *you* okay? Was anyone hurt?"

"Cosky—" His voice thickened and simply stopped.

Oh, God. Beth squeezed her eyes shut. Poor Zane. It had been obvious how close the two were.

What was she going to tell Marion? She took a shallow breath, so hypersensitive to the woman behind her; she could hear the catch in Marion's breathing, followed by the lack of breathing altogether.

"Is he alive?" Beth whispered.

"For now." The words were dull, as though Cosky's death was a foregone conclusion. Already accepted and grieved over. "I'll come get you," he said, that thick tightness still roughening the syllables.

Sacred Hearts was over an hour away. If they waited for him to come get them, they might not make it to the hospital in time for Marion to say a last—she broke off that pessimistic line of thinking.

"We'll borrow a car. We'll be there as soon as we can." She hung up before the argument could start.

Turning to face Marion was one of the hardest things she'd done, but she didn't have to say the words. From the fear and pain burning in her eyes, Cosky's mother already knew.

"Marion, I am so sorry."

The phone started ringing. Beth ignored it.

"But he's alive?" Fear and hope battled openly on her ashen face.

"He's alive. But it sounds pretty bad. You need to—" To what? Prepare herself? Was that even possible? "We need to get to the hospital."

"Of course." Mrs. Simcosky suddenly swayed and bent at the waist, cradling her abdomen, as though someone had kicked her in the belly.

Beth rushed over to wrap an arm around Marion's waist, suddenly wondering where they were going to get a car. From the looks of Jane Micelles, her driving days were over.

She'd have to call Zane back and have him come get them after all.

"We need to get to the hospital. I don't suppose you have a car we could borrow?" she asked Mrs. Micelles as she guided Marion toward a kitchen chair.

"In the garage. You're welcome to it." Mrs. Micelles released the handle of her walker long enough to wave a hand toward a key ring hanging next to the door.

How about that? At least something had gone right. Assuming the car wasn't as old as its owner, and undrivable.

"Thank you, Mrs. Micelles. I'll get it back to you as soon as possible." She changed course in midstream and guided Marion toward the keychain. "How do we get to the garage?"

"Through the pantry." The old woman nodded toward an archway to their right.

"Marcus is a strong one," Marion said as they hurried through a well-stocked pantry and into a narrow garage. "He'll pull through this. You'll see."

The car waiting for them was a rusted sedan. Beth prayed the thing would start as she led Marion to the passenger door and helped the woman inside. She hurried over to the driver's side. The key with the Ford insignia slipped into the ignition and the engine roared to life. Thank God.

She hit the garage door opener and shifted the Ford into reverse, waiting impatiently for the door to finish climbing, trying not to wonder if Cosky would still be alive when she got his mother to his bedside for her last good-byes.

Or whether they would stumble into more men with MP5s on their way to the hospital.

———————————

Mac braced himself and waited for a landslide of pain followed by lights-out Mackenzie.

Instead, another burst of gunfire sounded from his right and a quarter-sized bloom of red erupted in the middle of Tattoo's chest. The red stain spread to the size of a dinner plate. Slowly Tattoo's legs folded. He dropped to the carpet of pine needles with a dull thud.

Groaning, and without the benefit of either arm, Mac struggled into a sitting position. Tattoo's eyes were wide and glossy, staring at him from across the forest floor.

He turned his head, stared at the redheaded woman standing frozen and silent to his right. The Glock she held was still trained on Tattoo's body. Even as he watched, she gave herself a hard shake and stepped forward. After kicking the gun away, she bent and placed two fingers against the side of Tattoo's thick neck.

When Amy Chastain straightened, her gaze was locked on her attacker's blood-soaked crotch. A hand slowly crept up to her cheek, stroked the bruised flesh, and just for a moment her fingers shook. And then she stiffened. He could actually see the cloak of composure come down. When she turned to him, there was nothing but cool confidence on her face.

"You should've gone with the double tap," she said.

Un-fucking-believable.

"My hand slipped," he snapped.

She lifted an eyebrow. "That's quite a slip."

Had it escaped her attention that he'd been shot? Or that he'd broken his fucking shoulder?

"He was bound and gagged." Which wasn't quite true, but close enough. He glared down at his legs, wondering if he could trust them to him get upright. "It hardly seemed sporting."

"And shooting his dick off was?"

"Maybe not sporting, but sure as hell fitting."

His answer hung—throbbing—in the air between them. Her eyes touched his, and he could see the pain there. The horror. And then she looked away, broke the connection.

With her habitual smooth coordination, she swooped to pick up Tattoo's gun and the abandoned cell phone. When she turned back, her mask was firmly in place.

"Let me take a look at your shoulder. How bad is it?"

It hurt like a motherfucker. "It's fine. Let's get to the damn car."

Ignoring him, she dropped to her knees and grasped the hem of his T-shirt.

"I'm fine," he grated out, punctuating each word with a hiss as she maneuvered his right arm out of its hole and then over his head. When she eased the shirt down his left shoulder, the agony rolled through him in a dense, black wave. Nausea twisted his belly and started up his throat. Christ, he was about to vomit.

How fucking humiliating.

He would have pushed her hands away, but his left arm wouldn't work and he didn't want to stab her with the piece of kindling sticking out of his right hand.

"Yeah," she agreed, after examining his shoulder. "The bullet passed through. It's barely even bleeding. You dislocated your shoulder when you fell."

Well, hell...she could have shown a little concern.

"I'll call for an ambulance?" She rocked back on her heels and rose to her feet.

With a scowl, he fought to get his legs beneath him. "I can walk to the damn car."

She lifted the phone.

Swearing, he reached out to stop her, only to lose his balance and bobble, stabbing himself in the thigh in the process.

Jesus. Fucking. Christ.

He bit back a howl of pain and fought to keep from blacking out.

"I'm calling for an ambulance."

"I *said*, I'm *fine*."

"Sure," she agreed dryly. "Pasty green is your natural skin tone?" She punched in 911, identified herself, gave a quick recap of the situation, and asked for the nearest available ambulance.

*And he was attracted to this? What the fuck was wrong with him? She was the most aggravating, mouthy, bossy...*She was also right. The adrenaline suddenly drained away, leaving him weak as an infant.

"Just give me a fucking minute," he muttered, lowering his shoulders back to the damp pine needles.

What the hell. She'd already called for the ambulance. He might as well make use of it.

———————————

Russ turned in his rental at the airport and headed up to the third level of the parking dome. His Ford Expedition still sat where he'd parked it the day before. As he unlocked the SUV and slid inside, he ignored the urge to drag the Smith & Wesson out from under the driver's seat. He'd arm himself after he'd removed himself from the airport and the possibility of being picked up for another round of questioning.

He backed sedately out of his slot and exited the dome. After picking up his parking ticket, he pulled into the tollbooth with the shortest line. While he waited for his turn at the window, he tried Jilly's number again. The call rang and rang, and the answering machine picked up. He tried her cell phone next. This time the call went straight to voice mail.

She was probably out with the kids. Shopping. Maybe taking in a movie. There was no sense in worrying. But his stomach churned and sweat glued his shirt to his spine.

He punched in Tyler Carey's number next. What the hell was happening out in Enumclaw? But Carey's phone just rang and rang too, eventually going to voice mail.

Didn't anybody answer their damn phones?

He paid his toll and headed out of the airport, merging onto the highway to Burien. It would be a while before his team arrived at the rendezvous point with his new hostage, so he exited the highway, pulled into a diner, and ordered some grub. He tried Jilly's number again. Still no answer. An hour later, just before leaving, he tried her again. With the same result.

A cold, hard knot constricted his chest. *Damn it, where the fuck was she?*

Several miles from Burien, he slowed and angled the SUV to the right, into an industrial section full of trucking companies, warehouses, and automobile dealerships. A run-down storage facility came into view.

Stopping the SUV in front of a chain-link gate, he checked his cell's caller ID. Yeah. Not one fucking call. Swearing, he dragged the Smith & Wesson from beneath the seat, checked the magazine, and shoved the gun beneath the waistband at the small of his back. Then he leaned out to punch his code into the security panel. The gate rattled to life, rolling off the driveway in jerky, uneven increments.

The storage facility made a perfect rendezvous point. The place was ringed with steel units, which shielded the interior from outside eyes. While the owner claimed the property was protected by state-of-the-art security, in truth the only protection offered was the fence surrounding it. The video cameras so visible throughout the interior were nothing more than shells, meant to convince the patrons their valuables were being watched over. None of the cameras actually worked. Which suited Russ fine, as did the facility's seclusion.

The space he'd rented was at the very back, which meant he had to pass all ten rows of units. By the time his SUV rounded the last corner and crunched its way down the gravel lane, he knew the place was empty.

As expected.

Also, as expected, a green four-door sedan blocked the driveway in front of him. Two of his crew members leaned against the trunk. Willie, the one on the left, tossed down the glowing butt of a cigarette. The backseat of the sedan was empty.

A spurt of frustrated fury heated his veins. Was it too much to ask that one thing go right today? Just one fucking thing?

He stomped on the Expedition's brake and shoved the gearshift into park. Without Marion Simcosky, he had no way of forcing SEAL Team 7 to hand over Chastain's family.

Without Chastain's wife and kids, he had no leverage with which to force Mr. Fucking Agent in Charge to hand over the passengers on the bosses' "must have" list.

Which meant his neck was on the fucking chopping block.

The barrel of the Smith & Wesson dug into his spine as his feet hit the gravel.

Maybe it was time to distance himself from this mess. He had enough money squirreled away to last him, Jilly, and the kids a good long time. They could hole up somewhere. Wait things out.

The unanswered calls to Jilly flitted through his mind, and his heart skipped a beat.

"Marion Simcosky better be in that trunk," he said.

The two incompetent assholes glanced at each other, all superior and smug. Exactly the kind of attitude that got a person in trouble.

Willie straightened from his slouch. "We had some trouble—"

Enough with the excuses. Russ reached back, palmed the Smith & Wesson, and in one smooth move, he nailed the motherfucker right between the eyes.

As the body teetered and fell backwards onto the trunk, his second man jerked upright. "Are you a fucking moron?" Russ snapped as the asshole's hand dived beneath his bomber jacket. "You'll be dead before you can draw the damn thing."

The guy froze, then withdrew his hand in slow motion.

"Good choice. Now let's try this again. Where the fuck is Marion Simcosky?"

Flat, cautious eyes moved from Russ's gun up to his face. "We didn't get a chance to grab her. She was with someone."

"You had MP5s. There were two of you. Unless her visitor was ST7, you aren't doing yourself any favors."

"The other woman was looking out the window when I came around the corner. She saw me. It gave them time to run."

The news gave Russ pause. His finger loosened on the trigger. "What did she look like?"

"How 'bout you point that thing somewhere else and we'll talk about her?"

That was the whole problem with alpha personalities; they were constantly trying to take charge. Russ dropped the barrel of the gun and pulled the trigger. The round plowed into the bastard's right shoulder. He dropped the barrel again, this time shattering his right hand, and waited for the screaming to stop.

"How about we talk about her now?" he asked affably as the shrieks diminished to throaty moans. "What did this other woman look like?"

Blood welled between the fingers the driver had clamped over his shattered right hand. He ungritted his jaw long enough to force the description out. "Blonde. Slender. Late twenties."

Ah, Miss Beth Brown.

"Thank you." Russ smiled. "You've been most helpful."

He shifted the muzzle toward the bastard's sternum and squeezed the trigger. The guy dropped like a saturated log, dead before he hit the gravel.

Russ backtracked to the SUV and pulled a pair of leather driving gloves from the glove compartment. He popped the trunk on the sedan and carefully heaved the bodies inside, making sure he didn't smear himself with blood in the process. After parking the sedan in the rental space, he kicked a mound of gravel over the pools of blood.

No sense in advertising what had happened here. The bodies would alert people soon enough. It might take a couple of days, but someone would eventually question the smell. Decomposing flesh left a pungent calling card. But he'd be long gone by then. He'd leased the unit under Russ Branson, and as of this moment, Branson no longer existed.

He'd never abandoned a mission before, but this disaster had all the earmarks of a massive clusterfuck. His hostages had to be free. If Tyler had saved the day, he would have heard from him by now.

Which meant he'd lost all but one of the cogs he'd set in place. And the one FBI agent still in place was a psychotic powder keg on the verge of blowing. Besides, without Chastain, the man was of no use to him. He wasn't high enough up the food chain to step into Chastain's position and transfer those fucking passengers over. It was time to cut and run. He'd have to start over, but he'd done it before. He could do it again.

He'd have to be very careful, though. The bastards he worked for had long memories and held nasty grudges.

He climbed in the SUV, picked up the phone, and highlighted Jilly's number again. His sister was not going to be happy with him. In fact, he suspected the adjectives most likely to describe her reaction to his news would be "seriously pissed."

This time the call was picked up immediately. He breathed a sigh of relief.

"Hello, Russell Remburg."

The relief was short-lived. The voice was not his sister's. Every muscle in Russ's body clenched. His stomach plummeted and tightened in dread.

"Manheim," he said tightly. "Where's Jilly?"

"Your twin is fine." A cold pause chilled the line. "For now. You seemed quite concerned over her. Six calls in just over an hour?" A *tsk-tsk* echoed. "It's best you concentrate on the matter we hired you for. We'll keep an eye on your sister."

Russ unlocked his jaw. "I want to talk to her."

"That wouldn't be advisable. We wouldn't want to upset you."

What the fuck was that supposed to mean?

Russ took a shallow, raw breath. "I'm warning you, Manheim, if you hurt her, if you hurt any of them—"

"You, of all people, should know how useless such threats are. Let's dispense with them, shall we? We want what you promised. Once we have it, you'll get your sister and her family back—minus one of the children."

The line went dead.

Jesus. Jesus.

Russ's hand went numb. He dropped the phone.

Minus one of the children? Had those fucking bastards killed one of the kids?

He scrubbed shaking hands down his face and held his breath, forcing the panic deep. There was nothing he could do about what had already taken place. But to stop it from happening again, he had to get hold of those fucking passengers.

His mind circled back to Chastain's family. Considering the ordeal the women had survived, they'd take them to a hospital. But which one?

He frowned, letting the question roll around in his mind. There would have been casualties too. As good as those four SEALs were, they'd gone up against trained professionals armed with MP5s. Someone would have taken the lead. So while the women could have been taken anywhere, serious injuries would be rushed to the nearest emergency room. Odds were good that they'd take the hostages with them.

He snatched his phone off the floor and did a Google search for the closest ER to his Enumclaw setup. Google identified the hospital as Sacred Hearts. He called the number listed for information and hit pay dirt with the first person he talked to.

Two gunshot victims had been admitted within the last hour.

Okay, so he had a starting point to salvage something from this fucking mess. He just needed to infiltrate Sacred Hearts and grab Amy Chastain. He could still manage this. Still get his hands on those passengers the bosses were so twitchy about.

Unless...unless that unstable bastard shadowing Chastain moved too early. Hell, if he took Chastain out, Russ would lose any chance of getting Jilly and the kids back alive. Sweating, he called the intermediary number and hung up. The agent would call back as soon as he freed some time, which happened to be five minutes later.

"What the hell's going on?" his contact snapped. "Chastain's getting nosy. We need to move on him now."

"Negative," Russ stressed sharply. "We still need him. He is not to be taken out yet. Do you understand?"

The breathing on the other end of the line turned choppy. "Amy Chastain?"

Russ's fingers cramped around the phone. He drew a careful breath. "There's a possibility she's been freed."

Silence descended. No breathing. Nothing.

"Her kids?"

Russ ran a rigid hand over his heart. "I don't know."

"You promised—" The tone climbed. Broke in midpitch.

The guy's tone sent a chill down Russ's spine. "I have every intention of keeping my promise."

"If you kept your promises, they'd be dead."

The dial tone buzzed.

Shit.

Russ dialed the intermediary number again, his heart rattling the insides of his rib cage. To trust his sister's life, the lives of his nieces and nephews to that maniac…

Maybe he should head back to the airport. Put a bullet in the freak's brain. To demand the lives of innocent children in order to satisfy some perverted sense of retribution…Unfortunately, he didn't have time to take the sick bastard out. But then he didn't need to actually kill the guy, did he? Exposing him would work just as well.

Without hesitation, he highlighted Chastain's phone number.

The call went straight to voice mail.

Chapter Sixteen

S WEARING, ZANE HIT REDIAL AND PLASTERED THE CELL PHONE against his ear. It rang and rang, but Beth didn't pick up.

"Goddamn it." He snapped the phone shut.

"My mom says swearing is a sign of unintelligence," a young voice said from behind him.

Zane swung around, studying the boy sitting on one of the blue upholstered benches strewn throughout the waiting room. The kid had his right arm around the shoulders of another child—a younger version of himself—in a clasp both protective and comforting and far too adult for a child of his years. But then the kid's dark eyes were too old for the thin face too. Almost ancient.

What age had Chastain said his son was? Nine? Ten? Old enough to know what those bastards had done to his mother. Old enough for the knowledge to haunt him.

"That was smart thinking, leaving your note in the crack of the gun's stock," Zane told him, glancing toward the emergency room's pneumatic doors and then down the white hall to the left. "Without it, we would never have found you."

"It was Mom's idea," Brendan Chastain said, with absolutely no inflection in his voice.

"She couldn't have known about the crack on the stock. Hiding it there showed initiative. So did taking that gun from Ginny. By stepping up, you saved everyone's life in that room."

The kid didn't respond, just watched him with those too old, too dark eyes.

Uncertain what to say, Zane lifted his hand, started to rake it through his hair, but a flash of red stopped him. He froze, focusing. His hand was stained crimson, crusted with Cosky's blood.

He lifted his right hand—the one still clamped around his cell phone—and stared, the blood a dark blur beneath his burning eyes. His mind flashed back. *The breathless grunt as that first bullet struck...Cosky lurching forward...the wet thwack thwack thwack as round after round struck...the twitch of dying muscles...the blood...so much fucking blood.*

Jesus, not Cosky.

Not Cos.

When his hands started to shake, he forced them to stillness.

By the time they'd reached the ambulance, the backseat of the Chrysler had been spongy with blood. Cosky's face had bleached to bone, gaunt as death.

"Is your friend going to die?" Brendan asked in his oddly adult voice.

Zane didn't bother lying. The kid would see right through it.

"Yeah." He forced the admission through the lead pipe in his throat, surprised at how badly the admission burned. He'd thought he'd accepted the inevitability of Cosky's death during that endless race to rendezvous with the ambulance.

Nobody could lose that much blood and survive. Not even Cosky, the stubborn son of a bitch. It was a testament to Cosky's stubbornness he'd had a pulse when they'd wheeled him into the

ER. But stubbornness could only carry a person so far. Human frailty had the final say. And the human body could not lose over half its blood volume and survive.

He'd lost friends before. Watched them bleed out on scorching foreign sands or in tangled jungles fighting other peoples' problems.

But this wasn't the same. Cosky was more than a friend. He was a brother in every way that mattered. This was like losing a piece of himself. A piece that could never be patched. An emptiness he'd carry inside him until the day he followed Cos into the grave.

"My grandpa died when I was little. After a while you don't miss them so much."

Hell, if that didn't beat it all. The kid was trying to comfort *him*.

Zane took a deep breath, staring at the blood crusted on his hands. He needed to clean up before Beth arrived with Marion. He'd hit the restroom as soon as Rawls returned.

For the first time, he took a good hard look at himself. His bare chest looked like some weird Rorschach test in patterns of crimson and bronze. His jeans were stiff with drying blood. Hell, even his boots were spattered with red. It would take more than a stint at the sink to get the blood off. Plus he needed a change of clothing. Maybe he could borrow a pair of scrubs.

Rawls, he discovered a few minutes later, had had the same idea. Zane straightened against the wall, watching his lieutenant walk toward him, blond hair gleaming damply beneath the fluorescent lights, blood noticeably absent from hands and arms, a fresh pair of green scrubs hanging loosely from his shoulders and hips.

"Where did you shower?" he asked as Rawls joined him in the mouth of the waiting room.

"The emergency room has a guest shower. Ask the nurse at the kiosk. She'll find you a pair of scrubs." Rawls scanned the waiting room, his gaze settling on the two children cuddled together on the blue bench. "Any word?"

Zane silently shook his head.

Rawls studied his face. Frowned. "It's not your fault. Those damn flashes of yours never give us enough to work with."

Zane turned away.

With a sigh, Rawls scanned the emergency room's double doors. "What about Marion?"

"Beth's bringing her in."

Rawls nodded. "Mac?"

"Haven't heard from him. They should be here any minute."

Another quick scan of the waiting room and Rawls turned back to Zane. Dropped his voice. "Ginny Clancy and Kyle?"

"One of the nurses came for her. Her son insisted on accompanying her."

"Hell," Rawls frowned. "She's not going to want him in there when they do the exam." He glanced at Zane's bloody chest. "Clean up. I'll get him when you return."

Zane showered in record time, dressed in the surgical scrubs he'd been given, and checked the caller ID on his phone. Nothing.

"Anything?" he asked the minute he rejoined Rawls.

"One of the docs came out." Rawls turned his head toward Zane, grief a livid bruise in his blue eyes. "They've used twenty units so far on the stubborn bastard."

Twenty bags of blood? Jesus. "He's still alive?"

"For now. He's bleeding it out as fast as they're dumping it in." With a baffled shake of his head, Rawls turned to stare down the blindingly white hall. "With all the blood he lost before, how the hell he's managed..." He trailed off with another headshake. Squared his shoulders. "Mac arrived. By ambulance. Went straight into surgery."

"What the hell—"

Rawls cut into Zane's rising voice. "Apparently Tattoo hadn't checked out as we assumed. Surprised them in the woods."

"Jesus." Zane ran a hand down his face. "What's the damage?"

"In and out through the shoulder. Dislocated socket."

Zane relaxed. No doubt they hurt like a son of a bitch, but both injuries were survivable.

"Tattoo?"

"Chastain's wife took him out."

Zane paused to reflect on the poetic justice of that, and then turned to check on the three kids camped on the dark benches. "Where is she?"

Brendan hadn't moved from his position on the bench, although he now had his free arm around Kyle Clancy's frail shoulders in an embrace as protective as the one he had wrapped around his own sibling.

"In with the docs." Rawls followed Zane's gaze to the silent, redheaded child. "One of the nurses brought him back."

"My mom's okay," Brendan suddenly said, his dark eyes fixed on Zane's face. He phrased it as a statement, but there was a question in the tone of his voice.

"She will be," Zane said. "It won't happen overnight, but she will be."

A slight nod dipped the boy's chin. The tense curl in his stocky shoulders eased, and Zane knew he'd called it right by giving the kid the truth. He wouldn't have believed platitudes.

Suddenly something feral slipped into the gaze lifted to Zane's face. Something vicious. "I'm glad they're dead," the boy said, his flat intonation at odds with the fierce rage gleaming from his eyes. "I wish I'd killed them *all*."

Zane exchanged glances with Rawls. Christ, how did you respond to that? The kid had every right to his rage.

Apparently Brendan didn't need a response, because he leaned his head back on his bench and closed his eyes—effectively shutting them out.

Zane glanced toward the ER's entrance as the steel and glass doors whooshed open. Beth walked in. She had her left arm around Marion's shoulder. From the wobble in Cosky's mother's stride, the support was as much physical as emotional. Mrs. Simcosky looked like she'd aged two decades since they'd left the house. Deep lines bracketed her mouth, and her skin stretched tight and shiny across her cheekbones.

One moment Zane was standing beside Rawls, the next he had Beth in his arms. Christ, she felt so good against him. Warm and soft. Her body heat warming him from the inside out. He crushed her against him, craving her fresh, clean strawberry scent—and frowned.

Fragrant was right. But not fresh or clean or smelling of strawberries.

What the hell? She smelled of stale sweat, like she'd finished a hardcore workout but hadn't showered yet.

He thrust her out at arm's length and got his first good look at her scratched and bruised arms. Ice trickled down his spine.

Slowly he turned his head. Marion's arms sported the same bloody scratches and mottled bruises.

"What happened?" he asked, surprised at the calmness of the question.

"Marcus?" Marion's gray eyes locked blindly on Zane's face. Her throat trembled as she swallowed.

Zane took a deep breath, shook his head to clear the freezing fog from his mind, and turned to envelop Cosky's mother in a hard hug. "He's still in surgery," he told her roughly. "I'm so sorry, Marion. I should have—"

He broke off. Should have what? Taken the bullet himself? He glanced toward Beth, toward the future she represented. A wife. Children. A home. All lost if that gun had turned to the right instead of the left.

"He'll be fine." Mrs. Simcosky pulled out of his embrace and patted his arm. "You wait. My boy's strong. Stubborn. He'll get through this."

Zane worked his jaw and thought about warning her of the gravity of the wound, of the sheer impossibility of anyone surviving this kind of massive blood loss. But he couldn't do it, couldn't rip the blinders from her eyes. The hope from her face.

Instead, he turned to Beth. "What happened?"

She followed his gaze down to her scratched and bloody arms. "Remember the fifth and sixth hijackers from my dream? The two we didn't see at the airport? Somehow they followed us to Vivian's home."

Every muscle in Zane's body seized. *Jesus Christ!* The hijackers had gone after Beth? His mind flashed back to the images that had reeled through his mind during the shootout. *The kitchen window. An MP5 cradled in muscled arms. The wild flight down a narrow hall.*

Christ. He *had* connected with her. He'd picked up what she was seeing. What she was feeling. She'd been terrified, as he'd originally sensed, but when she hadn't said a damn word about it on the phone...

"They broke into the house, but we climbed out a bedroom window and hid in the bushes. We need to call the police. Send them out there. The stove's still on."

Fuck the stove.

His hands shook as he realized how close he'd come to losing her. A blast of fury incinerated the fear. "What the hell were you thinking?" His voice climbed with each word. "You should have waited for me to come get you."

Her shoulders stiffened. "What I was *thinking*," she said in a glacial tone, her chin tilting toward the ceiling, "was that Marion needed to get to her son ASAP. What I was thinking was that you needed to stay with your friend."

Zane barely heard her; he was too busy piecing the puzzle together. She'd called from a different number and said something about visiting one of Marion's neighbors. They must have run there. Chills swept him. Christ, those bastards had proved they didn't hold back when innocent lives were at stake. They'd been willing to slaughter an entire plane of civilians, hadn't blinked at killing children. They'd probably swept the neighborhood looking for the escaped women. Beth could have been taken the moment she hit the street.

"You should have told me what was happening," he told her, his voice as calm as he could manage when every inclination was to yell. "They could have been trolling the streets. One bullet to the tires and you'd have been at their mercy."

Which they'd proved they didn't possess.

Instead of looking contrite, she scowled and stepped back. "They weren't looking for us. End of discussion."

"Goddamn it, Beth—" He broke off, realizing his mistake the moment the words burst from his mouth. But it was too late. She shot him a dirty look and turned her back on him.

"Come on, Marion." She took hold of the other woman's arm and led her toward the benches. "Let's go wait among more pleasant company."

Zane braced his hands on his hips and scowled after her.

Kyle stirred, lifted his head, and caught sight of Beth. With a shout, he erupted from beneath Brendan's arm.

"Aunt Beth!"

Beth swooped and caught him when he launched himself at her. Lifting the frail body, she smothered his face with kisses, then pushed him back and scanned his face. Kyle wrapped his legs around her waist and held on tight.

"Hey, Bugaboo. I am so glad to see you." A quaver trembled in her voice.

In response, the boy wrapped thin arms around her neck and smothered her beneath the strength of his grasp. He shot an uncertain glance toward Zane and Rawls and leaned forward until his mouth was right next to Beth's ear. "They won't let me see Mommy."

Beth turned with the boy in her arms, her moist gaze seeking Zane's face.

Zane gave a slight shake of his head. "The doctors are with her."

She looked so natural holding the child, at ease, as though she'd held him like that hundreds of times before. An image abruptly rose in his mind. Another child. This one a little girl, with his dark hair and Beth's lavender eyes. The image fractured and dissipated.

"Where's Daddy?" Kyle asked when her attention returned to him. "I want Daddy."

Zane watched her catch her breath. Her arms tightened around the boy's frail body and her gaze flew back up to Zane's face. He shook his head. They hadn't had a chance to break the news to Ginny Clancy.

Beth turned back to Kyle. "I tell you what, Bugaboo. We'll go find your mom as soon as the nurses say it's okay."

The reddish-gold head ducked shyly in affirmation. "Then can we go find Daddy?"

Beth's chin trembled. "Let's find your mommy first, okay?"

"Who's that?" Kyle asked, staring at Marion.

"She's a friend of mine, honey."

Rawls stepped toward Cosky's mother, his face tight, a muscle twitching in his cheek. "Mrs. Simcosky—Marion—"

Marion saved him the trouble of trying to express himself. She caught Rawls's hand in a tight grip, squeezing his fingers, and then reached out to grab hold of Zane's left hand, squeezing it just as hard.

"You boys need to stop worrying. Marcus will surprise you. Just wait. He'll pull through this. My boy's a fighter."

The pneumatic whoosh of the clinic doors sounded. Zane glanced over and straightened as a pair of uniformed policemen headed toward them. Gunshot wounds were automatically reported, so he'd expected the cops to eventually show up. But he'd hoped to have Chastain's backing by the time they arrived. Hell, he'd expected Chastain to beat the cops to the emergency room. After what the man had gone through to get his family back, you'd think he'd be the first to welcome them home. Where the fuck was the man?

———————————

Beth brushed a strand of fire-engine-red hair off Kyle's forehead and shifted his weight in her lap. A nurse pushed open the swinging doors separating the ER from the waiting room. Zane and Rawls straightened against the wall, probably hoping for news of their teammates. Nobody had updated them on Cosky's or Mac's condition for almost an hour.

The nurse cast a lingering glance over Zane's athletic frame, and a distinctly carnal glint warmed her watery blue eyes. Beth shifted Kyle's weight again, a spurt of annoyance heating her belly. When the woman's eyes drifted back up Zane's tall, lean body instead of looking away—as good manners and professionalism dictated—the annoyance gained strength and velocity.

Which was ridiculous. She had no claim on the man. No reason to feel so possessive.

When Zane didn't return the nurse's interest, some of the irritation evaporated. The nurse herself noticed his lack of attention and, with a sigh clearly expressing regret, turned her head, scanning the benches.

"Beth Brown? Kyle?" Her gaze skimmed Beth's face and moved on.

"I'm Beth." She stroked Kyle's cheek. "This is Kyle."

The nurse's pale eyes returned and she smiled—an aloof stretch of her lips. "Ginny Clancy has been admitted. She's asking for you and her son."

Zane pushed away from the wall and headed in Beth's direction with that wickedly lethal stride full of power and masculine grace. The twit of a nurse had her eyes glued to Zane's approaching figure. Could she get any more obvious? Or annoying?

"I'll carry him." Zane closed in on Beth's bench. "He's too heavy for you."

As he bent to slide his arms beneath the sleeping child, his neck was right next to Beth's mouth. She had the unsettling urge to press her lips against that muscled column. To taste his warm, salty, oh-so-masculine skin.

She took a deep breath, and his smoky, male scent hit her like a triple shot of espresso. Her nipples tingled. The blood pounded through her veins. His dark head jerked up. His gaze dropped to hers and an echoing hunger brightened the green eyes until they glittered.

His attention dropped to her mouth, lingered.

As he leaned closer, his scent intensified until it surrounded her. *Oh, God, he smells so good.* Like soap and musk and healthy male. Her eyes latched on his face as it came closer. On his lips as they parted and aimed for hers.

And then Kyle stirred in her arms. Lifting his head, he smacked Zane in the chin. "Daddy?"

The sleepy question ruptured the cocoon of intimacy. She pulled back, her hunger splintering into grief. Kyle would never feel his father's arms again, smell his father's skin, hear his voice. Todd was lost to Kyle forever. To Ginny as well.

Oh, God. How was she going to tell Ginny?

A hot, aching pressure rose, washed away the tingles and chills. Zane shifted Kyle out of the way and pressed a soft kiss to Beth's lips, but the caress held solace rather than lust. He straightened, lifting Kyle easily into his arms. The child fell asleep again, his face nuzzled into Zane's throat, his frail body limp and utterly trusting as it slumped against Zane's broad chest.

Beth stared up at them. The muscled warrior and the little boy.

Suddenly her head spun, and she could swear the child cradled so gently in those muscular arms was no longer Kyle, but a girl—her dark hair captured in an untidy ponytail, staring back at her with sleepy lavender eyes.

"Are you okay?" Zane asked quietly.

She squeezed her eyes shut, waited a heartbeat, and opened them again, relaxing at the sight of the redheaded child nestled in his arms.

"I'm fine." She rose to her feet.

He hesitated and scanned her face before joining the nurse at the steel doors.

They followed the woman's periwinkle-clad figure across an open stretch of ER and down a hall to the left.

"This is the observation wing." The nurse half turned, darting a flirtatious look in Zane's direction. "You're very good with him." Her gaze lingered on the muscled biceps rather than the child they cradled. "Do you have any of your own?"

"Not yet," Zane said in that deep, calm voice that played like electricity across Beth's nerves. And then he turned his head, snaring Beth's gaze with gleaming, hungry eyes.

Eventually the nurse stopped beside an open door on the right. A blue curtain was pulled across the middle of the room, providing privacy for the bed behind it. Zane waited until Beth stepped into the room before following her inside.

"She's awake," the nurse said quietly as Beth hesitated in front of the fabric curtain. "She's expecting you."

"Beth? Is that you? Do you have Kyle?" a thin, strained voice asked—one only vaguely resembling Ginny's rich, warm tone.

Her chest tight, Beth pushed the fabric aside.

Ginny's hair looked vibrantly red against the hospital white of the pillows, but her face was wan. The skin stretched tight and translucent in places—splotched with ugly bruises in others.

Tears stung at the haunted darkness in those normally cheerful blue eyes.

"Hey." Beth's voice was thick, uncertain. For the first time ever, an awkward silence stretched between them.

"Hey." Ginny's voice emerged as dull as her eyes. Empty.

Beth took a deep breath and stepped forward, reaching past the uncertainty and awkwardness. "Oh, God, Ginny. I'm so sorry."

Which was apparently the wrong thing to say since Ginny flinched, her gaze recoiling from Beth's face.

Suddenly Ginny froze, her attention focused to Beth's right, and something flashed across her face. Flared in her shadowed gaze. Something molten and violent.

Startled, Beth turned. Zane was standing behind her. Maybe Ginny hadn't recognized him and was reacting to the sight of her child in the arms of a strange man.

"Ginny, this is Zane Winters." She lifted an uneasy hand. "He was one of the—"

"I remember," Ginny broke in, her gaze still fixed on the strong arms cradling her son, but that volcanic burn glowed brighter.

Zane shot Beth a frowning look. Ginny's attention shifted to Zane's face and the odd ferocity vanished. "How is your friend?"

"Still in surgery." Zane stepped up to the bed. When Ginny scooted to the left and patted the mattress in front of her, he leaned over and gently deposited Kyle's sleeping form beside her. "He wouldn't have made it to the ambulance without your help," he added.

"It was the least I could do." But the words were vacant rather than heartfelt.

After a moment, Zane turned to Beth and raised his eyebrows, and she knew he was asking if she wanted him to break the news of Todd's death.

Nausea swelled. The offer was tempting. Oh, so tempting, but Beth shook her head. Such devastating news should come from someone who loved her, not a virtual stranger.

Zane nodded slightly, as though he understood and agreed. "I'll wait outside."

He stopped long enough to stroke the back of his hand against her cheek and then left the room. The door closed quietly behind him.

Beth turned to stare at the woman lying so silent in the bed, her hand stroking her son's bright head in a repetitious motion that looked robotic rather than tender. Silence swelled until it throbbed in the air between them.

"Why didn't Todd come?" Ginny's fingers never faltering in their stroking. "No. Let me guess. Something came up at work and he can't get away, but he'll be here as soon as he can." Bitterness sharpened each word.

"Ginny..." Beth's knees wobbled as she stepped closer to the bed. "Todd's..."

She couldn't force the rest of the sentence out.

"He's what? Busy? In the middle of something? In a meeting?" Ginny's voice climbed with each word, sharp as barbed wire, brittle as an autumn leaf.

"No, he's…" Beth started to reach for that robotic hand, but a tight, distant sheen in those blue eyes told her the contact wouldn't be welcome. Instead, she gathered her courage and forced the admission out. "He's dead, Ginny."

Thick silence pulsed in the room.

"When?"

The flat, empty question sent unease skittering up Beth's spine. *Where was the pain? The grief?* She glanced toward the tense fingers and their mindless, repetitive motion.

"Yesterday morning or afternoon. I'm so sorry." Unable to stand another minute of that robotic stroking, she reached out, grasping the white hand between both of her own. The moment she captured it, the flesh went still and frozen in her grasp.

"How did he die?" Still no emotion. Just flat curiosity.

"He was shot. In your van. In PacAtlantic's parking lot. By the same people who kidnapped you."

The hand lying so rigid between her palms tensed. That eerie molten heat flooded the blue gaze again.

"He was still going to work? Still obsessed with his damn planes? Did he even notice we were gone?"

Beth's heart clenched. For the first time she recognized that volcanic glow. Rage. Pure, incandescent rage.

Ginny had once complained that Todd spent more time at work with his planes or in his shed with his inventions than he did with his own family. But the complaint had been half-hearted. Laughing. She wasn't laughing now. She was obviously reeling from what had been done to her, looking for someone to blame.

"He loved you, Ginny. You know he loved you."

With a sharp yank, Ginny tore her hand lose. "Yeah. Sure. I bet he didn't miss a day of work. I bet he was relieved I wasn't there to nag him into leaving his shop and coming to bed."

Beth's breath hissed out. There was a world of fury in the accusation. A universe of hurt. "That's not true. He had to go to work. It was the only way to get you and Kyle back."

A shrill laugh pierced the room. "Is that what he told you?"

Beth collapsed onto the chair beside the bed.

There was too much anger in Ginny's eyes, in the frozen white tundra of her face. An anger beyond what those bastards had done to her. Such pain didn't happen overnight. It didn't erupt full-blown following a crisis. It developed through the years. The foundation had already been laid, seething below the surface. The kidnapping may have ripped the mask away, but the emotions had already been there. Waiting.

How could she have been so blind to her best friend's pain?

"Is that what he told you?" Ginny repeated, almost accusing. "That he had to work?"

"No," Beth whispered back. "He didn't tell me anything. He was dead by the time I knew what was happening, but he had to go to work. To get you back he had to hide half a dozen guns on PacAtlantic's flight to Hawaii."

With another of those shrill, violent laughs, Ginny dragged her forearm across her eyes. "I bet those hijackers were pretty pissed then, which explains why the rules changed yesterday. Too bad they didn't explain why they took us. I could have told them Todd would never do anything to hurt one of his fucking planes."

Beth's mouth fell open in shock. She leaned forward to touch Ginny's arm, but pulled back at the last moment. "He planted those guns. Every last one of them. He emptied your bank account. He did everything they told him to in the hope of getting you and Kyle back."

Ginny's forearm rose and Beth could clearly see the disbelief in her dark, raw eyes.

"You're lying. Trying to make me feel better. I've known for years where we stood on Todd's priority list, which is right there at the bottom."

Beth's head whirled. A falling sensation hit her, as if the ground had just disappeared beneath her feet. "That's not true. You know it's not. Todd's always been there for you."

"*When?* When was he *ever* there for me? You spend more time with us than Todd did. You're the one who remembered my birthday, Kyle's birthday. You're the one who was my birthing coach."

"He would have been there for Kyle's birth, but he was away, remember? At that conference."

"Which I begged him not to go to. I was a week away from giving birth. To our first child." With a shallow breath, Ginny looked down at her son. Reached out to touch his face. This time her fingers trembled. "But he left anyway. Told me not to worry so much." Her voice dropped to a whisper, as though the rage had burned away and taken her strength with it. "I told him I wanted a divorce. The morning before they came and took us? I told him I wanted a divorce. I wanted to wake him up. You know what he said? That we'd talk about it *when he got home from work.*" Stormy, pained eyes rose to Beth's face. "It was always work, or his inventions, or a conference. Anything before his family. Amy never doubted John was doing everything possible to get them back. If it had been left to Todd, Kyle and I would have died in that awful place."

Beth stared at the disillusionment on her best friend's face. How could she convince Ginny her husband had loved her, had tried to get her back? Maybe she could get hold of the picture Chastain had showed her, the one of Todd sneaking on board the plane with a parts crate. Maybe the evidence the FBI were using to implicate him would prove to Ginny that, in the end, he'd put his family before his job, his planes, his inventions, even his own life.

"Why didn't you tell me you felt like this? What was going on between you and Todd?"

"What good would it have done?" With a roll of her head, Ginny stared up at the ceiling. "Nothing would have changed. All it would have done was set you more firmly against trusting another man, opening yourself to love."

Beth reeled beneath another tsunami of shock. "I've *always* been open to love, to finding the right man."

Ginny's red hair shimmered as she rolled her head on the pillow.

"Beth," she said gently, in the manner of people delivering crushing news. "You locked yourself behind a wall the moment you caught Brad with Shelby in that closet just before your wedding. You haven't let another man get close since."

"That's not true." This time Beth's voice rose. "I go on plenty of dates. I've let plenty of men close. They've just never been right for me. I want what your parents had. What I thought you had with Todd."

"You go on one date. At the most, two. But before things have a chance to develop, you back off. You claim you want a friendship that turns into love, but you break off the relationship before anything has a chance to deepen."

Beth sat frozen. The protest locked inside her aching throat. That wasn't true. That couldn't possibly be true.

Regret flickered in Ginny's eyes.

"Beth." She reached out, but a knock on the door shattered the moment. "Come in," she called instead, her hand dropping to the mattress.

A middle-aged woman with graying, no-nonsense hair and an ill-fitting maroon pantsuit stepped into the room. Tired eyes swept Beth's face and moved on to Ginny. "Mrs. Clancy? I'm Detective Meacham. I need to ask you some questions."

"Of course."

Beth rose to her feet, her legs numb beneath her. She glanced toward Kyle. "Do you want me to take Kyle? I can bring him back when you're done…"

Ginny settled a gentle hand over her son's head. "I doubt he'll wake up." She raised her head, met Beth's stare, regret clear in her eyes. Slowly her arm lifted and her hand stretched out. "I'm sorry. It wasn't fair to unload on you. Just ignore everything I said."

Without hesitation, Beth squeezed her friend's fragile fingers. She forced a smile. "Sure. Is there anything I can get you? Something to eat? A change of clothes?"

Ginny's face twisted, and she looked away. "Some clothes."

Of course, they'd probably taken what she'd been wearing. Beth winced. She should have thought of that earlier and picked something up without mentioning it.

Zane took one look at Beth's face as she came out of Ginny's room and straightened against the wall. Without saying a word he stepped forward, snagged the nape of her neck, and hauled her into his arms, simply holding her. Beth buried her face in the hollow where his throat met his neck and breathed in his musky, smoky scent. The world stopped spinning. The ground grew solid and stable beneath her feet.

"You want to talk about it?" he asked, running soothing palms up and down her spine.

She shook her head against his throat. He had enough on his mind with Cosky and Mac. The last thing he needed was a heap of her uncertainties as well. They were pressed so tightly together she felt the current of tension roll through him. His hands ceased their comforting slide. Frowning, she lifted her head. The moment she moved he released her.

Had he equated the silent shake of her head as a rejection? She hadn't meant it as such. She opened her mouth to explain, but he was already talking.

"I need to get back to the waiting room." His green eyes were muted. "Do you want to wait here?"

Beth slowly closed her mouth. It was foolish to presume his tension had anything to do with her. He had two friends in emergency surgery. It was more likely he was worried about them.

"I'm going to Ginny's house to pick up a change of clothes for her and Kyle."

He straightened. "I'll take you."

"I can do this alone. You should stay with your friends."

"I'm taking you," he said again, his tone flat.

There was no sense in arguing. He'd made up his mind, and the sooner they left, they quicker they'd be back. She nodded.

He stirred, but instead of heading for the waiting room, his gaze touched on the emergency exit, and the skin of his forehead wrinkled.

Could someone access the observation wing through the exit door? Was Ginny still in danger?

"Do you think she's still in danger?"

Zane glanced down. "She should be safe. They took her to force Todd Clancy to smuggle the guns on board. He's dead now. The hijacking's been aborted. They'd have no use for her."

"But she saw her kidnappers—"

With a shake of his head, he reached toward her cheek. His hand dropped before making contact. "Most of them are dead, the rest in custody." But he glanced toward the exit door and frowned. "Still, we need to make sure no one can access this hall from the outside."

Beth followed him down the corridor to the emergency exit and waited on the inside while he stepped outside and closed the door behind him. A few seconds later, he pounded on the steel door and she let him back inside. From the satisfied expression on his face, the hall was secure enough for his tastes.

By the time they got back to Ginny's room, Detective Meacham was stepping through the door. She stopped and studied Zane. Her weary gaze sharpened. "And you are?"

"Lieutenant Commander Zane Winters." He offered his hand. "United States Navy."

She shook it once and dropped it. "You're one of the men Virginia Clancy claims rescued her?" she asked in a voice more acerbic than admiring.

Zane's expression didn't change. "That's correct."

"I have some questions for you and your team."

"Of course. If you'll follow me to the waiting room you can question Lieutenant Rawlings as well."

"We need to take this to the station." The acidic bite in Meacham's tone strengthened. "Legally the US military cannot, under Posse Comitatus, conduct law enforcement operations. You should have let the local PD handle the situation."

"We didn't act beneath the umbrella of the Naval Spec War Office," Zane countered without raising his voice. "We acted beneath the direction of Federal Agent John Chastain—Special Agent in Charge of Seattle's Counterterrorism Division."

Detective Meacham flipped open her small notebook and glanced at a page of scribbled notes. "Agent Chastain, as in husband to Amy Chastain, a second kidnapping victim?"

"That's correct," Zane confirmed, and raised an eyebrow.

"And it didn't occur to you to report the situation to an agency that could *legally* act? It didn't occur to you that Agent Chastain could be emotionally and mentally compromised—"

"What occurred to us," Zane broke in, his voice retaining its level flatness, "is that Agent Chastain would have contacted another agency if he'd felt he could trust them."

The detective scowled and flipped her notebook shut.

"They saved Ginny's life," Beth reminded her. "As well as the lives of three children and Amy Chastain. Two of their teammates were wounded in the process."

Detective Meacham's gaze shifted to Beth's face. Her expression wasn't tired any longer. It was irritated. Frustrated. "I've got a house in flames, apparently with multiple bodies inside. I've got another dead body in the woods and two gunshot victims in surgery. If they'd called the incident in, as they should have, perhaps the body count wouldn't be so high."

Beth crossed her arms and raised her eyebrows, holding those irritated eyes squarely. "Or perhaps you'd have two dead women, three dead children, and no sign of the kidnappers."

A nurse approached them and cleared her throat. "This discussion needs to be taken elsewhere. Mrs. Clancy needs her rest."

With a small nod, Zane stepped back, obviously waiting for Detective Meacham to precede him down the hall. After a moment of hesitation, she strode off. Beth and Zane followed. When they reached the waiting room, Beth went to talk to Marion.

"The doctors are checking them out," Marion said as Beth's gaze settled on the vacant bench the Chastain boys had been sitting on. "I imagine they'll go see their mother afterwards."

"How are you doing?" she asked Marion. "Do you want some coffee? Something to eat?"

"I'm fine, dear." Marion's eyes drifted toward the steel doors to the ER.

Beth's gaze followed. "Has anyone updated you?"

"Not yet. That's good though, don't you think? It means they're concentrating on Marcus. On making him better."

That was one way of looking at it.

Her attention shifted to the mouth of the waiting room. A second detective had joined Meacham beside Zane and Rawls. After several minutes of intense conversation, the two detectives walked away. Something told her they'd be back.

She watched Zane scrub his hands down his face and just stand there for a minute, perfectly still, before dropping his hands and heading toward her with a resolute cast to his face.

It wasn't fair to drag him away from the emergency room. He'd want to talk to the doctor. He'd want to be there for Marion. What if the unthinkable happened and Cosky died while they were gone? Beth studied the other woman's lined, haggard face. If the news was…bad…when the doctor came out, she wanted to be here for her. She wanted Zane to be here. Cosky would want Zane here too.

"Are you ready?" Zane asked, stopping in front of her chair.

"Why don't we wait until the surgeon comes out? There's no hurry. Ginny's been admitted, so she won't need a change of clothes until morning."

From the gratitude that softened his taut face, she knew she'd made the right choice. As they settled in to wait, she could see Zane's tension escalate, see the anxiety cinch tighter and tighter until the corded muscles of his arms were clearly defined. A nerve twitched in his cheek. His silence and the tautness of his body illustrated how badly he was hurting. How much he dreaded the appearance of the surgeon and the words he seemed certain they would hear.

Chapter Seventeen

BETH DROPPED THE OVERNIGHT CASE FULL OF GINNY'S AND Kyle's clothes beside the master bedroom's door and shifted to watch Zane. He'd entered the room before her and was just standing there, next to the king-size bed, staring at the carpet.

He'd been withdrawn and silent since the surgeon had spoken with them. Unlike Marion, the news that Cosky has survived the surgery hadn't brought relief to his face. But then the doctor hadn't looked relieved either. In fact, the doctor had looked resigned. Even while filling them in on the good news, he'd stressed repeatedly that Cosky's short-term and long-term prognoses remained *uncertain*. Beth thought the more accurate word would be *grim*—which also described Zane.

He looked so somber and lonely standing there, desperately in need of a hug.

But maybe he didn't want comfort from her. Things weren't exactly easy between them. Nor did she want to lead him on, give him hopes she couldn't honor...which sounded like a bunch of crappy excuses.

Before things have a chance to develop, you back off. You claim you want a friendship that turns into love, but you break the relationship off before it has a chance to deepen.

Ginny's words whispered through her mind. Sharp-tipped and shredding. Beth tried to shove them away, except...there was an uncomfortable ring of truth to them.

"I keep trying to imagine what it's going to be like without the stubborn son of a bitch around," he said without turning his head.

She made a soft sound and headed for him. He turned toward her, the movement smooth and coordinated. Even in his grief he retained that natural grace.

His eyes were dry but raw. Burning.

Reaching out, she caught his hand. "He survived the surgery. Maybe he'll surprise you."

Zane shook his head. "He took two rounds to the back. They exited through his chest. It was a level four hemorrhage. He lost over half his blood volume. Nobody is capable of surviving such a massive blood loss."

She squeezed his hand. "But he made it through surgery. They would have given him blood. There has to be a chance."

Zane shook his head again. "He bled it out as fast as they put it in. Best case? Massive brain damage from lack of oxygen. Christ, Cosky would rather be dead than a vegetable."

For the first time Beth understood Zane and Rawls's utter lack of hope. Even if Marcus Simcosky survived, he'd still be lost to them.

"Oh, God, Zane. I'm so sorry." The pressure in Beth's chest swelled. She squeezed his hand and raised it to her lips, wishing there was some way she could comfort him. Ease the anguish burning in those grass-green eyes.

He released a rough sound and reached for her.

The kiss started out gentle. Comforting. The warm press of lips. The clasp of arms. A connection forged in grief and pain.

Until his tongue surged past her lips to stroke the inside of her mouth. Arms tightened. Hearts accelerated. She caught his tongue with her teeth and suckled, his dark-chocolate taste exploding in her mouth. Lord, he felt perfect. More perfect than anyone ever before. Hard as concrete. Hot as a furnace with that smoky masculine scent so uniquely his own, intensifying as his skin warmed, until she felt steeped in his smell.

With a soft, needy moan, her arms tightened around his waist and she pressed closer, wanting to climb inside his strong warm body. His mouth hardened and his arms convulsed, crushing her to him. He dropped his palms to the curves of her rear and cupped her, squeezing and releasing. Squeezing and releasing. Only to lift her with abrupt urgency, until he could rub the rigid bulge of his penis against her belly.

Her fingers knotted in the material of his scrubs as her muscles loosened, flushing with liquid fire. The damp flesh between her legs swelled. Throbbed in time to her heart.

God, she ached for him. Ached for the long, hot stroke of him.

She released his shirt and slid her hands up the hard plane of his back, relishing the way his muscles bunched beneath her fingertips. A sense of power engulfed her. *She* had done this to him. The way his heart thundered against his chest was because of her. Her touch, even through cloth, made this strong man quiver.

"My weapon." The warning came on the tail end of a groan as she wrestled the hem of his shirt up.

Avoiding the waistband and the gun tucked at the small of his back, she glided her hands up his spine, smiling as taut flesh rippled like velvet steel beneath her fingertips.

A grunt erupted from him and pulsed in her mouth.

The ache between her legs turned vicious.

Feeling wicked and powerful and more feminine than she'd ever felt before in her life, she scraped her nails down the muscled curve of his spine.

You'd think she'd electrified him, the way his body seized. If her nails on his back evoked such a storm, what kind of reaction would they elicit if she concentrated on more sensitive areas? She couldn't wait to find out.

But first she needed to breathe.

She dragged her mouth from his and gulped down a breath, resenting the necessity of feeding her starved lungs.

His mouth dropped to the side of her neck and feathered kisses up to her earlobe, where he stopped to suckle. Each damp tug shot an answering pulse to the flesh throbbing between her thighs.

Christ, it was a damn good thing the FBI had finished with the house.

The strange thought was suddenly just there. In Beth's mind. Not her own. But he distracted her by running his tongue down the length of her neck. When he caught the flesh with his teeth and gently bore down, she was the one to quiver.

An electrical pulse spiked through her, raising goose bumps and chills. He lifted her higher, until her toes left the carpet, and stepped to the right, his mouth suckling her neck. One of his hands disappeared from her butt to brace against the bed. He eased her down to the mattress and followed, settling between her splayed legs.

Calloused fingers brushed hers as he pulled the gun from his waistband and stashed it on top of the nightstand.

And then both his hands were back, pulling the hem of her blouse loose from her slacks. He slid his palms inside, along her ribs, his fingers scratchy and erotic against her bare skin. Tingles exploded in their wake, coursed up and down her spine, electrifying every nerve. The sheath between her legs clenched, only to melt in a molten rush. When he reached the straps of her bra those sandpapery fingers slipped around back, concentrating on the clasp.

She lifted slightly to allow him access, her breath catching as her bra loosened.

The warm silence of the shadowed bedroom seemed to heighten each sensation. His touch. His taste. His scent. Until every memory of past kisses, past touches, past lovemaking fell from her mind.

There was only Zane. Only now.

His mouth found hers and he drove his tongue between her lips in a parody of lovemaking—the thrust and retreat, the urgent stroking—while her tongue met each thrust with teasing little flicks and flirty little rubs.

She waited with caged breath for those calloused hands to slide around front and cup her swollen, tight breasts. Instead, the moment her bra loosened, his hands dropped to the hem of her blouse and tried to tug it up. She wrenched her lips from his.

"Buttons," she reminded him on a breathless rush.

His soft curse echoed through the room and a bubble of laughter escaped her.

While he fought to release the row of buttons, she tugged his shirt up. He swore again when the material of his scrubs trapped his hands, and quit working on her blouse long enough to tug his shirt over his head and toss it to the floor.

His bare skin was hot beneath her palms. Surprisingly smooth. She ran her fingers up the ridges of his muscled abdomen, smiling as his skin rippled beneath her touch.

A rumble broke from him. An urgent sound of need.

Somewhere, in the vicinity of her heart, something cracked. A thick, liquid heat spread out in waves. He was so responsive to her touch. So responsive to her.

Suddenly she needed to taste him, to connect with him in the most elemental of ways. He froze as her mouth found the muscles of his throat. She licked the damp, salty skin. Felt as well as heard the groan rip through him, the way his breathing literally stopped and his whole body shuddered.

An image suddenly exploded in her mind. A vision of herself—on her knees, her hands wrapped around the shaft of his penis, while her mouth worked the head.

She jerked upright. What in the world? And then another one of those weird, alien thoughts swallowed her mind.

Jesus. Jesus. Stop it. Imagining her going down on you isn't helping. Keep it up and the first time you come with her is going to be in your pants.

She froze beneath him, unease prickling. She had to be losing her mind. She could swear she'd just heard Zane's voice in her head.

Before the alarm had a chance to escalate, he worked the last button free and her shirt fell open. He lifted her, stripping both blouse and bra down her arms, his mouth finding her breast with unerring accuracy.

She choked back a shriek of shocked pleasure, her disquiet vanishing. With each moist tug on her breast, an answering twinge throbbed between her legs. In an effort to ease the aching pressure, she lifted her legs and wrapped them around his hips so she could rub her burning core against the bulge between his legs.

Christ. She tastes like strawberries.

This time the foreign thought barely registered. She was too focused on the rhythmic suckling against her breast and the echoing pulse between her legs. Oh God, she needed him inside her, filling that hungry void. She needed him to take away this empty yearning.

She arched in his arms, widening her thighs so she could get closer.

If we were naked, she'd be riding my cock right now.

Her fingernails scraped down the small of his back to the waistband of his scrubs. She loosened her legs and pushed his pants down, only to find herself distracted by the surprisingly cool globes of his butt. She cupped them. Raked her nails across the taut flesh. He was full of delicious contrasts. Hard yet smooth, hot yet devilishly cool.

He spread his legs as she explored lower, giving her access and encouragement. Her hand slid around his hip, down the crease at the top of his thigh. When her fingertips found the heavy weight of his testicles he hissed and arched into her hand.

She's killing me.

While she fondled him he shoved her pants down, slid his fingers into her panties and rubbed her damp slit. She shuddered at the rough caress, her hand tightening around his sack, smiling as his big body twitched—at least until he took her nipple between his teeth and delicately applied pressure.

An inferno rolled through her, settled in the heated void between her thighs. With a soft groan, Beth loosened her legs, holding her breath as his hand started moving again. The finger he pushed inside her felt huge, rough, scraping the sides of her sensitive sheath in an erotic caress that rippled through her like quicksilver.

She choked back a shriek, arched against his chest, forcing his finger deeper. Oh God, he felt so good. So perfect. But she needed more of him.

His lips sucked hard at her breast while he worked a second finger up in her. Only to withdraw both and thrust them in again. He repeated the motion over and over, then shifted his thumb to the bud of her sex and rubbed.

Flames caught, billowed through her in waves, and a thin scream erupted from her tight throat. She pressed down, straining against his hand, a current of energy twining tighter and tighter, tangling her in gossamer strands of urgency.

With a thick curse, his hand withdrew. She moaned in protest and rocked against his arm.

Christ, she's seconds from flying. I'm damn well going to be inside her when she does.

The words were clear as a bell in her head. Except he hadn't spoken them. She was certain of it.

And then he shifted, kicked off his scrubs, jerked her pants and panties down her legs, and settled back down, crushing her into the mattress. Something huge and hard pressed against her molten core, parted the swollen, slick folds and nudged inside.

She flinched from the contact, her breath exploding in shocked realization.

Oh God. They were about to make love. Something stirred in the back of her mind, a fragment of a memory, something she needed to remember.

"Wait." The plea emerged slurred but recognizable.

She has got to be fucking kidding.

His muscles clenched in protest. He stopped breathing. For a moment he froze beneath her, and then he suddenly rolled until she was on top.

His hunger pounded at her; she could actually feel his urgent need to thrust, to bury himself deep. But he'd stopped because she'd asked it—had shifted their position to give her the control.

The crack in her heart widened. Wept something tender. Something she didn't want to explore too closely.

He shook as he waited beneath her, perfectly still, the head of his penis burning against her. If she pressed down, she'd take him inside. The realization tantalized her. Driven by instinct, she rocked against him.

The head of his shaft slipped inside. Lodged there. Hot. Hard. Throbbing. They both groaned. She rocked again, forcing him deeper.

Ah, Christ, I can't hold back much longer.

This time the alien thought didn't faze her. She braced her hands against his wet chest and pushed down, taking him deeper still, the muscles of her sheath clamping around his invading length.

He arched up, his hips flexing.

She's killing me, killing me.

Her heart pounding so hard she could hear it, she lifted her hips and bore down again, hearing his hiss as she took him the deepest yet. The muscles of his chest bulged against her palms as he fought to rein himself in. Sweat ran down his skin.

But he held himself in check. For her. That crack in her heart split wide open.

So fucking tight. So fucking hot. So fucking perfect.

Distantly she was aware of his rigidity as she rocked against him, lifting herself up and pressing herself down. The awareness he was holding himself in check for her sake, for her comfort, added to the pleasure. His hand slipped between her legs, his calloused fingertips tracing her tightly stretched opening.

A current of electricity jolted through her at the intimate, rough caress. She stifled a scream and threw her head back. Her core clenching.

Jesus. I need…I need…ah…Christ.

His hips bucked, driving his penis deeper. He stroked her sensitive opening again, eliciting another muffled shriek, and then rubbed the tight bud of her sex.

She needed…she needed…oh God, she needed.

This time she couldn't hold back her scream, but he was waiting and dragged her down flat to swallow it with his mouth.

She felt the moment his control snapped. Felt him roll again, crushing her beneath him, and welcomed his hard thrust with tight arms, clutching hands, and coiled legs.

She was only taking half of him, riding the front of his cock with increasing urgency as she reached for her peak. With each surge of her hips, he fought the instinct to thrust. To bury himself in her tight, satin depths.

Holy Mother of God.

Her thoughts swam through his mind. Fragmented. Urgent. Proof the bond between them was finally and irrevocably intact. Only when the bond was fully formed did telepathy between partners come into play.

She was moments from coming. He could sense the coil of her approaching orgasm as clearly as he sensed his own. Could feel the pleasure pouring into her with every thrust of her hips.

She dug her fingers into his chest and his hips lunged. Light-headed, he tried to rein himself back, but his body had broken its leash and was firmly in control, refusing to take direction from his brain.

His hips surged again, rising to meet her.

Christ. He was out of time.

He scraped her clit with his thumbnail and pressed his shoulders against the mattress, feeling the tingles gathering in the base of his spine.

Oh God! Oh God. Oh God.

The feminine wail ripped through his mind and she jerked wildly against him. He pulled her flat, caught her scream with his mouth, and rolled, then thrust hard. Penetrating her to the core.

Dragging his hand from between her legs, he shifted his grip, tilted her slightly, and thrust again. Pulled out, thrust harder. Pulled out. Hammered into her again and again, vaguely aware of the headboard banging against the wall.

She convulsed, clamping down, milking him as wave after wave of contractions swept through her. And then his own release slammed into him. He drove into her one last time, his balls tight against her ass, and bucked—straining. His climax boiled up and out as he lodged himself deep, spilling himself into her swollen, convulsing depths.

Gave her everything he had to give. His seed. His heart. *His life.*

When he regained awareness, his cock still twitched. Tremors shook his arms and legs. His limp body crushed her into the mattress.

"Christ," he said, shocked at the breathlessness of the word.

He shifted to the side but kept her slight body anchored to him. Once settled, he pressed his sweaty forehead against her neck and breathed in the thick, earthy scent of strawberries and sex. Contentment spread through him. Finally. He had her exactly where he needed her. In his arms. Their bodies merged. Their minds mingling.

His cock, still locked within her sleek depths, twitched. His hips flexed.

She hummed in contentment. "I can't believe we did it here. In Ginny's bedroom."

"It could be worse," he murmured, licking the damp skin of her neck. "At least we have a bed and a shower. Too bad we can't say the same for condoms."

The taste of her, salty and seasoned with strawberry, hit him like a shot of whiskey. His cock hardened. His brothers hadn't exaggerated the potency of the bond. It was a natural aphrodisiac. He thrust again, and the headboard rattled.

She groaned, her arms tightening around his shoulders. Her head turned, her mouth seeking the sweaty skin of his collarbone. He doubted he tasted nearly as good.

"Condoms?" she repeated absently. Her thighs tightened around his hips and she arched into his next thrust.

He grunted. Kept the roll of his hips slow and lazy. But the urgency was already building.

"Yeah. I don't have any. I'll pick some up later today," he managed. Christ, she felt so perfect. Sleek and hot and tight.

Suddenly her breath caught. She froze in his arms. "You didn't use a condom?" The question emerged sharp enough to skewer him.

Zane frowned at the change in her tone, but his hips were already moving.

Only this time his thrust tore a curse from her. She shoved two determined palms against his chest and pushed. "Stop it."

Shit. But Zane's hips stilled.

"You didn't use a condom?"

Obviously it wasn't a question. Her body had tightened to rigidity. He reached out with his mind, tried to reestablish that earlier connection between them, but she'd locked herself down tight.

"I couldn't. We don't have any."

She flinched. The link cracked open and allowed a wave of horror to roll through.

Hell. His stomach tightened.

He'd never been so careless before. Never. Not even during the horny days of adolescence when he'd been a walking, talking erection. And Christ, he hadn't planned this. Condoms had simply been the last thing on his mind.

"Oh *God.*" Her voice thinned. She banged the back of her head against the bed.

He tried to cradle her close, but she jerked back. Hard.

"Look, it's okay. We'll face whatever comes of this together. If you're pregnant, we'll move the timeline up and get married sooner."

Which suited him just fine.

A vision took root in his mind, an image of her belly rounding, filling with his child. Christ, he hoped she was pregnant.

His cock swelled at the thought. His hips flexed. Except another wave of horror rolled through her. She shoved her hands hard against his chest.

"Are you crazy?" She pushed harder. "We are not doing this again. Get off me!"

Frustration boiled, but he eased off her, feeling the gush of fluid that followed—his and hers—and straightened to his full height beside the bed. Christ, his knees were actually weak.

She grabbed the comforter and wrapped it around herself with shaking hands. Some of his frustration eased. There was an odd panic in her eyes and a hitch to her breathing.

It was a damn shame he couldn't read her thoughts now. At least then he'd know what the hell was going on in her mind. "Look, if you're worried about disease—"

She choked on a strangled sound. "It's a little late for that, don't you think?"

Frowning, he studied her face, the tremor in the fingers clutching the comforter.

What the hell was going on?

Avoiding Zane's gaze, she scooted off the bed.

"Beth," Zane said softly, his stomach tightening at the red flags burning across her cheekbones. Jesus, he didn't want her ashamed of what had happened between them. He stepped toward her, touched her arm, his stomach knotting even tighter as she jerked away.

Lowering his hand, he forced calmness into his voice. "Talk to me. What's going on?"

"Isn't it obvious?"

"Not to me."

"You didn't wear a condom."

He studied the shake in her fingers, the fragile paleness of her face. This wasn't about a condom—or lack thereof.

"I'm clean, if that's what you're worried about. I haven't infected you with anything."

"Yeah, well. What if I'm not! This is stuff we should have talked about before, you know…we…well before." She swooped down and snatched up her blouse and pants from the floor.

"I don't care."

Her head snapped up. Startled eyes locked on his face. "You what?"

"I don't care if you infected me with something."

Her eyes softened, filled with warmth. But just for a moment, then that odd panic flared again. "You should care. You don't even know me."

He swallowed a curse at the edge of hysteria in her voice and flashed back to what he'd heard outside Ginny Clancy's room. How Beth always broke things off before her relationships had a chance to develop. That skittishness had worked in his favor after she'd broken it off with her ex—since it had kept her single and uninvolved—but he couldn't chance her retreating from *him* now.

"Look, sweetheart, if you're pregnant, we'll just get married sooner. If you—"

"I never said I'd marry you! We've only known each other a day. It's too soon to think about marriage."

The need to touch her, to soothe her, to reestablish their bond, overrode his caution. He stepped up, took her hands. "We know the important things about each other. The rest will come."

"Really?" Her voice went eerily flat, her hands utterly lifeless between his. "What's my favorite color? Where do I live? Do I like my job? How many kids do I want?"

He squeezed her fingers. "Those aren't the important things."

"How many kids I want isn't important?" She wrenched her hands free.

"That's not what I meant."

"You don't know anything about me," she continued in that emotionless monotone, her gaze never straying from his face.

Frustration rose again, and his voice emerged harsher than he'd intended. "I know you don't like lying. You do the right thing, no matter what it costs you. You're loyal, you'd go through hell and back for your friends. I know you're practical. That you'll stand up for yourself when you have to. I know you have a core of compassion." His gaze dropped to her belly. "I know you'll make a wonderful mother."

There was no change in her expression. "And you know all this, how? By this soul mate connection you claim we share?"

His jaw tightened at the disbelief in her tone. "I don't deny I recognized you the moment you stepped into the gate room, but the qualities I listed didn't come through our connection. They came through observation."

"We don't have a connection. What we have is good ol' fashioned lust, which isn't enough to build a marriage on."

A flash of hurt mixed with his frustration. How could she so easily dismiss what they'd shared? Zane studied her tight face. There was a hell of a lot more between them than lust, but she wasn't going to believe that. Not anytime soon.

"Marriage is hard enough when the couple's in love." A distant look filtered through her eyes. "When they know each other, when they accept each other's foibles." Her gaze focused again, centered on his face. "You don't even know what my foibles are."

He rocked on the balls of his feet and crossed his arms over his chest. "What I feel for you goes deeper than lust. We're connected."

Her snort of disbelief hung in the small room.

His hands fisted. He fought back a burst of anger. "We're connected, Beth. Whether you'll admit it or not, there is a link between us. You felt it when I was inside you. You felt me in your head, just as I felt you inside mine."

Frowning, she dropped her gaze. "I don't know what you're talking about."

"Bullshit." He caught her chin and forced it up. "You were picking up on my thoughts, just like I was picking up on yours. That's part of the bond. The connection we share. It will strengthen as we spend more time together. You can deny it all you want, but in your heart you know we're connected. *You felt it.*"

She jerked her chin loose and stumbled back. "I didn't feel anything other than lust. Do you seriously think some mystical connection is going to hold us together once the chemistry fades? I bet your family is full of divorces."

He ungritted his teeth. "That mystical connection, as you call it, is exactly why my family has never had a divorce. Not one. My parents just celebrated their fortieth anniversary." An edge sharpened his tone. "You're big on knowing each other? Well, the men and women in my family know their partners at a deeper level than what you're talking about. They can share thoughts, share minds, share emotions. You can't hide anything when you share a consciousness. That exchange while I was inside you is just a taste of what we could have."

"But it's not real," she whispered.

"It's a hell of a lot more real than your version of love. And I can damn well guarantee you'd never find me in a closet with another woman."

She flinched, dismay overtaking the flatness as she realized he'd heard her conversation with Ginny Clancy.

He fought to rein his temper in. "Look—"

She didn't wait around for his apology. Instead, she rushed for the master bathroom, the comforter trailing along the carpet. The door slammed behind her. Zane started after her, but the memory of her face stopped him. He wasn't going to convince her of anything while emotions were flying high.

The shower turned on.

Swearing, he spun around, fought the urge to drive his fist through the wall.

He hadn't lost her. Once she calmed down and had a chance to think, to remember, to relive what had just happened between them, she'd realize how special it had been. He needed to back off. Let her come to that realization on her own.

Giving her space was the smart thing to do. So why did it feel like he was making the biggest mistake of his life?

Chapter Eighteen

*B*ETH STOOD UNDER THE HOT SPRAY, PANIC BEATING AT HER chest.

Liquid trickled down the inside of her thighs. Liquid that wasn't water, liquid that reminded her of what had happened. What she'd let happen. What she'd actively encouraged and participated in.

She closed her eyes and tipped her face up to the water. An image of her mother rose in her mind, the deep lines of exhaustion creasing her forehead and bracketing her mouth. Her skin wan and dull from too much time spent indoors. She remembered the way her mother would stagger into the living room between shifts and collapse into her recliner, soaking her aching feet, too tired to get up and head into her bedroom for a nap.

Raising a child on her own, with no emotional or monetary support, had leached the life out of her. She'd been so busy providing everything—a home, food, clothing, health care, the hundreds of odds and ends a family needed to survive—that she'd stood on the sidelines while life drifted by.

Although, in truth, life hadn't passed her by. It had ground her up instead, drained every ounce of strength and ambition, and then spit her out. Surviving from day to day had withered away

Rebecca Brown's energy reserves until she'd had nothing left with which to fight the cancer that had eventually taken her life.

After everything she'd witnessed her mother go through, how could she have been so foolish? How could she have made the same mistake?

At least with Brad she hadn't had to worry about an unplanned pregnancy. She'd gone on birth control long before they'd become lovers. But then she'd never gone up in flames with Brad either. Or lost control, or allowed passion to sweep her away.

Unlike Zane, who'd swept her away so completely, she hadn't even thought about birth control.

Hadn't thought about anything except feeling him move inside her.

Was their child already growing inside her? A dark-haired, green-eyed little boy?

She flashed back to that odd vision while he'd been carrying Kyle.

Or a dark-haired, purple-eyed little girl?

Some deep maternal instinct whispered *yes*. She was carrying his child.

The hard knot in her stomach loosened beneath a surge of warmth. Of wonder.

She'd always wanted children, had enjoyed Kyle's company as much as she'd enjoyed Ginny's. She loved watching the world through Kyle's eyes. Loved his uncomplicated take on life. Yeah, she'd always wanted kids.

Only not like this. On her own. Unprepared. In the same situation her mother had been in. Although…

Beth frowned, her chin lowering until the spray hit the top of her head.

She wasn't actually in the same situation. Her mother had been uneducated and ill-prepared for the job market. She'd never finished high school, nor had she gone back to pick up a GED. Her lack of education had convinced her the only jobs she was qualified for were menial ones. Jobs that paid little better than minimum wage, which meant she had to pick up extra shifts or second jobs in order to support them. Perhaps, if Beth's father had been alive...but he'd died within months of the divorce, leaving her mother to struggle along on her own.

But if her mother had tried for a higher-paying job, she wouldn't have had to work so many extra hours. A job like, say, clerical support at PacAtlantic.

While far from exciting, her job as engineering support boasted a generous salary with excellent benefits. She wouldn't need to work extra shifts to make ends meet. In fact, she made more than enough money to support a family. Plus the company's medical insurance would cover any clinic bills. Sure, once the maternity leave was up, she'd have to find some kind of child care, but she'd be able to afford that as well.

In fact, raising this child alone would be eminently possible.

She relaxed as the realization set in. Until it occurred to her that she'd been standing in the shower for so long it was a miracle Zane hadn't barged in to make sure she was okay. Not to mention Zane probably wanted to wash up too. Plus they needed to get back to the hospital. She washed and rinsed, toweled off, dressed, and ran Ginny's brush through her hair before twisting the wet stands into a knot at the back of her head and pinning them in place with a hairpin she found in the top drawer.

Then she braced herself and stepped into the bedroom. The empty bedroom. Zane's clothes were gone from the floor; so was the overnight case she'd packed for Ginny. And then there was the bed. It had been stripped. She backtracked to the bathroom and grabbed the comforter, turned off the lights, and headed through the darkening mansion to the laundry room.

Zane turned to face her when she walked through the door. His eyes watchful, hair damp. He must have washed up in a sink. A thick, unbearable pulse of tension arced between them.

He turned back to the washing machine without saying a word and picked up the detergent. Beth breathed a sigh of relief, thankful he hadn't launched back into the argument, although there was little doubt the discussion was far from over.

He might have backed off for the moment, but her instincts warned that he hadn't given up.

They left the house side by side, accompanied by a silence denser and more uncomfortable than Beth had ever endured before. While Zane walked her to the passenger seat of Marion's SUV and opened the door for her, he didn't touch her. Not even a light caress against her back to guide her inside.

After stowing the overnight case in the backseat, he slid behind the wheel and started the car, all without looking at her even once. The trip back to the hospital seemed to take forever, the silence stretching on and on between periodic polite exchanges that left Beth utterly exhausted.

Before they separated at the hospital, with Beth taking the overnight case to Ginny and Zane hunting down Marion and Rawls to find out where they'd moved Cosky, Zane caught Beth's elbow. He dropped it immediately once he had her attention.

"We need to talk."

She took a deep breath, let it out slowly, and nodded. "I know. But not here, not now."

His face lost some of its flatness. An expression close to relief lightened the darkness in his eyes. He gave her a half smile. "Soon."

"Soon," Beth echoed.

That horrible, thick tension eased slightly. Beth swallowed hard. Suddenly she wanted to walk into his arms and hold on tight.

"I'll come and get you as soon as I know where Rawls and Marion are. Wait for me?"

She nodded, then headed for Ginny's room before she did something she'd regret. Like kiss him, which would probably end with them locked in the supply closet. If she wasn't already pregnant, she would be by the time they came out.

If she were pregnant, she wouldn't be raising this child on her own. Zane wouldn't let her. He'd just keep coming back—calmly, assuredly, ignoring her attempts to push him away.

He'd be there for her and their child, whether she wanted him to or not.

And it wouldn't matter if they were married or living together or not sharing a home at all. He would always be there for her. Just as he'd been there for Cosky when he'd needed help painting Marion's house, just as he'd been there for Ginny and Kyle and Chastain's family when they needed rescuing, just as he was here for Marion while Cosky was in the hospital.

Zane had a core of honor that made him incapable of skirting his responsibility, even when the responsibility wasn't actually his. The knowledge settled, warm and comforting, inside her: Zane would never abandon his child or his child's mother. He'd come running with one phone call.

Of course, how long it took him to arrive depended on multiple variables. Like how far away he was and whether a phone call would even reach him. Best-case scenario? He lived in San Diego. It would take him hours to arrive in an emergency, and how often would he actually make it up to visit? A half-dozen times a year? Plus he faced deployment at a moment's notice, missions that could last for months at a time.

No matter what, she'd still be raising this child on her own.

You could marry him, an insidious voice whispered. *At least you'd be with him when he was on base. Your child would have a father more than a couple of times a year.*

Assuming he made it back from those deployments. SEALs took the most dangerous missions. No matter how highly trained, how eminently capable, there was always the possibility they wouldn't return.

Her thoughts shifted to Cosky. Those bullets could have brought Zane down just as easily. It could be Zane fighting for his life in the ER. Someday it probably would be. If she married him, how often would she be waiting in a hospital, terrified of what the surgeon might say? How many times would their children have to fear they'd lost their father?

The urge to run hit. To escape this man who made her body hunger in ways she didn't understand. Who wrung emotions from her she didn't want to feel. Who was dangerous to her in the most elemental of ways.

Before things have a chance to develop, you back off. You claim you want a relationship based on trust, forged from friendship, yet you break things off before anything has a chance to develop.

Beth stopped dead in the hall and closed her eyes. *Oh God.* Ginny was right.

Here was a good man, an honest man, a dependable man. A sexy-as-hell man, who curled her toes and gave her chills and only had eyes for her. Who'd made it crystal clear he wanted to marry her, to start a family with her. Who insisted she was his soul mate.

Yet she was the one in full flight. She was the one throwing up excuses as to why they shouldn't be together.

Wasn't there something wrong with this picture? Why wasn't she giving him a chance?

She raised shaky hands and pressed them against her temples. She might lie to Zane, but she couldn't lie to herself. Something had passed between them on that bed. Something beyond sex. She had recognized him inside her mind, had heard his thoughts, experienced his hunger.

In the distance, down the long white corridor, a male figure in periwinkle scrubs ambled toward her. Was he a surgeon, on his way to update the others about Cosky or Mac?

Which brought to mind Zane's teammates. It would be difficult to find two more suspicious men than Cosky and Mac. Yet Cosky had trusted Beth's nightmare and taken down the hijacker at the airport—all because Zane's intuition had warned them something was about to happen. Mac had contacted the feds on nothing more substantial than Zane's supposed dream. For such cold, pragmatic men to trust Zane's psychic abilities so completely…well, those abilities must have come into play before, and often enough to instill immediate belief. Immediate trust.

And Zane claimed that ability—that same psychic intuition—had recognized her. Something *had* happened in Ginny's bedroom. She *had* heard his voice inside her head…Maybe it was time to stop running. Maybe, just maybe, she should let go and stop being such a coward and see where this connection led them. She didn't have to marry him. She didn't have to quit her job and move down to San Diego. They had time to get to know each other. She'd just let things flow and see what developed.

A smile broke over her, the relief so sweet she wanted to find Zane right then and share it with him. She started to turn when the approaching figure in the periwinkle scrubs caught her attention. Beth frowned, watching him stride closer. Something about the way he moved looked familiar. He walked with a loose amble, a roll through the hips and knees—unhurried—which seemed odd for a doctor in a trauma unit.

Her frown deepened as she watched him come closer. It wasn't just his walk that seemed so familiar. His structure did too; the length of torso to limbs, the breadth of shoulders. It was the shoulders that clicked the memory into place. Russ Branson had been built like that. Long legs, long arms. Quarterback shoulders on a computer geek's frame.

A chill of unease prickled. Her gaze lifted to his face. Russ Branson had worn glasses and combed his hair to the side instead of back, but the thin face and angular nose looked the same. So did the mahogany hair.

She flashed back to Zane's reaction to the man. Something about Russ had set off Zane's internal alarm. He'd been suspicious of her Good Samaritan immediately.

Trying to act casual, she turned and headed down the corridor at a brisk pace, the overnight case suddenly a dead weight in her hand. Every instinct she possessed screamed she needed to find Zane. Now. The impact of her shoes bounced between the walls. Yet nothing echoed behind her. Nothing at all.

The man trailing her moved as silently as a ghost.

Which wasn't natural...unless...well, unless he had some kind of stealth training. Like Zane and his teammates.

She swallowed hard, increasing her pace. She was imagining things—that's all. Even if Russ Branson had been involved in the aborted hijacking, why show up here? He wouldn't be able to take control of the flight, so the hostages would be useless to him. It made no sense to risk exposure by showing up here, by showing up now.

Ergo, it wasn't him. Her imagination was running wild. They'd have a good laugh over her panic attack once she reached Zane's side.

She was still trying to convince herself of that when a hand landed on her shoulder, tightened, and swung her around, slamming her up against the tile wall. She dropped the overnight case, took a deep breath, and prepared to scream.

He slapped his palm over her open mouth and leaned into her with such pressure she couldn't close her jaw to bite him.

"Tsk, tsk," Russ said with a cold chuckle. "No biting. Do you feel that?"

Something hard dug into her side.

"It's fully loaded. The cartridge holds eight rounds, but I only need one. I'm a very good shot." It wasn't a boast, more a statement of fact. "Of course, from this distance a toddler wouldn't miss." Something dark and haunted slipped through the brown eyes above hers. "But a toddler wouldn't know human anatomy. For example—" The gun dropped a couple of inches and dug back into her side. "If I were to pull the trigger here, the bullet would sever the hepatic artery leading into your liver. You'd bleed out in seconds. Which would be rather ironic, don't you think, considering you're seconds from the ER?" Flat eyes watched her face. "Trust me. Nobody would reach you in time." He lifted an eyebrow. "You ready to play smart?"

When she nodded, the pressure against her side eased. "Excellent. I'm going to let go of your mouth. One scream and you're dead."

Beth stared into his utterly cold, utterly empty eyes. She was dead anyway. Scream or no scream, he had no intention of letting her live. Once she served whatever purpose he had planned, she would be as disposable as Todd, as his coconspirator at the airport.

On the other hand, her scream might warn Zane and Rawls.

He must have read her intentions on her face, because he smiled. A chilling, anticipatory stretch of thin lips. "Go ahead. That SEAL of yours will come running. It will be easy to take him out. He'll have no cover, while I'll have you. He can wait for you at Saint Peter's gate. Assuming that's where you'll both be headed." A flash of rage flitted across his angular face and melted the chill from his eyes. "Go ahead. Scream. The bastard deserves a couple of rounds for all the trouble he's caused me."

A cold, hard weight filled her chest. He was right. Zane would come running and die the moment he rounded the bend. He'd never risk shooting if there was a chance of hitting her, and if Russ used her as a shield...

"What do you want?" she asked when his hand dropped from her mouth. To think she'd thought him so nice at the airport, to think she'd thought he was her type.

"I want Amy Chastain." He kicked the overnight case out of their way, wrapped hard fingers around her elbow, and jerked her around until they faced the opposite direction. "Amy, unfortunately, is difficult to reach, and I don't have time to wait until she's released from this damn place. So you, my dear Beth Brown, are my bargaining chip. If Zane Winters wants to see you again, he'll trade you for Amy."

Beth digested that as he tugged her back the direction they'd come. "Whatever you have planned isn't going to work." She bit back a hiss of pain as his fingers tightened with brutal strength around her elbow. "There's no way you can hijack the plane now. Not even with Agent Chastain's family as hostages. Surely you realize that? There are too many other agencies involved. Your guns have been discovered. Your crew taken into custody."

He didn't slow, just propelled her forward. "This was never about that damn plane."

They reached an intersection between corridors, and he took the narrower hall to the right. Beth glanced behind her. If only she could send Zane a warning. The thought had barely registered when the memory of what he'd told her in the closet raced through her mind. He'd claimed the bond connecting them allowed them to share thoughts.

Something had passed between them while they were making love. His thoughts had been in her head. So, going out on a limb and assuming the exchange actually had taken place, that it hadn't been a product of her oversexed imagination, that she had picked up on his thoughts and he'd picked up on hers—well... how, exactly, had they done it?

Could she access this link again?

Zane was almost back to the waiting room when a thick wave of unease rolled through him. He slowed, recognizing the emotional signature. Beth. Halting, he raked tense fingers through his hair. Beth only broadcasted during moments of intense emotion. What had happened between them had sent her into a full-blown panic, but he'd thought she'd recovered from that.

Suddenly a hazy image flashed through his mind. The figure was male. Distorted. Walking down a long, white hall. Periwinkle scrubs flashed beneath the overhead lights. The image flashed through his mind again. Sharpened. Coalesced into arms, legs, broad shoulders. Unquestionably male. Something about the proportions of the frame was off.

He frowned harder, straining to place the image. The figure's build was familiar—he flashed back to another corridor. An airport corridor. And another man. Only this asshole had been walking away.

He froze as the sense of familiarity snapped into place.

Fuck. This asshole's build was identical to Branson's. He moved like Branson too. What were the odds of that? A face crystallized in his mind. Narrow and long. A beak of a nose. Brown eyes. He was lacking the glasses and had parted his hair differently, but there was no doubt who that face belonged to.

Russ. Fucking. Branson. Here, in the hospital, headed toward Beth.

There was no good reason for Russ Branson to show up at the hospital. Something Beth must have recognized instinctively, hence the unease, which had escalated to fear.

Zane spun, shook the image from his mind, and sprinted for the hallway Beth had taken to Ginny's room. He should never have let her go alone. Damn it. He should have gone with her.

The corridor unraveled behind him in a blur. He rounded another corner and skidded to a stop in front of Ginny's overnight bag. The corridor branched to the right and the left, but Beth wasn't in either of them.

He had absolutely no idea which corridor she'd taken.

Russ propelled her down the hall. At first Beth had hoped they'd run into someone, until it occurred to her that Russ would eliminate anyone who tried to interfere. He had no compunction about killing, as evidenced by Todd and the hijacker at the airport.

"If this was never about the plane, why are you doing this? Nobody knows you were involved. You haven't been implicated, which means you still have time to escape."

He snorted and amusement kicked up the corners of his mouth. "You mean other than kidnapping you?"

His amusement quickly vanished. An ugly rawness darkened his eyes. "I was hired to acquire several people on that plane. My employers don't tolerate failure. If I can't provide these passengers through the hijacking, then I'll have to acquire them through other means."

Chastain had mentioned a list of names. So this was Russ's new plan? To use her to get hold of Amy Chastain and use Amy to force John to hand over the names on his list?

She needed to figure out how to contact Zane fast, because she wouldn't survive long once Russ dragged her out of the hospital.

How, exactly, did one go about sending a message with one's mind? Did you just think that person's name? Focus on it extra hard? Feeling foolish, she concentrated on Zane's name. Reciting it over and over in her mind.

Nothing happened. Big surprise. Mentally she shrugged. It wasn't as if she had many options; there was nothing in the hallway to grab and use as a weapon. If she tried to snatch the gun, he'd shoot her. If she wrenched loose and ran, he'd shoot her.

Calming herself, she focused her mind and visualized Zane's face while reciting his name over and over in her head.

Again nothing happened.

But then, what good did saying his name do? She should be sending him clues, visualizing where Russ was taking her and sending him those images. She visualized the entry to the corridor Russ had steered her into, painted it in her mind, adding details until it was crystal clear. Then she expelled it from her subconscious as though she were expelling air from her lungs.

This time something stirred in her head. Something alien. Something other than her own consciousness. She was so shocked, she instinctively flinched, her entire body clenching.

The stirring vanished.

"What's wrong?" Russ's grip tightened on her elbow and jerked her to a stop. He glanced behind them and turned his head to frown down at her.

Pain shrieked through her arm as he ground her elbow into the socket. "You're hurting me."

He frowned and released her elbow, moving his hand higher up her arm. "Better?"

Yeah, like she was going to buy solicitousness from him, considering what he'd already done. Considering what he still planned to do. "Not really. If you let go of my arm, I promise to be a good girl and walk beside you."

He didn't bother replying, just jerked her forward and started walking again.

She focused on a drinking fountain. Visualized it to crystal clarity and pushed it from her thoughts, then waited with anticipation to see if anything stirred in her mind.

Nothing.

"Tell me something." Russ pulled her to a stop in front of an elevator and punched the down button.

Beth focused on the elevator, visualized the green arrow pointing down.

"How did Mackenzie know about the hijacking? Who tipped him off?"

She shrugged. If telling him would keep him talking, why not? "I did."

He glanced down, raised an eyebrow, but there was no surprise on his face. "How'd you find out? From Clancy? Why go to Mackenzie instead of the FBI?"

Rage stirred at the thought of Todd, followed by a burst of grief. The image of the elevator she'd been so carefully visualizing wavered and collapsed into fragmented wisps. Swearing beneath her breath, she forced the anger and pain aside. She needed to focus on the visualization. If Zane was picking up on what she was trying to send him, she needed to make sure she was feeding him useful information, not empty emotion.

"Todd didn't tell me anything." She focused on the glowing elevator button again and rebuilt the image in her mind. "I dreamed about the hijacking two nights ago. Watched your men slaughter everyone in coach."

Once the image of the elevator with its lit panel was sharp and focused in her mind, she pushed it out, as she had before. This time, when that alien stirring whispered through the depths of her mind, she caught herself before tensing.

"Bullshit." The elevator chimed and the door whooshed open. Russ yanked her inside and punched the basement button. "You're psychic?"

There were equal measures of curiosity and disbelief on his angular face.

"No." She stared at the glowing basement button. The elevator doors whooshed shut again. With a jerk, the car dropped. "I've never had a dream like that before."

"Too bad," he said after a minute, dry amusement rounding his vowels. "If you were psychic, you could have avoided this."

He didn't believe her. Not that it mattered. In fact, it might even work to her advantage. If he didn't believe in ESP or psychic phenomena, it wouldn't occur to him she could communicate with Zane through their minds.

She concentrated on the elevator panel again. Visualized it. Pushed it out. And tried not to dwell on the fact she was pinning all her hopes on a psychic connection she'd scoffed at a mere sixty minutes earlier.

Chapter Nineteen

FROZEN IN THE HOSPITAL CORRIDOR, ZANE RAN BATTLE scenarios.

Beth wouldn't head toward Ginny's room; she'd try to lead him away. And if Russ was in control, he'd head away from people. Odds were they'd take the corridor to the left. Zane broke into a light, soundless jog. He couldn't assume the bastard had come alone, and if he pulled Rawls off the waiting room, Marion and the kids would be vulnerable.

Mac was out of commission.

While Hollister, Trammell, and Russo—the leadership from Delta and Echo platoons—were on their way up, they had an ETA of a couple of hours.

He'd have to handle Branson on his own.

As he increased his speed, another image flickered through his mind. *A white tile corridor. An impression of movement. A dull, throbbing pain and a band of pressure around his right elbow.* He glanced at his arm but knew the sensations were coming from Beth. His pulse accelerated.

Branson looked down, brown eyes flat and hard. "Go ahead. Scream. The bastard deserves a couple of rounds for all the trouble he's caused me."

That bastard had her. Fear reared up and seized him by the throat. He locked it down. Forced himself to concentrate. To

346

think. The son of a bitch was dragging Beth somewhere. But where?

Light shimmered across a stainless steel drinking fountain. The image vanished as quickly as it bloomed.

There was no drinking fountain anchored to either of the walls on this corridor, nor was there a couple walking side by side in the distance. Maybe he'd taken a wrong turn, but the passage also curved to the right. Maybe the fountain was farther down. Maybe Beth was just past that bend. He increased his stride and kept going.

An elevator. Panel lit. A bright-green arrow pointing down. "Tell me something," Russ said. "How did Mackenzie know about the hijacking? Who tipped them off?"

His blood pressure skyrocketed. The bastard was forcing her into a fucking elevator. If he managed to get her out of the hospital before Zane could stop him…

Ignoring the tight clench of his heart, Zane warped around the bend. Twenty feet up, a stainless steel drinking fountain was affixed to the white wall, but neither Beth nor Branson were in sight. Neither was an elevator. What were the chances this was the same drinking fountain? He could still be wasting his time on the wrong hallway.

Just ahead was another curve in the passage. The elevator could be up there. He sure as hell couldn't turn back without finding out.

As he headed for the next bend, he strained to catch even a whisper of voices. Anything to assure him he was headed in the right direction.

The square steel box of the elevator pressing in on him. A control panel. A round button with a B painted on glowing white.

Branson was taking her to the basement.

He took the corner at a dead run. An elevator came into view, but the green arrow pointing down was unlit. Either this was a different elevator or they were several minutes ahead of him. Either way, he needed to access the basement level. He blew through the stairway door and took the steps four at a time.

As the stainless steel rails flew past, it occurred to him the images flickering through his mind were too steady and too detailed to be a fluke. It was almost as if Beth was sending them to him, feeding him a map to find her.

Wishful thinking? Or had she actually opened herself to the connection linking them?

When the elevator doors whooshed open, Russ jerked Beth back and propped the doors open with his shoulder. A quick glance to the right then left, and he stepped out, dragging Beth with him.

A huge, fat *B* framed by a circle announced they'd arrived at the basement. She concentrated on the image. Focused. Pushed it out. A few feet down from the elevator was a fire extinguisher encased in a glass shell; she visualized that as well.

Russ noticed her interest in the canister as they passed and shook his head with a chuckle. "It's not as easy to grab those things as the movies make it look. You'd be dead before you managed to pull it loose from the wall."

Beth ignored him. She had no intention of letting him victimize her, but she didn't intend to get herself killed by acting foolishly either. She'd wait for an opportunity before acting.

And hope Zane was picking up on the images she was sending him.

Every once in a while, she caught a flash of alien thoughts—a flicker of a subconscious that didn't feel like her own. But it was gone so quickly it could have been her imagination.

The corridor curved to the left. When it straightened again, double steel and glass doors came into view. *MORGUE* was painted in bold, black letters above the entrance. Beth's stomach tightened. Somewhere, in another hospital, Todd's body was lying behind a pair of doors like those.

Russ noticed her sudden tension and glanced down with another chuckle. "Not to worry. Your continued good behavior will keep you out of there."

Liar.

Concentrating on the steel and glass doors with the sign above, she built the image in her mind and pushed it out. A whisper of sensations flickered in the depth of her mind. This time she caught herself before tensing up, before shutting it out. Suddenly an image exploded in her head.

Stairs. Rails flashing past in silver streaks of burnished light. The sensation of speed. The urgent pump of blood. Adrenaline, but caged by calm purpose. A steel door flying open. A huge B painted on a white wall.

Zane!

Excitement crested as the images flashed through her mind. There was absolutely no doubt that the images and sensations were coming from him. She could feel him inside her mind. The calm, cool focus of him. How his adrenaline spiked and surged yet remained leashed by the strength of his control. By his coolness.

Holy Mother of God, she could sense him inside her head. See what he was seeing, feel what he was feeling. They really were connected.

When they reached the morgue's entrance, Russ tugged her to the right, around the corner, and down another long, white corridor. A new set of double doors glinted in the distance.

Worry mingled with the excitement as it occurred to her that Zane wasn't far behind them. In fact, at the rate he was moving, he'd overtake them momentarily. And the instant he turned that corner in front of the morgue, he'd be exposed. Russ would use her body as a shield. Zane would be a sitting duck.

She needed to get Russ talking again. At least their voices would give Zane a reference point. She strained but couldn't hear footsteps behind them. Which wasn't a surprise: SEALs were trained for stealth. He could be right behind them, and she wouldn't know it.

Zane? She formed his name in her mind. At the same time, she glanced up at Russ. Her kidnapper was staring straight ahead, fixed on the double set of steel doors in the distance.

"Where are you taking me?"

Zane! She thought his name again in her mind, enunciating it with crystal clarity, and pushed it out.

That odd stirring flickered through the depths of her mind and she caught a flash of the morgue's steel and glass doors. If he could see the morgue, he was very close. A burst of panic swallowed the excitement.

She concentrated harder. *Zane. Slow down. Up ahead. No cover.*

"I'm taking you outside," Russ said.

She barely heard him; she was so intent on that alien stirring in her mind. *Zane.* The ripple swelled. Her subconscious brushed up against his, mingled with his cool intellect.

Coming. It was his voice. Calm as a priest. Clear as glass. In her head.

Slow down, she told him. *We're just ahead. Gun. No cover.*

Nothing for an agonizingly long moment. Then a single word. *Copy.*

The word was clear as a bell, and just like that she could feel him inside her again. His calm focus. His keen intelligence. She could sense his thoughts brushing against her mind.

The walls ceased flashing past. The impression of speed diminished.

Where is he taking you?

She marveled at how clearly she heard the words, as though he'd spoken them directly into her ear.

Outside.

A ripple of masculine amusement undulated through her mind. Apparently he'd already guessed where they were headed.

A door, down the hall from the morgue.

She concentrated on the double doors at the end of the hall, visualized them. She could sense Zane studying the doors with that cool focus.

"What the fuck are you smiling about?" Russ clamped his hand around her arm and jerked her to a stop.

She hadn't realized she'd been smiling. He twisted her elbow and gave her a hard shake. Agony screamed up her arm and through her shoulder.

Zane's calm vanished, swamped by molten ferocity. His rage rolled through her subconscious—a violent red mist.

I'm okay, she hastened to assure him, startled by his instinctive, protective response to her pain. *He just surprised me.*

Liar. The fury didn't abate, simply hardened into cold, hard purpose. *He's dead.*

"I asked you a goddamn question." Russ dragged her to a stop.

Luckily, this time he didn't twist her arm; she doubted she could hold Zane back if Russ hurt her again.

See how well you already know me? But there was grimness rather than humor in his tone.

Beth held Russ's suspicious gaze. "I was just thinking about how much I'm going to enjoy watching Zane tear you apart."

He studied her face and laughed. "I'm afraid I'll have to rob you of that pleasure."

Beth released a pent-up breath. They couldn't afford to raise Russ's guard. Zane needed every advantage they had. And their biggest advantage was that Russ didn't have a clue how close he was or that they could communicate without talking.

My biggest advantage is you.

Beth's chest melted beneath an explosion of warmth. It wasn't just the compliment. It was reading the absolute sincerity behind it and knowing he meant every word.

It should have been terrifying having Zane's consciousness mingling with her own. Reading his thoughts, his feelings as clearly as her own. But for some odd reason, rather than feeling unbearably exposed, it felt comforting. Natural. As though they'd been blended like this since the beginning of time.

For the first time in her life, she felt connected to someone.

Gun in hand, Zane pressed his back against the wall in front of the morgue. He glanced down at the 9mm. He had a full cartridge, but the Glock was a bitch when it came to long-range targets. Russ had already dragged Beth far enough down the hallway to make a kill shot problematic, and if he didn't drop the bastard immediately, the risk to Beth increased astronomically. He needed to get closer. Make sure his first round took the asshole down.

But therein lay the problem. Russ would hear him coming and use her as a shield.

He needed another approach. His gaze shifted to the morgue. What were the chances the morgue employees had their own entrance to the facility, one bypassing the interior corridors? If he could find another exit, he could beat Russ to the parking lot, set up an ambush, and take the prick out.

He rolled forward and took a quick peek down the hall. Russ still faced forward, focused on the exit. Zane darted across the mouth of the corridor, eased open the door to the morgue, slipped through, and eased it shut behind him.

A narrow white counter stuck out of the wall down the hall to the right. A sliding glass window was behind it; a door flanked it. Zane yanked open the door and bolted through, trading stealth for speed.

He raced down another, narrower hall, burst through a second door, and found himself in the morgue. The stink of death, body fluids, and the acidic bite of astringents swelled with each step. Stainless steel body tables and rolling carts shimmered beneath the harsh fluorescent lights. White sheets and toe tags brushed his scrubs as he cut through the narrow space between tables.

The rear right corner of the room didn't boast equipment or walls. He raced in that direction, thankful that the place appeared empty. It took seconds to reach the back of the morgue and the hallway that led into the bowels of the building. A line of lockers buzzed past. The rear entrance was steel. Thick. Not a goddamn window in sight.

He reached for Beth with his mind. *How close to the entry?*

She responded instantly. *Ten feet?*

Which gave him seconds to set up an ambush.

Forgoing caution in favor of speed, he thrust open the heavy door and bolted onto the landing. Steep steps led down to the parking lot, but there were no cars close enough to provide cover.

The ambulance bay was to his right. Wide enough to accommodate four rigs, it had a shallow ledge that wasn't deep enough to hide him. The double doors Russ was dragging Beth toward were set back ten feet, right next to the morgue's employee entrance.

Again, no cover.

To his left, however, was a five-foot drop. He'd have to use the employee landing as his ambush point and hope like hell Russ used the steps immediately in front of them rather than the ones to the far left of the ambulance bay.

Zane vaulted the railing to his left and landed on the balls of his feet in a crouch just as the steel doors to his right screeched open. Too bad he hadn't had time to set up a distraction, something to draw Russ's attention from this corner of the bay.

He's not holding me very tight. Do you want me to pull loose? I could try to knock the gun from his hand. Would that be enough of a distraction?

Sheer horror sent his heart into overdrive. *No!*

But I can help. I can distract him for you.

The horror congealed in his chest and his heart stopped beating. *Stand down. Do nothing. Do you copy me? Nothing!*

A disgusted *hrummmph* rolled through his mind.

Scowling, Zane crab-walked along the side of the retaining wall. Footsteps started across the ambulance landing and down the shallow flight of stairs.

So far, so good. They were headed right for him, but on the other side of the landing.

He concentrated on the sound of Beth's footsteps. Russ's feet were completely silent on the concrete. Which pointed to a military background. Who the hell was this asshole?

As Beth's footsteps grew louder, Zane crouched lower and waited for them to pass. Beth's adrenaline crested, flooded the link between them with nervous energy, but her stride never faltered.

"Where's your car?" she asked, and Zane tensed.

"Don't you worry about that," Russ said. "We'll be there soon enough."

Their voices were in front now. Zane carefully rose. Luck remained with him. Russ hadn't changed positions. He still gripped Beth's left arm, which meant he was walking on the right, the back of his head in plain view.

He'd have preferred a chest tap. Head shots were a bitch. Too much chance the bullet would glance off the skull. But he had no choice. The landing shielded Russ from the neck down. Barely breathing, Zane raised the Glock, steadied it against the edge of the landing, and lined up his shot.

Head tap or not, this bastard was going down.

Slowly, delicately, his finger tightened on the trigger.

"Behind you! He's got a gun!" The scream came from across the parking lot.

Son of a bitch.

He squeezed off the round, but Branson was already moving. Ducking, the asshole clamped his arm around Beth's waist and swung the two of them in Zane's direction. The bullet whizzed past his head, missing Beth by inches.

Russ fired back, simultaneously dragging Beth in front of him.

The round plowed into the landing next to Zane's cheek, peppering him with concrete fragments. Zane ducked.

"You're fucked," Russ shouted. "You go after me, you kill her. So how about we handle this all civilized? You'll get her back after you've given me what I want."

"How about you hand her over now and I let you go to prison instead of the morgue," Zane yelled back, reaching out to Beth with his mind.

She was calm, waiting for him to tell her what to do.

The way Russ had Beth pinned against him didn't leave much of a target. The chances of dropping him had just plummeted to nil. However, while that arm around Beth's chest might hold her in place, it wouldn't stop her from slumping forward, over his arm. She could expose enough of Russ's head to do some serious damage.

The timing would have to be perfect, though. Russ was obviously well trained, with killer instincts. He'd compensate as soon as he felt Beth fold. They'd have maybe a second before he adjusted position. Zane would have to take the shot at the exact moment Beth moved. It was the only way they'd catch Russ off guard.

On my word slump forward, bend over his arm. He sent a visual image along with the order.

He expected nervous trepidation. Fuck, if their timing was off by even a fraction of a second, that bullet would kill her as well. But calmness brushed his mind. Absolute trust.

He was the one to hesitate. Christ, if she didn't move fast enough. If he fired too soon—

I trust you. Trust me.

Her faith steadied him.

In the distance, a siren started screaming.

He wanted to close his eyes and take a moment to pray, even though he hadn't prayed in…well…ever…but he didn't dare. Instead, he took a deep breath. Then eased up, sighting on Beth's head.

"I'm warning you," Russ started dragging her backwards, "you try anything and I will kill her."

Now!

He squeezed off the shot.

Beth executed the movement perfectly, slumping and folding over Russ's arm. Zane was expecting the move. His target was not. As Beth's shoulders and neck dipped, Russ's head was exposed. The first bullet took him in the forehead. The second plowed into his throat.

In slow motion, Russ's arm dropped from Beth's waist and he fell backwards.

The sirens screamed closer.

Zane vaulted the stairway, caught Beth around the waist, and swung her behind him, away from Russ's splayed body.

"Is he dead?" Beth asked as he bent to snatch the weapon from the bastard's limp hand.

He checked for a pulse, surprised to find a weak beat against his fingertips, even more surprised to find Branson's brown eyes locked on his face, some kind of entreaty in their glazing depths. A wavering hand reached for him. "Find Jil—" The rest of the garbled sentence drowned beneath a gurgle of blood. The brown eyes went fixed and vacant.

"What did he say?" Beth asked.

"Hell, I don't know. I couldn't make it out." Straightening, he surveyed the parking lot. The woman who'd screamed the warning was half-hidden by a car, cell phone pressed to her ear. Otherwise the parking lot was empty.

If Russ had backup, they would have moved by now.

Turning, he took hold of Beth's shoulders and pushed her back so he could get a good visual.

I'm fine.

He wasn't sure if the words were spoken out loud or whispered through his mind.

There was blood glistening in her hair and splattered across her face. Gritty shards of Russ's skull spattered the side of her neck and ground into his palms. She was the most beautiful thing he'd ever seen.

Please. She snorted with disbelief.

This time he heard it with his ears *and* inside his head. Felt it with his heart. Suddenly his hands were trembling. He tried to drag her into his arms.

Ducking, she wrenched herself loose. "Zane! For God's sake, I've seen what I look like."

She meant through his eyes. "Then you know you're beautiful."

She rolled her eyes and backed out of reach. "I'm filthy. I'm covered in blood." Her voice started to shake. "And other...things."

He stepped forward, ignoring her attempts to evade him, and dragged her into his arms, next to his heart. "They'll let us use the shower in the emergency room. The blood will come off."

He'd make sure of it. He'd wash every inch of her and then pin her against the wall and make sure she didn't associate their first shower together with death and gore.

A shimmer of arousal rippled through their link. *I'm not going to shower with you in a public place!*

Did she realize she hadn't voiced the protest but had sent it through their connection?

I do now. A certain dryness laced the words.

She was adapting to the bond more quickly than Zane had expected.

A sudden wave of trembling shook him. His arms tightened. He wished he could drag her inside his skin, where he could keep her safe...forever.

"Jesus," he whispered, his voice raw. "I thought I lost you."

He wasn't just talking about her abduction.

She sighed and wrapped her arms around his waist. "It's kind of hard to deny this bond, considering it saved my life."

Instead of easing, another wave of shakes coursed through him. He felt her mind brush his and knew she read his fear, the terror he'd kept caged—the realization of how easily Russ could have taken her from him.

Taken her life. Which equaled taking his, since she was his life.

But he didn't. I'm still here. She was the one to soothe.

Twin sighs shook them. Slowly his trembling eased as he rested against her, their minds mingled, their bodies touching, their breathing in sync.

The only way they could be any closer would be if they were naked, and he was inside her.

I'm still not taking that shower with you.

And then images exploded through the link.

Steam. Soapy hands sliding down his chest, cupping his balls, stroking his cock. Her lips following the teasing path of her fingers and taking him into her mouth.

He went rock hard and throbbing in an instant.

Jesus, he was liable to be a walking, talking erection for the rest of his life if she kept that up.

Amused feminine laugher rang out in his mind.

Lips against her forehead, he smiled. It was a damn good thing SEALs were trained for stamina, because it looked like that training was going to come in handy.

Chapter Twenty

MAC FROWNED, STRAIGHTENING IN HIS HOSPITAL BED AS BETH Brown followed his LC into the private room. "Rawls will be here any minute." Mac alternated his glare between Zane and the damn woman who'd trapped him. "I'm sure Miss Brown would like to spend some time with her friend."

"We just came from Ginny's room." Ignoring the less than subtle hint, she shot him a serene smile and let Zane steer her toward the foot of the bed.

Mac's jaw tightened. "We've got things to discuss that don't concern you."

Rather than retreating from his glare, she lifted her eyebrows and leaned back against Zane's chest. "Considering I was kidnapped and a friend of mine was killed—" A shadow slipped through her eyes. "I'd say this *does* concern me."

With a snarl, Mac transferred his scowl to Zane, but from the shit-eating expression on his LC's face, the damn fool wasn't ready to see reason...yet.

Before he had a chance to enlighten the pair with exactly why this wasn't any of her fucking business, the door swung open again. This time Rawls stepped through, followed by Trammell, Hollister, and Russo—Delta and Echo Platoon's leadership.

Three pairs of hard eyes zeroed in on Beth.

Mac's scowl collapsed into a smirk. He settled back to enjoy the show. He had to give the woman credit, though. She matched the suspicious stares without flinching, cool as you please. Zane looked on with amused calm.

Russo was the first to break the confrontation. After a hard look at Zane, he checked Beth out again—slowly, thoroughly. Finally he stepped forward, hand outstretched.

"Devlin Russo," Zane's counterpart from Echo Platoon told Beth as she accepted his hand.

Mac's smirk vanished. Did the damn woman have them all fooled? Apparently so; Hollister and Trammell offered hands and names as well.

"When the hell did you boys arrive?" he asked, knowing they hadn't made the trip up from Coronado to check on him. Cosky's absence in the room was an open, festering wound.

"Last night, while you were getting your beauty sleep," Russo said. Dark eyes sharp with intelligence swept Mac's face and dropped to his bandaged shoulder. "It didn't help. You look like shit. Any news on Cos?"

Mac swiped a hand down his face and locked the grief behind a mask of control. "He's still breathing."

Hollister shook his head. "He always was a stubborn cuss."

An aching silence fell.

And then six throats cleared.

"They found John Chastain's body in a supply closet a couple of doors down from where he interviewed us," Mac said.

Zane frowned, straightening sharply. "How was he taken out?"

"A knife." Since his shoulder was screaming like a mother-fucker, Mac settled back against the pillows. "Which means who-ever grabbed him is flat-ass crazy, or a fucking genius."

"Or both," Russo said thoughtfully. He rocked back on his heels, his black hair shining like obsidian beneath the fluorescent lights.

"Whoever killed him has some serious brass balls," Zane explained after Beth glanced up at him, a small frown pleating her forehead. "They grabbed him in a high-traffic zone, killed him with a knife, which can be messy and loud, and escaped without catching anyone's attention."

"Which means not only does he know what he's doing, he's damn good at it," Mac added grimly. "With both Branson and Chastain gone, it's unlikely we'll find out what the hell was going on." He transferred his ire to Zane. "You just had to take the kill shot, didn't you? You couldn't clip him, leave him for question-ing?"

Zane offered an unapologetic shrug. "The bastard had a gun to Beth's head."

"You have the two who were watching Ginny and Kyle," Beth interjected, settling back against Zane's chest again.

"Hired muscle. They won't know a damn thing." Mac turned his scowl on Beth.

Their lack of leads was her fault anyway. If Zane hadn't been so concerned about saving the damn woman's life, he would have left his target alive enough to talk. "We don't even know who Branson was or what the fuck he was up to."

He was still glaring when the door opened.

"We need to find that out."

At the sound of Amy Chastain's cool, feminine voice, Mac stiffened. In more than one place. Thank God for the blankets and the fact everyone's attention was turned toward the door. It gave him time to kick up his knee, which tented the bedding and hid the storm taking place under the sheets. Why the fuck did this woman rattle his libido like this? He'd convinced himself his earlier reaction had been adrenaline based. Yet here he was, all revved up and raring to go—because of her voice.

Luckily he had a secret weapon at his disposal when it came to dealing with this particular female. A plane ticket. A couple thousand miles between them ought to do the trick.

"I'm sorry about your husband," he told her in a gruff voice, meeting hazel eyes so flat and controlled they looked more like glass than flesh and blood.

A slash of grief brightened the hazel before they turned hard. She closed the door and turned to stand in front of it—arms crossed, feet slightly spread, as though she were barricading everyone inside.

"I want to know why," she said without preamble, her attention locked on Mac's face. "Why *that* plane? *Those* passengers. What did he want John to do? I want to know why he did this. I want to know who he was."

Mac frowned. Her words sounded uncomfortably close to a demand for help, which would play hell with his intentions of a full-scale retreat. "The FBI and DHS will be launching an investigation."

He'd been fielding calls from both agencies all morning.

"Their findings can't be trusted," she countered flatly. "John said his department was compromised. He had the same fears for DHS. That's why he approached *you*."

All true. But it didn't change a damn thing. Perfectly still, Mac watched her, aware their little showdown held every eye in the room. "Look, I don't know what the hell you're asking, but the answer is no."

She leaned back against the door and raised a russet eyebrow. "It benefits you as much as me to uncover what this operation was about."

"How the hell do you figure that?" Mac raised his right hand to run it over his hair, remembered it was bandaged, and put it down with a grimace.

"Because the only person who can corroborate your version of events is dead." Her voice didn't waver. "Whoever is behind this is already painting you and your team as out-of-control vigilantes who acted without authorization."

Mac smiled grimly. No way in *hell* was she dragging him back into this mess. "We got the green light from Admiral McKay. He'll testify the request came from your husband."

Shock flooded Hollister's face and narrowed his eyes. "Jesus. When was this?"

Frowning, Mac watched stunned glances pass between his Delta and Echo leadership. *What the hell...?* "Before we left for the fairgrounds."

"Son of a bitch." Russo ran a hand over his head. He turned, exchanged grim looks with Trammell and then Hollister. "This can't be a coincidence."

"No shit." Trammell's agreement was clipped.

"Someone want to fill me in?" Mac asked between his teeth, splitting his glare between his Delta and Echo officers.

Russo scrubbed a hand down his face. He stood there for a moment, apparently thinking, and then dropped his arm. Squaring his shoulders, he turned to Mac. "McKay was targeted last night. Car bomb. NCIS locked the incident down pending investigation. We were gagged."

A blast of shock ripped through Mac, followed by a hard kick of grief.

"He's dead?" he asked, after he was certain his vocal cords wouldn't cut out on him. "Why in the *goddamn fuck* wasn't I notified?"

He'd talked to Captain Gillomay that morning, reported on Cosky's condition. Why the hell had Gillo kept silent about McKay's death? A gag order? He was the fucking commander of ST7. The captain knew they'd been friends. If the platoons had been notified, he should have been too.

Another round of those grim, tense glances passed between Russo, Hollister, and Trammell.

Ice prickled his spine. "What aren't you telling me?"

Russo paced toward the bed, his dark eyes somber. "Gillomay doesn't know you got the green light from McKay."

Mac's face tightened. "I went to Gillo first—when he hedged, I took it to McKay. He knows." Rigid silence descended over the room. "Jesus fucking Christ," Mac finally said. "The bastard's goat-fucked us. He's cutting us off."

Christ, it was unbelievable. Yeah, he and the captain had had their differences, but for the motherfucker to turn on his own team…

It was against federal law for United States military personnel to act within a law enforcement capacity. Acting under SAC John Chastain's umbrella had been dicey enough, but without Chastain and McKay to back their story they were well and truly fucked.

He took a deep breath. Focused. Since the statute they'd be accused of breaking was a federal one, the FBI would investigate. And wasn't that just fucking beautiful, since the FBI was compromised and covering their asses. Still, NCIS would investigate as well. He just had to prove he'd gone up the ladder and received approval. He just had to prove Gillomay was a lying, hypocritical prick.

"They have any idea who took McKay out?" Mac wasn't surprised by the silent shake of Russo's dark head.

He locked this newest grief behind a frown and glared down at his blankets. His boys were right. The timing of the admiral's hit was too much of a coincidence. Somehow McKay's murder had to be connected to this mess with the FBI, and Gillomay's fucking lie would swing the investigation in the wrong direction.

McKay deserved justice. Mac intended to make sure he got it. But that meant pointing NCIS toward the right debris field.

Mac's gaze lifted, locked on the silent redheaded woman across the room. "What the fuck did your husband drag us into?"

Hazel eyes met and held his own. "To find that out, you're going to have to help me. It looks like your CO's hanging you out to dry. The FBI gets pretty pissy when officers within the United States military turn renegade."

She was right. Rage heated his belly. Cosky was somewhere in the bowels of the hospital fighting for his life. Damn if he was going to let his team take the fall when the whitewashing commenced.

"Those bullets they pulled from us will corroborate our version of events." He'd stuff those damn bullets down any bureaucratic naysayer's throat if he had to. "You and Ginny Clancy can testify on our behalf."

"About our kidnapping? Sure. The fact you rescued us? Sure." She shrugged and settled against the door. "First question will be why you didn't contact the proper authorities and let them handle the extraction. Without John and McKay to verify your story, you and your team are screwed."

"The detective who interviewed us yesterday raised these questions," Zane said quietly. "We knew we were climbing out on a limb when we agreed to help. Chastain and the admiral's deaths chopped that limb down."

Russo nodded in agreement and turned to stare at Mac. "We need to prove Chastain's and McKay's murders are linked, which means we need to prove Chastain asked for help because he had no alternative."

Mac growled and thumped the back of his head against the pillow.

Motherfucking son of a bitch.

Gillomay had jammed his escape hatch.

Looking into the hijacking and subsequent murders was one thing, but something told him Amy Chastain wasn't going to be content watching from the sidelines. Which meant he'd be spending far too much time up close and personal with the only woman since his ex-wife who made his skin itch and his palms sweat. Just. Fucking. Beautiful.

As if he didn't have enough on his plate extracting his team from this volcanic mess Chastain had dragged them into, now he had to worry about the damn man's widow too.

Chapter Twenty-One

*E*IGHT WEEKS LATER

Beth woke with a smile, her body sated, her muscles lethargic, her mind reaching out to Zane. She caught a glimpse of intense focus, burning muscles, laboring lungs, feet pounding the pavement. She broke the connection and rolled over. He was on the tail end of his run then. He'd head to the gym next. It would be a couple hours before he returned home.

She smiled at the memory of how focused he'd been, ignoring the pain and fatigue of burning muscles—fixated on the task at hand. SEAL training taught control, focus, and stamina—a potent cocktail when those traits were locked on something more sensual than exercise. When you added in the heightened emotional and physical connection courtesy of the bond between them, it was a miracle he hadn't killed her this morning, or last night. Or the night before.

She stretched again, still smiling, the sheets cool and silky against her skin. She needed to get moving, get that first emergency rush to the bathroom over with and some crackers and tea down to settle her stomach before Zane returned.

And she needed to take that pregnancy test, which had been sitting in her purse for the last week.

The test was rather redundant, though; she already knew she was pregnant. Just as she knew, he knew. It was the giant, invisible rabbit they'd both been tiptoeing around for the past eight weeks. Not because it was unwelcome, but because it would change everything.

They both knew she was going to have this baby and he was going to be a father to this baby. The question was *where* was he going to be a father? Up here in Seattle or down in San Diego? And was he going to be married to the baby's mother?

If it had been up to Zane, they'd have been married weeks ago and she'd be sharing his bed down in Coronado instead of him sharing her bed up here in Burien. It said a lot about his patience that he hadn't broached the subject. Not once. Not yet anyway. But it was coming. They both knew it was coming. These last eight weeks had been a vacation from worry and stress and life-altering choices. But his leave was almost over.

The choices had to be made. They both knew it.

In the end the decision had been remarkably easy. It had seeped into her consciousness a little each day as she basked in his attention and got to know his mind and soul as intimately as she knew his body.

She missed Zane when he was gone. She missed him so intensely it was almost a mental ache.

She didn't miss her job. Her job was just a job. Sure, the pay was good, so were the benefits. But she could find other work with good pay and good benefits. As for her condo...she could build another home. *They* could build another home...together.

But Zane?

He was one of a kind. She'd never find another Zane. What she felt for him went beyond chemistry, beyond sex; it was a connection at the cellular level. Just as he'd claimed all those weeks ago, to think she'd been so damn afraid of something so…perfect.

And while she might not be emotionally invested in her job, he was in his. His team was a part of him. He'd give the team life up for her, she knew that instinctively, and he wouldn't ever resent her for it, she knew that as well—but it would haunt him. He'd regret that particular choice until the day he died.

She couldn't do that to him. She wouldn't do that to him.

So she'd move down to Coronado and push the fear of his eventual deployment to the back of her mind and enjoy him for every second she had him. At least they'd be together when he was on base.

Her only regret was Ginny and Kyle—but apparently they weren't going to remain in Seattle anyway. With that lingering grief still heavy in her heart, she forced herself out of bed, which brought an immediate wave of nausea. She bolted to the bathroom, spent several miserable minutes in front of the toilet until her stomach settled enough to wash her face and brush her teeth.

In the kitchen she munched on saltine crackers while she brewed a pot of ginger tea, which the homeopathic website had sworn would alleviate morning sickness.

She'd just sat down at the kitchen table with a pile of crackers and her first cup of tea when the front door opened and Zane walked in. He looked terrible—pale, tight-faced, sweaty.

He dropped the plastic grocery sack he was carrying on the table without saying a word and reached for a cracker before sitting down across from her.

"What's wrong?" she asked in alarm, even as she reached for his mind. She relaxed when a sea of calm greeted her. Whatever it was, it wasn't serious.

He gave her the strangest look. Half disgusted, half stoic, maybe a tinge of grim. "My stomach's giving me hell." He stole another cracker from her pile, pulled a huge box of saltines out of his bag, and set them on the table in front of her.

She stared at the box of crackers. He'd obviously noticed her morning sickness; talk about an in-your-face challenge. She wondered what else he had in the bag, perhaps a pregnancy test?

"Did you pick up some kind of bug?" she asked absently, trying to see through the semitransparent plastic. A strange sound brought her head up. "Zane?"

"I wouldn't call it a bug...exactly." He picked up another cracker.

"What—" Her stomach suddenly cramped and a surge of nausea climbed her throat. She froze, concentrated on breathing, and once it had settled took another sip of tea and a bite of cracker.

"Are you okay?" Zane's voice sounded strangled. "It's getting worse. You need to see a doctor."

There was no sense in ignoring the giant white rabbit now; it wasn't so invisible anymore. "It'll settle down in a minute."

Something about the silence struck her as odd. She turned her attention to Zane. He'd gone a pasty white and was eying her ginger tea like a desperate man. She opened their link a crack and felt the wave of nausea roll through.

"Oh. My. God." She choked and felt her stomach roll.

"For Christ's sake, calm down." He grabbed another cracker and shoved it in his mouth.

"You too?" It couldn't be possible...but then again...she shared his physical and emotional reactions during lovemaking as well as at various other times through the day. They were linked somehow, so perhaps it was possible. "How long?"

"A week? Give or take." He sounded disgusted.

Which was about when her morning sickness had started.

"I think it's getting worse. We need to go see the doctor." There were equal parts concern and desperation in the look he gave her.

She nibbled her saltine and stared at him. "It's perfectly normal from what I've read and it's not getting any worse." At least not for her. She swallowed a giggle. God. This was just…perfect.

The concern on his face gave way to ire.

"So I take it this sharing of symptoms is because of our psychic link? How long does it last?" She tried to keep the rising glee out of her voice, but from the look he gave her she didn't quite manage.

"We're connected. They don't go away."

She choked back another giggle. He sounded frustrated as hell. Apparently there were certain things he didn't want to share with her, which reminded her.

"Uh—labor?" She coughed delicately and desperately tried to hold the laughter in.

"Jesus." A look of profound dread crossed his face.

She couldn't help it: the laughter pealed out of her in waves.

He erupted from his chair and stalked toward her. "Christ." He sounded grim. "Why the hell do you women always find that so amusing."

Which sent her into gales of laughter.

He swooped down and lifted her, which sent her stomach rolling. They both froze and held their breath until the moment passed.

Swearing beneath his breath, he carried her to the bedroom, but much more sedately. When he reached the bedroom he yanked back the sheet, carefully set her down, and went to working stripping them both. Flat on her back, the dizziness and nausea instantly subsided.

Naked, she lazily stretched, watching with appreciation as his long, lean body with its corded strength was revealed to her. "Isn't this how we got into this predicament in the first place?"

"Your stomach's fine as long as you're flat on your back." A gleam lit his eyes as he came down on top of her. He feathered a kiss across her lips and nibbled his way down her neck to murmur in her ear. "The sensible thing would be to keep you flat on your back as much as possible." He nibbled a path across her shoulder to her breast.

She sighed as he went to work seducing her. He knew all her secrets now. All those erogenous spots that yielded a sigh or a squirm or a scream. He knew just how to build the urgency into frenzy before setting her free.

An hour later, after dragging an entire litany of oh-my-Gods and an entire symphony of screams from her, he collapsed beside her, his body slick with sweat, his heart racing like he'd run a marathon, his arms tight around her cooling body.

With a sigh, she pressed her cheek against his damp chest. She could feel his heart pounding. Strong. Enduring. Hers.

Suddenly it occurred to her that they hadn't gotten sick once. Maybe staying flat on her back for the next seven months wasn't such a bad idea. There were certainly side benefits.

His chuckle was raspy and filled with masculine arrogance. "I'm game."

Since she hadn't spoken that last thought aloud, he must have picked it up from her mind. What else had he picked up? It was time to find out.

"I suppose I should move in with you so we can continue this unique form of bed rest after you return to base."

He went absolutely still beneath her. For a moment even his heart seemed to stop beating. "Beth?"

Her name was more breath than whisper.

She propped her forearms on his chest. His eyes were intensely green in the dim light. "Yes. I'm going to marry you. Yes. I'm going to move down to Coronado to be with you."

The hand he lifted to her face was rock steady and unbearably gentle as it stroked the hair from her cheek. "What about your job? Your house."

She smiled, leaning into his touch. "They aren't important. You're important. Our daughter is important."

His palm slid around the nape of her neck. He drew her down to his mouth. "I love you."

"I know. I love you too." She whispered the words against his lips.

He smiled, his mouth brushing hers. "I know."

Suddenly he rolled, taking her with him until she was flat on her back again, his warm, heavy weight anchoring her to the bed. She sighed in pleasure. Yeah, he was her anchor.

"How soon can we do this?" He dropped a kiss on her lips.

"As soon as Cosky can walk. You'll want him to be your best man."

Relief brightened his eyes. "Rawls says he's already mobile, although his knee's still giving him hell."

"He checked out of the hospital too soon. At the very least he should have stayed with Marion longer. You guys should have waited a couple more weeks before taking him down to Coronado."

Zane shrugged. "He insisted. When Cos sets his mind to something, it saves time to give in. Look *bullheaded* up in Webster, you'll find a picture of Cosky."

No doubt that very bullheadedness was why he was walking already. Heck, it was probably why he was still alive, with no mental effects, which had shocked everyone.

Of course Cosky wasn't the only bullheaded member of the teams. The past eight weeks had taught her the *S* in SEAL actually stood for stubbornness. It was a trait they all shared.

"Are you going to ask Ginny to be your matron of honor?" he asked quietly, and the kiss he feathered across her lips held solace rather than hunger.

"Yeah, but she'll find an excuse to say no. She's still avoiding me." Tears stung.

He swore softly and cradled her close. "You can't help her until she's ready to let herself be helped."

He was right. She knew that. But that didn't stop the ache.

Suddenly Zane pulled back, a frown creasing his face. "We should wait a few weeks. Mac talked to Amy. The DOJ is about to announce a full-scale investigation into our actions regarding the hostages of flight 2077."

The hostages of flight 2077.

It was what the media had nicknamed Ginny and Kyle and Chastain's family, even though technically they hadn't been booked on the flight.

"Considering the media frenzy right after the news leaked last time, reporters are bound to start hounding everyone involved again. I don't want you anywhere near the cameras."

They'd known the investigation was on the horizon. Maybe it wasn't such a bad idea for Ginny to get out of town.

She could feel the gathering tension in him. Except it wasn't concern over himself and what might happen if the DOJ actually leveled a case against them. No, the concern was for her. He'd been using extreme caution since they'd started seeing each other, paranoid some past enemy was going to use her to exact revenge against him.

Why, damn it—why—had the Naval Special War Office allowed their names and faces to be splashed across the press like that? They'd pinned massive bull's-eyes on all four men. They could have torpedoed the news reports, refused to cooperate under the guise of national security. Instead, they'd hung four good men out in the public eye.

On the plus side, the public for the most part were just as furious over the betrayal as Beth was.

Mac said Captain Gillomay was behind it. But it didn't matter who was behind it; the betrayal sank so deep it made her furious and sick to her stomach at the same time.

"Did Amy find out which passengers Russ was after?"

"No. Chastain's laptop's missing. But odds are they're scientists. Most of the passengers in first class were Pacific Northwest scientists on their way to Dynamic Enterprises' annual show-and-tell in the hopes of procuring research funding."

"Dynamic Enterprises. I've never heard of them."

"They keep a low profile. They're one of the leading corporations in cutting-edge technology. Nanotechnology mostly. Since Russ tried to take the bird first, they were likely after the research as well as the scientists. Grabbing the plane would have made it possible to acquire both at the same time. Such technology is kept under lock and key. It would have been nearly impossible to grab both the researchers and the data unless the researchers had the data with them."

"Like a research funding trip," Beth said slowly. "They'd have to present their research in order to procure the funding."

"Exactly. But that leaves thirty-one different scientists with various areas of expertise. Christ, there were scientists working on everything from medical nanotechnology to environmental technology to warfare on that plane."

"Warfare," Beth repeated, a chill going down her spine.

Zane nodded grimly. "To complicate matters the feds are claiming there's no evidence they were after any passengers."

Beth bolted up. "But I told them what Russ said." When the dizziness hit, she flopped back down. "What are we going to do?"

With a grunt, Zane stopped talking for a moment. "We're going to find the damn scientists Branson was after. If we find them, we might be able to identify who's behind this. The feds sure as hell aren't going to identify them, not when they're more concerned with covering their asses than finding out what the hell's going on."

The FBI and Homeland Security probably hadn't believed her because of her bogus engagement to Zane. They'd all but accused her of making the list up to protect him. Although how that was supposed to protect him, she wasn't quite sure.

Suddenly it occurred to her that their bogus engagement had just turned real.

Zane apparently took her slow smile to mean she had other things on her mind than nanotechnology and federal whitewashing. As he bent over her, all that wonderful intense focus fixated on her, Beth's body started to hum in anticipation.

She'd been wrong all those weeks ago. Her secret weakness in literary escapism translated just fine into reality. Every woman needed a bonded alpha male in her life.

About the Author

Trish McCallan was born in Eugene, Oregon, and grew up in Washington State, where she began crafting stories at an early age. Her first books were illustrated in crayon, bound with red yarn, and sold for a nickel at her lemonade stand. Trish grew up to earn a bachelor's degree in English literature with a concentration in creative writing from Western Washington University, taking jobs as a bookkeeper and human-resource specialist before finally quitting her day job to write full time. *Forged in Fire* came about after a marathon reading session, and a bottle of Nyquil that sparked a vivid dream. She lives today in eastern Washington.

Read on for a sneak peek of Cosky's story, FORGED IN ASH

Available March 2013 on Amazon.com

Lieutenant Marcus Simcosky cranked the wheel to the right and punched the accelerator, bracing his elbow against the door handle as his pickup shot forward. From behind him, around the corner, a car backfired. The explosive sound echoed in the air, as staccato as a gunshot. A rusted two-door sedan, the same one that had been riding his ass for the last mile, took the corner on a greasy plume of exhaust and settled in behind his bumper, tailing him so closely he could clearly see the driver—a thin, jaundiced woman with ratty brown hair.

There was no question now. He'd picked up a tail.

She was of European descent, which didn't mean shit these days with domestic terrorists giving the foreign ones some serious competition for murder and mayhem. Although he doubted she was a tango. Terrorists trained their cell members better than this. Christ, the woman was a complete amateur. Or an idiot. Or both. Only a moron would tail him so closely he could identify her face. Anyone with the barest rudiments of training, or a kernel of common sense, would keep a couple of car lengths between them.

He glanced in the rearview mirror as the sedan backfired again, and studied the greasy plume of smoke slicking the street behind him. At the very least a professional would choose a less conspicuous ride.

"Un-fucking-believable." Grimly, he glared into the rearview mirror, and then reached down to massage the knot in his cramping thigh.

He'd noticed her the moment she'd pulled onto Silver Strand Boulevard behind him. She'd been impossible to miss. If the backfiring hadn't caught his attention, the squealing brakes would have, or the jet engine muffler. The damn thing was the noisiest car on the street, which was why he hadn't realized at first that she was following him. Sure she'd mirrored him turn for turn, but coincidences happened. By the fourth turn he'd started to wonder, so he'd tested her by taking sudden random corners, by speeding up and slowing down, sailing through yellow lights and stopping at green. She'd matched every maneuver.

Yep, he was being tailed. By an idiot.

It would have been laughable, if he still possessed a sense of humor, if his knee wasn't howling and his thigh charley horsing and his life dangling on the edge of disaster.

She was probably a reporter, another vulture eager to pick over the carcass of his Navy career. He scowled, as a python of frustration wrapped around his chest and slowly squeezed the air from his lungs.

Damn it!

The media shitfest was finally settling down. They were able to step off base without being mobbed by the press. Yeah, this press hiatus would disappear once the DOJ handed down their verdict, but for the moment at least they'd been given room to breathe...and investigate. The last thing they needed was another opinionated piece hitting the papers, or airing across the networks.

Another cramp ripped into his thigh. He shifted in an effort to take some weight off the leg. When that didn't ease the pain, he dug his fingers into the spasming muscle. He'd overdone it at the gym, worked the damaged muscles and joints longer and harder than he should have. But babying the sucker wasn't working. The leg wasn't any stronger than it had been four months earlier when he'd limped his way to his mother's Lexus from the hospital entrance. It was time for some tough love, to force the fucker to hold its weight and do its job.

His mind shifted to Kait Littlehorse, to long aristocratic fingers and a waterfall of sleek, pale hair. To the appointment with her massage table he was on his way to keep.

Possibly, just possibly, there may have been another instinct at work in the gym. The urge to work his body to the point of exhaustion so it wouldn't have the energy to react to the hour of torture he'd signed it up for.

Grimacing, he released a frustrated groan. Christ, this visit was a bad idea. As bad an idea as he'd ever had. There was a reason he'd avoided Kait for the past five years. But he didn't turn the truck around. Apparently his need for a miracle overrode his sense of self-preservation.

The last thing he wanted, though, was to bring the press down on Kait's door. With a quick shake of his head, he studied the woman in the sedan behind him; she looked pretty disheveled for a reporter. And then there was that monstrosity of a car. Would any self-respecting reporter try to catch a story with that piece of junk? Maybe she was some whack job who'd been following his story on the news, caught sight of him on the road and decided to run him down for a "howdy, how 'ya doing?"

Either way, he didn't want Kait caught up in this mess, so when he came to her apartment complex he drove past. He'd dump his tail and then circle back to keep his appointment. Of course, losing his tail wasn't much of a plan. She'd just attach herself to him again, later. Or maybe next time she'd fixate on Rawls, or Zane, or heaven help them—Beth. Zane would blow a gasket if some whack job started tailing Beth. He might as well put an end to this woman's game now and send her on her noisy way.

With that in mind, he pulled into Coronado Mall's parking lot. His tail had to wait for several cars to pass before she could follow. He cruised around the center parking isle and picked a space on the far left of the lot for the coming confrontation. The woman behind him chose a spot in front of the sidewalk that ran the length of the mall. Perfect, she'd have to cross the incoming and outgoing lanes and the center parking isle to reach him, giving him plenty of time to assess her approach.

After parking the truck, he released his seat belt and hit the latch to the glove box. The compartment fell open, exposing his Glock. He stashed the weapon under the waistband of his jeans and slid out of the truck, doing his best to ignore the slivers of molten fire piercing his kneecap.

When his feet hit the pavement, his knee wobbled and refused to take his weight. Grimly, Cosky wavered there, bracing his shoulders against the open door. How fucking humiliating. He'd fall flat on his face if he tried to take a step. Best to let his tail come to him.

He tucked his T-shirt behind the Glock for easier access, watching as the woman slammed the rusted door of the sedan and started toward him.

Marcus Simcosky, or Cosky as his teammates and friends called him, was even better looking in person than he'd been in the newspapers or on the television. There was a cold intensity to the flesh-and-blood man that the digital and print images lacked.

Jilly Michaels shoved her hands into the pockets of the poncho she'd liberated from a clothesline south of Portland, Oregon. The poncho was in the same poor shape as the rusting sedan she'd liberated at the same time. She hadn't expected the rusting bucket of bolts to actually carry her all the way to San Diego. But she'd figured every mile those worn tires rolled was a mile she didn't have to hitchhike.

She studied the man she'd come thousands of miles to kill— or at least, one of the men—as she headed across the parking lot. She hadn't expected him to be so tall or tanned or muscular. She hadn't expected the confidence and strength he exuded, or the subtle sense of threat. She hadn't expected him to look so damn… capable.

He'd hovered near death for days. Spent weeks in the hospital. But he didn't look sick or weak or sallow. Not like she did. But then he'd had the luxury of recovering in the hospital, or in the homes of family and friends. Nor was he on the run, sleeping in stolen cars, scrounging out of trash cans or ransacking empty houses in the hope of finding enough cash to fill her gas tank or enough food to fill her belly.

A horn suddenly blared. The squeal of brakes followed. Jilly jumped back, realizing she'd stepped in front of an oncoming car. Shaken, she glanced across the pavement and found her soon-to-be-victim watching her with cold detachment. He must have seen the car headed directly for her, but he hadn't bothered to yell a warning.

The bastard.

A flush of rage warmed her. Her fingers curled into claws. She shoved them deeper into the pockets of her poncho. When her right hand bumped against the cold steel of the revolver, she forced her fingers to unfurl and take hold. The voluptuous folds of the poncho hid the bulge from the gun. She wouldn't even have to pull the revolver out; she'd just point it and fire through the cotton. He wouldn't have a clue what she was planning until it was too late.

And while he lay dying there, the murdering, lying bastard, she would shoot him again. And again. And again. One shot for each of her babies and another for her brother.

He'd be the first to pay for what they'd done to her. For what they'd taken from her.

He'd be the first, but they were all going to pay. Every last one of them. She was going to make sure of it.

18185782R00228

Made in the USA
Charleston, SC
21 March 2013